For all my boys.

...SURE BOOK®

...r 2002

...ed by

...ster Publishing Co., Inc.
...th Avenue
...rk, NY 10001

...3439-5114-1

...e "Leisure Books" and the stylized "L" with design are
...ks of Dorchester Publishing Co., Inc.

... the United States of America.

...isit us on the web at www.dorchesterpub.com.

ANGEL OF LIGHT

"Faith." His breathing was ragged, his voice hoarse with desire. "I need you so much."

"I know, I know," she whispered. She moved under him. He started to undo the ribbons on her camisole, but she stopped him and pulled it over her head. The moon shone down on her, and he drew in his breath at the sight.

"You're my angel of light, Faith. I don't think I could live without you. Do you know what that means?"

A tear left a silver trail on her cheek as she whispered, "Yes, I know I can't live without you either. You consume me."

"Are you ready to go then?"

"Whenever you say."

CHASE THE WIND

CINDY HOLBY

A LE...

Octob...

Publis...

Dorch...
276 Fi...
New Y...

If you...
that th...
destroy...
publish...

Copyrig...

All righ...
transmi...
includin...
and ret...
publishe...

ISBN 0-...

The nam...
trademar...

Printed i...

LEISURE BOOKS

ACKNOWLEDGMENTS

Thank you, Bill and Linda. You made a difference in my life.

My family, you are the best support group in the world.

Rob, Josh, Drew, Justin, Mike, Gib, Chris, Travis and Jake, you never doubted.

Christine Anderson, Mike and Debbie Shea, Christine Zdon and Karen Tally, thank you for the encouragement. I could not have done it without you.

Wilson Smith for the story of Good King Wenceslas and everyone at RHMC.

CHASE
THE WIND

Part One
Western Virginia, 1838

Chapter One

Ian Duncan was hot and thirsty, and he had a feeling his horse was too. He turned the tall gray from the track and headed down the bank to the wide expanse of the Kanawha River. While the stallion buried his muzzle in the cool water, Ian took the canteen from the horn of his saddle and refreshed himself with water taken earlier that day from a spring he had passed. He took a kerchief from his pocket and wiped the sweat from his face. Then deciding he needed to do a better job of it, he bent down to dip it in the water and bathed his face and neck. He combed his thick, straight, russet-colored hair back from his forehead with his long, lean fingers and swore to himself that the next time it flopped over into his eyes he would cut it all off.

But Faith had said she loved his hair. He closed his eyes and remembered the soft touch of her slender hand as it smoothed the rebellious locks back. He shook his head to clear away the thoughts of her that threatened to run rampant in his mind and busied himself with checking the girth on the saddle. He turned his darkly lashed sapphire-blue eyes to the canopy of branches overhead. The midday sun tried to burn through, but luckily failed to find the way down to the track. The weather was hot enough without the

3

sun adding to the discomfort. Ian had just passed through Charleston and was anxious to press on; his goal was Point Pleasant by nightfall, and he was determined to make it.

"I can't wait to hear what Faith has to say about you," he said to the gray as they once again headed west towards Ohio. "She has always had an eye for a fine horse, and you definitely fit the bill." The gray responded by flicking his ears and nodding his head up and down in agreement. Ian chuckled and rubbed the fine arched neck of the thoroughbred. He had raised the horse himself and swore to everyone that the two of them could understand each other.

Though he had had the pleasure of the gray's company since the day he was foaled, Ian had just recently come into legal possession of the fine animal. His former employer had left the stallion to Ian in his will in gratitude for twelve years of service in his stables. Ian had a gift with horses and an eye for lines and breeding. His employer's stables and reputation for fine quality horses had grown in the time Ian had spent with him. The man had given him a home in the stables at the age of thirteen when Ian's parents had died; Ian gave him all the knowledge of horses that had been passed down from Duncan father to Duncan son since the first one came from Scotland as a bondsman some hundred years earlier.

Now, at last, it was time for a Duncan to use his knowledge for his own profit. Each generation had worked his magic for another. Each generation had dreamed of breeding his own horses in his own way on his own land. Finally, Ian had the opportunity to fulfill the dreams of his father and his father's father and each one before. He had beneath him a fine stud to sire many a fine foal. In his boot he had 500 dollars that he had won racing the gray. Before him was the West, with land aplenty for anyone who wanted to take on the risks. All he needed now was Faith.

His mind wandered back to the last time he had seen her. They were in the barn behind her father's house. Her sky-blue eyes were full of tears as her father berated him. She was not permitted to see Ian, her father had shouted; he hadn't invested all his time and money raising her just to see her married off to some stable hand. He had higher aspirations for her future, and Ian was not part of them. "More like he wants to sell her to the highest bidder," Ian said to the gray. Her father's words still bothered him because not once had he mentioned Faith's happiness, just his own ambitions for Faith to make a good marriage.

"If only she'd come with me that day," Ian said to himself, not for the first time. The gray shook his head again as if to agree that life would be sweet if only Faith were with them. Ian grinned. "Soon enough she'll be admiring your fine form. Let's pick up the pace a bit so she doesn't have to wait." The gray obliged by moving into a slow canter on the well-traveled road. Ian noticed the leaves moving a bit and felt sure there would be rain soon. He began to whistle a familiar tune, and the gray flicked his ears in response to the music. Ian was sure he would reach Point Pleasant by nightfall.

Faith lifted the mass of silvery blonde hair from her slender neck in hopes that some stray breeze would cool her. The air was heavy and still, the humidity weighing down on her like a woolen blanket. She felt as if she were about to suffocate. She glanced over at her stepmother, Miriam, who was engrossed with several stacks of papers at the desk. She looked as fresh as the morning in her high-necked, long-sleeved gown, her only sign of discomfort a slight tic at the corner of her mouth. It seemed to coincide with the movement of papers from stack to stack.

How can she stay so cool and calm? Faith thought to herself. At this point in time, all she could think about was running down to the Ohio River and throwing herself into the churning waters to escape the heat, and to escape the wedding that was to be held on the morrow. A slight movement at the window caught her eye, and she rose as if in a trance from the straight-backed chair that had been her prison for most of the day. The sewing that had occupied her slid unheeded to the floor, and she nearly stepped on the heap of white satin and lace as she moved to the window. Her eyes, usually the color of a summer sky, seemed pale and lifeless as she stared at the small stirring of leaves on the oak tree at the north-eastern side of the house. The leaves were calling her, they were calling his name. "Ian," they sighed. "Ian." The lace curtains of the window fluttered so lightly that she would have missed the movement if her attention had not been focused on the window.

"Faith, what ever are you doing? You're going to ruin your dress," Miriam scolded. Faith didn't answer, just kept her eyes on the dancing leaves of the tree. All at once the movement stopped, and she leaned her forehead against the pane of glass, hoping it would help to cool her feverish brow. She closed her eyes and saw hair the color of copper falling over eyes so blue she could drown in them. "Faith, come away from there. You're going to smudge the window, and it will have to be cleaned again."

"I thought perhaps it might rain," Faith said as she turned away from the window, from the flash of a smile in a sun-bronzed face. *Why, oh why didn't I go with him?* she wondered to herself. She knew the reason why, but now she thought there might have been a way.

Miriam gave her a pensive look. The chit's attitude would really need improving before tomorrow. She made a mental note to have her husband talk to the girl. There was too much at stake for the event to be ruined by an apathetic bride. Perhaps there was a tonic they could give her to lighten her mood. The girl's gloomy manner was too obvious to be put down to nerves.

"It wouldn't dare rain on the event of the season," Miriam assured her as she rose from her desk and gathered the dress up from the floor. "Now come and finish this hem. We must get your dress done before dinner."

Faith wearily returned to her chair and searched the hem of the dress for the last stitch she had placed. She rubbed the back of her hand against her damp forehead and wiped the moisture on the side of her skirt. She knew she couldn't take another stitch if her life depended on it.

"Miriam, I need to go lie down for a while. I'll finish this later, when it's cooler." Before Miriam could voice a protest, Faith was out the door and fleeing up the stairs to her room.

A slight tic twitched the corner of Miriam's mouth as she contemplated the chores remaining to be done. Having Faith make her own wedding dress had been one way to cut costs. And cost was definitely an issue, even when one was putting on the wedding of the year. Perhaps it would rain, and some of the guests would be deterred, cutting the expense some more. The whole event had been funded with credit extended on the expectations of Faith marrying the richest bachelor on this side of the Ohio. Randolph Mason was a good catch, she thought to herself. If she had been a few years younger, and a bit prettier, she would have considered going after him herself. After all, Faith didn't have the good sense to appreciate the wealth and prestige she was about to command. As for herself, she had settled for Faith's father, the owner of the local mercantile, who had brought a load of debt to their marriage.

Of course she hadn't known about that until well after the event. Ironically, she had married him for money and he had married her for the same reason. "I guess we had more in common that I realized," she remarked to no one in particular.

As soon as Faith reached the landing in the stairs, she knew she had made a mistake. The temperature upstairs seemed at least ten degrees higher than in the drawing room. She fled into her room before Miriam had a chance to call after her and hastily shed the skirt and blouse that were plastered to her skin. The windows were open to catch any breath of air and she stood between them to see if it was cooler there. She might as well have stood in an oven, she decided. A tepid pitcher of water was on the washstand, so she poured some in the bowl to splash on her face. Her camisole and pantalets clung to her skin, and she plucked the offending fabric away as best she could. She wrung out a cloth and wiped around her neck and down her arms, and felt a tiny bit of relief.

At the foot of her bed was a patchwork quilt that had belonged to her mother. It was a double wedding ring design, pieced in shades of blue with just a touch of pink. Her mother had made it in anticipation of her own wedding, and it was Faith's most treasured possession. She smoothed it on top of her bedspread and lay on top of it, face down. She pulled her hair back off her neck and pulled a corner of the quilt up under her arm, as she would a doll to comfort her. The quilt, a family Bible and some memories were all she had left of her mother. Jenny Taylor had died five years ago, right after Faith's fifteenth birthday. She closed her eyes to summon her mother's dear face. Most of Faith's memories were of a sad woman, one who did all the proper things that the wife of an upstanding citizen was supposed to do. She obeyed her husband and made sure that life was peaceful at all times. For the life of her, Faith could not imagine where her own restless spirit had come from. She felt as if all she wanted to do was rebel. She could not believe that she would be able to live the life her mother had lived, not even if she was married to the richest man in this part of Virginia. Faith pulled the quilt up closer and brought to mind the last happy time she had spent with her mother. Her mother was helping her dress for a wedding they were to attend. Faith was sitting on a chair in her mother's room while her mother brushed her hair.

7

"Momma, how do you know you want to get married?"

"You just do, my darling girl." Her mother continued brushing Faith's silvery blond hair. "When you meet the man you love, you'll know."

"How will I know if I love a man?" Faith asked, turning her head slightly to see her mother's response. Her mother put her hand on the back of Faith's head to straighten it and busied herself with tying a blue ribbon. "Momma?"

Her mother came around to the front of the chair and knelt in front of Faith. She gathered the girl's slender hands in her own and caressed the pale skin that so resembled hers. She looked up into her daughter's face and saw there all the hopes and dreams that she had lost. "Faith, you will have lots of men courting you, and they will make all kinds of promises, but when you meet the man you love, the man you should marry, you will know by his kiss that he is the one."

Faith made a face at the thought of kissing any man. Her mother reached her hand up to stroke the skin of her porcelain cheek. "My darling girl, when the man you love kisses you, you will feel it down in your very soul, and you will know he is the one."

"What will it feel like in my soul?" Faith asked, her curiosity awakened. Her mother got a faraway look in her pale blue eyes, and a smile came over her face. "Your toes will curl," she said with a soft smile.

Faith looked at her mother as if she had lost her mind, then she looked down at her own toes, encased in a pair of blue satin shoes. Her mother's laughter bubbled up, and Faith put her hands over her mouth. She had never heard her mother laugh before, at least not like this, not with spontaneity and spirit. Her mother pulled her close and hugged her. Then her laughter was gone, as fast as it had come. "Faith, when you find the man you love, don't ever let him go. Promise me."

Faith wondered why her mother sounded so desperate. "I promise, Momma."

Six weeks later her mother was dead from a fall down the back stairs. Faith tried as hard as she could to imagine what it was like to feel a kiss in her soul, but as she had never seen her parents kiss at all, she had no reference to go by.

That all changed five years later when she met Ian Duncan. She had been walking to her father's mercantile to pick up a few items when she first saw him. He was riding down the road on the back of a tall chestnut and leading a group of fine mares. He had caught her attention because he was whistling "Good King Wenceslas" and Christmas was still quite a few weeks away. The mares were beautiful, with gleaming coats and fine lines, and were only outmatched by the chestnut, which seemed determined to break into a trot. The hands on the reins were steady, however, and the chestnut did as he was told. She stood at the side of the road to admire the animals, her hand shielding her eyes from the morning sun, as the chestnut stopped before her. The rider pulled his hat off, pushed a handful of copper hair back off his forehead and flashed a cocky grin at her.

"Excuse me, miss, but I am looking for the Mason estate," he said, his voice deep and strong. Faith took a step to the right so that the sun was behind his body and found herself looking up into the bluest eyes she had ever seen. A moment passed while she seemed to consider his question, and she realized that she was grinning right back at him.

"Follow the river road; it's around five miles north of here, on the right. You can't miss it; it's the biggest house around," she finally managed to say. The hair had fallen back over his eyes and he pushed it away again before he clamped his hat down firmly to keep the hair in place.

"Thank you, Miss . . ." he said, the inquiry plain on his face.

"Taylor. Faith Taylor. My father owns the mercantile," she replied and wondered why she couldn't seem to control the stupid grin that had taken over her face.

"Ian Duncan at your service, Miss Taylor. I'm here to help the Masons develop their breeding stock." He motioned to the string of horses waiting behind him. "These are some of the best that Richmond has to offer."

Faith took a step towards the group. "They're beautiful. May I?" she asked, holding her hand out to indicate she would like to take a closer look.

"Go ahead, they're tame. I raised them myself." Faith heard the pride in his voice as she reached out to stroke the neck of the fine-boned bay mare that had stepped up next to her. The soft brown eyes were full of intelligence, and she noticed the ears were turned towards the man in the saddle as he spoke. "Do you ride, Miss Taylor?"

"Yes, I love to, although I don't have a riding horse. I'm afraid my father travels strictly by carriage."

" 'Tis a shame. This one would be perfect for you."

"Yes, she would," Faith replied as she stroked the velvety nose. The mare made soft whuffing sounds and nudged Faith's hand when she stopped. Ian laughed at the mare's antics, and Faith looked up at him. She realized that she didn't hear laughter enough and his was wonderful. It made her want to laugh, too, and she didn't know why. Her cheeks felt hot, and she wondered if they were flushed. The mare was shaking her head up and down, and Faith took a step back. For the life of her, she didn't know what she should say next and realized that she was perfectly content to stand there in the road talking to a stranger about breeding horses. He must think her an absolute wanton. Meanwhile, he was still looking down on her with that cocky grin on his face. Faith struggled to get her own face under control. She stepped back and shielded her eyes again. "It shouldn't take you long to find the place."

"It sounds easy enough." He tipped his hat and gathered the reins. "I'll be staying at their place for the next few months; perhaps I'll see you again."

"It's a small town, Mr. Duncan, I'm sure we will run into each other."

"I'm sure we shall." He made a slight motion with his knees, and the chestnut started up the road. Faith stood watching his progress, and he turned around and gave her a wave. The whistling started again, and Faith softly hummed the tune along with him. She watched until he disappeared around a bend in the road.

Chapter Two

Faith rolled up on her side, her hand still clutching a corner of the quilt. The frown that had creased her face was gone, replaced by a peaceful smile. She was drifting into sleep, images of Ian flashing through her mind.

The next time she had seem him was Sunday morning at church. He had come in around ten minutes late, which turned several heads. She stole a glance at him from her seat in the fourth pew, and he flashed a grin at her. His hair was slicked back with water, and his blue eyes twinkled with laughter. Faith looked down at her gloved hands so no one would see her own wide grin, which she was having trouble suppressing. She looked sideways at Miriam and saw the tic that hit the corner of her mouth when she was annoyed.

"Please, God," Faith began to pray, and then realized she didn't have any idea what she was praying for. She took a deep breath to steady her nerves and decided to try concentrating on the sermon.

I wonder why he is here, she thought as the minister droned on. *Surely he's not here to see me.* The idea made her cheeks burn, and she decided the tip of her shoe needed instant perusal. After a moment she raised her head and quickly glanced over her shoulder. The grin flashed again, and beside her the corner of Miriam's mouth twitched angrily. Faith crossed her arms and grabbed her elbows. She felt as if something in her was going to overflow, and it took every bit of her willpower to sit calmly listening to the minister while her insides were turning cartwheels.

Finally, after an eternity, the sermon was over, the last hymn sung and the congregation was making its way towards the door. Faith caught the back of a copper-colored head above the mass filing down the aisle. Ian stopped to shake the minister's hand and pushed his hair back before putting on his hat. The hair had flashed with gold when the autumn sun hit it, and Faith felt as if the same sun had gone behind a cloud when Ian's head disappeared from view. She looked at the ponderous backside of Mrs. Johnson, who was blocking her way. Behind her, Miriam and her father were engaged in conversation with the Masons. Mrs. Johnson turned to say something to her husband, and Faith took advantage of the small opening and squeezed through. She managed to miss the minister by timing her exit with the introduction of Mary Higgins's new fiancé and was out the door. She flew down the steps and skidded to a halt in the road, looking left and right to see where he had gone. Her ears caught a hint of a whistle, and she bounded across to where the carriages were waiting. He was there, standing by the chestnut, the reins in his hand. She stopped suddenly, her skirts billowing out at her sudden halt.

"I went to the wrong church," he said.

"What?" she asked, suddenly embarrassed by her pursuit of him.

"I was late because I figured you for a Presbyterian." He motioned to the left, where up the road the Presbyterians were still inside worshiping. "When you didn't show up, I thought I'd try here."

"No, we're Methodists to the bone."

"And what do Methodists to the bone do after they're done worshiping?" he asked, his blue eyes suddenly intense.

"Some of us have been known to take a book and quilt down by the river so as not to disturb older folks' Sunday afternoon nap," she said. The corners of her mouth lifted in a smile and her dimples flashed.

"Sounds like a pleasant way to spend an afternoon. Perhaps I should try it."

"There's a lovely place off the river trail near a grove of hemlocks."

He effortlessly swung up in the saddle. The grin flashed, and he tilted his hat. "It doesn't sound hard to find."

An hour later Faith flew out the back of her house with her mother's quilt and a book of poetry under her arm. She had made an appearance at dinner, but her father and Miriam were so distracted that they hardly knew she was there. They actually seemed relieved when she asked to be excused and said she wanted to get out and enjoy the day before winter set in. They had their heads together in the drawing room when she came flying down the stairs, and Miriam didn't even frown at her for rushing about. As soon as she got behind the barn, she broke into a run. She came upon the Ohio a few minutes later and turned north. Some ten minutes later she reached a bend to the left where a grove of hemlocks grew on the bank.

He was there, sitting on the bank. Apparently, he had eaten his dinner there, for the remains were lying beside him. The chestnut was browsing among the trees, the reins dangling from the bridle. Ian stood up when she came into the clearing and dusted his hands down the sides of his pants. Faith walked up to him and tilted her head up. She hadn't realized how tall he was. She reached out for the quilt and spread it on the bank, kicking the remains of his meal out of the way as he did so. When the quilt was spread to his satisfaction, he held out his hand to her and with a courtly bow indicated that she should sit. Faith giggled and daintily stepped on the quilt. As she settled down, her skirts and petticoats billowed out around her. Ian came down beside her with her hand still gripped in his. Her skin glowed like a pearl against the bronze color of his, and she marveled at how fragile her hand looked in his big one. He could crush it if he wanted to. A million thoughts raced through her mind. He could murder her and dump her in the river and no one would know it, but here she sat on the banks of the Ohio with a complete stranger who had the gentlest hands, the bluest eyes and the cockiest grin she had ever seen.

They spent the afternoon talking about everything. They shared stories about their lives, shared the grief of losing parents, and talked about their dreams. Ian wanted to go west and breed horses on his own land. He lived as cheaply as he could, over his employer's stable, so he could save enough money to buy a stud. He had his eye on one now, a four-year-old he had raised from birth. Faith marveled at his outlook on life. His conversation was witty, and she found herself laughing time and time again. Occasionally she caught him gazing at her with a serious look in those deep blue eyes, and she felt absolutely helpless. The afternoon flew by, and as the sun dipped behind the trees across the river a chill entered the air. Ian pulled Faith to her feet and wrapped the quilt around her shoulders.

"I don't suppose your father would let a stable hand call on you?" he asked, the hair falling into his eyes again.

Faith tentatively reached her hand up to smooth the silky locks back. "No, I don't think he would approve." She cast her eyes to the ground. Ian put a long bronzed finger under her chin and lifted her face up to his.

"Then I guess we just won't tell him about it." He flashed his grin, and Faith answered with one of her own. "Should I see you home?"

Faith had a mental image of her father's face if she showed up with Ian. "No, I'll be fine."

He adjusted the quilt around her again and stood with his hands on her arms. He lowered his head towards hers, and Faith felt the hair come down on his forehead when his lips touched hers. She tilted her head back to give him better access to her mouth, and he pulled her into his arms. Her own arms went around his neck, and her fingers made their way into the close-cropped hair at the back of his head. One of his hands came up behind her head, and she marveled again at the gentleness of his touch. He took his mouth from hers and drew in a ragged breath. Their foreheads touched, and Faith realized she was breathing in the very essence of him.

"You'd best be off," he said after a moment. She nodded, afraid to speak, and turned to step away. Instead of making a graceful exit, she tripped over the ends of the quilt and fell to her hands and knees. Ian instantly dropped beside her. "Are you all right?" he asked, concern all over his face. Faith started to giggle and looked up at him in wonder. He joined her laughter as he pulled her to her feet. "What's so funny?" he asked when she covered her mouth with her hand to halt the tide that was overflowing from within.

"I'll tell you later," she managed to get out and started down the trail. She gathered the quilt around her and broke into a run. When she finally reached the safety of her room, she jumped on her bed and kicked off her shoes. She stretched her legs out in front of her and wiggled her stocking-covered toes. "Oh, Momma, my toes curled!" She laughed and fell back on the bed.

A breeze had gently come down from the north and its soft caress cooled Faith's body. She relaxed into slumber, the weeks she had spent with Ian passing as seconds in her dream. After that first Sunday afternoon, she had spent time feverishly praying for beautiful weather. God had answered each week, and after Sunday dinner she had sped down the trail behind the barn to meet him. Ian had faithfully attended church each week and waited across the road after service for her to make her appearance at the door. While her father was shaking the minister's hand, Faith was watching for the tip of Ian's hat that said he would be there waiting for her. He had taken to riding the chestnut closer to her house each week, until he was soon waiting under the maples right behind the barn. One time he had brought the bay mare with him, and they had spent the cool, crisp fall day exploring the hills that rolled down to the river.

Faith's life became a cycle. She was with Ian or waiting to be with Ian. There was nothing else. The time she was spending outdoors had brought a golden hue to her porcelain skin, and her sky-blue eyes sparkled with a life they had never shown before. She felt as if a piece of her had been missing and Ian had miraculously put it in place. She had a glow about her now, one that was hard to ignore, and she noticed Miriam studying her when she thought she wasn't looking.

The time they spent together was precious, and they talked about everything. Ian had a way of bringing humor into every conversation, and Faith soon found that she had her own sharp wit. When she voiced her observations, Ian would flash his grin and wink, as if they shared a deep secret. The best part about being with Ian, however, was his kisses. They left her breathless and excited, and wanting so much more. She knew Ian felt the same way because each week he had a harder time pulling away. The last beautiful fall day they shared was especially difficult. They were in the grove of hemlocks again, on the quilt, when he pulled her to him. The touch of his lips to hers was intoxicating as always, but this time she felt an urgency in him. He pulled her down beside him, so that she was on her back looking up at him when he pulled away.

"God, Faith, do you know what you do to me?" he asked, his voice husky with emotion.

"Probably the same thing you do to me," she whispered, losing herself in his gaze. He placed his hands on either side of her heart-shaped face and looked into her eyes.

"I love you, Faith. Since the first time I saw you, I loved you." She looked up at him and saw everything that was Ian reflected in his deep blue eyes. She knew he was good and she knew there would never be another for her as long as she lived. Her mother's words came back to her. *When you find the man you love, don't ever let him go.*

"I love you too." Her hand caressed his cheek, and he lowered his face to hers, their lips barely touching, their eyes open, searching the depths of each other. His hands on her head became possessive, and he suddenly bore down on her lips, asking her to respond in kind. She opened her mouth to receive his kiss, and Faith felt as if her very soul was being drained out by the play of his tongue on hers. Her arms wrapped themselves around his neck, her fingers wove through his hair, and she felt herself suffocating. He dragged his lips away and began to kiss her neck. Faith tilted her head back and gasped for air. Her head was spinning, and she felt as if she was being sucked down into a whirlpool. His hand caressed her arm and moved around to take possession of her breast. It surged up to meet his touch, the heart beneath it pounding frantically.

Suddenly he was gone. In the seconds it took for Faith to get her raging body under control, she realized that he had removed himself from her. He was sitting on the edge of the blanket with his back to her, running his hands through his hair. She rose to her knees and tentatively touched his shoulder. A shudder ran through him at her touch, and she dropped her hand. She gathered her skirt around her and sat beside him, facing him. His face was flushed, and he turned away to look up the river.

"Would you come away with me then?" he finally asked, when the color in his face had returned to its normal bronze hue.

"To Richmond?" she asked, her face curious as to what he had in mind.

"Aye, to Richmond, to live over a stable, with a trainer of horses as your husband."

"Husband?" she asked, a smile turning up the corners of her mouth.

He gave her an exasperated look. "Yes, husband. I mean to be your husband, if you'll have me, and I mean to do better for you than what I can offer now."

"I think what you're offering now sounds just fine," she said with a laugh.

"Are you having fun with me?" he asked, his exasperation turning to annoyance.

"Yes, I am, and I'd like to have fun with you for the rest of my life, if that was indeed a proposal of marriage. Was it?"

He looked down at her. Her face was positively merry, her smile wide, her eyes tilted up at the corners with happiness.

"It will be," he said. He became very serious. "Faith, I mean to make you my wife, but it will have to wait until I can make us a home. Can you wait?" His eyes were desperate as they searched hers. She reached up and smoothed his hair back.

"Ian, all I want is to be with you. I can wait. I don't want to, but I will." He took his hand in hers and raised it to his lips. Their eyes met and made promises to each other. He pulled her up from the quilt and gathered it around her.

"Off you go," he said and kissed the end of her nose. He turned her in the direction of her house and swatted her backside. "Try not to trip."

She turned back around and stuck her tongue out at him.

"I'm going to think things through, and we'll talk next Sunday," he said as he gracefully swung up on the chestnut and turned around to give her a salute. "See you in church." And then he was off.

Faith watched him disappear through the trees and turned towards home. The wind had picked up—it was now the middle of November—and she realized that they had probably exhausted their supply of beautiful Sundays. Winter was sure to come, and then what would they do? Ian would think of something, she was sure.

The next Sunday it rained. Faith stood with Miriam in the portico of the church waiting for her father to bring the carriage around. Ian rode by on the chestnut, his brown suit covered with a dark rain slicker. The brim of his hat barely tilted as he rode past, and

17

Faith's mind whirled with confusion. "He sure is dedicated for someone who's not from these parts," Miriam mused as she watched his progress up the rutted road.

"Who?" Faith asked, although she knew the answer. Miriam indicated the darkly garbed figure that was melting into the sheets of rain.

"The Masons' new trainer, or should I say trainer on loan? They speak very highly of his ability," Miriam said with the authority of one who had knowledge of every happening in town.

"I hadn't noticed," Faith answered and anxiously looked for their carriage in the procession that was lined up in front of the church. When Faith turned back, she caught Miriam staring at her. Faith instantly wondered if all her secrets were showing on her face. Miriam did not look pleased, and the corner of her mouth gave way to the tic. She would have to be more careful now, now that there was so much at stake. There was no doubt in her mind that her father would never approve of Ian. She knew the only way they could ever be together was if she ran away with him. But there had to be a place to run to, and she had to trust Ian to take care of that. He had said he would have some answers for her today. She knew he would find a way for them to be together.

Once again the family's Sunday dinner was a stilted affair. Faith shoved her food around on her plate and complained that the rain had made her sleepy. Miriam frowned at her when she excused herself and fled up the stairs. She shivered as she entered her room and realized that her window had been left open. She rubbed her arms to erase the chill and crossed over to lower the sash. The rain had blown in and left a wet patch on the floor, wetness that led to the dressing screen placed in the corner. She cautiously approached the screen and peered around the side. Ian was standing there, dripping wet, his shirt unbuttoned, drying his face and hair with a towel she had left there earlier that day. He brought the towel down the front of his chest and flashed his grin at her. He tossed the towel over the screen and pulled her into his arms for a kiss.

"What are you doing here?" she asked when they finally came up for air.

"I didn't think you should be prancing out for a bit of poetry on such a rainy day, so I came up with an alternative."

"How did you know which was my room?" she asked incredulously.

18

"I've known since that first Sunday," he replied. "I've come by every night to bid you sweet dreams."

Faith looked up into his deep blue eyes with wonder. She knew in that moment that she didn't care where they went; she would follow him into hell, as long as they could be together.

"Let me tell you what I've decided." He led her over to the bed and they sat down together on the side. "Any chance we'll be disturbed?"

"No, the door's locked. I always lock it when I'm in here, and it used to be my habit to spend Sunday afternoons in my room."

Ian leaned back against the pillows and pulled Faith up against him. She waited patiently for him to speak, content to have her cheek against the bare skin of his broad chest, listening to his heart beat within. She wrapped her arm around his waist, and he squeezed her closer. She was quite sure there was no better place on earth to be at that moment.

"There are two possibilities before us," he began. "The first involves me getting you with child as soon as possible and making the deed right as soon as it becomes known."

A smile split Faith's face at that delicious thought. "I don't think you would survive the telling," she replied, poking a slim finger into his bronzed chest to drive the point home.

"Me either," he agreed, rubbing his hand over the injured area. "The second involves going to my employer for help. I know he thinks highly of me and would lend me a small amount for us to find a place of our own. I have some money saved, but I will need to buy stock so we can support ourselves. Without an income, we would be sorely pressed in a short time. The only problem with this plan is that we will have to wait until my job here is done. I cannot tell the man I have failed him and then ask for a loan the same day."

"I agree, it would not be a good way to start out." Faith sat up to look at him. "You know that we will have to steal away. My father has hopes I will make a good marriage." Ian frowned at this. "I mean he wants me to marry a rich man so he will have no worries. I'm actually surprised that I've reached the age of twenty without being promised to someone."

"I am so glad you have. It would be much more difficult for me to steal you away from some rich old man who would totter after us with his cane." Faith smacked him with a pillow. He flipped the

19

weapon out of her hand and pulled her back down on his chest. "We could leave right after Christmas," he mused. "Everyone should be busy enough that they will not immediately notice our going, and perhaps the weather will discourage any chase."

"I don't know if I can wait that long." Faith sighed. The rain had indeed made her sleepy, and the combination of the pounding on the tin roof and Ian's heartbeat was lulling her into dreamland. She yawned against his chest, and he kissed the top of her head.

"The Masons are having a big gathering soon to celebrate their son's homecoming. Maybe we can spend some time alone together then."

Faith nodded in agreement. She felt so at peace. Ian slid down on the bed a bit and rolled over on his side. She fit up against him in spoon fashion, and he reached down to the foot of the bed and pulled the quilt over both of them. His arm went over her and slid under her waist. Faith nestled down in the pillows and felt his soft breath in her ear.

"I love you," he whispered.

Faith nodded her head in perfect agreement. "I love you."

He barely heard her.

When Faith woke up later that afternoon, Ian was gone. For a moment she wasn't sure that he had actually been there, but the towel was still hanging where he had left it and her window was not quite closed. She wrapped her quilt around her and went to the window. She realized that it was no easy feat for Ian to have climbed the oak tree and opened her window. If not for his height it could not have been done. She decided to make it easier for him next time by leaving the window open.

She twirled away from the window and flung the quilt on the bed. Christmas was just six weeks away, and then they would be leaving. Oddly, she felt no sadness at the thought of leaving her home. Actually, it hadn't felt like home since her mother died. She felt absolutely no connection to the man who was her father. He had never treated her with affection, she was just another responsibility to him, someone to be clothed, schooled and married off. Even her looks did not connect her to him. She had her mother's eyes and nose, but the rest of her bore no resemblance to her sire. Maybe her height came from him, but upon reflection, she remembered her mother had been petite, too. His hair was brown, his eyes brown, his legs and arms were short, and he had a paunch. There was nothing of Melvin Taylor in Faith, certainly none of his personality. Why had her mother married the man?

A knock at the door interrupted her musings. It was Miriam.

"Did you have a nice nap?" she asked as Faith opened the door.

"Yes, I did." Faith looked in confusion at the back of Miriam's head as she came into her room. Miriam never came to her room; no one did.

"Your father and I have some good news." Miriam smiled, an expression that never quite reached her eyes. "The Masons are having a ball to celebrate Randolph's return from Europe and we've been invited. Your father has even decided that you will have a new dress."

"A new dress?" Faith couldn't believe her ears. The only new dresses she'd had recently were ones she had made over from her mother's wardrobe.

Miriam examined the towel that was hanging over the dressing screen. "Yes, a new dress. How did this get so wet?" She held the towel out with the question.

"I left the window open a bit and the rain came in. I cleaned it up with the towel." Miriam gave Faith a piercing look and dropped the towel in the chair.

"Tomorrow morning we shall visit the dressmakers and see what we can find," Miriam said and made her way back to the door. She paused and looked around the room as if seeing it for the first time. The bedspread was rumpled and the pillows flattened. The quilt was hanging off the end of the bed where Faith had dropped it in her celebration spin. "Clean up this mess," Miriam ordered and left the room.

The following Sunday there was a slight dusting of snow on the ground. Ian rode by the carriage as Faith was getting in after church and tipped his hat. He had left a note under her pillow the previous Sunday that said he would meet her in the loft of the barn. That was easy enough; she had only to wait until her father and Miriam retired for their afternoon nap. Then she would pay a visit to the necessary. With luck, they wouldn't notice when she didn't come back right away.

She found Ian sitting on a bale, looking out a small window that

21

had been left ajar. He seemed tired. There was no wide grin, just a slight smile as he held out his arms to her.

"What's wrong?" she asked when she was safely in the circle of his arms.

"The young prince has returned," he said into her hair.

"Randolph?"

"Yes, the royal Mason heir, returned from his education and his world tour. The man is a brute."

"What happened?" Faith leaned back on her heels to better see his face. He rose from the bale and ran his hands through his hair.

"He came into the stables with his stud," he began. "He doesn't know a thing about horses; he's brought this big black war horse from England, calls him Armageddon." His movements became agitated. "He wants to use him for breeding with my mares—I mean his mares." His face was anguished, and Faith's heart hurt for him. She knew how much he loved his charges, how he nurtured them. "He decided to ride Katrina yesterday. I told him she was too young and he was too big for her, but he wouldn't hear anything but he was going to ride her." He scrubbed his hands through his hair again. "The man near ruined her wind, and she's lame in the foreleg." Ian dropped back down on the bale and put his head in his hands. Faith rose up and put her arms around him. He wrapped his arms around her waist and put his head to her breast. She sensed the anger and frustration coursing through him and felt it too. Katrina was the bay that she had ridden. The mare was long-legged and delicate, made for a woman to ride, not a burly man like Randolph Mason.

"Perhaps you could talk to his father?" she suggested.

"I've tried, but in his father's eyes he can do no wrong. He's like the prodigal son come back. Everyone's all atwitter with the ball, and nothing else matters. It seems that they've invited all the eligible young maidens for his perusal. They want him to pick a wife."

Faith felt a chill run down her spine. A thousand coincidences came flooding into her head. Her father and Miriam suddenly being so friendly to the Masons at church, Miriam's constant perusal of her, the ball gown that was cut much too low in front. She recalled now the many conferences her father and Miriam had held in her father's study. Surely they were not planning to marry her off to Randolph Mason. She shook her head to clear away the horrible thought. Ian was looking up at her.

"He won't have you," he said, and Faith shivered again. For the first time since she had met him, Ian scared her. His eyes had gone black in the shadows of the winter day, and his face was hard and closed.

Faith put her hand to her mouth to press back a sob that threatened to erupt. She noticed that her hand was trembling. "Ian, what are we to do?"

"We'll bide our time. Surely they can't marry you off before Christmas."

She shook her head. No, they couldn't make this happen, and she wouldn't let it happen. Maybe she and Ian were being foolish; there were plenty of young ladies around who would happily marry Randolph. She knew deep inside, though, that he would choose her. He had always watched her with his black eyes, and she had always made sure that she kept plenty of distance between them.

Ian pulled her down on his lap, and she laid her head on his shoulder. "Tell me about Richmond, and the ocean." He had told her all about it before, but she loved to hear his voice and she wanted to take his mind off Randolph. Soon he was talking about swimming in the waters of the Atlantic, but she knew his rival was ever present in his mind. They tried to come up with a plan to meet the following Saturday evening at the ball, but decided they would just have to see what happened. Ian promised to stay close to her and left it at that.

The breeze that had caressed Faith earlier strengthened, bringing a hint of moisture. She roused from her sleep enough to pull the quilt over her and settled back to her dreams.

It was the night of the Masons' ball and she had just gotten out of the carriage. She held her satin wrap up under her chin as she surveyed the grounds, searching for a glimpse of Ian. The stables were down the drive to the left and seemed to be the center of some activity. The area was well lit, and there seemed to be a conference of some sort going on in the opening of the wide double doors. No one in the group gathered there towered above the rest, so Faith assumed that Ian was elsewhere, probably inside the huge building. He had promised to be close, and she knew he would be.

Her father took her arm and led her up the wide brick steps that led to the Masons' mansion. The family was standing inside the drawing room receiving their guests, and the Taylors joined the line. Faith nervously clutched the wrap up over the expanse of breast that her dress revealed. She just knew that Miriam had had it altered after her last fitting. When it was her turn to greet Mrs. Mason, the woman made such a production over the butler's failure to take Faith's wrap that she had to surrender it to the chastised man so as not to draw further attention to herself. The next person in line was Randolph Mason. He took her hand and bent over it for a courtly kiss, but his black eyes never left the creamy expanse of skin that she knew was covered with goose bumps. She also knew, without a doubt, that the tip of his tongue had touched the back of her hand. She tried to snatch it away, but he held it in an iron grip.

"I hope you will do me the honor of a dance tonight, Miss Taylor," he said in an oily voice, and Faith's hand curled into a fist within the folds of her dress.

"I'm afraid I don't dance very well," she lied. "I wouldn't want to cause you undo embarrassment at your party."

"A woman of your beauty needn't worry about that." Faith managed to wrestle her hand from his grip and massaged her wounded fingers with the other. Randolph just smiled at her as Faith looked around for the nearest escape route, but before she could find one, Miriam had her arm.

"Good idea, Faith," she hissed in her ear.

"What?" Faith asked incredulously. Her stepmother was actually smiling at her.

"Playing hard to get will just make a man like Randolph more interested."

Faith pulled Miriam into a corner, then jerked her arm out of her grasp. She had only been at the ball ten minutes and felt absolutely mauled. "I don't know what you are plotting, Miriam, but I tell you now, I want no part of it, and I especially want no part of Randolph Mason." Her teeth were clenched so tight, she had to grind out the words.

"Don't be ridiculous," Miriam hissed back. "Why do you think you're here?"

"I did not come here to be pawed by the likes of him." Faith indicated the man with her chin.

"It is way past time for you to marry, and you will marry well. Do not think that you will spend the rest of your life up in your

24

room waiting for some prince to come rescue you like your mother did." Miriam was spitting the words out and her eyes were narrowed with anger. "I know you've been pining after someone, and I know that whoever it is has been snooping around. I saw tracks in the yard a few weeks ago under the tree by your window." Faith prayed that the shock she was feeling didn't show on her face. Miriam suddenly realized that people were watching them and she reached up a hand to smooth her hair. She smiled at Faith, a brittle smile that didn't reach her eyes. "Let's go view the buffet, dear."

"No thanks, I've lost my appetite." Faith walked away. She could feel Miriam's eyes on her as she went into the hall. She crossed her arms over her breasts and looked around to see if she could find her wrap, a coat, blanket, tablecloth, anything to cover herself with. The doors to the library were open, and she decided to take shelter there until she could find a way to get to Ian.

Something stopped her in her tracks. Ian was here. He was standing behind Mr. Mason, talking into his ear. Mason was shaking a guest's hand, but he had his head tilted back to catch Ian's words. He asked a quick question, and Ian shook his head. Mason turned to the next guest, and Ian stood patiently behind him. His face was haggard, his hair nearly standing on end, the set of his broad shoulders showed how tired he was. Faith stood in the hall watching him while the guests eddied around her.

Ian's eyes found her. She could feel them burning into her. She stood in the middle of the crowd and felt them all disappear. The only other person in the world was Ian, and his deep blue eyes were devouring her soul.

Mason turned to say something, and Ian tore his eyes away from Faith and nodded assent to the man. He looked at her again and Faith felt the impact of his pain; then he left.

Faith ducked into the library. The windows faced the front of the house, and she hid between one and a heavily lined drape to watch Ian's progress down the drive. He turned once, but she knew he couldn't see her in the dark window. She watched him disappear in the night, then reappear in the light of the barn door. There was a flash of copper from his hair and he was gone.

She knew that in order to get to the barn she would have to disguise herself somehow. She was just considering the merits of ripping the draperies down when she heard someone come into the room. She ducked back to the side of the window and saw

Randolph's reflection in the glass. He stood there with a drink in his hand and carefully surveyed the area. Faith held her breath. Someone called to him from the hall, and he turned to leave. She realized that her legs were shaking and she slid to the floor, the satin of her dress pooling around her. She had to get a grip on herself. Her teeth were chattering. She needed a plan.

The first order of business was to get to Ian. The best route would be through the back of the house. Perhaps the servants had left a cloak lying about she could make use of that. All she had to do was get past Randolph, Miriam, her father and the multitude of guests who would think it strange that she wanted to be in the stables instead of the house. She took a deep breath and readied herself for the charge.

It was easier than she thought. She ducked out into the hall and made polite conversation with the first person she saw. She flitted from group to group, keeping a watchful eye out for the enemy. A maid came out of the kitchen, and she slid behind her. She pleaded a nervous stomach to the cook, who directed her to the outhouse and, as luck would have it, gave her a dark cape to wear. She was soon skimming over the frozen ground by the line of trees with her skirts bunched up in her arms. She cautiously peered through the rear door into the dim light of the stable. The place had been well lit earlier but now seemed dim and deserted. Ian's chestnut was standing in the first stall to her left. His head was out over the door, and he was looking down the row. His ears were flicking and turning, picking up the soft murmur of Ian's voice. The horse turned his head to her, and then turned back. Faith gently touched his forehead when she went by.

She found Ian two stalls down. He was sitting in the straw with Katrina's head cradled in his lap. He was speaking gentle words to her. The mare's eyes were glazed over with pain, and her breathing was labored. Beside him there was a gun. Ian lovingly stroked the mare's head and neck, and then stood, taking the gun in his hand. "Faith, wait for me outside," he said without looking up. Faith turned and ran out the way she'd come. She waited in the corner of the fence and stable, her back pressed against the wall. The shot, when it came, made her jump. A few minutes passed, and she waited, trembling in the frosty air. Then he was there. He wrapped his arms around the inside of the cape, and she drew the folds of it around his back. All he was wearing against the frigid night air was his shirt.

"I must get you back to the house," he finally said. Faith tried to search his eyes but could see nothing in the darkness. He took her hand and helped her back through the fence. He walked in front of her, pulling her along. He didn't say a word, but when they got to the garden, he kissed her and faded back into the trees.

Faith scampered breathlessly back into the kitchen. The cook gave her a once-over and shook her head. "Straighten your skirts, missy," she said and pushed Faith into the back hall. "I'm sure they didn't even miss you in that crowd." Faith smiled her gratitude and went back in. She took a position by the window, where she hoped the soft pink of her dress would blend into the ivory drapes.

Chapter Three

Faith wearily climbed the stairs to her room. The ball was over, and she reminded herself to thank God in her nightly prayers that she had survived. She had been unable to find a graceful way to escape Randolph's advances, so she had tolerated them, reminding herself that Ian would soon take her away. Randolph had pulled her out on the dance floor, leered down her dress, tried to get familiar with her behind by sliding his meaty hands down her back while escorting her to a chair. Her head was hurting, her feet were hurting, and her wrist was raw from the grip of his hand. She had in no way encouraged him, but he had hung on to the bitter end, even to the point of handing her into the carriage and calling her his "ice princess." When they had finally driven home, the stable was quiet and dark. Her father commented that the stable hands had put a horse down that night. Faith had been too weary to reply.

She gratefully shut her door and locked it. The pink satin gown slid to the floor, and she kicked the hated thing into a corner. She pulled the pins out of her hair and picked up her brush. That was when she caught his reflection in the mirror.

Ian was sitting in the chair in the corner between the two windows. She had missed him in the darkness. She crossed over to where he sat and picked up the hand resting wearily on the arm of the chair. He pulled her down onto his lap and buried his face in her hair.

"How long have you been here?" Her finger traced the curve of his ear.

"Since I took you to the house. I just couldn't stay there any longer." His voice cracked as he spoke. She felt the heat of his arms through the thin silk of her camisole. Her stocking-clad legs hung over the side of the chair, and Ian was running his hand down the length of them.

"Miriam found your footprints before," she said softly in his ear.

"The ground is frozen; there will be no sign tonight." He drew his head back to look at her. The moon reflecting in her eyes made them turn silver. He ran his hands back up the length of her legs until he came to the top of her stockings. He hooked a finger in the top of one and pulled it down. Faith felt a stiffening underneath her and caught her breath. In the next instant she was on the bed and he was on top of her, kissing her, pressing her into the mattress. His hands were wild in her hair, and his kisses were draining her. She held on to him, because that was the only way she could keep herself from spinning off into space.

His hand took possession of her breast, and his mouth trailed down to the valley between. She could feel him pressed against her thighs and she became desperate to have him. She pulled his shirt up and ran her hands over his wide chest, down his narrow waist, and dipped her fingers under the waistband of his pants.

"Faith." His breathing was ragged, his voice hoarse with desire. "I need you so much."

"I know, I know," she whispered. She moved under him. He rose up over her and began to undo his trousers. She tried to help, but his hand got in her way. He left her hands to accomplish the task and pulled her pantalets down. He started to undo the ribbons on her camisole, but she stopped him and pulled it over her head. The moon shone down on her nakedness, and he drew in his breath at the sight of her. He freed himself from his pants and bent over her, his mouth coming to hers for a kiss.

"Faith, I would like to talk to you." It was Miriam knocking on the door. She rattled the knob. Faith and Ian froze where they were, not even breathing. "Faith?" The word was whispered, not insistent. Miriam tried the door again, and then they heard her footsteps fading away. Ian reclaimed his clothes and moved to the chair, running his hands through his hair. Faith sat in the middle of the bed, her quilt gathered around her.

"Do you remember the song I whistle to the horses?" he asked when a stillness had finally settled over the house. His voice was hushed but clear.

"Good King Wenceslas?" He leaned forward in the chair, and Faith moved to the side of the bed, the quilt still gathered around her.

"Do you know the legend?" Faith shook her head. "King Wenceslas was a good king, and one night he and his servant went out to deliver Christmas gifts to the people of the kingdom. They became lost in a blizzard, and an angel of light came and showed them the way to safety." Ian ran his hands through his hair again and reached out to take one of hers. "You're my angel of light, Faith; I don't think I could live without you. Do you know what that means?"

A tear left a silver trail on her cheek as she whispered, "Yes, I know I can't live without you either. You consume me."

"Are you ready to go, then?"

"Whenever you say."

"Meet me in the woods tomorrow; I need some time to think." He went to the window and was gone without a sound. Faith could hardly follow his progress down the tree and across the yard, he was that quiet. She closed the window behind him and curled up on her bed and wept.

The Taylors did not attend church the next day. It was doubtful if anyone of any importance in town did; the cream of society had all been present at the ball the night before. Faith had not slept well. She was haunted by visions of Randolph chasing her, then nightmares of fruitlessly searching the woods for Ian. She finally came down to Sunday dinner, but soon decided that the fare would do nothing for her mood. She needed to get out of the house to meet Ian. She hoped that her father and Miriam were still feeling the effects of the previous night and would retire to their rooms. Before she could excuse herself from the table, however, there was a knocking at the front door. They looked at each other in surprise before her father threw his napkin down in disgust and went to answer the summons. They hardly ever had callers, and never had had one on a Sunday afternoon.

It was Randolph Mason. Faith's stomach heaved into her throat and she was overcome with nausea. She wouldn't have to look for an excuse to leave the house, she was about to provide one on the dining room floor. Miriam gave her a look that would kill as her father escorted the man into the dining room. Her stepmother rose from the table to greet their guest. A few pleasantries were exchanged about the ball, and then Mason turned to Faith, who had turned a shade of pale green.

"I should like to get to the purpose of my visit, Miss Taylor," he said as he came around to where Faith was sitting.

"And what would that be, Mr. Mason?" Miriam asked sweetly. Faith didn't dare open her mouth for fear of what would come out.

"I would like to have permission to pay court to Faith," he said, smiling broadly. Faith jumped out of her chair so quickly, it hit the floor with a bang that echoed through the big, silent house. She ran into the kitchen with her hand over her mouth. Miriam found her as the last of her dinner came up into a bowl on the counter.

"What is wrong with you?"

"Something disagreed with me," Faith gasped from her position over the bowl.

Miriam flung a cloth at her. "Clean yourself up. Maybe we can still save the day."

Faith looked at her as if she had lost her mind. "I am not going out there, Miriam. I will throw myself in the river before I spend one minute with that man."

"Do you know what's at stake here?" Miriam's tone was venomous.

"Yes, I do. The rest of my life is at stake."

Miriam slapped her. "You ungrateful little bitch." The words were pure evil.

Faith took the cloth Miriam had thrown at her and wiped her mouth. She took the bowl she had retched in and washed it out at the pump. She looked out the window at the woods, where she knew Ian was waiting. Her heart ached because she knew she couldn't go to him now, not with them all watching, not with Mason here. She knew Ian would fight the man if he had a chance, and she couldn't take the risk.

"Please give Mr. Mason my apologies." Faith took the back staircase to her room.

*   *   *

It started sleeting later that afternoon. When the sleet came, Mason left. He had visited with her father and Miriam in the room below hers. She could occasionally hear their laughter drifting up through the floor. She was trapped. As long as they were below her, Ian couldn't use the tree to come up. She curled up on the bed with her quilt and hoped he'd been safely gone when the sleet came. She didn't want him out in the woods waiting for her in this weather. He was smart enough to see what was going on and wait for a better time.

The next Sunday was the first in Advent. It was a beautiful winter day with the sun sparkling on the coating of ice on the trees. Ian had been at church, in the back row as usual, and his grin flashed as he rode by her carriage after church. Faith realized it had been a while since she had seen it. She couldn't wait to meet him. She began imagining the moment, and then realized that their carriage had passed the turn to their house.

"Where are we going?" she asked her father. He had just urged the horse into a trot on the frozen ground. Ahead of them was the Masons' carriage, with Randolph riding alongside on Armageddon.

"We've been invited to dinner." Miriam smiled sweetly at her from her perch beside her husband.

Once again, Faith was trapped. She narrowed her eyes at the back of Miriam's head. She knew Ian would wait for her in the woods, but she also knew that he would look for her when she didn't come. He would see that their carriage had not returned. When they made the turn into the Masons' drive, she surreptitiously dropped her glove over the side of the carriage.

Later that afternoon, the two families were gathered in the library. Faith had chosen a straight-backed chair to sit in, the rest were casually arranged on sofas around the fireplace. The men were enjoying snifters of brandy while the women sipped sherry. Faith had declined the offer of a drink. Her perch gave her a view of the drive, and her heart began to pound when she saw Ian coming up it on the chestnut. He dismounted in front of the house, and they soon heard his steady knock on the door. The butler hastened to answer it and soon presented Ian.

"Yes, Duncan, what is it?" the elder Mason asked, and then quickly explained who Ian was to his guests.

"I found this out on the drive." Ian stepped into the room with the glove in his hand. "I thought perhaps it might belong to one of your guests."

Faith put her hand to her mouth in pretend surprise. "I believe that could be mine!" she exclaimed and rose from her chair. "Let me check my cloak to see if one is missing." She was out in the hall before anyone could protest, and the butler led her to where her cloak was hanging. She examined her pockets and held one glove up to the man. He stepped aside to let Ian hand her the other. Ian gave him a look, and the man raised his eyebrows and went back to his post.

"Leave your window open," he said with a wink and went out the front door.

"We believe he's found a girl in town. He spends every Sunday afternoon there," Mrs. Mason was saying to Miriam when Faith came back into the library.

"He's good with horses, that's for sure," Mr. Mason added.

Randolph snorted his contribution. "His horses don't have any stamina. That mare of his failed the first time I rode her. He's going to weaken our stock, I tell you."

Mrs. Mason apologized for her son. "He thinks every horse should be like his Armageddon," she explained.

Faith mentally compared the big, bulky horse with the delicate Katrina, or even the tall chestnut, and found the black lacking in every category except size. She looked up to find Randolph gazing at her. He tilted his glass to her in a silent toast, and Faith shivered.

"Are you cold, my dear?" Mrs. Mason asked, concern written on her face.

"A little," Faith answered. "I really haven't felt well since last Sunday. I guess I just need to rest." She looked pointedly at her father. "It looks like it might snow again." The clouds were indeed starting to gather outside.

Shrugging, her father got up to leave. It was obvious Faith was not going to cooperate today, so they might as well go home.

Faith was sound asleep when Ian crept into her room later that night. She had left her window wide open and was buried under the covers. It had indeed snowed again, and wet flakes dripped off his hair and into her face when he moved the covers down to find her. She came up out of the bed and threw her arms around him.

"Silly thing, I just meant for you to leave it cracked, not wide open to let all the weather in."

"Oh, Ian, when can we leave?" she cried into his neck. He pushed her back so he could see her face. He smoothed her hair back and smiled tenderly at her.

"Next Sunday eve, at bedtime," he said. "The moon will be starting its cycle again, so we'll be able to travel at night." He kissed her forehead. "Make your bed up so if they check Monday morning they'll think you're still sleeping." He hugged her again. "I just hope I can make it through another week without wringing Mason's neck."

Faith put a pillow over her mouth to stifle her laugh. "Me too," she squeaked.

Clouds were gathering in the summer sky. Tall thunderheads began stacking one upon the other on the Ohio side of the river. In the upstairs corner bedroom of the Taylor house, Faith's sleep became troubled, her face lined with stress as she dreamed about a winter's day in mid-December.

They were leaving that night. Ian had ridden past her after church and included a wink with the standard grin. After the usual quiet Sunday dinner, Faith had escaped to her room to pack. Her warmest clothes were waiting in the bottom of her wardrobe. In a small carpetbag she placed a few essentials, along with her mother's Bible and the quilt. There was nothing left to do now but wait. She had nothing to hold her there. The only relation she had in this world was a father who had barely noticed her in the twenty years of her life. She realized she wouldn't miss him a bit.

She restlessly puttered about the room, straightening odds and ends, and then decided to try to rest. She knew that they would be riding all night, so it was best to sleep now, but slumber eluded her. The anticipation of being with Ian filled her mind. Eventually she did doze off and was awakened some time later by a feeling of disquiet. She lay there a minute, trying to decipher the mood of the house, but all was still. Maybe her father and Miriam had gone out, she thought.

She decided to visit the kitchen to see what kind of stores she could collect for their escape. She crept down the back stairs and had started into the kitchen when a flash of color caught her eye. She peered around a corner and saw Miriam standing in the main hall, her ear pressed to the closed door of the drawing room. Something was going on.

34

Faith went around into the dining room and crept up on the closed double doors that separated the two rooms. There was a crack between the doors, and she peered through. She saw her father deep in conference with Randolph Mason. She put her ear to the crack to hear.

"I tell you the bastard is planning to steal her away." Randolph's words hung viciously in the air.

"How can you say that?" Her father's voice was desperate.

"He has a bad habit of talking to his horses. I overheard him myself today."

"But she doesn't even know the man," her father exclaimed.

"How many women named Faith are there that look like a silver angel?" Mason sneered.

"What are we to do?" Her father dropped wearily into a chair.

"You keep your daughter in line, and I will take care of him."

"What do you mean?"

"He's threatened to kill me over that worthless mare. It would be a simple thing for me to gun him down and claim self-defense." Mason seemed to relish the idea. "There were witnesses to the threat, and I'm sure some could convinced to say they saw the deed—perhaps even you, Taylor."

Her father wrung his hands.

Faith felt as if she were sliding into a hole.

"Of course you know I can't pay you as much now, since she will be a tainted bride." The words hung heavy in the room.

"I swear to you, she's not been with any man." Her father was practically begging.

"I won't know that for sure until our wedding night, and by then it will be too late to return the damaged goods," Mason continued. "You'd best take what I give you and be happy with it."

Her father's face was that of a man who had just made and lost a fortune. Faith could not believe it. Her father had sold her to Randolph Mason.

"Do you have to kill him?" the beleaguered man finally asked.

"I would hate for this death to be connected to our name somehow. It would be a shame to tarnish the reputation of your bride."

Apparently, Mason hadn't thought of that. "No, we can't have that. We'll just have to make sure she stays out of it."

"Perhaps we can convince him that she won't go with him."

"I plan on having a talk with him myself about that very thing,"

Mason said with relish. "I have a few men in my employ who are even now arranging a surprise for that arrogant stable boy." Mason rubbed his fist as if in anticipation of using it against Ian's strong bronze jaw. "I also have men posted on the road to the east. If he's decided to take her back to Richmond, he will be killed on sight and she will be returned posthaste."

Faith looked out the window in panic. Dusk was coming, and Ian would arrive soon, to wait for her in the barn. She knew beyond a doubt that Mason would kill him, and no one would care or do anything about it. Worse, if Ian killed Mason, he would be hanged right before her eyes. She had to protect him, and the only way to do that was to send him away without her. She wiped her tears with the back of her hand and went out through the kitchen to the barn.

Ian arrived nearly an hour later. Faith had taken shelter in the stall with their one horse for warmth. She was standing with her arms around the animal's neck when she heard a soft creak from the back of the building. She came out of the stall and saw him standing in the shadows.

He stepped out into the light. His hair had fallen over his eyes again and he pushed the mass back. "You're hardly dressed for traveling," he said, moving his hand to indicate the Sunday dress she was still wearing.

"I can't go with you." Her voice broke on the words, and she clenched her fists together in the folds of her dress. She couldn't cry now or he would know she was lying and do something foolish.

Ian grabbed her shoulders and gently shook her. "What do you mean?" His deep blue eyes bored into her soul, and anguish covered his face.

"I can't go with you. I need to know that I'll have a home, a nice home, and clothes, and parties and . . ."

"All the things that a man like Randolph Mason can give you." He ground the man's name out between clenched teeth.

She tremblingly nodded her assent, and he pushed her away in disgust. She caught herself and put her hand over her mouth to cover the sob that erupted from within. Ian had his back to her.

"Was it all a lie, then?"

She couldn't answer; she had to make him leave before it was too late.

"What's going on here?" It was her father, coming through the

36

door in a rush. Faith prayed that Mason wasn't with him. Her father walked up between them. Ian turned and looked beyond him at Faith, who could not control the flood of tears that burst from her eyes.

"I don't know what you're doing here, Duncan, but if you've come for my daughter, you're wasting your time. I haven't invested all this money raising her to see her take up with the likes of you."

Ian never took his eyes off Faith.

"Please go," she cried. Ian's dark blue eyes were fixed on her. He finally turned and went to the door that opened into the woods. He paused, his hand gripping the jamb, and then he ducked out into the darkness beyond.

When Ian faded into the night, Faith felt all the light and warmth go out of her. She became aware that her father was shaking her when her head snapped forward and she bit her tongue.

"Do you hear me?" he screamed. She looked at him as if she had never seen him before. "Do you understand me?" His face was red with anger. "You are never to speak of him again."

Faith nodded in agreement. That was fine with her, she couldn't bear it if she heard them say his name. "Father, let go of me," she begged. He released her, and she fell to the floor of the stable.

"I expect we'll have no more of your nonsense where Mason is concerned."

She shook her head again. Anything, she'd agree to anything. Just please, God, don't let them hurt Ian.

She didn't know how long she sat huddled on the floor after her father left. She finally realized she was cold. She wondered if she could remember how to stand, to walk, to breathe. She managed to climb to her feet and lurched unsteadily into the house and up the stairs to her room. She pulled the quilt out of the carpetbag and climbed into her bed.

The two families announced the engagement of Faith to Randolph on New Year's Eve. The wedding was set for mid-June so the groom could enjoy the spring racing season back East without the burden of a wife.

Chapter Four

"Damn!" Ian exclaimed when the first droplets of rain came through the canopy of trees. He searched through the swaying branches overhead and frowned at the thunderheads piled in the sky. There was going to be a deluge, and soon. He didn't want to risk the gray in the bad weather, especially when he didn't know what lay ahead of them when they arrived in Point Pleasant.

There was a tavern up ahead where they could take shelter. It was just a summer storm, and it shouldn't last long. Ian parted with a few precious coins to stable his horse, then went inside for his own meal just as the skies opened up in a deluge that hadn't been seen in that area for weeks. He took a table in a corner next to a window so he could watch the weather. He planned on leaving as soon as the rain stopped.

He ordered a portion of stew, and a young woman delivered it with a pint of ale and a loaf of crusty bread. He laid his coins on the table and ignored her. She left with a frown and quickly turned her charms on a table of rough-looking men in the corner. They seemed inclined to stay for a while, and she was hoping the tips would flow as freely as the ale they were drinking.

Ian watched quietly as the raindrops gathered on the window

panes. They would hit the glass, become suspended for a split second, then trail down like a tear on a cheek; like the tears that had shone silver on Faith's cheek on the moonlit night when he told her a story about an angel in a blizzard, the night that he had almost made love to her. . . .

Ian stirred the spoon around in the bowl, taking inventory of the contents. It seemed palatable, and he began to eat because he needed the fuel, nothing more. That was the only reason he did anything anymore, because of need. The need to eat, the need to drink, the need to sleep, the need for Faith. He broke off a crust of bread and dipped it in the stew and ate it, his eyes on the window, willing the rain to stop.

Faith. She was constantly running through his mind, he could no more control thinking of her than he could breathing. He had nothing else to do at the moment, so he let his mind drift. He envisioned the first time he had seen her, standing in the road, and that first Sunday when she had come rushing into the clearing with her quilt under her arm. He remembered Faith riding beside him on a cool autumn day with her cheeks pink from the crisp air. Faith at the Masons' ball, her breasts threatening to overflow the bounds of her soft pink gown. He felt a familiar tightening in his loins at the thought of that image.

His mind then drifted to later that night, when her passion had been awakened and she had innocently reached for him in her need. He wondered what would have happened if they hadn't been interrupted, and realized that he had crushed the loaf of bread between his hands. He didn't even remember reaching for it. He cleared the mess away to the other side of the table and picked up the pewter mug. The rain was coming harder now, with massive bolts of lightning and thunder that rolled through the trees. He hoped it would soon be over.

The table in the corner burst into boisterous laughter. He caught Mason's name among the guffaws, and his hand tightened around the tankard. *Mason* he thought to himself. *I should have killed him the first time I saw him.* He slammed the tankard down and turned to the window. The barmaid gave him a look, then turned back to the others.

The first time he had seen Mason was the day he came striding into the stable shouting instructions about the care of the great stud he had brought back from England. The horse was pure evil, as brutal as his master. Mason had insinuated that Ian wasn't man enough to handle the beast. Ian simply didn't care to; it was too late to undo the damage that had been done to the animal. Mason had strutted about the place checking out the new stock, studying the new mares as if they were food at a buffet.

The next day he had taken Katrina while Ian was working with one of the other mares. Ian had been livid when he returned and found out. He had immediately set off to find Mason before the mare was damaged beyond repair. He had come upon them in a small field. Mason was ruthlessly hitting her with his crop, trying to get her to jump a low stone wall. The mare was shaking her head and turning from side to side, limping in the front. Ian hadn't hesitated; he kicked the chestnut into a run and took Mason off the back of the mare with a tackle launched from the back of his flying horse. Mason had landed face down in a pile of wet leaves and come up spitting and snarling. Ian got to his feet and went to check Katrina. The mare was trembling with fright, and her breath was coming in wheezing gasps. Mason came up behind Ian with his crop raised. The mare snorted in fright, and Ian turned, snatched the crop from the man and sent it sailing into the field. Mason swung on him and Ian countered with his forearm and followed with a punch that sent his adversary to his knees. Mason stayed there, testing his jaw, while Ian stood over him with his legs apart and fists ready.

"I shall have you fired," Mason threatened.

"I don't work for you," Ian replied, dismissing the threat. He led the hobbling mare over to where the chestnut was waiting. He bent over to check her foreleg and looked back at Mason in disgust. He swung up on the chestnut's back and slowly started back to the barn, Katrina limping badly beside him. He had spent all of that day nursing her. She had patiently let him tend to her, but Ian knew the trust she had for him was gone, he could see it in her eyes. She felt he had betrayed her by bringing her to this place of pain. He had stayed up with her all night, and then gone on to Sunday services and his rendezvous with Faith.

Faith had understood his pain and frustration. She'd also shared his antipathy to Mason. Just the thought of Mason's rough hands on her satin skin made Ian want to kill him. There was no way in this world he would let Mason touch her, use her the way he had Katrina. Ian knew Mason would use any woman that way, he was a taker, he knew no mercy and would give no quarter. All he was after was his own satisfaction. He would not have Faith.

Ian had spent the week before the ball working with Katrina. Every available minute he spent with her, even sleeping in her stall at night. He periodically heard Randolph coming and going in the stable. Ian ignored him for the most part. He would soon be gone, and the future was too precious to risk over a beast like Mason. Ian had no illusions about what would happen if he was to go head to head with Mason. He could possibly beat him in a fight, but he wouldn't have a chance against the entire county coming down on him if he did. It was best to steer clear of the man and finish his job.

On Friday night, despite his best efforts, Katrina went down. The entire estate was involved in getting ready for the upcoming ball, but Ian's world began and ended in Katrina's stall. The Masons' stable hands supported him the best they could. They respected his abilities and felt his frustration at the senseless waste of such a fine animal. Unfortunately, they had been dealing with the like for years. Ian nursed the mare throughout the early morning hours and into the afternoon. By dusk he realized that he was just prolonging the inevitable. Katrina's spirit was gone; he could see it in her eyes. All that was left in the soft brown of her eyes was suffering; it was best to end it now.

That decision, however, belonged to her owner. He washed up and changed into a clean shirt, dragging his wet hands through his hair to rake it into some kind of order. The drive of the house was lined with carriages, dropping the well-dressed elite of the county off in front of the massive stairs that led to the mansion. Ian wondered briefly if Faith had arrived as he ducked around the back into the garden. He came in through the kitchen and shook his head at the cook as she looked up from her platters of food. The dear woman had taken a liking to him and made sure that he ate well. She always packed him a lunch for his Sunday trips to town and had been sending special treats down to the stable this week just to keep him on his feet. Ian made his way through the crowd and came up behind the receiving line where the Masons were greeting their guests. The younger Mason rolled his eyes at him, but Ian ignored him and waited patiently for the elder to acknowledge his presence. Mr. Mason finally inclined his head towards Ian, and he related the mare's prognosis in a few short words.

"Can she be saved?" Mr. Mason asked. Ian shook his head and waited while the man's attention was drawn back to his guests.

Faith was standing in the hall. At the sight of her his loins tightened with such an impact that it took his breath away. She was angel and temptress rolled into one. The pink satin of her gown shimmered around her, giving her skin the glow of a pearl. He could see the rise and fall of her breath in the exposed part of her breasts. Randolph was looking at her. He wanted to kill him.

"Put the mare down," Mr. Mason told him. Ian tore his eyes away and looked at the man. "Do it now."

Ian nodded in agreement. He looked at Faith again. He wanted to whisk her away from this place, from Mason's lecherous gaze. He had to go. Katrina needed him more now. He went out through the kitchen.

"I've asked God to send you an angel to help you through this, laddie," the cook said as he came through the doors. She gave his arm a squeeze. Ian brushed a kiss on her sweaty forehead as he went out. He felt as if he was being watched as he went down the drive, but he saw no sign of anyone when he turned to look at the well-lit house. Every room was ablaze with light except for the library, which showed only a soft glow from the fireplace.

When he got back to the stable he went to his room in the loft and removed a revolver from his saddlebag. He sat on the edge of his cot and looked at the piece, the soft light from the lantern gleaming off the well-oiled barrel. He contemplated what it would feel like to use the piece on Randolph Mason, deciding that beating the man to a pulp with his fists would be much more satisfying.

When he came down with the gun, the hands saw his intent and quietly cleared the area, turning down the lanterns as they went. He went into the stall, dropped on the straw and lifted Katrina's head into his lap.

"I wish I could have saved you for Faith," he whispered into her ear as he rubbed her sweet face. There was no response. Her spirit was gone, leaving behind a shell that wheezed with every breath. He took the gun in his hand and stood over the mare.

Faith was there. He hadn't seen her but he knew she was there; he didn't want her to see this. "Faith, wait for me outside," he commanded softly. He took careful aim at the mare's head. "I'm sorry, Katrina," he said and fired the gun.

* * *

The barmaid came to check on Ian. The rain was still pounding, the water gathering in ruts and depressions in the road outside. Ian waved the girl away before she had a chance to speak, and she went back to the group at the other table.

Ian turned back to the window. He prayed again for the rain to stop. He needed to be on his way. If only he could have left Point Pleasant the night of the ball, then maybe she would have gone with him. He would have had her away before Mason had had a chance to work his wiles on her.

He would never forget the way she'd looked that night in the barn, when he'd finally come to take her to Richmond. She had come out of the stall, her eyes swollen, as if she had been crying. He had known right away that something was terribly wrong; he could feel it in his heart.

It had been six months since that night. Six months since his heart had been torn out of his chest by her words, yet all he could do was think of her. She had said she needed more, so now he had more to give. He hoped it was enough. If it wasn't, he would go on without her, but it wouldn't be the same. He looked around the rough walls of the tavern. It had been six months since his last stop here also. He barely remembered the first visit.

He had left Faith's that night in a daze. He could not believe it. After all the time spent together, all the planning, she just didn't want him anymore? Could it be that simple? He had mounted the chestnut and turned him to the east, the road back to Richmond. His mind was in a whirl. What had gone wrong? Where had he made his mistake? He had been so careful of her and her feelings, treating her gently, letting her make her own discoveries of her feelings. He rode as if he were asleep, his body functioning automatically as he sought to make sense of what had happened. He couldn't deny the tears she had shed, but he also couldn't deny that she had clearly wanted him to leave. He left the town without a backwards glance. The trail was well lit by the moon, and he let the chestnut set his own pace.

He had ridden close to an hour when he was knocked from the saddle by an impact that left him lying breathless in the snow. A shadowed figure loomed over him, and a few others stood behind.

"Randolph Mason sends his regards," the shadow jeered. Ian was hauled to his feet and punched in the stomach before he had a chance to regain his breath. He fell to his knees. Another shadow grabbed his hair and pulled his head up.

"Mr. Mason would like you to know that he plans on riding all of your mares." The shadow punched his jaw, causing Ian's ears to ring.

"Mr. Mason said to tell you he's especially fond of the mare you call silver angel," another shadow said into his ear. Ian closed his eyes. Another punch was coming, and he didn't care.

Ian had awakened the next morning stiff and cold. He had dragged himself onto the chestnut and made his way to the same tavern where he now sat. He had spent the day recovering there before heading home to Richmond.

Now the rain was tapering off. Ian scanned the sky through the window to see if there was a break in the clouds. There was, but more bad weather was in store. At least for the moment the heavy pounding had given way to a light pattering against the pane. He needed to leave; he had lingered long enough. Ian rose from the table and made his way to the door.

"A toast!" The table of revelers exclaimed. "A toast to Randolph Mason and his marriage to the Ice Princess!"

Ian froze in his tracks.

"I guess she won't be the Ice Princess after tomorrow night," one of them offered.

"Mason will thaw her out right quick!" another added, and the entire table burst into laughter.

Ian stood in the door as the realization hit him. Faith had remarked at one time that Mason had called her the Ice Princess. She was marrying the bastard tomorrow. He stumbled out into the yard. The rain was lightly falling, and he turned his face up to the sky to let the drops splatter on his face and trickle down his collar. He stood there for a moment blinking up to the heavens. Then he squared his shoulders and shoved his hair back before setting his hat firmly on his head. He was going to see Faith. He wanted to hear from her lips that she loved Randolph Mason.

Chapter Five

Faith woke with a start. The thunder had awakened her as it rolled across the river and rumbled through the treetops. The rain was coming down hard, and the wind was blowing it in her open windows. She kicked the quilt off and quickly closed the window at the front of the house. She stopped, however, when she got to the side window. She stared at the oak tree as the wind blew the rain in on her body. Was it possible for her to escape by way of the tree?

The realization of what she was thinking hit Faith like the raindrops hitting her body. She had been living as a sleepwalker these past six months. Since the day she'd asked Ian to leave, her emotions had been dead. It hadn't mattered what anyone said or did, if only they left her alone so she could dream of Ian. But Ian was in Richmond where Mason couldn't touch him. It was that simple, she realized. She could go to Ian, be with him if he still wanted her. If he didn't, well, she'd just worry about that then.

Faith wheeled around and surveyed the room. The carpetbag came out of the wardrobe. She packed it as she had before with a few essentials, her mother's Bible and the quilt. She hastily dressed and then stood at the window braiding her hair, her mind racing over the best way down. If she could make it to the tree, the rest would be easy. A bolt of lightning split the air. She began to count, and when the thunder started to rumble she dropped the carpetbag to the ground. She straddled the sill and surveyed her options. If she could reach the branch above, she could swing her feet over to the one below, possibly going hand over hand to bring her body into the center of the tree.

She took a breath and stood up on the sill, grabbing the frame with her left hand. She took a deep breath and reached out. A gust of wind took the branch out of her reach. The rain was running into her eyes. She looked down at the ground two stories below. The wind died. She reached out again, then leaned, letting go of the window frame. Now she was dangling from the limb, the wind whipping the leaves against her. She swung her feet into the tree and managed to brush the limb below with the toe of her boot. The rain was making the branches slick, and she tightened her grip. She crossed hand over hand until she could get a foothold on the branch below. She made her way into the center of the tree and wrapped her arms around the wide trunk. She needed to keep the trunk between her and the house in case someone was in the drawing room. On her way down, she noticed that the rain that had been blowing moments before had almost stopped. The only remaining problem was hitting the ground without breaking a bone. She managed to land gracefully without any damage to life or limb, and she smiled to herself as she looked over the route she had just come. If only the trek to Richmond could be that easy. She crept up to the house to retrieve her bag. She heard voices inside and stood next to the open window, listening.

"When are you to collect the money?" Miriam was asking.

"I told you, after the ceremony." It was her father, sounding very impatient.

"Will it be enough?"

Faith heard her father's bitter laugh. "Is it ever? I thought the price Jenny's father gave me to marry her when she was carrying her little bastard daughter would be enough to last a lifetime, but it was gone in a few short years."

Faith listened to the revelation without batting an eye. It made perfect sense. Her mother had loved someone else. She picked up her bag and headed towards the woods behind the barn.

*　　*　　*

The rain had not really stopped. It continued in a slow drizzle, just enough to make Ian's last few miles uncomfortable. Night was coming early, the clouds that had gathered to the west canceling out the evening sun. He routed himself around the north side of town and came down the river trail to the woods behind Faith's house. He left the gray in the usual place, the grove of trees being well sheltered now with the undergrowth that was common in the summer. He came around the outside of the barn and quietly made his way to the oak tree. He stood with it between him and the house and studied the situation. It sounded as if a row was going on inside the house. He saw the big black, Armageddon, tied to the fence post and a horse and buggy stationed beyond. He heard words being exchanged but was unable to make sense of the conversation. *If they're unhappy now, wait until I get through with them*, he thought to himself as he swung up in the tree.

He had climbed up to Faith's window in a matter of seconds and had to smile when he saw the sash wide open. No doubt there was a puddle on the floor beyond. He reached out for the sill and quickly scanned the room. The door was barely hanging by one hinge, but something else was wrong. Something tickled the back of his mind. His eyes went round the room again and settled on the bed. The quilt was gone. Ian knew Faith well enough to know that she wouldn't go anywhere without that quilt. It was gone, so therefore she was gone. She must have changed her mind about the wedding at the last minute, and that was what the uproar was about. The thing to do now was to find her before Mason did.

He was hanging from the lowest branch, ready to hit the ground, when he saw her boot prints in the soft earth beneath the tree. He landed gently and looked back up at the route he had taken. He smiled at the picture that formed in his mind. He couldn't wait to hear about her tackling the tree. The prints went to the window and then took off around the barn. He had practically walked over them on his way in. He heard movement at the window above him and flattened himself against the wall. The heated conference had moved from the front hall to the salon.

"I thought you had her under control, Taylor." That was Mason speaking.

"She never gave any sign," Faith's father replied.

"Now, Randolph, I'm sure it's just a case of pre-wedding jitters," Mason's mother suggested.

"We must find her before anyone discovers she's missing," Miriam was adding. "It would be most embarrassing for both families if word of this got out."

Ian quietly moved away from the window. There was only one place he could think of that she would go, and that was to find him in Richmond. He'd probably ridden right by her on his way into town. There were several routes available to her, and he needed to consider them quickly before Mason found her. Since he had come in on the road from the east and north, he would check the ferry to the south across the Kanawha. She probably didn't have much money and would need to pass in secret. Those constraints would reduce the transportation available to her.

He made his way around the barn, practically walking in her footprints. They disappeared in the leaves and debris that covered the ground in the woods. He mounted the gray and followed the path out, scanning the earth as he went. There, she had turned to the south, she was going to cross the river and go east on the other side. He kicked the gray into a gallop along the trail, his churning hooves flinging up mud and erasing the signs of Faith's passage. The trail ended where the business district began. Ian rode down the main street now, the buildings here backing up to the river.

He came to the place where the two rivers met and he turned east, searching for the path that led down to the ferry. He spied the trail and urged the gray down. The ferry was gone, the place deserted. Ian jumped from the back of the gray to better scan the earth around the dock. It was nearly dark, and the rain was picking up. The shack that housed the ferry master looked empty, and he could only surmise that the man had already crossed the river. It was too dark to see if the ferry was docked on the other bank. Ian wanted to make sure, so he went to knock on the door. The door was unlatched and he pushed it open, cautiously sticking his head into the one room shack. He caught the flash of some projectile and raised his arm to block a pewter pitcher that was aimed at his head. He launched his body into the corner from which the weapon had come and crashed into a body. He tried to find a purchase on his squirming attacker and found his hand curved around a soft breast.

"Faith?" he asked the darkness. He heard a small intake of breath and sat back on his heels. The body moved away, and he heard fumbling across the room. A lantern came to life, spreading a small circle of warmth in the dreary shack. She walked up to him, carry-ing the lantern, and held it up to his face in the darkness. The hair had fallen across his eyes and he pushed it back. Her face went from bewilderment to joy in a matter of seconds, and she flung herself into his arms, dropping the lantern in the process. Ian held her to him, then instantly shoved her away and began stamping out the flames that were dancing across the floor from the broken lantern. When they were out, he found her again and drew her within the circle of his arms.

"What are—" she began, but he put his finger to her lips.

"We'll talk about it later; we must be away before they find us."

"I never stopped loving you," she said in the darkness.

"I know," he replied. "Let's go." He pulled her out the door, giving her a second to scoop up her bag. He mounted the gray and pulled her up behind. He hooked the bag on the horn as she wrapped her arms around him. Her cheek settled against his shoul-der, and he caressed her hand as he gathered the reins.

"I hope you don't mind going west," he said as they went up the embankment to the road.

"As long as we're together, I don't care where we go," she said against his shoulder.

"We will be, I promise." He kicked the gray into a canter. "We'll go north and take the ferry across."

"But that will take us by the Masons place."

"I know. They're all at your house now." She laughed at that, a laugh that bubbled up from within and made Ian's heart leap.

The streets were mostly deserted due to the rain that had now increased in tempo. They were both soaked through, but neither seemed to care. They had soon passed through the town and were on the road to the north. The rain was getting worse, with the wind picking up again, and the far-off rumble of thunder could be heard. Ian slowed the gray on the road; it was almost impossible for him to see and he couldn't risk the animal stumbling.

"Is there any place around here where we can take shelter?" he asked Faith over his shoulder. She raised her head to get her bear-ings. He heard her talking, but the wind snatched the words away before he could hear them. She finally pointed to a cutoff to the right and he took it. The path led them into a tunnel of trees. The rain let up a bit, but the wind howled through the passage with a vengeance. The limbs above them swayed and creaked, and the gray danced a bit when a wayward branch landed on his rump. The path opened into a clearing, and Ian made out the remains of a barn when a bolt of lightning lit the sky. He dismounted and led the gray to the leaning structure. One wall was completely gone, causing the other three to lean in at odd angles. He led the gray into the opening, Faith having to duck down over his neck to make it safely in. Ian reached up to help her down, and noticed she was smiling when another bolt of lightning ripped through the sky.

"What is this place?" he asked above the roar of the rain.

"My mother had a friend who lived here. We used to visit when I was small," Faith explained. "The lady died when her cabin burned—I was ten, I think."

"Does anyone know about this place?" Ian asked. He was briskly rubbing Faith's arms to keep her warm.

"I don't think so; it's pretty much been forgotten."

"We can't stay here long; we have to move on before they get all the roads covered."

Faith nodded in agreement. Her teeth were chattering, and she leaned her head against Ian's chest. "You know I am supposed to get married tomorrow," she said into his damp shirt.

"I guess I showed up just in time, then," he replied.

"To stop it?" she asked, looking up at his face in the darkened barn.

"To be the groom. You weren't planning on it being someone else, were you?" She caught the flash of his cocky grin in the darkness. He lowered his head and kissed her, and all the emotion she had held in check flooded to the surface.

"Oh, Ian, I had to send you away. They were going to kill you." The words were followed by small, shuddering sobs. "They found out about us, and Randolph had hired men to get you, but he wanted to kill you himself, and my father sold me to him to get out of debt, only he's really not my father, and I realized I couldn't marry"—a big sob came out—"and I had to get to you—" Ian pushed her head back into his chest. He was so soaked, a few tears wouldn't matter.

"How did they find out?" he asked.

"I heard Randolph tell"—she couldn't call the man Father—"Melvin." The name sounded obscene to her. "He heard you talking to your horse about us."

Ian looked at her incredulously, and then his mind flashed back to a stall and a tall chestnut he was brushing and a noise he heard in the stable that day.

"Faith, I am so sorry. I am an idiot at times, especially around my animals."

"I was just so afraid they were going to kill you."

"They nearly did," he said, remembering the rest of that day.

"They did?" She sobbed again, "Oh, Ian."

"Don't worry, I survived. Besides, only the good die young, haven't you ever heard that?"

"That's what scares me so." He pulled her close again. The storm was now directly over them, the thunder coming so fast that it was impossible to talk. The wind shook the old timbers, and Ian surveyed the rafters, wondering how much abuse the old place could stand. They stood together in the barn, Ian holding Faith close, stroking her hair. The gray sidled up to Ian's back, he too wanted the comfort of the man.

When the lightning seemed to have moved off a bit and the thunder didn't sound like it was on top of them, they emerged from the rickety shelter. The rain was still falling, but they could travel. They needed to cross the river before they were found. Ian didn't even want to think about what all this rain was doing to the waters of the Ohio. He just knew they needed to get across. Then maybe he could breathe easier. There was no doubt in his mind about what would happen if they were caught.

They made their way back up the trail and were soon halted by a tree that had fallen across the path. Ian backed the gray up and sent him into the underbrush towards the trunk end to get around the mess. They floundered about a bit, and then found the path again. They soon were on the road, heading north to the ferry that would take them across to Ohio and safety. Ian regretted running the gray so hard, but felt that the need to escape was greater than the need for caution. Faith clung to his waist, her face buried against his shoulder, his wide frame protecting her from the rain that pelted his face.

Ian saw lights shining up ahead. He hoped it was a sign that they had come to the small river town that was home to the ferry. That hope turned to dismay when he saw a group of men on horseback holding torches and sheltered under the limbs of a sprawling oak next to the road.

The men came out to meet him. He touched his heels to the

gray's flanks and the horse burst though the mob, scattering the group in all directions. Faith held on for dear life. Ian heard the sound of pursuit behind. He leaned over the gray's neck, Faith leaning with him, and looked back under his arm.

It was Mason. The big hooves of Armageddon were eating up the road, quickly closing the distance between them. The gray was no match. He was tired and he was carrying two on a wet track. Armageddon was in his element; he was born and bred for conditions such as this. Ian knew he had to stop and fight. He reached his arm back and wrapped it around Faith's waist.

"When we stop, you run."

"No!" she screamed in his ear. Ian pulled up on the reins with his left hand and swung Faith to the ground with his right.

"Run!" he yelled at the top of his lungs. He wheeled the gray around and kicked him towards the big black that was looming up on them before Faith hit the ground. She dashed into the woods by the road and took shelter behind a tree. Ian could practically see the smile on Mason's face as he headed Armageddon right for them. Ian knew his gray couldn't survive a full charge from the animal. At the last minute he flexed his right knee and the gray turned from the charge. Ian leaned into Mason as he passed by and pulled him off the back of his horse, both of them going down into the muddy road. They struggled to get a hold on each other, rolling around in the mud, each looking for an opening.

"She's mine," Mason ground out as he went for Ian's throat with his meaty hands.

"She doesn't belong to anyone but herself," Ian returned as he pushed Mason away with a forearm. Ian rolled out from under Mason's body and staggered to his feet, the mud clinging to him, sucking against him. Mason reached out a hand and tripped Ian, and he went down on his hands and knees. Mason made to grab Ian's waist, but Ian slipped away, rolling. Mason lurched after him.

Faith came out of her hiding place and grabbed the reins of the gray. Both men were so covered with mud that the only way she could tell them apart was by their builds. Ian was leaner and taller than Mason, while Mason had a good thirty to forty pounds more on his frame. She anxiously watched the men rolling and slipping, as neither one could press an advantage. She frantically wondered what she could do to help Ian, but realized that if Mason got his hands on her it would seriously jeopardize their escape. If only she had a weapon . . .

Ian had a gun. She had seen it the night he had put Katrina down. She began to search his saddlebags, sticking her hand in one to see if she could feel anything. It wasn't there, so she tried the other side, the gray dancing away from her as the fighters rolled under his forelegs. She jerked him around and began to search the other saddlebag; Her hand closed around the cold, hard barrel at the same time that she felt something else cold and hard pressed against her back.

"I should have killed you along with your mother." It was the man she had referred to as her father all these years.

Faith leaned her head against the gray, her hand still in the bag. "You killed my mother?" she said in an icy voice.

"Yes. I pushed her down the stairs. I needed to find a new wife with some money, and hers had run out."

While the voice belonged to the man Faith knew as Melvin Taylor, the tone was one she had never heard before. It was the voice of one who would do anything to get what he wanted. "Now step away from that horse. We've got to get you home for your wedding."

"I am not going to marry Randolph Mason," she said between gritted teeth. She pulled the gun out of the bag and in one motion swung around and struck Taylor in the jaw with it. The man staggered back, his gun flying out of his hands into the muck. She hit him again, this time sending him into the mud with his weapon.

She turned to focus on the fight. Mason had used his greater weight to force Ian onto his back, his hands wrapped around his neck, choking him. Faith raised the gun and fired.

The bullet hit Mason in the right shoulder, the impact sending him off Ian and onto the ground. He clutched his shoulder and rolled in agony. Ian staggered to his feet, trying to draw air into his bruised throat.

"I'll get you for this," Mason gasped. His right arm was hanging uselessly at his side; the bullet must have broken a bone.

Faith ran to Ian, throwing her arms around his waist. Ian grabbed her shoulders and turned her to the horse.

"If it's the last thing I do, I'll hunt you down and make you pay," Mason growled as he climbed to his feet, still clutching his shoulder.

Ian mounted and swung Faith up behind him.

"No matter where you go, you won't be safe!" Mason was screaming at them now.

Ian stopped the horse by Mason. "She chooses me," he said calmly. "If you come after us, I'll kill you."

"You won't see me coming," Mason screamed. Ian kicked the gray with his heels and they took off toward the ferry.

Chapter Six

The ferry master looked at them in disbelief when the mud-covered couple begged to be taken across. The storm had made the waters of the Ohio swirl and turn, so passage would be hazardous at best. It wasn't until the young woman with the pale blue eyes laid her hand on his arm and said, "Please, sir, it means everything to us," that he agreed. He shook his head as he swung the boat out into the river. The couple just stood with their arms around each other, the horse hanging his head over the man's shoulder, the three of them seeking comfort from each other. They were quite a bedraggled sight. The captain wondered what had made them take flight on a night like this. It probably was best that he did not know. The ferry dipped and lurched in the raging waters, taking every bit of his strength and knowledge to keep the course straight and true. The couple still stood, wrapped in each other's arms. The horse seemed a bit nervous with the water swirling around, but the man stood tall and spoke soothing words to the animal. When the ferry finally came to a halt against the bank, the couple hesitated. It seemed they didn't know what to do next.

"Do you need some shelter for the night?" the ferry master asked. "I'm goin' to my sister's, you're welcome to come along." There was something about these two that had struck a chord in his heart.

Ian looked down at Faith, who wearily nodded. "That would be very nice," he said. "I could pay her for a bed and bath."

"I'll let you work that out with her," the man replied. "Come along; let's get out of this weather."

Ian and Faith followed the man, leading the horse with them. They walked a few blocks through the town, Faith wearily wondering if she would ever be dry again. The rain had washed most of the mud off of Ian, but he was still in sore need of a bath. They soon came to a cheerfully lit cottage. The man led them around to the back and directed Ian to a shed where he could bed the horse. He guided Faith to the back door, where a well-rounded woman stood with a lantern in her hand.

"Jonas, I can't believe you made the crossing in this weather," she scolded.

"At the time it seemed like the right thing to do," he replied dryly. "I've brought you some company."

The woman held her lantern up to Faith's face and immediately started fussing over her like a mother hen. "Oh, you poor thing, what are you doing out on a night like tonight? Get in this house and let me get you dried off." She took Faith's arm and led her into the kitchen, where a huge pot of soup was bubbling merrily on the stove. Faith stood in the middle of the room, blinking like an owl.

"Her man's in the shed puttin' his horse away." Jonas jerked his thumb in that direction. "I told him you'd give 'em shelter. He has some coin," he added.

"The first thing you need is a bath," the woman began. Faith didn't know or care if the mention of Ian's coin had motivated her. She just knew that at the moment a bath would be wonderful. The woman sent her brother off to get the tub with instructions on where to put it. She then put some water on to heat.

Ian appeared at the back door with their bags. The woman gave him a good look up and down. "I take it you have stolen this lassie away." Ian flashed his grin at her through his mud-smeared face. She looked at Faith and winked. "He's a keeper, for sure." Faith smiled at her, and the woman took her arm and led her into a small room off the kitchen. "We'll do your bath in here and then let your man have the leftovers."

Jonas came clanking in with a tin washtub and deposited it in the middle of the floor. He returned shortly with the water that had been heating and filled up the tub. Faith could see Ian in the kitchen beyond, inspecting the pot of soup on the stove.

After Jonas left, the woman said, "Let me take your clothes. We'll get them washed and dried before morning comes." Faith let the woman help her out of her wet clothes, wondering if this was what it would have been like to have had a grandmother. The woman left, and Faith settled into the tub with a sigh of relief and let the hot water soak the chill out of her aching bones. She finally felt inspired enough to wash her hair, and rinsed it with a bucket of water that had been left for that purpose. She dried herself with a towel and wondered what she was to put on when the woman showed up with a huge robe.

"I know it's a mite big, but it'll do for tonight," she explained. Faith smiled at her gratefully and wrapped the thing around her. She went into the kitchen and found Ian sitting at the table wrapped in a blanket. He motioned with his eyes at the heap of wet clothing on the floor by the door. He flashed his grin and went back to work on the bowl of soup in front of him, ignoring the wet and matted hair that hung over his eyes. The woman set a bowl of soup in front of Faith.

"Molly here is famous for her soups," Jonas commented from his place at the table. His own bowl was nearly empty.

"I can see why," Ian added, and the woman beamed.

"Why don't you go on to your bath and have another bowl when you come out," she suggested. Ian hastily finished his bowl and, gathering the blanket around him, disappeared into the other room. When he was safely behind the closed door, Molly sat down at the table. "Is anyone chasing after you two?" she asked Faith.

Faith looked at the brother and sister, who were gazing back at her with some concern. Behind her in the bath she could hear Ian whistling, and she imagined him lathering himself with the soap. She set her spoon down and folded her hands in her lap. "Yes," she said quietly. "I was supposed to marry Randolph Mason tomorrow."

Jonas began to laugh. "I told you, Molly. I told you she was the one."

Faith's eyes grew wide with fear as she looked at the two who were laughing at the table. Surely they hadn't come all this way just to be betrayed now.

"Jonas, you're scarin' the girl," Molly said and reached out her

57

hand to comfort Faith. "Randolph Mason is not my brother's favorite person."

"If takin' you two in can cause him any pain, then I'm glad I did it, the cheap bastard," Jonas sputtered out between his laughter. "I never had dealin's with such a spoilt brat in all my life."

"Jonas can carry a grudge for years," Molly said.

"Well, then you'll be pleased to know we left him lying in the mud with a bullet in his shoulder," Faith said with a smile.

"Yer man took care of him?" Jonas asked.

"He put him in the mud. I added the bullet," Faith explained. Brother and sister exchanged looks, then broke into uproarious laughter. Jonas began to choke, and Molly came to his aid by heartily pounding on his back. Ian chose that moment to come back into the room. He had on a pair of pants that Jonas had loaned him. They sagged dangerously low at the waist, and the hem hit him at mid-calf. The sight of him standing there clad in only the pants made all three of them burst into laughter again. Ian looked down at himself and tugged the trousers up to a decent level. He grabbed the blanket and wrapped it around himself and sat down at the table.

"I believe you promised me another bowl of soup," he said to Molly when the laughter had subsided a bit.

"Yes, I did." Molly hastily filled his bowl. She gathered up the wet clothes and went to make good use of the remaining bathwater. In no time she had the muddy pile clean and hanging over the stove to dry.

Faith sat at the table listening as Molly and Jonas pressed Ian for the story of their adventure. He filled them in briefly on their history and got to the evening's escape fairly quickly. Her mind wandered back to their afternoons on the riverbank when they were sharing their dreams. The next thing she knew, she was in Ian's arms and he was following Molly down a hallway to a room. Molly turned back a bed and set a candle on the stand. Ian safely deposited her on the mattress and pulled the covers up over her. He gently kissed her and blew out the candle.

"Where are you going?" she asked sleepily. "Stay with me."

"I will when we are man and wife," he replied.

"When will that be?" Faith yawned.

"As soon as possible," he said from the door. Faith was asleep before he closed it.

* * *

Faith awakened the next morning to the sight of Ian leaning over her. He had a daisy in his hand and had been using it to tickle her nose.

"Are you going to lie here all day?" he asked when she finally focused her eyes. She rubbed the end of her offended nose and tried to ignore him. "Come on, sleepyhead, it's your wedding day, or did you forget?"

"It depends." She yawned. "Exactly who am I marrying today?"

Ian lowered his face so that it was inches from her own. "Ian Duncan, him and no other. Perhaps a sound beating would help you to remember."

Faith reached around to rub her backside. "I believe I've already had one, from the way I feel," she mumbled.

"Not even a full day in the saddle and you're already complaining." Ian shook his head. "It looks like I'm going to have to toughen you up." He pulled her up from the bed. "Come on. The day's awasting."

"Ian, do you think they could still be after us?"

"I don't think Mason will be after what you did to him. However, I wouldn't put it past him to sic the law on us. At least we don't have to worry this morning, since Jonas has the only ferry on this part of the river."

"I found something out last night about my mother."

Ian came and put his arms around her. "What?"

"Melvin Taylor murdered her." Ian looked down into her face. Tears were brimming in her eyes. "He said he should have killed me along with her, that he had pushed her down the stairs because her money had run out. He was paid by my mother's family to marry her because she was with child. I don't even know who my real father is."

"Perhaps the fact that you know he's a murderer will keep him from pursuing us." Ian didn't want to add that it might also make Taylor want to kill them. "Your mother must have been very special, to have raised you the way she did."

Faith wiped her eyes on a corner of the oversize robe she was still wearing. "She was, but she was always so sad. I guess now I know why."

"Is there no one you could ask?"

"No. Her family was all taken in a flood. I have no one."

"You have me, Faith. We're both orphans, but we have each other, and that's all I need." Ian gently kissed her, then stuck the daisy in her hair. "Now get dressed. We need to find a preacher."

Faith quickly dressed and braided her hair. When she reached the kitchen, Molly had just set a plate of eggs on the table. Jonas and Ian had their heads together over a map. Jonas was showing Ian the best route west.

"I need to find Faith a good mount. I might as well get a mare so we'll have a start on our herd."

Jonas recommended a few places for Ian to look. Ian, however, felt that there wasn't enough distance between them and Mason and decided to move on a ways first. Molly handed them a sack with enough provisions for the next few days, and the couple bade the brother and sister goodbye, Molly giving both of them a teary hug.

The day was beautiful. The storm had washed all the humidity away, leaving the air clear and cool. The gray was feeling good and rested and was inclined to prance about a bit as they hit the trail west.

"Is this the horse you always talked about?" Faith asked Ian after they had laughed over the horse's antics.

"Yes, he's the one. I delivered him from his momma and raised him up to be the fine upstanding young stud you see today."

"What do you call him?"

"Storm. I thought he looked like one, all black and gray mixed up together."

"Sounds appropriate after last night."

Ian laughed. "Yes, it does."

"You haven't told me yet why you came back." Faith tilted her head around Ian's shoulder as she asked him.

Ian caressed the arms that were wrapped tightly around his waist. "You said you wanted things I couldn't give you. I came to tell you I could give them to you now."

"I don't care about that. I never did," Faith said against his back.

"It didn't make a whole lot of sense when you said it last December. Now I know why you said it, but I guess I just let my pride take me on out of town."

"I was so afraid of what they would do. Randolph seemed to enjoy talking about killing you, and I just couldn't let that happen."

"The man is a bit mad, I'm afraid. It's past us now. We're together and we have a future before us."

"Is there any particular place we're going?"

"I've heard that Iowa territory is nice—lots of land to be had for those who aren't afraid of hard work."

"Sounds wonderful. Do you think we'll get there before my backside gives out?"

Ian looked over his shoulder in an attempt to peruse Faith's posterior. "You leave your backside to me," he said with a flash of his grin. Faith pinched what little she could grab of his.

"You'd best make me your wife before you start on my backside or anything else."

"That's my plan, as soon as we can come up with someone to do it."

They rode on towards the west, stopping once to enjoy the lunch Molly had prepared for them. When late afternoon came they were on the outskirts of Chillicothe. They rode past a church in a grove of oaks by the road. Ian turned the gray down the drive to the small white church. An elderly couple came out of the door as they rode up.

"Can I help you?" the man asked.

"Are you the minister?" Ian asked as he took off his hat.

"I am. Do you need my services?" the man answered.

"We'd like to get married," Faith volunteered.

"As you can see, the bride is most anxious," Ian added dryly. Faith pinched him again and dared him to react.

"Is there a reason for the rush? Have you no home where you can do this?" the minister asked.

"The rush is we've waited some six months and don't want to wait any longer," Ian explained. "We're on our way west to find a home, and we'd like to do that as man and wife."

The minister looked at his wife, who nodded in agreement. "Come on down and let's get you ready," she said to Faith.

Ian helped Faith to dismount, and the woman led them into the church. It was a quaint little sanctuary, light and airy and sweet-smelling with a vase full of flowers on the altar table. The woman selected several blooms from the display, wrapped her lace handkerchief around them and handed the bouquet to Faith. Ian had left the church while this was going on and returned with a very satisfied look on his face and his hair flopped over into his eyes.

61

Faith pushed the locks back, and he flashed his grin.

The minister directed them to a place in front of him and opened his prayer book. "Dearly beloved," he began. Faith and Ian followed the ceremony, responding when directed. When the minister called for the ring, Ian produced a carved silver band from his pocket and slipped it on Faith's finger.

"It was my mother's," he explained. Faith looked at it in wonder, then lost herself in his deep blue eyes. The next thing she knew, Ian was kissing her and the minister was calling them man and wife. Ian shook the minister's hand and gave the man a coin. The woman gave Faith a hug and a kiss on the cheek. They waited while the minister filled out a marriage certificate.

Before they mounted, Ian discreetly placed Storm between them and the church and gave Faith a kiss that would not have been appropriate inside the sanctuary, a kiss full of promise for the night to come. When he finally stopped, Faith dreamily leaned into him for more.

"If I start again, I won't be able to stop," he whispered into her ear.

"I don't want you to stop," she replied, turning her face up to his. She was surprised when instead of kissing her again, he mounted Storm and soon had her up behind him. "This is not what I had in mind," she said mournfully.

"You'll get your way soon enough," he said suggestively. They waved to the minister and his wife, who had been watching the exchange from the steps of the church.

"I think they found us just in time," the wife said to her husband. The minister looked at her with a pained expression for her facetious reference to sin, and then took her hand. They watched the Duncans as they rode out of sight.

When they were back on the trail, Faith decided to try out the role of wife. With her arms wrapped securely around Ian's waist, she took advantage of the proximity to do some exploring. Each small foray below his waist made him jerk just a little, which sent Storm dancing around on the road. And each time, he took his wife's hand and put it firmly back in place, where it stayed for a minute or two before it was back testing the waters again, going further and further each time. He finally stopped the horse in the middle of the road.

"Faith," he said slowly, as he would to a child. "Do you wish to spend your wedding night under yon bush?"

Faith examined the bush he was indicating. "I don't think so," she finally answered. "Why?"

"If you don't stop what you're doing, I will have to drag you into the woods and have my way with you. I had something else in mind for our first night together," he patiently explained.

Faith let out a disappointed sigh. "I'll be good."

Ian checked to make sure her hands were in their proper place and moved on, leaving one hand over Faith's as they rode. They soon came into Chillicothe without further incident. Ian stopped to ask a local for some information, and he directed them to a little inn off the main trail. They checked into a small room at the back of the building. Ian took quick inventory of the windows and closest exit.

"You're afraid they might still be after us, aren't you?" Faith asked when he was done with his examination. He came to her and took her in his arms.

• "I don't want to take any chances where you are concerned." He kissed the top of her head. "Yes, he could still be after us. We're not making good time doubling up on Storm."

"When do you think we'll be safe?"

"I don't know. Maybe when we cross the Mississippi, maybe we're safe now, I just don't know."

"I feel safe now, here in your arms."

Ian squeezed her tighter. "Can you wait a while longer?" he asked. "I need to take care of some business and find us some supper."

Faith looked at him incredulously. "I'm beginning to wonder why you married me," she said, pushing him away and placing her hands on her hips. She looked him up and down and could find nothing lacking in his manly form. "The problem must be in your head," she finally declared.

Ian grabbed her arms and pulled her to him, hard. She let out a little gasp, and his mouth came down on hers before she could draw in a breath. His tongue pushed its way into her mouth, taking possession of her. His hands moved down her back and caressed her behind, pulling her against his thighs. She felt him pressing against her stomach, felt the heat of him. One hand moved up and ravaged her hair, pulling locks of it out of the neat braid she was

63

wearing. Her knees buckled under her, and he pulled her up with one hand cupped under her buttocks. He turned, and she felt the back of her legs hit the edge of the bed. He pushed her down on it and broke off the kiss. He leaned over her; his arms braced on either side of her, his hair flopped into his eyes. Faith lay on the bed, panting to regain her breath.

"When I come back, you will have my undivided attention. You will have it for so long that you will beg me to stop." His dark blue eyes were shooting sparks into her pale blue ones. "You will never again doubt why I married you, do you understand?"

Faith nodded her understanding. He flashed his grin at her and kissed her forehead.

"Lock the door behind me," he cautioned, and he was gone.

Faith made good use of her time while Ian was away. She carefully examined the few articles of clothing he had packed in his saddlebags and made use of the needle she'd brought with her toiletries to do some mending. She changed into the one nightgown she had brought with her. It wasn't the creation that Miriam had picked out for her wedding night with Randolph; instead it was plain and practical, the first one out of the drawer when she had hastily packed. She was sitting on the bed brushing her hair when she heard his knock on the door.

"Where have you been?" she cried when he entered with a basket of food in one hand and a package wrapped in brown paper in the other.

"I went to buy you a wedding gift." He pulled her into his lap and handed her the package. Faith carefully held the gift, the weight of it heavy in her hands. "Open it," he urged. She pulled the paper off and saw a wooden box. The top was carved with an angel reaching out her hands as if waiting to pull someone into her arms. "Remember the story of the angel?" he asked. "I saw this box and knew we had to have it. It's to put the story of our lives in." He pulled their marriage certificate out of his coat pocket. "We can start with this."

"Ian, it's beautiful. I—" Tears welled up in her eyes. She took the certificate from Ian and placed it in the box. She gently closed the lid and held the gift in her lap, her hands on either side. Ian placed his hands over hers. She leaned her head back to kiss him. As they were kissing, he took the box and set it on the bedside stand, then pulled her down on the bed beside him. The basket of food got in their way and it was soon on the floor, followed closely by his boots.

The next few seconds were spent hastily removing his clothes and her gown. When they were both undressed, Faith felt suddenly shy. He was beautiful, she realized, like a warrior angel, or one of the gods of mythology she had read about in school. He was lean and well muscled, his chest and back smooth, his legs long and straight, with a reddish tinge of hair starting at his navel and traveling down to his groin. She tentatively reached out her hand and let it trail across his chest. He closed his eyes, and she continued following the path of hair. He took her hand in his and guided it to his shaft.

"Ian, show me. I want to . . . I love you . . ." she began. Ian pulled her to him and they lay side by side, his hands exploring her, his lips following his hands until she was quivering beneath him, breathless, begging, urging him, her hands imitating his, driving him to the same place she was going. He raised himself over her, preparing her for the initial pain. "Please," she whispered, tears overflowing the corners of her eyes. He entered her, slowly, letting her adjust herself to him, and when he felt her ease, he began to move. Faith clung to him as if she were drowning. She felt herself whirling in space, a thousand stars spinning around her. Ian was her lifeline, without him she would go on into the beyond, never coming to earth again.

"Faith, look at me," he gasped. She opened her eyes and saw the deep blue of his above her, his hair hanging down over them. She held his gaze until her world exploded and she heard his cry above her.

When her world stopped spinning, she was lying in his arms. "I love you," he said softly, his mouth against her forehead.

"Don't ever stop," she whispered, her mouth against his neck. She marveled at the essence of him, the taste of his skin on her lips, the smell of sunshine, hay and the faint hint of soap. He rubbed her back and buttocks, making her body arch against his in pleasure. He chuckled at her antics, and she rubbed against him again, making use of her hands. She was trailing her fingers across the hard plane of his stomach when it issued a growl. He placed his hand over the rumbles.

65

"If we're going to keep this up, I will have to have some nourishment," he said, feigning a weakened condition.

Faith gathered her quilt around her and went searching for the basket of food. It was hidden beneath their clothes, which had been hurriedly tossed aside. Ian piled the pillows against the headboard and discreetly pulled the sheet up over his waist. Faith placed the basket between them on the bed.

"I told the cook downstairs that it was our wedding night, and she took pity on me," he explained as they unpacked roasted chicken, cheese and bread. There was also a jar of lemonade and some apple tarts wrapped in a cloth to keep them warm.

"You seem to have a way with cooks," Faith remarked as she tore off a piece of chicken. "I recall the Masons' cook was quite taken with you." Ian flashed his grin at her.

"I never asked if you could cook, did I?"

"If I can't, are you going to send me back?" She held up a piece of chicken and fed it to him.

"If you can't, you'll just have to make up for it in other ways," he said with a leer.

"Just try to keep on the cook's good side," she answered with a leer of her own.

They soon ate their fill and Faith began to clean up the leftovers, trying to save them for their lunch on the trail. Ian had other ideas, however, and she barely had their supper cleaned up before he had her in his arms.

He had been right earlier. Sometime before dawn, she begged him to stop; her body was so sensitive she couldn't stand any more. He wrapped her in her quilt and pulled her to him. She was soon asleep and so was he, with a very satisfied smile on his face.

When Faith woke up the next morning, she was totally disoriented. She was in a strange bed in a strange place, and her body felt as if it had tumbled along in the flood waters of the Ohio. She was still wrapped in her quilt, but she felt as if something was missing. Her eyes focused on the wooden box sitting on the table next to the bed. "Ian," she whispered to herself and searched the room for him. He was gone, along with the clothes that had been scattered about. She stretched in the bed, taking careful inventory of all her muscles and marveling that she could move at all, after the passionate attention he had given her. She sat up and pushed her hair back from her face.

"Oh, so you're alive," Ian said as he came into the room. "You were sleeping so soundly, I thought you were dead."

"It's a miracle I am alive after the abuse I suffered last night," Faith retorted dryly.

"Oh, abuse is it? A man shows a wife how much he loves her and she screams abuse?" Ian's grin flashed dangerously, causing Faith to pull the quilt up under her chin. He sat down on the bed and pulled the quilt off her in one quick motion, leaving her exposed to his reaching hands. He had her pinned under him before she knew what had happened and was trailing kisses down her neck while his hands roamed her body. Faith made use of her own hands to unbuckle his belt and unbutton his pants.

"We're never going to make it to Iowa territory at this pace," he said later when they were both lying spent and sated on the bed.

"Ian, please don't make me ride on the back of your saddle again today," Faith groaned. He raised himself up and kissed the tip of her nose.

"Get dressed. I won't make you ride on the back of my saddle again unless you want to." He pulled her up from the bed and handed her hairbrush to her. "You're going to need this too." He grinned and tugged on a strand of her hair. Faith used the brush to smack his behind as he turned away, and then began to work on her hair. She soon had it tamed into a braid, and Ian busied himself packing up the leftover cheese, bread and the forgotten apple tarts. Faith dressed and gathered her things into her bag. When she came to the box, she stopped. She searched in her bag for her mother's Bible and carefully placed it inside the box, along with their marriage certificate. She closed the lid and ran her fingers over the surface, feeling the carving of the angel. When she looked up, she saw Ian watching her, a gentle smile on his face. She stood and went into his arms.

"I love you so much," she said. He held her tenderly, as if she would break.

"I love you more than my life," he said. They stood in each other's arms like that for a moment.

Then they went down to the dining room and had a late breakfast. Faith knew Ian was still worried that Mason might come after them. Even though they were now married, she knew Mason was not the type to give up easily. He would come after them just for revenge. Ian was keeping to the lesser known roads, but she knew that neither of them would rest easy until there were several more miles and a couple more rivers behind them.

"I was thinking, Ian, there's no reason for Randolph to know we were headed west. Wouldn't he think we were going back to Richmond?" she asked as they ate breakfast.

"I think Mason is the type to cover all the options." He reached across the table and took her hand. "I won't hide it from you, Faith. I'm not afraid of anything in this life but losing you, and he's not the type to stop, especially now, after you put that bullet in him. It isn't easy for us to hide, either. People notice you because of your beauty, they notice me because of my height, and they'll notice Storm because of his unusual coloring. That's something I can't change, so I'm hoping to stay clear of places where we will be seen. From now on, we're going to stick to ourselves and travel the less known routes and hope he gets tired of looking."

"I know you'll do everything you can to protect us," she said. As long as Ian was next to her, she felt as if nothing could hurt her.

"I've got another surprise for you." He smiled across the table.

"Ian, all your money will be gone before we get to where we're going," Faith protested. Ian just grinned at her and pulled her up from the table. He led her out back to where Storm was waiting, saddled and ready to go. Storm wasn't interested in Ian, however; his attention was devoted to a black mare standing next to him at the rail. She had the same delicate look as Katrina, and was very flashy with a white blaze and four white stockings.

"Mrs. Duncan," Ian said with a bow and a wave of his hand, "I'd like to present to you the founding members of the Duncan horse family—and by the way, your ride for the rest of the trip."

"She's lovely," Faith exclaimed as she made friends with the mare. "Is this what you were up to last night?"

"Since it's Sunday, I thought I should get us provisioned before today. I noticed her down by the livery, and the man was willing to strike a deal."

"I love her. What's her name?"

"I'll leave that up to you." He gently lifted Faith up to the saddle. She noticed that her rig included saddlebags that seemed well stocked with supplies. Ian's own rig held a pack where she had been sitting and a rifle attached to the side. Ian noticed Faith's survey of their belongings and he shrugged his shoulders. "I guess it's better to have it and not need it, than to need it and not have it," he explained and hung her bag over her saddle horn. He finished putting his belongings on Storm and gracefully mounted. They rode off, the cook coming out to wish them well as they left. Ian just grinned at Faith as they rode by the waving woman.

"I guess I won't have to worry about starving to death," she said, and Ian laughed. The day was pleasant, the weather still mild from the storm a few days past. Faith was much more comfortable riding on her own, although she did miss the contact with Ian. They followed a route that was a bit north of the main trail that most settlers took. They passed a lot of farms and small communities and were for the most part the only people on the road. The rolling hills and valleys they were used to had given way to flat land that stretched for miles before them, occasionally broken by groups of trees.

The riding was easy, for which Faith was grateful, and the two mounts traversed the miles rapidly. Ian and Faith took notice of everything, Ian often pointing out a house that caught his attention or a barn design that looked practical. He was planning their home—he could see it in his mind—and he wanted Faith to see it too.

Faith, meanwhile, was trying out several names for her mare and finally settled on Tess. Ian approved, and she christened the mare with a rub on her finely arched neck. The mare responded by shaking her head, causing her mane to fly out in all directions. Storm thought she was flirting with him and began to show off, jumping into a trot. Ian steadied him with a firm hand.

"I guess I'll be spending our trip keeping this rutting beast in line," he said when the horse had settled beneath him.

"Just as long as he's the one acting up and not you," Faith said with a lecherous look on her face. Ian flashed his grin and then got down to the business of finding a place to stay for the night. He finally settled on a sandy creek bank along a deserted stretch of the road, and they set about making camp. After a quick meal Faith decided that a bath was just what she needed, and the creek offered the perfect opportunity. Ian joined her and they were soon on the bank, rolled up in the quilt, enjoying the benefits of matrimony.

Day after day passed in much the same manner. The weather would change on them from one day to the next, they were either seeking shelter from passing thunderstorms or seeking relief from the heat. Ian found Faith a straw hat with a wide brim to help keep the sun off her delicate features. He just turned more bronze in the sun, his hair now shot through with streaks of gold. They traveled on, Ian growing more relaxed each day as the threat of pursuit became unlikely. Faith was just content to be with Ian, no matter what the weather or the traveling conditions. They stayed to themselves, occasionally stopping in a town for provisions, mostly making do with what they could find or catch.

After a few weeks they found themselves facing the Mississippi River and turned south to cross over into St. Louis. After the days of traveling on their own, they were overwhelmed by the number of people making the passage. Ian began to seek out large groups of men, to listen in on their conversations. He would mingle into the group, make a few comments about heading west and then let the others ramble on, each one having an opinion on where the best settlements were, where the best land was, where the safest place was. It was a trick he had learned when he had been racing Storm, and it had served him well.

The most important thing was to be settled somewhere before winter. That ruled out going to Oregon or California, where most of these people seemed headed. Iowa territory seemed to be the place for them, probably the western part. It had just been opened to settlers, and if he could believe what he heard, the land would be good for what he wanted. Also, there were a lot of forts in the area to protect against Indian attacks, and the army would need horses, as would with all the travelers heading further west. He decided the best course was to go on to Independence, then north to St. Jo. It was midsummer now; they could be settled before autumn was upon them, he was sure.

They spent the night in St. Louis at a small inexpensive hotel that Ian found after asking around at the docks. Faith protested at spending the money, but he insisted, not knowing when he would have a chance to treat her again. They enjoyed the benefits of a bath and a fine meal, and especially enjoyed the comforts of a soft bed after spending many a hard night on the ground. They finally fell into an exhausted sleep sometime after midnight, Faith wrapped securely in Ian's arms.

The morning was soon upon them. Ian, always an early riser, woke up his usual cheery self. Faith was hard to rouse, and when she finally did wake up, she bolted directly to the chamber pot and lost the expensive dinner she had eaten the night before. Ian held her until the heaves were over and carried her back to the bed. He rinsed out a cloth at the washstand and cleaned her face. Faith just lay there under his careful touch.

"I guess the food was too rich after what we've been eating lately," she finally managed to say when the room stopped spinning before her.

Ian didn't respond; he just looked at her tenderly and kissed her forehead. She sent him on down to breakfast, the thought of eating anything sending her stomach into spasms. He returned a short time later with a biscuit and helped her to sit up and take a few bites of it along with some sips of water. She soon felt better, and insisted that they be on their way.

They joined the caravan of people traveling west out of the city, but soon overtook them, making better time on horseback than the wagons loaded down with children and household items. By nightfall they had caught up with another group and decided to make camp with them, Ian liking the safety of numbers now that he was in unfamiliar surroundings. The group was lively, excited about the future. This was their first night out on the trail, and they were making the most of it with music and dancing around the fire. They readily included Ian and Faith, who was feeling much better, her eyes sparkling when Ian whirled her around to the music. Afterward, they curled up in her quilt by their own fire and counted the stars above. Ian talked some more about his dreams for their place, and Faith was soon lulled to sleep by the sound of his voice.

The next morning she was awake for the first time in their marriage before he was. She carefully slid out of his arms and lost the contents of her stomach behind a tree.

"Poor child," she heard behind her when the spasms had stopped. She wiped her mouth with the back of her hand and felt a comforting hand on her back. It was one of the women from the group; she was around ten years older than Faith and was traveling with a husband and two almost grown sons. "It's hard at first, but you'll soon get used to it."

"What . . . what are you talking about?" Faith asked. Her mouth felt like the inside of a horse's hoof, and she was having trouble making polite conversation.

"Having a baby, of course. It always starts out this way."

Faith dropped to the ground and put her head on her knees. She began mentally counting in her head. They had been together close to a month, and she had last had her time a week before Ian had found her. She must have conceived right at the beginning of their marriage. She was going to have a baby. The woman was still hovering over her.

"Didn't you know?" she asked.

"I didn't even think about it," Faith admitted. "There were too many other things going on."

The woman shared an understanding look with Faith. "It was like that with me and my first son, and here he is near grown, practically a man himself, and I wasn't much more than fifteen when I had him. Got with him right off, probably our first night together."

Faith just blinked at the woman's ramblings.

"Where is your mother?" the woman asked her.

"Dead a long time," Faith replied.

"Poor child, let me give you some advice." Faith leaned against the tree while the woman shared her experiences with her. Some of what she said seemed to make sense, some of it Faith decided didn't need repeating or remembering. She began to feel better after she had sat for a while and decided that, like the morning before, a biscuit might do her some good. She thanked the woman for her kindness and went back to where Ian was packing up their camp. He flashed his grin at her and handed her the remainder of the biscuit from the previous morning. He had wrapped it and stuck it in his pocket when she was done with it. Faith looked at him in amazement.

"How did you know?" she asked.

"Oh, come on now, Faith, it had to happen sooner or later. There's a purpose to what we've been doing besides pleasure." He took her in his arms. "Getting sick two mornings in a row is a sure sign. The stable master back in Richmond had seven children. I don't think I'd know his wife unless I saw her losing her dinner over the fence."

Faith playfully attempted to punch the iron chest in front of her. "Don't you think this will make things harder on us now, trying to start a place, with me having a baby?"

Ian kissed the top of her head. "It will just make things more wonderful. We'll have a baby in the spring, and hopefully foals running around soon after that. It sounds like paradise to me."

"Let's just hope it's a boy, because from the way you talk about our place, you're going to need lots of help."

"It makes no matter to me," he cheerfully replied. "And it's too late to change it now, whatever it is."

Faith took a nibble out of the biscuit and decided she could stand this condition for now. Pregnancy had always seemed like something a long way off, but since it had happened, it would be wonderful. She changed her mind, however, the next morning when she crawled away from their bed and was sick again. Ian took care of her with his usual good patience. Faith just looked at him from under her half-closed eyes and wondered why he got to have all the fun.

They continued on the trail to Independence, making camp close to other travelers, Faith being sick in the mornings, Ian caring for her until her good humor was restored. They turned north at Independence and traveled to St. Joseph. Ian was worried about Faith by now; she had huge circles under her eyes, and her cheeks were sunken in. He took her to a doctor as soon as they reached St. Jo. The man pronounced her healthy but in serious need of rest. He directed them to a boardinghouse, where the landlady promptly decided that they both needed fattening up.

"I should have known that you'd find a cook who would fall madly in love with you even all the way out here," Faith said as Ian pulled the covers over her weary body.

"I guess I just look like I need mothering," Ian replied with a grin.

Faith looked up at him. His cheeks had gotten a bit gaunt also, and he was badly in need of a haircut. The hair that used to flop in his eyes was now touching his nose. She reached up and smoothed it back.

"I'm going to do a bit of exploring while you rest. We can stay here for a bit and get the lay of the land," he said.

Faith yawned in agreement. They were close now, Iowa territory was right ahead of them, and they would soon have a home. Ian took her wooden box out of her bag and placed it on the table by the bed. She was asleep before he left the room.

Chapter Seven

Ian left Faith to sleep and went directly to the livery stable. After arranging for the care of the horses, he wandered around the town, checking out the mercantile and the land office and then picking up a newspaper. He went into the saloon and hung out for a while just to pick up on the local gossip. After that he went to the barber and felt a bit more civilized once his hair was cut. He made it back to the boardinghouse just as the landlady, Elizabeth, was starting dinner. She invited him into the kitchen, and he sat at the table enjoying milk and oatmeal cookies while she worked on the meal.

Elizabeth and her husband, along with his family, had been some of the earliest settlers to come to St. Joseph. Both she and her sister-in-law were widowed now, her sister-in-law having the blessing of a married daughter to take care of her and her dress shop. Elizabeth had turned her home into a boardinghouse, which at present only had one other boarder, the local schoolteacher. Elizabeth's one child, a son, had died of scarlet fever many years ago.

Ian shared parts of his and Faith's story with her, leaving out the part about Mason chasing them. He had just reached the part where they realized Faith was pregnant when she came into the kitchen.

"Are you feeling better, my dear?" Elizabeth asked her.

"I think I could sleep for a week," Faith said and looked pointedly at the cookies and milk. Ian just grinned at her.

"You need your rest now," Elizabeth said and set a glass of milk on the table for Faith. Faith slid into the chair and helped herself to one of Ian's cookies.

"We need to get you healthy," Elizabeth declared with her hands on her hips. She went back to preparing the meal, and Ian shared his day's adventures with Faith.

That evening, Ian made dinner a fun experience with his dry observations on the things he had seen in town. He even had the schoolmarm laughing into her napkin, and Faith could have sworn she saw the old maid bat her eyes at him. Faith ate as if she were starving and then couldn't keep her eyes open when they moved out onto the porch to enjoy the cool evening air. Ian said he felt a bit tired himself, and the two retired to their room.

"I'm sorry, Ian," Faith said when she was beneath the covers. Ian was sitting up, perusing the newspaper.

"For what?" he asked, setting the paper aside.

"For this—for messing up our plans."

"This isn't messing up our plans," he said.

"But we're sitting here instead of finding a place."

"Faith, taking care of you and our baby is the most important thing right now. The land is out there, it's not going anywhere. I want to look around and see what's here, instead of just rushing out and settling on the first place we see." He pulled her up into his arms. "Besides, what would happen if we were out there on our own and you had trouble giving birth? I wouldn't be able to help you or the baby."

"What are you saying?"

"I guess I'm thinking that maybe we should stay in St. Jo this winter. It would be hard starting out in the fall anyway. It would take all our money just for provisions, and getting a house and barn built before the snows come would be close to impossible without help. I could get a job at the livery. It would give me a chance to see a lot of stock and maybe buy some more mares. It would be nice to have the herd under way when we found a place to call our own."

"I think Elizabeth would like it if we stayed—she seems to really care—and I know the schoolmarm would like it. She has a crush on you." Ian laughed at her comment. "I have to admit, Ian, I've been a little scared, thinking about going out on the plains and having a baby all by myself."

"I'll talk to Elizabeth tomorrow and see if maybe she'll reduce the rent in exchange for my doing chores. There's a lot around here that needs to be done."

"And what am I supposed to do while you're doing all this work?" Faith yawned against his chest.

"Get fat and healthy and keep me warm at night."

"Is that all?" She snuggled up closer to him. "I think I can handle that."

The next day, Ian charmed Elizabeth over the breakfast table and soon had her convinced that she couldn't make it another day without his help about the place. He drew up a list of improvements, and she was trying to decide how much credit she could get from the bank. Ian's days were full with his job at the livery and the chores around the boardinghouse. Sundays he left free for exploring the surrounding countryside.

Faith really didn't know how to cook and begged Elizabeth to teach her, without letting Ian know. She began to fill out, and with rest was feeling much better. She now had a glow about her and was quite content. She helped Elizabeth where she could, and when her talent with a needle was discovered, she found herself employed by Elizabeth's sister-in-law making dresses and shirts for the well-to-do in town. Every Sunday they went out to explore, Ian simply couldn't get enough of it. He was leaning towards the north and west territory and wanted to make a trip to Council Bluffs to see what it was like.

As Faith's condition began to show, she left him to wander about on his own, and he returned after each expedition with exciting stories of game and scenery. He also began to practice with his rifle and revolver and took to wearing the revolver in a holster on his hip when he was out of the house. At first it bothered Faith, but she soon became used to it, and remembered his adage about having it and not needing it instead of needing it and not having it. Faith used the money she earned to buy fabric so she could make Ian shirts and clothes for the baby. Elizabeth became so attached to the couple that she was soon referring to the baby as her grandchild and spent all her free time knitting caps, stockings and blankets.

By the time winter arrived, Faith was feeling cumbersome and Elizabeth admitted that she was rather large for being just six months along. The baby was constantly kicking or pushing against her, and Ian was amazed at the antics going on inside her extended belly. He loved to watch the movements in the morning before they started the day and would lay his hands on her to determine which end was up.

"I swear, Faith, I think you're going to have a foal," he said one morning as he watched a major protrusion come out on her side.

"Feels more like a full-grown horse to me," Faith groaned. The baby was pressing on her lungs, making it hard to breathe. Christmas was coming and Elizabeth was full of plans, but Faith was having a hard time keeping up with the older woman.

Ian just grinned at her, his hand roaming over her stomach.

In all her life Faith couldn't remember being as happy as she was now. She hadn't had many joyful Christmases as a child, but since she had married Ian, it seemed like Christmas was all year long. He was constantly scavenging things for her. The shed behind the boardinghouse was full of furniture he had found and repaired, and one day he even came home with a buckboard he had earned by doing chores. He also became quite a hunter and often contributed to the larder. As the Christmas season approached, he became as giddy as a child with all the preparations. He was constantly snooping around in the kitchen to see what treat Elizabeth was working on, and she would shoo him out with her broom or towel, any tool that was handy. She adored Ian, and doted on Faith.

Christmas came with all the trappings. Ian found what he called the perfect tree, and the three of them decorated it on Christmas Eve. They all went to the church service, Ian and Elizabeth on either side of Faith to help her walk through the light dusting of snow. The next morning they exchanged presents. Faith gave Ian a knife and scabbard. He gave her a lovely shawl and a cradle he had found and restored. They both gave Elizabeth a rather impressive looking bonnet, which she promptly put on and wore while fixing breakfast. They spent the day in peace, and after their bountiful dinner, featuring a wild turkey that Ian had shot, Ian read the Christmas story from Faith's Bible.

"Please, God," Faith prayed as she listened to the rich timbre of his voice. "Let us always be this happy." She felt the baby move beneath her hands. Ian caught the movement out of the corner of his eye and laid his hand over hers as he continued reading the passage. Elizabeth watched the two and gave thanks that they had been sent into her life.

Winter was soon upon them, but it didn't stop Ian from his Sunday adventures. He had purchased a gelding to use on his forays and made sure that he was prepared for any contingency on his outings. Faith, meanwhile, was finding it harder and harder to get around. She couldn't make it to the dress shop anymore and worked on things at the boardinghouse, when she had the energy. She was now seven months pregnant but looked more like nine.

There were a couple inches of snow on the ground when. Ian rose to begin his preparations for another exploration of the countryside. He was quite familiar with the area now and was beginning to venture further out to the north and west. Faith was buried under the covers, only the tip of her nose sticking out. Earlier she had complained about being hot, but now she looked as if she were hibernating. He kissed her and placed his hand on her belly to feel the baby before he left. For once the babe was quiet. He hoped again that it was a boy, because of its size. Once again he was glad they had stayed in town; he knew that this delivery would be difficult for Faith.

He set out on the gelding, heading northwest as usual. The air was crisp, his breath showing in the air, and the hooves of the horse crunched through the snow. The sun was shining in the winter sky, but it was not having any impact on the temperature. Ian rode for a while, taking note of various landmarks, and how different they looked in the snow. This area was pretty well settled, he had seen it all before. The place he was going was north of the Platte; it was wide-open there, with plenty of range for the herd he envisioned. This was to be his last trip for a while. He had promised Faith that he wouldn't range far now that winter storms were more likely. He had also told her not to expect him back for a few days. He would choose his land on this last trip; he wanted to be ready when he took his small family north to Council Bluffs.

He camped by the river that night. He found a depression near some trees and soon had a cheery fire going to ward off the cold.

The air was so clear that he felt as if he could hear for miles around. He briefly wondered what Faith was doing before he fell asleep. This was the first night they had spent apart since their marriage. It wasn't something he wanted to do often.

Faith was very restless that night. She missed Ian's presence in the bed. She was unsettled, and the baby was restless, rolling around inside her every time she thought she was comfortable. "Please, God, keep him safe," she said again. It had been a litany in her head ever since she woke up that morning.

Ian awoke the next morning to overcast skies. He hoped the pending storm would stay away at least another day. There was a particular valley he wanted to explore. It would take him all day and then the next to get home. He had ridden a few hours when he came to the small rise that overlooked the valley. There was a stream running through the middle, with land that gently tapered down. Beyond the stream the land curved out to the southeast, and there was a grove of trees. He could envision a drive leading up to the house that he would build there, just in front of the trees. The barn would be situated to the left. He rode the gelding down into the small valley and turned him upstream. He wanted to see how far the stream went, where the game trails were, and check for Indian signs. This land had belonged to the Sioux, and there were still several tribes around. The horse crunched through the snow, and Ian scanned the ground for tracks. He hadn't traveled far when he heard a shot from somewhere up ahead. He pulled his rifle from its scabbard and kicked the gelding into a run.

He had about given up on finding anything when he came across an Indian pony standing in a small depression. He slowly approached the horse and managed to catch hold of the tether that dragged the ground, tying it to his own saddle horn. He followed the tracks until he spotted blood in a patch of torn-up ground. He followed the trail of blood to where it disappeared into some brush. He dismounted, traded his rifle for his revolver, and cautiously entered the brush.

He found an Indian, a man about his age, curled under a tree, a rifle in his hands. He was bleeding badly from a wound in his side. He tried to turn his gun on Ian, but didn't have the strength to hold it up. Ian held up one hand and slowly holstered his gun with the other. He then lowered himself to his haunches and held both hands out to the man. The Indian dropped his gun to the ground. Ian slowly approached the man, who kept his dark eyes focused on his face.

"Let me see what happened to you." Ian said in the same soothing tones he would use with his horses.

"I speak English," the Indian panted. The blood was flowing quite freely and pooling on the ground.

"Well, that should make things a bit easier," Ian said with his customary grin. He carefully inspected the wound. The bullet had entered the man's back and passed through the body, apparently hitting some blood vessels on the way. "We've got to get this bleeding stopped." The Indian just grunted in response. Ian whistled, and the gelding came crashing through the brush, leading the other horse along with him. Ian grabbed his extra shirt out of his saddlebags and ripped it apart to bind the man's wound. He padded it several times in front and back and tied it tightly to put pressure on. When the job was done to his satisfaction he wrapped his blanket around his patient and leaned him against a tree, then went about the job of making a camp. The light was beginning to fade, and he had a feeling the weather was going to turn against him.

"Do you know who shot you?" he asked when he had a fire going and bacon frying in a pan.

"A coward," the man replied. They were the first words he had said since Ian had bandaged his wound.

"Was he white?"

"He was not of my people, nor of yours."

"An Indian but a different tribe?" Ian asked.

"Yes."

"Do you think he's still around?"

The Indian shrugged his shoulders, the brief conversation having taken most of his strength. The wind began to pick up a bit, and Ian pulled the collar on his coat up. They were in the middle of a dense thicket of trees and brush. Ian hoped it would be enough to shelter them from the next blast of winter that was bearing down on them. He handed the man some bacon and a cup of coffee. He ate quietly, his eyes never leaving Ian. Ian went to check on the horses. They seemed content, each one gathering warmth from the other. "If only people could be as smart as animals are sometimes," Ian thought to himself and pulled his hat down further on his head. Luckily, he had added an extra blanket to his pack. It was going to be a long, cold night.

He thought about Faith. She was probably tossing about in the bed right now, complaining about being hot but ready to stick her ice-cold feet in the small of his back. He smiled at the thought. With luck, tomorrow, he'd be there with her.

He went back to the fire. The Indian had finished his meal and was sitting with his eyes closed. Ian picked up the tin mug and poured himself a cup of coffee. He leaned back against his saddle and cradled the cup, letting the small heat warm his hands. The sky above the trees was black as pitch. He wasn't surprised when a few flakes of snow floated down and landed on his coat. He was just glad the heavy brush was keeping out most of the wind.

Ian awoke the next morning wearing a heavy blanket of snow. The fire had managed to make it through the night, the flames melting the flakes before they had a chance to pile up around it. Ian stood and shook the snow off, stamping and flailing his arms to get the circulation going. The Indian looked as still as death. Ian gently prodded the man with the toe of his boot. The black eyes flew open, and then closed again when he saw Ian. Ian crouched down and tentatively checked the bandages. The blood had dried the padding to his side, but it had not bled through. Ian thought it best to leave it alone; trying to pull it off might start the bleeding again.

"I am called Gray Horse."

Ian couldn't help smiling. "I'm Ian Duncan." He extended his hand. "I think fate brought us together."

"What do you mean, fate?" The man was curious as he took Ian's hand.

"I have a gray horse." The Indian looked over to where the horses were standing. "He's back in St. Jo."

"I am grateful that your fate has joined our paths. You saved my life."

"I was glad to do it."

"Why are you here?" Gray Horse asked, his arm motioning to the general area.

"I'm looking for a place to settle, to build a home. I had just found it when I heard the shot."

"You have a family?"

"Yes, a wife, and soon a child. How about you?"

"My family was taken last winter by the pox. My wife and my son."

"I'm sorry; I have a friend who lost her son to the pox."

They were both quiet for a moment.

"Where is your home?" Ian finally asked.

"North, half a day's ride." Gray Horse weakly tried to stand, and Ian helped him to his feet. "I owe you a great debt, Ian Duncan." His name sounded like music on the Indian's tongue. "The land you want is south of here, where the stream cuts through the small valley?"

"Yes."

"It is good land." He handed Ian the blanket.

"Keep it," Ian said. Gray Horse went to his horse and swung up, taking a moment to straighten himself, his hand gripping his side over the bandage.

"I will see you again." He rode off. Ian watched his passage through the maze of shrubs, and then turned to pack up his own belongings. It was a two-day ride home, and Faith would be worried. He'd best get started.

Chapter Eight

Faith was frantic by the time Ian got back. The snow had drifted so deep that he didn't get home until Friday. He arrived after dark, weak and exhausted but alive. Faith alternated between raging at him because he had worried her so much and smothering him with kisses because he was safe. Elizabeth finally sent her waddling off to the kitchen to fix him a plate, and sent Ian off for a much-needed bath. Faith was much calmer when Ian came to the table, his hair slicked back and his jaw freshly shaved. Her eyes had dark circles under them and seemed huge and colorless in her pale face. Ian laid his hand on her cheek.

"I promise I won't go off again like that," he told her tenderly. Faith burst into tears and climbed into his lap, her face buried against his shoulder. He tried to pull her close, but the baby pressed against him. Elizabeth shook her head and left the kitchen, leaving him to reap the rewards of his transgressions. He gave Elizabeth a sheepish grin over Faith's head as she left.

The next day was better for everyone. Ian shared his story with the group at the breakfast table and talked on and on about the land he had found. Lynora, the schoolmarm, shuddered in apprehension when he told of finding Gray Horse. Faith and Elizabeth exchanged worried looks behind Ian's back as he talked of spending the night in the brush with the injured Indian. He couldn't say enough about the land he wanted, and couldn't wait to get to the land office on Monday to stake a claim on it. Faith moved slowly around the kitchen as he talked, her hand pressed against the middle of her back to relieve the cramp she had awakened with. Elizabeth watched her painful movements with a look of concern. Ian noticed Elizabeth's worry and turned to see what the cause was. About that time, Faith doubled over and wrapped her arms around her stomach. Ian flew out of his chair and had his arms around her in an instant.

"What is it?" he asked as he took her weight upon himself.

"I don't know, it just hurts," Faith gasped.

"Elizabeth, it's too soon. What is it?" Ian asked, panic-stricken.

"We'd better send for the doc," Elizabeth said. Lynora grabbed her coat and was out the door, her eyes wide in her head. "Let's get her up to your room."

Faith doubled over in pain again, and Ian scooped her up in his arms and carried her up to their room. He kicked the door open and deposited Faith on the freshly made-up bed. She clutched his arm as the pain rolled over her.

"Ian, it's not time. It's too soon," she cried.

"Hush, darling, it will be all right. We've sent for the doctor." Ian pulled her close and smoothed her hair. Elizabeth came around on the other side of the bed and picked up Faith's hand.

"Where is the pain, Faith?"

"My back." Faith motioned around her extended belly. "Here, Oh—" Another wave of pain came over her. Elizabeth looked at Ian over Faith, whose whole body was tensed with pain, and shook her head. The baby was not going to wait another six weeks; it was coming now.

"We need to get her undressed." Elizabeth jumped into action. Ian started to undo the back of Faith's dress, which he had just helped her button before breakfast. Elizabeth drew off Faith's shoes and stockings and stood ready with a nightgown to pull over her head as soon as Ian had removed the dress. Faith bore their attentions bravely, grabbing on to Ian's arm as each wave of pain came over her. Ian lifted her off the bed, and Elizabeth pulled back the covers and placed an old blanket on top of the sheets. They heard the doctor and Lynora come clattering up the stairs as Ian was putting her down on the bed.

"I hear this baby is in a rush to arrive," the doctor said as he came into the room. He took Faith's hand and patted it reassuringly. "How far along are you?"

"Almost eight months," Faith gasped. "Is it too soon?"

"Hard to say. It looks like he's pretty well grown already." The doctor moved his hands over Faith's abdomen, and then bent to pull up her gown. "We need to have a look-see," he said to Ian, who nodded, his usually bronzed complexion pale. Faith sucked in her breath as the man poked and prodded. "Yes, ma'am, this baby is coming," he announced. "And he's coming now."

"Lynora, go fix a kettle of water," Elizabeth commanded. "Then bring up those old towels in the washroom. Ian, you'd best go down and wait."

"No-o-o-o," Faith wailed grabbing his arm.

"I've birthed many a foal, Elizabeth. I'll stay for this," he said calmly.

"Then stay out of the way," the doctor said.

Ian settled down at the head of the bed and supported Faith against his body. He wrapped his arm around her chest, and she hung on to him, her fingernails digging into his arm each time a pain hit her. He lowered his head over hers and talked gently into her ear. She was now soaked with sweat, and her hair was in wild disarray around her pale face. Elizabeth handed Ian a wet cloth and he wiped her face with it. The pains were coming closer and closer until she could hardly draw a breath before the next one consumed her. Her water broke and came out onto the bed in a rush.

"There's no going back now," the doctor exclaimed and bent to examine her again. He pulled her legs up and apart and announced, "I see a head."

"Faith, you're going to have to push now," Elizabeth directed her. Faith nodded, her eyes pale and colorless in her face.

"What do I do?" Ian asked.

"Sit her up."

Ian moved behind Faith on the bed and propped her up against him. Her gown was pushed up over her waist, and Elizabeth was mopping up the flood on the bed with the old towels.

"When you feel the next pain, push," the doctor said and moved down to the end of the bed. Faith nodded and grabbed her knees. The pain was already there. She gritted her teeth and pushed, her body arching against Ian.

"Again," the doctor commanded. She drew in a breath and pushed, her body trembling with the effort.

"Again," he shouted, his hands moving into place to catch the baby when it came out.

Faith pushed again, screaming with the effort, tears streaming from eyes that were squeezed tightly shut.

"I see it!" Elizabeth exclaimed.

"Push again."

Ian didn't think she had it in her, but she gathered herself again and pushed, her voice hoarse with another scream.

"It's a boy," the doctor said. "Will you look at that!" As he pulled the little body out of Faith, a small arm followed, its hand wrapped around the ankle of the baby boy. Ian leaned forward to see, but Elizabeth blocked his view.

"There are two," she explained simply.

The doctor disengaged the tiny fist from the baby's ankle and gently pushed it back into the womb.

"This might hurt," he said. He placed his hand on Faith's abdomen and inserted his arm inside her. Faith's back arched off the bed as he probed. Elizabeth pulled the baby away as he withdrew his arm, along with the afterbirth. Ian looked at the goings-on incredulously. Elizabeth was smiling so he knew the boy was all right. The doctor cut the cord, and Elizabeth bundled the baby in a blanket, his small wails filling the room. She handed him to Lynora, who had watched the entire episode wide-eyed from the door. She didn't seem to know what to do with him.

"Just hold him," Elizabeth said as she wiped the baby's face with a wet cloth.

"Here comes the other one," the doctor said. "Push!"

Faith gathered herself again and pushed.

"Well, look at that," Elizabeth said. "I think she was the one that was in a hurry." The baby had come out in one push, and Faith collapsed back against Ian, her job done.

"Lynora, give that baby to its mother," Elizabeth commanded as she worked over the little girl, whose wails were joining those of her brother. Lynora deposited the bundle into Faith's waiting arms. Ian pulled back the blanket to find a shock of copper-colored hair on the babe's head. His wide grin split his face, and he pulled the blanket down to find ten perfect fingers and ten perfect toes, and a huge display of manliness between his two perfect legs.

"No doubt who he belongs to," he said into Faith's ear as Elizabeth dropped a bundle into Faith's other arm.

This one had a swirl of golden curls over a delicate face and was screaming like a banshee. The boy was looking up into the faces of his parents with eyes the color of the deep blue ocean. Elizabeth took him to be cleaned up, and the doctor gave him a quick examination. The proud parents pulled the blanket back from their daughter to find the same perfect limbs that her brother had. Elizabeth had finished with the boy and quickly exchanged him for the girl, who protested loudly at the bath.

"What are you going to call them?" Lynora asked from her post at the door.

Faith looked down into the eyes of her son, eyes exactly like his father's. "James Ian after Ian's father."

"And the girl?" Elizabeth asked as she deposited his daughter into Ian's surprised grasp.

He looked down at the bundle, which had finally grown quiet. Her eyes were the same as her brother's, and were looking up at him in what he swore was complete adoration. "Jenny Elizabeth, after Faith's mother and after her grandmother, if you want the job."

Elizabeth burst into tears "I can't help it," she apologized. "I'm so happy."

"Are they all right, being born so early?" Faith asked the doctor.

"They seem fine to me. They're not even that small, really, and the lungs sounded healthy." He packed his tools into his bag. "I'll check on all of you again in a week or so. Elizabeth, take care of your family," he instructed and was off.

Elizabeth shooed Ian off the bed and into the rocking chair, which had been placed in the room that very week. She placed a baby in each arm, and he sat there grinning, looking from one to the other. They both stared up at him in blue-eyed fascination. Elizabeth gave Faith a quick cleaning and brought a fresh gown out of a drawer. Lynora helped her change the linens, and the new mother was soon back in the bed with her hair shining from the brushing Elizabeth had given it.

"Now it's time for them to eat," she announced, taking James from Ian. She placed him in Faith's arm and helped her to guide her breast into his gaping mouth. Ian chuckled at his antics from his place in the chair, his finger grasped in Jenny's tiny fist.

"What was all the fuss about when James came out?" he asked Elizabeth as she stood beaming down at Faith and the baby.

"Jenny had a hold of his ankle," she explained. "It was the darnedest thing I ever saw. It was like she was afraid he was going somewhere without her."

Ian looked down at the wide blue eyes of his daughter. "I have a feeling, my sweet little child, that you are going to be nothing but trouble." Jenny held tightly to his finger, her eyes gazing up into the face of her father.

When Elizabeth felt that James had had enough she traded him for Jenny, who took the breast with a fierceness that amazed them. "I'm afraid two of them might wear you out," she said to Faith. "Are there twins in your family anywhere?"

"I never heard of any. Ian?"

"Not that I know of."

"They usually skip a generation. Were either of your parents twins?" Elizabeth asked.

"I don't know who my real father was. Maybe he was a twin," Faith volunteered.

"It would have been nice to know beforehand. We're going to have to find another bed, and we'll definitely need more diapers." Elizabeth began a mental list in her head of all the things they would need with two babies in the household. Ian immediately solved the bed problem by emptying out a dresser drawer, lining it with a few blankets and placing it on top of a small chest. Elizabeth went off to see what other items she could come up with and left the new family to themselves. Jenny had stopped eating, and Ian joined his wife and babies on the bed.

"You've managed to double our family in one day," he said to Faith. She had curled on her side and had pulled Jenny up against her. Ian lay on the other side of James, so the two babes were sheltered between their parents' bodies.

"I believe you might have had a little to do with it," she said as she stroked the soft cheek of her daughter.

"I love you, Faith. You were so brave. I don't think I could have done it."

"I didn't have much choice," Faith laughed. "I love you." Ian leaned across the babies and kissed his wife. Jenny started to fuss beneath their joined lips.

"We're going to need a bigger bed," Ian said when the two parted.

Faith bent down to soothe her daughter, whose wide blue eyes were focused on Ian again. "At least young Jamie here knows what it's good for," she said. Jamie was sound asleep against his fussy sister.

A while later Elizabeth returned to find the entire family asleep on the bed. "Best get it now, because you'll sure miss it later," she said and shut the door.

Chapter Nine

The family soon settled into a routine. They found that Jenny was the demanding one of the twins. She would be the first to wake up, and Ian would scramble to get her before she set Jamie off. Jamie, on the other hand, was content with everything and seemed happy to do things at his parents' convenience. Ian and Faith's life for the moment was a cycle of taking care of babies and trying to catch up on sleep when the babies slept. Ian was also working at the livery, and the hard hours were taking a toll. Ian also was anxious for the weather to break so he could get about the business of claiming his land. Soon February had passed and March was upon them. The snow melted, the days were longer, and the twins were sleeping through the night. He began to gather the things he would need to begin their homestead.

Faith was ready to pack up the babies and go with him, but Ian wouldn't hear of it. He loaded the buckboard with supplies and hitched the gelding and another horse that he had bartered for to the front. Storm was tied to the back. He planned on using him to travel back and forth. He promised to return at the end of two weeks' time with a progress report. He hoped his family could join him before summer.

He kissed Faith long and hard before he climbed onto the seat of the buckboard. They had just rejoined again as man and wife, and that was the one thing he hated to do without. The circles under her eyes were gone now that the twins were sleeping more and she had regained her slim figure, except for the extra fullness in her breasts. He commented on that very fact as Faith leaned into him and pushed his hair back out of his eyes. He kissed her again, kissed the babies, whom Elizabeth was holding in her arms, and bussed Elizabeth on the forehead with instructions to take care of the Duncans for him.

He set off into the spring morning, finally seeing his lifelong dream with his reach. The land office in Council Bluffs confirmed what he had found out in St. Jo. The land was his, all he had to do was stake his claim. As he drove the buckboard around the gentle curve of the hill and saw before him all that he had dreamed about, he gave a prayer of thanksgiving. He now had everything he had ever wanted. Life was good.

Ian set to work laying out a foundation for a house, building a corral, carefully planning everything. He would dig a well after Faith arrived; he could get water from the stream until then. It was too early to think about a garden, besides, Elizabeth and Faith had been canning all fall and had enough to keep them well fed until they had their own crops. *With all the things we've been collecting, it will take me to next fall to get everything hauled out here*, he thought as he struggled with a stud to erect a wall in his house. He pushed against the section and slowly moved it into place. He bent to pick up his hammer, and froze when he saw a man on horseback on the rise above the house. He pulled his gun from his holster and dropped down from the foundation as the rider came down the slope.

It was Gray Horse. He rode up to what would be the front of the cabin and dismounted. Ian stepped out from behind the frame of the house and put his gun away.

"I came to see if you were the one who had settled here."

"None other," Ian replied. He followed Gray Horse, who was walking over to the small corral Ian had built.

"You do have a gray horse," the Indian commented as he admired Storm. "He should give you many strong foals."

"I hope so," Ian said. "How's your wound?"

Gray Horse touched the faint scar on his steely abdomen. "It healed well, thanks to you." He stood and surveyed all the work Ian had done. "I still owe you a life," he commented.

"I would be happy instead with your friendship," Ian replied, "You might get bored waiting around for me to get into trouble." The Indian looked at Ian and gave a heartfelt laugh, and soon Ian was laughing with him.

"Has your coffee gotten any better?" Gray Horse finally asked.

Gray Horse stayed the night with Ian and helped him set the framing in place for the walls of the cabin. Ian showed him the different rooms he had laid out and shared his future plans with him. He also told him about the twins, and Gray Horse was amazed when he heard about Jenny holding on to Jamie's ankle. The two men talked many hours, and Ian was amazed that despite the differences in their cultures, they were basically the same inside. With the help of the Indian, Ian was able to do a weeks work in one day, which meant that Faith would be able to join him that much sooner. He was in high spirits at the end of the first two weeks when he made the trip back to St. Jo.

As spring came to the area, Ian's homestead grew. The house was nearly complete. Gray Horse had shown up from time to time, sometimes with fresh game or fish that he had caught upstream. He always stayed the night and helped in whatever way he could. The bond between the two men grew stronger. Ian even allowed Storm to cover some mares that Gray Horse brought along, and in exchange the Indian gave him a mare. Like his family, Ian's herd was growing, with the expectation of two foals come next spring, one by Tess and one later on by the Indian pony. He soon had the house under roof, and the next trip out he would bring his family.

The twins were now three months old and growing as expected. Jamie was the first in everything, Jenny usually right behind him. Faith was anxious for her family to be back together, but at the same time hated the thought of leaving Elizabeth. The woman was as close to her as anyone had ever been, except for Ian, and she wasn't sure if she could cope with the babies without her steadying influence.

The time soon came for them to part. Ian, much to their disbelief, had been able to pack all of their collected household items into the buckboard. The babies were safely tucked into baskets beneath the seat among the last-minute items that Elizabeth kept adding to their load. Tess and Storm were tethered to the back. This was the first time Faith had ever felt regrets at leaving anywhere, and she held on to Elizabeth as tears filled her eyes.

"How will I manage without you?" she cried into the woman's shoulder.

"You'll be fine my dear, just use that pretty head of yours. Common sense is usually the answer." Elizabeth wiped her own eyes. "I promise to write, and I'll be out for a visit before you know it."

"We'll be back to see you," Ian promised. "You're our family." He handed Faith up into the buckboard and followed her up onto the seat. Faith checked on the twins, who were both asleep, and they started off for their new home. Faith was full of apprehension as they traveled, but she was so glad to be back with Ian that she soon relaxed and began to look forward to finally seeing the place that had captured Ian's heart.

She wasn't disappointed when early the next morning they rounded the hill into their little valley. The cabin was sitting all fresh and new in front of a grove of trees. There was a stream, close enough to be convenient, and off to the left were a corral and a small shed. Ian helped Faith down from the wagon, then swept her up into his arms.

"What are you doing?" she squealed as he pretended he was about to drop her.

"Carrying you across the threshold." He grinned as he kicked open the door and carried her into her home. He spun her around in the main room of the cabin until she was drunk with laughter. He deposited her in the middle of the floor and ran out to get the baskets with the twins. He handed Jamie to Faith and took Jenny in his own arms as he conducted them on a tour of their home. The cabin consisted of three rooms—a sitting room, a kitchen behind, and a bedroom off to the right. Above the sitting room and kitchen was a loft that would later become the twins' bedroom. Faith examined each room and admired the careful craftsmanship that had gone into the building of the place.

"I can't believe you did all this on your own," she said in amazement.

"Like I said, Gray Horse helped," Ian replied. He had gone to the wagon and carried in the rocking chair. Jenny was getting restless and was ready to be fed. He set the chair in front of the window, and Faith sat down to take care of Jenny. She still wasn't sure if she felt comfortable about Ian being friends with an Indian, but Ian seemed to have no concerns, so she would wait and see what happened. Faith nursed the babies while Ian carried in furniture and provisions. There were several things they still needed, but between the two of them they soon had the place looking like a home. They finished the basket of food Elizabeth had packed for their dinner and put the twins to bed, each one now having its own cradle at the foot of the bed. Faith's quilt was carefully folded at the end of the bed, and her box with the angel carved in the top was in its place on the bedside table.

Faith took the box into her lap after she had settled into bed for the night. Ian was out making sure the stock was content and the house was secure. She had her Bible open and was reading the pages in the front when he came into the room. He stopped at the door and surveyed the scene before him with a smile on his face. His children were contentedly sleeping in their beds, and his wife was before him, the glow from the lamp on the bedside stand making a halo around her head as she studied the Bible.

"Ian, look at this," she said without looking up. "I've never paid any attention to this until now." She laid the Bible beside her on the bed as Ian sat down to look. The book was opened to the front where births, marriages and deaths were recorded. It started with the marriage of what Faith assumed were her mother's parents; then there was her mother's birth, and another birth, soon followed by a death of the same baby. Her grandmother had died soon after that. The next recording was the marriage of her mother, Jenny Marie, to Melvin Taylor; then, not even five months later, her own birth was recorded. After that was the death of her mother, hastily scribbled in some fifteen years later before the book had been handed to her. "It was right here in front of me the entire time and I didn't even know it."

"You mean the fact that Taylor isn't your real father?" Ian asked. "I knew that the first time I saw you together." He pulled Faith into his arms. "I don't care who your father is, or was. I just care that he made you for me, and that you're here with me now. I've missed you so much."

"I'm just glad that we're finally here—" Faith motioned around the room—"home." She settled against his chest.

"I don't ever want to be apart from you again." Ian kissed his wife. She was here with him now, and they had all the time in the world.

It was a few days later that Faith met Gray Horse for the first time. She was out hanging the endless pile of wet diapers on the clothesline when he rode into the yard. She was startled at first, this being her first contact with an Indian, but soon felt comfortable in his presence. Ian had gone to town to buy a cow, and was happy to see his friend sitting on the front stoop with a twin in each arm when he arrived later that afternoon. Faith had taken advantage of his babysitting, and used the time to fix the three of them dinner. Gray Horse seemed uncomfortable inside the house now that it was furnished with all the civilized trappings of a family, so the three of them ate on the porch, juggling plates and babies.

What amazed Faith most was that the sun had bronzed Ian's skin to almost the same color as the Indian's. They both had the same sharp planes and angles to their faces, the only thing setting them apart was the color of their eyes and hair. Gray Horse was very polite and was quite taken with the babies. Jamie stared intently at the man with his deep blue eyes. Jenny seemed determined to take possession of Gray horse's hair, her tiny hand reaching for the braided and beaded strands that hung down to his chest. He agreed to stay the night but refused to sleep in the house, instead making camp down by the stream where he and Ian had spent many a night.

"I was afraid of him at first," Faith confessed to Ian when she was securely wrapped in his arms, safe in their bed.

"Why?" Ian asked. He rubbed his cheek against the top of her head.

"I guess it was just the whole idea of having an Indian in our home. When you first mentioned him, I as if we were going to the very edge of civilization, but now I realize, he's not so different."

"I didn't think about how much he must miss his own family until I saw him with the twins."

"It's a sad thing, to know that you've lost the ones you love."

"I know I'd die if anything happened to you," Ian said as he moved down on his side, taking Faith with him. His hand caressed the side of her face, his deep blue eyes pulling her once again into the very essence that was Ian. His mouth came down on hers, and she felt herself spinning as he poured his soul into her, as she poured hers back, as they once again came together in their love. At the foot of the bed, Jamie and Jenny slept on.

Ian decided to start on the well since Gray Horse was there and seemed inclined to help. He hadn't wanted to dig without knowing that someone was nearby to lend assistance in case of a cave-in. He had rock left over from the chimney and was hard at work when Faith called that breakfast was ready. Ian hastily cleaned his plate and jumped back into the well. Faith sat down on the porch steps with Gray Horse as he ate.

"How did you learn to speak English so well?" she asked.

"At the mission, my father thought it would be wise to learn the ways of our enemies."

Faith was taken aback by his admission. "Do you consider us your enemy?"

"Your husband saved my life. There are not many white men who would do that." Gray Horse put his plate down and watched Ian as he worked. Faith waited patiently for the man to continue. "I have found that there are good and bad in both worlds. If we have to share this land with someone, I would rather it be someone good, like your husband."

"He is good," Faith said as she watched Ian dig. The babies began to fret, and she went inside to get them. She returned with both and handed Jamie to Gray Horse. Faith sat down behind him and discreetly began to nurse Jenny, laying a blanket over her for modesty's sake. Gray Horse propped Jamie on his knee and began to bounce him. Jamie promptly stuck his chubby fist in his mouth and watched Gray Horse as he sang a little song to him. "Ian said you had a son," Faith said as she watched the two.

"Yes. He is gone now." Faith didn't pursue it, she could tell by the set of his shoulders that the subject was closed.

"You are really good with children," she finally said. Gray Horse glanced over his shoulder and saw Faith smiling at him. He pulled Jamie up to him and hugged him. Faith saw the deep blue eyes of her son gazing at her over the Indian's bare shoulder. She knew without a doubt that Gray Horse would be there for them.

Ian popped his head out of the well and flashed a grin at his wife. His hair was hanging down in his eyes again and he pushed it back, leaving a long streak of dirt on his forehead.

"Hey, how about some help?" he called to his friend.

Gray Horse held up Jamie and shook his head. "Some things are more important, my friend," he said and laughed.

Ian went back to his digging.

Ian's next plan was to raise a barn. He knew it was more than he could handle, even with Gray Horse's help. He had faithfully been taking his family to church each Sunday in Council Bluffs and had begun to make friends with the other new families in the community. His homestead was further along than most, so he volunteered his time in return for help with his barn. He also managed to increase their household by the addition of a pregnant sow and a flock of chickens. They had a successful barn-raising at the end of June, complete with a picnic under the trees behind the house. The women all fussed over the twins, and the men all admired Storm, who showed off for everyone by prancing around his corral, tossing his mane and tail.

Faith looked up once to see Gray Horse deep in the trees watching the proceedings. He faded back into the brush when he saw her. Faith knew he would not come to the house with so many people there. He appeared later that night, after everyone had left. Faith and Ian were sitting on the porch admiring the new building when he came around the corner of the house. He didn't say a word, just sat on the steps and looked at the barn. Faith kissed Ian and went into the house. She knew Gray Horse wouldn't say anything as long as she was there.

"You have many new friends who helped you today," Gray Horse remarked after Faith had left.

"That's the way it is. We all help each other," Ian said. He came down and sat next to his friend on the stoop. "Is there something I can help you with?"

"I have seen many horses out on the plains to the west."

"Running wild?" Ian asked.

"Yes, ours for the taking," Gray Horse replied. "Two men should be able to take some, if they had a plan."

"Tell me more," Ian said.

Faith looked out the window and saw the dark head and the russet one bent close together. Ian would tell her about it soon enough. She climbed into bed and went to sleep to the sounds of their voices talking into the night.

The next day, Ian was full of plans for going after the wild horses. Elizabeth was coming for a visit, so he decided to wait until she arrived so Faith would not be left alone with the babies. Ian picked Elizabeth up in town from the stage depot. She arrived with many packages and baskets full of food, bubbling over with excitement at getting to see her grandchildren. When the buckboard pulled into the yard, Faith ran out to meet her, letting herself be enfolded in the woman's loving arms. Ian grinned at Faith over Elizabeth's gray head as he loaded the packages into his arms.

Elizabeth immediately went to the babies upon entering the house. They were on the quilt in the middle of the floor in the sitting room. She plopped down between the two and scooped them both up into her arms. Jamie looked up at her with his deep blue eyes, Jenny wiggled around until Ian took her out of Elizabeth's arms. The only time Jenny seemed content was when her father was holding her. She was also quite fascinated with Gray Horse, and would stare at him for long minutes on end.

Gray Horse arrived soon after they had finished dinner and were sitting on the front porch enjoying the night air. Elizabeth gasped as the Indian seemed to appear magically out of the darkness. Ian had heard the bird call that usually announced Gray Horse's arrival but neglected to tell anyone that company was coming. Faith was by now used to the Indian turning up in the evenings and didn't bat an eye as he gently rubbed Jamie's head. Elizabeth was holding a sleeping Jenny in her arms and looked from Ian to Faith in bewilderment as Gray Horse sat down on the porch step next to Ian.

"We'll be leaving at first light," Ian informed the ladies. Faith just nodded, she dreaded the separation but knew it couldn't be helped. This was a way to expand their herd with little financial investment. Ian had confided that Gray Horse was hoping to take another wife and needed the horses to impress the girl's father.

"Well, it worked on me, didn't it?" Faith had laughed when he told her, remembering the first time she had seen him leading the string of horses.

"And here I was thinking it was my charm and good looks," he had replied as he advanced on her. She had just put the children down for a nap and was once again hanging diapers on the line when he had told her of the plans. He had grabbed her around the waist as she bent to get a diaper out of the basket, and she had squealed in mock fright, slapping the wet cloth against his chest. He flung the cloth over the line and picked her up, throwing her over his shoulder and carrying her into the house. They had made love while the children slept through the afternoon, smothering laughter in the pillows as they tickled each other.

Faith looked at her husband, who was now sitting on the steps of the porch with his friend, planning a roundup of wild horses. *God, please keep him safe*, she prayed silently.

Ian looked over at her from his perch and winked. She gathered the sleeping Jamie against her and took him to bed, Elizabeth following with Jenny. They had fixed Elizabeth a place to sleep in the sitting room, and she made her way to her bed after depositing Jenny in hers.

Faith brushed out her hair as she waited in their bed for Ian to come to her. She heard the creak of the boards as he came across the porch and through the door. He bade Elizabeth a quiet good night, entered their room and closed the door firmly behind him. He loved seeing Faith this way, with the light of the lantern making a halo behind her head, her hair shining silver around her shoulders. He sat down on the bed and pulled off his boots. He had taken to going without his shirt as he worked in the sun, and his chest and back were now as bronzed as Gray Horse's. Faith rubbed her hands over the muscles of his torso as he slid out of his pants, and he leaned back, pulling her down on top of him. Her hair pooled on either side of his face as he kissed her and rolled her over so that he was now on top of her, her hands once again kneading the muscles at the back of his neck, across his shoulders, down his spine to his waist. Her hands moved around to the front and he lifted her to pull her gown up. She adjusted her hips and he slid in, Faith letting out a little gasp as he did so. She wrapped her legs around him and he began to move, his hands holding her head gently between them, their foreheads touching, his hair hanging down on hers. Once again Faith held on to him for dear life as she felt her body begin to spin off into space, nothing but the stars around her.

Part Two
Iowa Territory, 1853

Chapter Ten

Ian Duncan looked up from the corral post he was replacing. A burst of laughter from Faith had caught his attention. She was on the porch with Jenny, their blond heads bent over some sewing. It was an uncommonly warm day for fall, and he could see Faith's bare toes peeking out from under her dress. Jenny's feet were also bare, her ankles sticking out of a pair of Jamie's hand-me-down pants. Jenny was perched on a stool beside her mother, watching the progression of intricate stitches that Faith was making in the fabric. He couldn't help smiling at the sight of them. He told himself again how rich he was, to have a wife who was silver and a daughter made of gold. Jenny closely resembled her mother in the shape of her nose and chin, but her coloring was more vibrant, possibly from all the time she spent in the sun. Jenny definitely had her father's deep blue eyes, as did her brother Jamie.

Jamie was trying to wrestle the corral post into the hole left by the broken one. At thirteen years of age the boy was shooting up so fast that Faith couldn't keep him in clothes. The endless eating that had been his hallmark for years was becoming evident, and he was already approaching his father in height, although he still needed to fill out quite a bit through the shoulders. He was the image of Ian, right down to the hair that wouldn't stay where it was supposed to. At present, Jamie's copper-streaked hair was wringing with sweat and hanging down in his eyes as he shoved against the post. Ian reached out a hand and braced the top of the post while Jamie pushed the bottom until it slid into the hole. Ian handed him a hammer and stepped back so the boy could nail the planks into place. Storm, who had been watching the proceedings, danced away in mock fright when the hammering started. Ian watched the stallion's antics, then began to whistle "Good King Wenceslas." Storm came over to where Ian was sitting on a barrel and placed his nose in the man's lap. Ian rubbed the horse's sooty-colored nose as he considered the years that had brought him to this place.

He had started his herd with a roundup of several horses that were running wild on the plains. Ian and Gray Horse had spent several days pursuing the bunch before they trapped them in a box canyon. They had camped there and cut the cream from the herd before turning the rest loose. They had then divided the animals between them and tamed them enough to get them home. They had returned home some three weeks later much richer for the trip. Faith had been beside herself with worry, but after one look at his satisfied grin she had declared it was all worth it.

Ian now had some of the finest horses in the whole territory, with the U.S. Army as one of his best customers. Gray Horse had also profited greatly from the trip and his friendship with Ian. He now had a wife, two fine sons and a daughter. He would occasionally bring his family along when he visited. His wife was still shy after all these years, but the twins got on quite well with the younger children and they would run all over the countryside until they dropped into their beds at the end of the day.

Once again Ian looked up at the house where Faith and Jenny were working. The house had aged until it looked as if it was part of the landscape. There had been talk at one time of building an additional room after the birth of another son, but he had died at the age of two from the pox. Another son, born a few years later, had died in his sleep one afternoon, for no apparent reason. The two tiny bodies were in the church cemetery in town. Faith had been devastated, especially after losing the second.

She was pregnant once again, however, her condition just beginning to show. Ian hoped it was a girl. Jamie was all anyone could every want in a son, but Ian knew Faith felt she had not done quite as good a job in raising Jenny.

Ian couldn't help grining when he thought about his daughter. From the very first steps she took, she had been on her brother's heels, following wherever he led. It was never practical to put her in a dress; she was constantly climbing trees and splashing through creeks and getting into as much mischief as any boy ever did. She also had an incredible sense of balance. She could walk across the corral rail without batting an eye, and Ian had once caught her swinging from the rafter outside the hayloft in the barn. Faith still didn't know about that one, she would have beat Jenny for a week if she had seen it.

Faith had instilled proper manners in the children so that they could be civil when they wanted. She had also managed to pass down her talent for sewing to Jenny. They had spent many a winter evening with Jenny working on a sampler while Jamie read out loud. It was the only time Jenny ever really sat still. Jamie, however, could sit for hours, reading a book, or just watching the clouds in the sky. He would be wrapped up in a world of his own making until Jenny couldn't stand it and would come pester him until he joined her in some adventure, both of them flying across the plains, usually bareback, Jenny's long golden hair flying in the wind.

They both had inherited the Duncan horse magic, as Faith called it, especially Jamie. He could tame a horse faster than anyone Ian had ever seen, and usually just by talking to it. He was constantly amazing Ian, who couldn't help looking on the boy with pride. He was proud of Jenny, too; he just hoped that as she grew older she would grow more ladylike. There was still time. They were only thirteen years old, on the threshold of growing up.

Jamie finished his work on the corral and stood back so his father could inspect his work. Ian carefully looked over the job and nudged the post with the toe of his boot. "Looks good to me," he finally announced. Jamie flashed a grin, and Ian put his arm around the boy's shoulder. "Let's go see what your mother has fixed us for dinner."

Faith looked up and smiled as she saw Ian and Jamie making their way to the house. They were so much alike that it scared her sometimes. Ian was so proud of the boy, she had caught him several times just watching him while he worked, or while he read, sometimes even as he slept.

105

"Like this, Momma?" Jenny asked. Faith turned from her musings to look at the sewing that was gathered in Jenny's lap.

"Yes, that's it," she answered as she inspected the small, neat stitches. Jenny might run wild like a savage, but she was most ladylike in her sewing, taking pride in the neatness of her work.

Something had caught Faith's attention, and Jenny looked up to see what it was. Her father and brother were at the well. Ian was working the pump so they could wash up for dinner, the lean muscles in his back working effortlessly. As always, Jenny's heart skipped a beat when she looked at her father. He was as glorious to her as a god, his easygoing ways and patience a calming influence in her otherwise hectic life. He had always been the one to calm her when her emotions got the better of her. Faith claimed she and her daughter were too much alike personality-wise for her to be able to reason with Jenny.

"Momma, how did you know you loved Dad?" she asked her mother. Faith was also watching the two briskly scrubbing their face and hands to wash off the sweat and grime. Faith had to take a minute to answer, her mind going back to when she had asked the same question of her own mother.

"I just knew. The first time I met him, I knew," Faith answered.

"How did you know?"

Faith remembered that Sunday on the riverbank, a warm fall day like today, when Ian had first kissed her. "My toes curled up when he kissed me," Faith said, a soft smile curving her face. Ian walked up on the porch and bent over Faith, putting his hands on the arms of her chair.

"What are you smiling about?" he asked, the grin flashing as he leaned over her.

"I was just remembering something," she replied. He lowered his face and planted a soft kiss on her curved lips. Jenny leaned forward and saw her mother's toes peeking out from between her father's booted feet. To her amazement, she saw Faith's toes curl up as if seeking a purchase on the aged wood of the porch.

"And what was that memory that made you smile?" he asked when he was done with the kiss.

"I'll tell you later," Faith answered. She extended her hands, and Ian pulled her up from the chair.

"What were you looking at?" Jamie asked his sister after their parents had gone into the house.

"Momma's toes curl up when Dad kisses her," Jenny informed him. Jamie looked at her as if she had lost her mind.

"You wouldn't understand. You're just a boy."

"Thank God," Jamie replied. Jenny stuck her tongue out at him as they went inside.

Later that night, when the twins were asleep in their loft and Ian and Faith had settled down for the night, Ian asked her again about what had made her smile.

"Do you remember the first time you kissed me?" Faith asked him.

"Yes, I do, it was that first Sunday, on the banks of the Ohio. I felt like I had been kicked by a horse." Faith punched his ribs at the crudeness of his comparison. "Ooof," he said, rubbing the injured area. "Yes, I remember," he said softly as he pulled her close.

"Remember when I tripped over the quilt?"

"Yes. Come to think of if, you never told me why you had the giggles that day."

"My mother told me I would know that I loved a man because my toes would curl up when he kissed me. That's why I tripped— my toes were all curled up." Ian burst into laughter. "Jenny was asking me the same thing today, and I told her that she would know she loved a man because her toes would curl up with his kiss." Ian couldn't smother his laughter; he let it out in whooping bursts. "What is so funny?" Faith asked, punching his ribs again.

"Oh, Faith, I love you," he said when he got himself under control. "Let me give this a try and see what happens." He pulled her down and began to rain kisses on her, stopping occasionally to see what condition her toes were in. He soon had Faith giggling out of control because he got confused and started kissing her toes. In the loft above, Jamie and Jenny listened in the dark to their parents' laughter.

"What is going on down there that is so funny?" Jamie asked softly from his bed. A blanket hung in the middle of the room as a partition between them. Jenny leaned up on her elbow and looked at where she knew Jamie was lying on the other side of the blanket.

"You know," she said into the darkness.

"No, I don't," Jamie replied. Jenny dropped back on her bed and kicked her blankets restlessly. "What?" he asked.

"Sometimes you are so stupid," Jenny said in frustration. "They're making love."

"What?"

"You heard me. How do you think we got here? Why do you think Momma is expecting right now?"

"I try not to think about that."

"You try not to think about anything, if you ask me."

Jamie threw the first thing he could find at the blanket. Jenny laughed as the blanket blew towards her with the impact of his boot.

Chapter Eleven

It was time for the fall visit with Elizabeth. Ian would bring a string of horses to trade, and Faith would shop for the special things that could only be found in the big city. Faith, Jenny and Jamie were out on the streets of St. Jo shopping for shoes. Jamie was being uncooperative because he had wanted to go horse trading with his father and Faith had insisted that he come with her so she could be sure of the fit. He was following her now, his arms full of packages. Jenny was behind him, occasionally smacking his bottom with the package she was carrying by a string. Jenny had decided that her misery was worse, because not only could she not go horse trading but she had also been made to wear a dress. Jamie had assured his sister that the minute they were back at their grandma's he was going to give her a thrashing that she wouldn't believe. Jenny had just stuck her tongue out at him, which drew a sharp look from her mother. Faith's patience was gone, and she was tired. Her back hurt, too, her pregnancy making the long day on her feet painful.

She was leading her family along to Elizabeth's when someone grabbed her arm.

"I thought that was you," hissed a voice from her past. The children, who had been bickering with each other, crashed into her from behind. She jerked her arm out of a claw-like grasp and turned to look at the woman who had grabbed her.

It was Miriam, and the fifteen years since she had last seen her had not been kind. Her hair, which had once been a deep brown, was now shot with gray, and her once perfect complexion was now full of bags and wrinkles. Her skin hung on her once well-proportioned frame, and her clothing was secondhand at best.

"I see you didn't waste any time getting brats from that bastard," Miriam said as she looked the twins over. "This one is that stable hand all over again." Jamie stepped back as the woman made a motion to grab him.

"I have nothing to say to you, Miriam," Faith said. She tried to step off the walk, but Miriam blocked her path.

"I have plenty to say to you, you selfish bitch." The hatred was plain on her face, and Jenny took off like a shot to find her father. Jamie drew himself up to his full height and stepped between them. Faith put her hand on his arm and pulled him back. "You and your lover ruined my life," Miriam began. "Do you even care that your father killed himself the night you ran off?"

"He wasn't my father," Faith said, her voice steady.

"He left me with all those bills, all that debt. I had to sneak out of town. I lost everything." Miriam's eyes had a faraway look to them. "Randolph Mason wouldn't help me; he said he would if I got you for him."

"You sold me to him," Faith cried, looking at the half-crazed face of the woman. Jamie's eyes were huge in his face as he watched the two of them.

"Randolph went crazy after you left." Miriam was whispering now, as if sharing a secret with Faith. "You messed him up real good when you shot him. It took him forever to heal. He swore he'd hunt you down and make you pay. I'm surprised he hasn't found you yet."

"It's been fifteen years." Faith felt her legs trembling beneath her.

"The funny thing is, after you left, he started putting his name on everything, he owned—his clothes, his shoes, his belt buckle, even a big old R M branded on the side of that devil horse of his. He said nobody would ever take anything of his again, he'd made sure of it."

The streets of St. Jo started spinning around Faith. She saw Ian running towards her, Jenny behind him, heard Jamie calling her, but it was all so far away. The last thing she remembered was Miriam's haggard face leering down at her, the tic, and then a bizarre smile that didn't quite reach her eyes.

Ian saw Faith slide to the ground as if in slow motion. Jamie dropped the packages he was holding and tried to stop her descent. There was a woman standing over her, but by the time Ian crossed the street, she was gone. Jenny was trying not to cry, and Jamie was looking up at Ian, his wide blue eyes full of fear. Ian gathered his wife into his arms and felt the wetness that had soaked through her gown. Jenny let out a sob when she saw the bloody water staining the walkway. She helped Jamie retrieve the packages, and they made their way after their father, who was trying to get Faith through the crowd that had gathered.

"Jenny, run on to Elizabeth's and tell her what happened. Jamie, run get the doctor," Ian barked as he carried his wife through the streets. The twins took off like shots out of a cannon, Jenny hiking her skirts up as she ran.

Ian arrived at the boardinghouse on Jenny's heels and carried his wife up to their room. Elizabeth followed behind, wringing her hands. He carefully laid Faith on the bed and sat down on the edge, taking her hand in his. Faith was still unconscious, but restless, her face pale.

"Jenny, tell me what happened."

"That woman grabbed Momma and started talking to her," she managed to get out, her voice shaky as she wiped tears away with the back of her hand.

"Think carefully, Jenny. What woman?" Ian asked, his voice steady and calm.

Jenny took a deep breath. "Miriam. Momma called her Miriam. Who was she?"

Ian felt a shiver go down his spine. "Go and wait for your brother. Send the doctor up here when he comes."

"Is the baby dead?" Jenny asked as she took a step closer. Ian held out his arms and she flew into them. He smoothed her hair back and kissed her forehead.

"Please just go and wait for your brother," Ian said gently. She turned and left the room just as they heard the pounding of feet up the stairs. Elizabeth stopped Jamie at the door, and the doctor came up behind him and entered.

"Go downstairs and wait with your sister," Elizabeth said to the boy. Jamie looked over Elizabeth's head as Ian stood up. Jamie saw the doctor raise his mother's skirts, and he turned and ran down the stairs, past Jenny and out the back. Jenny followed as usual, right behind him.

Ian found them later up in the old tree that had been their sanctuary since they had discovered they could climb it. He had to shake his head as he watched Jenny scramble down, her skirts tucked up into her waist. In his head he heard Faith saying that she came by it honestly, remembering the oak tree that grew outside her own bedroom window.

"Your mother is going to be all right," he began when they were standing in front of him, both sets of deep blue eyes moist from the tears they had been trying to hide. "But she lost the baby, and she's very upset."

"Who was that woman?" Jamie began. "The things she said . . ." Jamie and Jenny had discussed the event in depth and could make no sense of it at all. Ian looked at his children as they stood there before him, both on the verge of adulthood, both having been sheltered in a loving home. He took them into the kitchen and sat them down at the table.

"Your mother's family did not approve of me," he began.

"Was that woman family?" Jenny interrupted. Ian took her hand in his from across the table.

"That woman was your mother's stepmother. She married the man we thought was your real grandfather, after your real grandmother died. Do you understand?" Both twins nodded, their eyes wide, their faces pale. "They wanted your mother to marry a man named Randolph Mason. I met your mother when I worked for his family." Ian looked at his children to make sure they were following the story. "On the night before they were to marry, your mother ran away, and I found her. Mason chased us, and we fought before your mother and I got away. Your mother shot him in the shoulder to keep him from strangling me."

"Momma shot a man?" Jamie asked. He could not picture his mother with a gun in her hands.

"She did, to save me," Ian answered. "Apparently, the man Faith thought was her father owed a lot of money and was hoping that Mason would get him out of debt, in exchange for her hand in marriage."

"But Momma loved you instead," Jenny said.

"Yes, she did." Ian ran his hands through his hair to shove back the locks that had fallen over his eyes. Jenny got up from her chair and put her arms around his neck.

"Dad, I hope I marry someone like you," she said. Ian pulled her into his lap and held her tight.

"You can't," Jamie said. "I'm just like him, and you can't marry me because I'm your brother." Jenny gave her brother an exasperated look from the shelter of her father's arms.

"I think what she means is that she wants to marry a man who will love her the way I love your mother," Ian explained to his son. He hoped desperately that he did so without smiling too much at Jamie's innocence. Jenny nodded in agreement.

"You'd better hope that *you* can marry someone who can shoot," she added. "You'll probably need someone to save your life, too." Ian had to laugh at that.

"Do you think Mason will try to find Momma now?" Jamie asked.

"It's been fifteen years. Surely the man has gotten on with his life by now," Ian reassured them.

Jamie was not so sure. His father hadn't seen the woman, or seen the fear in his mother's eyes before she fainted.

Elizabeth came into the kitchen wiping away her tears. "She's asking for you." Ian kissed Jenny on the forehead and rose from his chair.

"Can we go too?" Jamie asked.

Elizabeth put her hand on his shoulder. "Let's leave them alone for now." Ian had already gone up the stairs.

Faith was dressed in a gown and propped up on the pillows when he reached their room. The doctor had finished up and left her with instructions to stay in bed the rest of the week. Ian sat down on the edge of the bed, took her hand in his and looked into her pale blue eyes. Her eyes were lifeless, and the person who was Faith seemed far, far away.

"Faith?" Ian lowered his head until his eyes were inches from hers, their noses practically touching. She was looking beyond him. "Faith?" he repeated, firmer this time. "Don't let them win."

Faith sucked in a shuddering breath; her eyes began to focus. She saw Ian before her and sobbed.

"The baby's gone?" she asked.

"Yes."

"What was it?"

"A girl. She never drew a breath, she was too little." Ian's hair fell down over his eyes again, and Faith felt it brush against her forehead. Her face crumpled in pain, and Ian pulled her close as sobs began to rack her body. He held her until she could cry no more, her grief giving way to exhaustion. Ian lay down next to her and held her in his arms as she slept.

The next day, Faith insisted on going to the cemetery for the burial of the baby girl. She leaned heavily on Ian as the tiny coffin was placed in the ground next to Elizabeth's husband and son. The twins were solemn, neither saying a word. Jamie took his mother's other arm as they turned to leave the cemetery.

When he had his family back safe at the boardinghouse, Ian left to see if he could find Miriam. He asked at every hotel and stage depot in town, but no one had heard of her. He finally decided that she was part of the endless stream of settlers heading west and decided to think no more about her. When Faith was strong enough to travel, he took his family home.

Faith was melancholy for a while after they settled back into their life. Ian did everything he could to cheer her up, but there were times when he would come upon her unexpectedly and catch her crying. He would hold her close, his hands caressing her silky hair, and she would sob into his shoulder. She could never tell him what she was crying for; she never knew herself—she was just sad. Ian knew deep inside that she was worried about Mason coming after them.

Ian was also determined that he wasn't going to give up everything he had worked so hard for on the chance that their old tormentor might come. He was going to stand his ground. If and when Mason came, he would fight him. He would not let his family live under the shadow of that fear. It had been fifteen years; surely the man had moved on with his life. Still, every time he saw Faith cry, he wished he had killed the man when he'd had the chance.

Amazingly, it was Jenny who helped her mother return to her old self. As winter came on, Jenny began to blossom. She had always been straight as a stick, with legs as long as Jamie's, but with the snow came a new softness about her. She began to develop curves, and Jamie was always looking at her as if he didn't recognize her. She also began to take an interest in doing things with her mother. They spent a lot of time in the kitchen, where Faith passed on the cooking skills that Elizabeth had taught her. They would talk and laugh about silly things, and they began to share a friendship that was beyond the mother-daughter bonds. Jenny started taking pride in preparing special treats for the men of her family, and they all began to look at her in a new light.

Jamie also began to change over the winter. His voice was deepening, much to the amusement of his family. He had always read to them in the evenings as they sat by the fire, but now it became a game as they waited for his voice to crack on the words. He would peer at them over the top of the book while they dissolved into fits of laughter at some particular squeak he had emitted. He would wait with the patience of a saint until the giggles subsided, then continue like a professor with an unruly class. He was also growing wider and more muscular with the hard work of keeping the ranch going. He became the image of his father as the winter passed, from his wide shoulders right down to his rock-hard stomach and slim hips. He even had Ian's unruly hair, which always managed to fall down in his eyes when he was trying to read or work on something that required a lot of attention.

He had developed a deep interest in learning how to shoot well, and was thrilled with his Christmas gift from Ian, a Colt revolver and holster. He spent hours shooting at empty cans lined up on a fallen tree.

Jenny followed along with him on these outings, still dressed in Jamie's hand-me-down pants, and would practice using Ian's revolver. She soon became good at hitting targets, both stationary and moving, but she knew she would never be as fast as Jamie. Ian was surprised that Faith never got upset over all the shooting and gunplay the twins were now involved in; but instead she seemed quite happy that they could now defend themselves and she would come out and watch their latest trick shooting.

When spring finally came to Iowa territory, Ian and Faith felt as if they had watched two butterflies emerge from their cocoons. Jamie was now taller than Ian and had a quiet strength about him that was amazing. Even Storm sensed the difference in him, and would respond to his commands as quickly as he did to Ian's. Ian watched him work the stock with the pride of knowing that all the Duncan horse magic had passed on to his son, tempered with the gentleness of his mother.

Then there was Jenny. Every time Ian looked at her, she took his breath away. She moved with the grace of a dancer and glowed with a golden beauty that was all her own. She was tall and slim, with just the right amount of curves. She had a perfectly oval face, wide, deep blue eyes that a man could drown in, and golden blond hair that hung in waves down to her hips. Ian knew it would have to be a very special man to win her heart; he prayed that he would be around to protect her from the ones who would want to break it.

Spring also brought bad news to the family. Word came from St. Jo that Elizabeth was very ill. The Duncans hastily packed their bags and took off for the city, but arrived too late; Elizabeth had died the night before. Ian arranged for her burial in the cemetery with her husband, son and the Duncans' baby girl. Faith grieved heavily for the woman who had been her only true friend, but comforted herself with the idea that Elizabeth would now take care of her lost daughter, along with the two little boys who were buried in the church yard at home. As soon as the service was over, the family returned home; there was too much work to be done in the spring to spend much time away.

It was amazing how much had changed in just the few days the family had been gone. Spring was coming out all over the prairie. All the flowers and trees were in bloom, and the fields were full of newborn calves and foals. The family made it home just as dusk was settling in. Jenny and Jamie bolted from the buckboard to see if there were any newborns in their own barn. Faith began to fuss at them because they were still dressed in their good clothes, but Ian stopped her by putting a finger to her lips as he helped her down from the wagon.

"Let them go. Their clothes will wash," he said as he pulled her into his arms. They stood in the gathering darkness and listened to the excited chattering of the twins. Jenny had heard kittens in the loft and was calling to Jamie to bring a lantern so they could find them in the gloom. A soft glow soon filtered through the slits in the barn, and they heard Jamie climbing up the ladder in haste.

"And who do you propose to do this washing?" Faith asked him pertly as they listened to the oohs and aahs coming from the loft.

Ian was glad that Faith was not dwelling on Elizabeth's passing. "I volunteer to do some washing, but I'm not interested in washing clothes," he said with a flash of his boyish grin.

"And what do you propose to wash?" Faith was flirting outright with him, and Ian felt the familiar tightening in his loins.

"Everything I can get my hands on," he replied and pulled her close for a kiss. Faith felt her world spinning, as she always did when he kissed her. She leaned heavily into him and let him have his way with her mouth, his hands pressing her into his hips. He finally pulled away and leaned his forehead down on hers. Faith looked up at the devilish glint twinkling in his deep blue eyes.

"I'd better fix us something to eat," she said.

"I'm not hungry."

"They will be." She inclined her head towards the barn, then let her eyes slide down the front of him and settle on the obvious bulge in his pants. "You can eat later," she said pointedly and turned to go into the house. As she reached the porch she gave him another look that took his breath away. Ian decided then and there that bedtime was coming early for everyone that night. The sooner he got the chores done, the sooner he could retire.

Faith went into the house to fix a quick supper for the family, and Ian turned to the business of unhitching the buckboard. He noticed that Storm seemed unduly agitated. At first he had thought that it was just the excitement of the family returning home, but then he decided that something else was bothering the stallion. He would restlessly dance about the corral, then stop, facing the darkness with his ears pricked. Ian whistled for him to come, thinking perhaps there was some wild animal stalking out in the brush beyond the yard. Storm came immediately to his master, but was still watching beyond the boundaries of the corral. Ian talked to the animal in soothing tones, hoping to calm him, but Storm just twitched his ears and tail and pawed the ground with his hoof. The animal suddenly danced away with a snort, and Ian realized that a rider was coming up the drive. Ian went over to light the lantern that hung by the barn door just as Faith stepped outside on the porch to call the family in for dinner. She came out into the yard when she realized they had company.

The man on horseback rode up to the corral and casually dismounted. It wasn't until he stepped around his horse and into the circle of light that Ian realized he was face to face with Randolph Mason. The years had changed the man, that much was obvious. He was leaner now, the once soft features harder and sharper. The look of rich boredom had been replaced with a callous cruelty around the eyes and mouth, and everything he wore was emblazoned with his initials, even down to the leather inlays in his boots. Ian felt a shiver run down his spine as the man stepped into the glow from the lantern, and he regretted he was not wearing his gun. It was under the seat of the buckboard, too far away to do him any good right now. Ian saw Faith stop in her tracks, her hands over her mouth as she realized who it was. Her eyes went to the barn behind Ian where she knew the twins were still engrossed in the kittens. Ian caught her eye as Mason spoke.

"I had given up on finding you, Duncan." The voice was pure evil.

"Why did you?" Ian asked. He needed to buy some time. He prayed that Jamie had heard the rider and would investigate before coming out of the barn. Faith was behind Mason and could perhaps signal him to bring out the rifle that was kept there for emergencies.

"I came for what you stole from me," Mason drawled. His fingers tickled the handle of the pistol strapped to his hip. "Lucky for me that Miriam saw you. Do you know how much money I've spent trying to track you down? I've hired people from Richmond all the way to California to look for you. I had to spend a pretty penny to get your location from her, but it was worth it." A look of pure glee came over him. "Of course, I made sure she won't be able to enjoy it."

"You are out of your mind," Ian ground out. He knew he shouldn't agitate the man, but he could not help it. Mason was crazy—he knew no boundaries and he felt no guilt. Ian saw that Faith, behind Mason, was stricken with terror. She kept looking at Ian, then looking up to the loft above his head. There was no sign of the children. She alternated between praying that they would stay hidden and hoping that Jamie would have the presence of mind to put a gun on Mason.

Mason began to laugh at Ian's statement. Ian stole a look at the buckboard, counting the paces. He was running out of time. His eyes went back to Mason and he saw him draw his gun. Ian felt his life go into slow motion. He dove towards the wagon, and heard Faith's screams beyond the blood pounding in his ears. He saw her as she rushed towards Mason, the impact of her body sending the bullet into the air.

Ian rolled away from the shot and gathered himself into a crouch. The buckboard was still out of his reach. He watched as

Mason landed a fist on Faith's jaw and she fell into a heap on the ground. Ian dove again as Mason fired once more, willing his body to reach the safety of the buckboard where he could get his hands on his gun. Behind him in the barn he heard a crash as the bullet penetrated the wood of the barn, then bloodcurdling screams—it had to be Jamie—rising in the night air.

Mason fired again as Ian was in midair, and the bullet caught him in the spine, flipping him over on his back. The next bullet hit his chest before he landed on the ground. He could feel nothing below his shoulders. His blood was pumping out of his chest and beginning to pool on the ground around him. He heard the furious cries of Storm from the corral, and the screams of his children above that.

Ian watched helplessly as Mason hauled Faith up beside him. She began to scream when she saw Ian on the ground, covered with blood. Mason slapped her and dragged her, kicking and screaming, into the house. The screams from the barn had stopped, replaced by a sob from Jenny and a moan from Jamie. Ian wondered how his son could be alive after all those screams. From the house he heard the cries and protests of Faith, along with the crashing of furniture. Tears gathered in Ian's eyes and ran down his face. He couldn't move anything, his life's blood was pouring out of him onto his land, his wife was being attacked by a madman, and his children were hurt. He heard the furious cries of Storm in his corral, the stomping on the ground and the horse racing around the pen. He heard the stallion gather himself and felt the impact on the ground beneath his head when Storm cleared the fence and landed in the soft dirt. *Go on, go free before he gets you too*, Ian thought.

The house was silent now. Ian felt his heart skip a beat; he felt a light go out inside him, and he was cold. There was a noise from the door and he heard Mason's footsteps—they were too heavy to be Faith's. Ian knew she would never come out of the house again.

Storm sensed the man and charged him. Ian watched as Mason dove away and drew his gun. Storm never broke stride as the shots sailed over his back; he just kept running until he disappeared into the darkness.

"Your wife is dead." Mason was standing over Ian with what was supposed to be a smile on his evil face. "She hit her head on the hearth when I slapped her. She never was any fun at all."

Mason looked at the barn door. "I heard you had a couple of brats. It sounded like I got both of them with one shot. I guess I should make sure they're finished. I wouldn't want any witnesses left to tell the tale." He started towards the barn.

"*No.*" Ian felt as if he had screamed it, but all he managed was a whisper.

Mason suddenly froze in his tracks as he heard the distinctive sound of a bullet entering a chamber. He cautiously stepped back towards Ian, his eyes never leaving the door of the barn. "Maybe it's better revenge to leave them as orphans. I've always heard that parents suffers more for their children than for themselves. As for me, I'd never want the nuisance." He backed away from Ian and mounted his horse. Ian heard the sounds of Mason riding off into the darkness. The darkness was closing in on him, too.

"Dad?" It was Jenny sobbing over him. Her left arm was held at a funny angle, and she was covered with soot and blood.

"Jenny," Ian managed to get out. "Jamie?"

"He's hurt—he's burned, but he's alive," Jenny cried. She reached up with her right hand and pushed Ian's hair out of his eyes.

"You're so much like your mother . . ." Ian smiled at her. He wasn't cold anymore, and it didn't seem to be as dark. Jenny looked towards the dark, silent house. "Do you know that your mother is an angel?" She could barely hear him. "Look, I see her now. She's waiting for me." Ian looked beyond Jenny, to where Faith was standing in the light, her arms outstretched towards him, like the angel on the carved box at their bedside. She was smiling, and the light had turned her to silver. He couldn't wait to be in her arms again, where he belonged. "Faith," he whispered as his deep blue eyes closed for the last time.

"Dad!" Jenny screamed. She fell against his chest, her hair dragging through the blood that had poured out of his body. His face looked so handsome, almost serene. He couldn't be dead—he was her father. Her cries filled the night.

Chapter Twelve

Jenny felt sick and dazed from the injury to her arm, and her head swirled with images of the events that had just taken place. She had been in the loft with Jamie playing with the kittens when the stranger had ridden into their yard. They were so absorbed with what they were doing that they had not realized anyone was there until they heard the bizarre sound of Mason's laughter. Jamie had taken one look out of the loft door and begun to scramble down the ladder to get the rifle. His dad needed help; he did not know who the man was, but one look had told him his intentions were not good. A bullet came whizzing into the barn through the boards and struck the lantern hanging on a hook by the ladder. Jamie was just even with the lantern in his descent when it exploded from the impact of the bullet, spraying flaming oil over the left side of his face, down his neck and onto his shoulder and chest. His clothes burst into flame, and he fell screaming from the ladder. Jenny watched in horror from the loft above as Jamie tried to put the flames out by rolling on the floor of the barn. Jenny scrambled down to help, but her usually agile feet got tangled in the dress she still wore and she fell to the floor, landing on her arm, the impact shattering the bone of her forearm. She didn't even look at her arm, she just threw herself on Jamie's screaming, squirming body, her dress finally smothering the flames. A sob came out as she raised herself and looked at his blistered, bleeding form. Jamie was blessedly unconscious, but the pain had penetrated his darkened state and he moaned as his sister examined the blackened skin under the tatters of his shirt. Jenny had heard the shots outside, heard her mother screaming, heard Storm giving voice to his fury and the pounding of his hooves. She staggered to her feet and pulled the rifle down from its place on the wall. She crept over to the door and looked through the cracks to see a man standing over her father. She tried to raise the rifle to shoot but couldn't manage it with her injured arm. She bit her lip and willed her trembling body to stay still as she saw the man start towards the barn. Without even thinking she cocked the rifle, its barrel still pointing into the ground. The man stopped when he heard the sound and backed away from the door. She watched him mount his horse and ride away into the night. As soon as he was gone, she ran to where her father lay.

She was still there, her sobs having given way to exhaustion, when Gray Horse rode into the yard the next morning. He quickly dismounted and pulled Jenny off Ian's body. The blood from his chest had dried in her hair, and he had to detach her unconscious form from his. A quick look told him that Ian was dead, and he turned his attention to his dear friend's daughter, who was now stirring in his arms. Her eyes fluttered open, and she turned her face into his bare shoulder when she recognized the sharp features of the Indian. Gray Horse let her cry a bit, then sat her up on the ground before him. Her left arm hung at a funny angle at her side as she pulled up the blackened bloody tail of her dress to wipe her tear-filled eyes.

"Your mother?" he asked.

"Dead, in the house." A sudden awareness hit Jenny. "Jamie—he's in the barn. He's hurt." She stumbled unsteadily to her feet. Gray Horse sprang up beside her and grabbed her waist as she swayed dizzily. She pushed him away and headed towards the barn. Jamie was lying where she had left him. She fell to her knees beside him and bent over to listen to the sound of his labored breathing. Gray Horse knelt beside her, but one look told him the boy's injuries were beyond his healing skills.

"Jenny, you must get him to a doctor," he said. Jenny was looking down at her brother's blistered face, her hand reaching out to smooth the charred ends of his hair off his forehead. Gray Horse grabbed her shoulders and turned her to face him. Jenny grimaced as pain shot down her broken arm, and she raised her tear-stained face to look at the best friend her family had. "I can't help him. He needs white medicine, do you understand?" Jenny looked down at her brother and then past Gray Horse to where her father's body was lying in the dirt. Gray Horse looked over his shoulder at his friend. "I will take care of your parents. Send someone out to get their bodies." Jenny nodded at the man's instructions. "Do you know who did this?"

"I don't know. It was a man I've never seen before. I didn't get a good look at him, and it was dark." Jenny wiped the back of her hand across her eyes and nose, smearing the soot even more. "Will Jamie live?"

Gray Horse looked down at Jamie's burned skin. "I don't know. It's in your God's hands now." Jamie moaned as they looked down at him. Gray Horse hated to think of the pain the boy must be in. It was good that he was unconscious. He got the buckboard ready for Jenny and then gently laid Jamie in the back.

He wouldn't let Jenny go in the house. He had seen Faith's body lying where she had landed against the hearth. The front of her dress was ripped away and there were bruises on her face and arms.

He had found a blanket and used it to help cushion the back of the wagon for Jamie. With the help of Gray Horse, Jenny climbed into the seat and took the reins into her one good hand, the other hanging at a strange angle on her left side. Gray Horse tenderly squeezed her right forearm, and she looked into the dark eyes of her father's best friend.

"Take the horses and take care of them for us. I don't want people coming here and helping themselves to our stock," she instructed him. "Storm has run off. You'll find him out there somewhere. Take care of him until Jamie can come for him." She broke into a sob at her brother's name. Gray Horse stood patiently while she talked. He hadn't seen the children during the long winter, and now he was overcome by how much she had matured in that one season, how much she had grown up in the past few hours.

Gray Horse nodded as Jenny slapped the reins against the backs of the team. The Indian watched the wagon roll out of sight; then he turned to gather up the body of his friend.

When the marshal arrived, he found the freshly washed bodies of Ian and Faith lying side by side on the bed they had shared. Any tracks that might have been left by the killer had disappeared among all the others on the well-used road to town.

The next few days passed in a blur for Jenny. She had told her story to the marshal, her parents had been buried, and decisions had been made for the twins. They were to be sent to the mission orphanage in St. Jo. There were people there who could help the still-unconscious Jamie through his long recovery, and perhaps the two of them would have a better chance of being adopted by someone in a large town. The truth of the matter was that no one was willing to invest the time that Jamie needed for his recovery. It was springtime and everyone's attention was on the work that needed to be done, not taking care of a young boy who might not recover from his injuries.

The Duncans' property was forfeited to the bank; there was no way Jamie and Jenny could make the payments on the small balance that was left. Jenny was thankful that the stock was under the care of Gray Horse, she knew her father would be happy about that. Someday they would come back and claim what was theirs. For now, she just needed to make sure Jamie recovered. She wondered briefly about Storm as she rode in the wagon that took them away from their home. She hoped he was still running free, or that Gray Horse had managed to find him. She hated the thought of anyone else having custody of the stallion.

Jenny held the carved box close to her as she watched the doctor and the minister carefully place Jamie in the back of the buckboard that would take them to St. Jo and their new life. He had been given enough morphine to keep him unconscious for the long trip. The marshal had packed their things, Jenny hadn't been able to stand the thought of going back. She still saw the dead body of her father every time she closed her eyes. The angel box held all the things her mother had thought important, along with the wedding ring that had been taken off her hand before she was buried. Jenny didn't even look up as the minister drove the wagon out of town. All of her attention was on her brother and the look of pain that crossed his face each time the wagon went over a bump in the road.

The minister counseled Jenny as best he could on the trip. He quoted scriptures and talked about God's plans. Jenny rode in silence. Too much had happened, she still couldn't absorb it all. She just prayed with all her might that God would not take Jamie too. They arrived at the mission soon enough and the minister left them in the care of a kind nun and a rather stern-looking priest. The nun, Sister Mary Frances, immediately took over the care of Jamie. Father Clarence, the priest, tried to send Jenny into another part of the mission with one of the younger nuns, but Jenny flatly refused to leave her brother's side.

"You will soon learn that we do not tolerate this kind of ungodly behavior," he said to Jenny as he peered over his glasses at her. Jenny was sitting on the edge of Jamie's bed, her good arm hooked through the headboard.

"I won't leave my brother," she told him fiercely.

"We believe here that if you spare the rod, you spoil the child. It is obvious that your parents neglected that part of your upbringing." The priest looked at Jenny as if she were a hardened criminal. "The sooner you learn the rules here, the sooner you will fit in with the other orphans that God has given into our care."

Jenny locked her arm tighter around the bed frame. She saw Sister Mary Frances make the sign of the cross and take up her rosary. The priest came around the bed and grabbed Jenny's arm above the splint and began to squeeze. Jenny grimaced as a pain shot down her arm, and she let go of the bed frame. "We will forgive your indiscretion this time due to the fact that you are new here and have yet to learn the commandments that we live by. Tomorrow we will begin your instruction."

His face was just inches from Jenny by this time, but she didn't blink, she just looked up at him with her wide blue eyes, eyes that had seen too much too soon. Something the priest saw in her eyes gave him pause, and he released her quickly. Jenny never said a word, and she never took her eyes off the man until he had left the room.

"Please go with Sister Abigail," Sister Mary Frances said. "I promise that you can visit your brother."

"When?" Jenny asked in an assertive tone. The nun's eyes widened at her voice, but as she looked at Jamie's bandaged face, she forgave the girl.

"We'll let you know. Now please go before Father Clarence comes back."

Jenny looked at the woman, then tenderly pushed Jamie's hair back off his forehead. She picked up her box and followed the sister to another wing of the mission, taking note of the way. She was led to a large room that was bare of any ornamentation, with cots lined up in rows and a washstand at the end.

Jenny's mind filled with images of the past as she wearily lay down on a cot and closed her eyes. She saw her father's grin as he came bouncing up on the porch, full of some story to tell them at dinner. She heard her mother's laughter ring in her head over some foolishness of her father's. She felt the wind blowing in her hair as she raced across the prairie on horseback, Jamie at her side. She remembered the good-night kisses her parents gave her and lying in her bed at night, listening to the sound of Jamie breathing across the room and the quiet murmurs of her parents drifting up from below. Tears came out from under the tightly closed lids and trickled down the side of her face.

Jamie felt as if he had been lost for an eternity. He knew he was dreaming, but that knowledge didn't help him. He was locked inside himself, trying to escape. He could hear his mother calling to him, he knew his father was standing there beside her, but he couldn't find his way around the flames. They were everywhere. No matter which way he turned, the flames seemed to shoot up and singe him with their heat. The flames were behind him too, licking at his heels, driving him on, but there was no place for him to go. He could hear Jenny crying and calling out to him, but he couldn't find her. He felt so tired, and he hurt, he couldn't remember what it was like when he didn't hurt. He knew there were bandages on his flesh, he knew someone was tenderly ministering to his needs, he felt the cool touch of gentle hands on his body, but he couldn't find his way through the haze of pain that consumed him. He needed an anchor, a landmark, someone to pull him back. He agonized at the loss he felt within: he felt himself crying, and he felt all the worse for it because he was too old to cry. He was lost.

Chapter Thirteen

Jenny was awakened by the sounds of movement in the room. It took her a few moments to orient herself to her new surroundings; then she remembered. She was in St. Jo, in a mission. Jamie . . . she needed to go to Jamie. She cautiously looked around the room to find the source of the noise. She saw several small girls taking turns at the washstand. It must be time for dinner, she thought to herself. Her stomach certainly indicated it.

There was a nun standing in the doorway who carefully inspected each set of hands and each face as they were presented to her. She occasionally looked at Jenny to see if she was awake. Jenny didn't move, she made her breathing steady, willing the nun to leave.

When Jenny heard the procession of girls going down the hall, she went to the door, peering around the frame to see if anyone was about. She didn't know the workings of the mission yet, but she hoped everyone was at dinner. She quietly made her way back to the infirmary and found Jamie, still as death in his bed. She curled up next to the side of his body that wasn't burned and put her arm around him. He turned his face towards her.

"Jamie, Jamie, can you hear me?" she whispered, afraid that

someone might hear. His mouth moved; he was trying to talk. Jenny sat up to see him better. "Jamie?" she asked, louder. She bent her head down to his mouth to catch the words he was trying to form.

"Hurts," he barely whispered.

"I know," Jenny pushed the ragged ends of his hair off his forehead. "Can you open your eyes? You need to wake up." She watched the struggle on his face as he tried to fight his way back to the living. "Jamie, wake up, please, I need you."

"Jenny?" he whispered, a bit stronger now. His eyelids began to flutter, the one on the left minus some lashes from the heat of the flames.

"Come on, Jamie, open your eyes," Jenny implored him. His blue eyes appeared beneath a crack in the lids. When his eyes swam out of focus, she lowered her face to his and caught his gaze with her own. "Hey," she said, smiling tenderly at her brother.

"Hey," he barely managed to get out. "What happened?"

Jenny squeezed back the tears that were threatening to spill out and shook her head against the onslaught of grief that welled up inside her. He didn't know, she realized. He had been unconscious since it happened.

"You got burned," was all she said. Jamie weakly lifted his bandaged arm and held his hand to his face for inspection. It was whole, with just a few scabbed places on the back of the palm. He lightly touched the bandages on his face, then trailed his hands down his neck and chest.

"How bad?" he asked, his voice hoarse.

"I don't know; we won't until they take the bandages off."

"Where's Momma?" he asked. His eyes were totally focused now and were searching the room. "Dad?" he asked, his voice cracking on the word. Jenny squeezed her eyes shut and shook her head again. "Jenny, where are they?"

"They died—they were murdered."

"What?" His eyes went wide, full of disbelief. Jenny sobbed. "They're dead?" he asked, not believing her.

"Yes," she cried, "Yes." She lowered her head to her chest and tried to wipe the tears away. Jamie looked up at the ceiling and ran his good hand through his hair. He reached out his arm to Jenny and pulled her down to him. He turned his face into her hair. He couldn't stop the tears that were coming; he hadn't even felt them

128

come. They were just there, running down his face.

"Where are we?" he finally asked when he felt Jenny's shuddering sobs subside.

"They sent us to an orphanage in St. Jo where you could be cared for."

"Who sent us?"

"The town."

"I don't understand, Jenny. What happened?" Jamie's voice was weak and wavering as he struggled to make sense of their situation. Jenny raised herself from his chest and pushed his hair back off his forehead. His dark-lashed eyes were enormous in his gaunt, pale face.

"I don't understand it either," she said soothingly. "When you feel better, we'll talk about it."

Jamie wearily closed his eyes and nodded his consent. The morphine was still in his system and he wasn't strong enough to fight it. Jenny stayed by his side, smoothing the ragged ends of his hair until she felt the steady breathing that meant he was asleep.

Jenny knew that she was being watched long before Jamie returned to the sleep he so desperately needed. When she was sure that he was sleeping soundly, she turned to find Sister Mary Frances standing in the doorway.

The woman shared a smile with Jenny and motioned for her to come nearer. Jenny checked on Jamie one more time and went over to the woman.

"Would you walk with me for a bit?" she asked Jenny, who nodded and followed the nun outside.

The mission was located a few miles outside of town, in the middle of a rolling field. The place was totally self-sufficient with a huge garden and a barn full of livestock. Jenny listened quietly as they walked around the grounds and the nun explained life at the mission. When they came to a small orchard of apple trees, Sister Mary Frances asked Jenny to take a seat on a bench under one of the bloom-filled branches. Jenny sat and patiently waited while the nun prepared herself.

"You and your brother have been through a great ordeal in the past week. I know you didn't ask to be sent here, but here you are, and here is where you will stay until you are adopted or of an age to leave." She hadn't yet said anything that Jenny didn't know already. "I have seen a great bond between you and Jamie."

"Yes," Jenny replied when the sister seemed to be waiting for an answer.

"I have seen his wounds. He will have scars, bad scars, and it will be a great struggle for him to adjust."

"I will help him," Jenny said firmly.

"I'm sure you will." The sister smiled at her determination. "But what about *your* scars?"

"I don't have any."

"Some scars are on the inside. You are scarred because of what you have seen."

"You don't know what I saw." Jenny raised her chin a notch. She didn't know this nun, and she knew that she wasn't ready to share her feelings with her.

"I know you saw your parents murdered, and your brother severely burned. I know that is more than any child of your age should see."

"I don't feel much like a child anymore." Jenny stood up. "I haven't eaten all day. Would it be possible for me to get some supper?" The nun carefully looked at the set of her shoulders and the grim lines on her face.

"Of course, we'll go find you something now." Jenny took off at a rapid pace for the mission, challenging the sister to keep up with her long-legged stride, but the nun fell in beside her, matching her step for step. "You will be expected to earn your keep here. All of the children contribute to the running of the mission."

"We're not afraid of hard work; we've done it all our lives." Jenny kept her eyes straight ahead as they walked back to the mission.

"I'm afraid we don't have any girls your age here. They are all younger than you."

"That's okay, I've never had much use for other girls anyway."

"There are a few boys your age," the sister continued as if she hadn't heard Jenny. "It will be nice to have some new students in our school. They always add a new perspective to things."

"We learned more from what our parents taught us at home than we ever did in school," Jenny told the nun.

"Then your knowledge will definitely be an asset to our classroom," the nun assured her. Jenny felt as if she were talking to a wall. Apparently, the woman didn't understand that as soon as Jamie was better, they were going to leave. Then, Jenny realized she hadn't known that herself until just this minute.

They came to the main building, and the sister led her to a huge room filled with tables and benches. "This is the girls' table, here; boys eat over there," the nun said. Jenny felt that this separation was a foolish notion, but she kept that opinion to herself for the moment. She took a seat at the girls' table, and the sister soon returned with a plate for her. The food was bland, but Jenny was starving, and she attacked it with gusto. "Beginning tomorrow, you will follow a set schedule."

Jenny felt the walls close in on her as the nun went over the schedule with her. Visions of long summer evenings filled her head—wading in the creek with Jamie, chasing frogs and lizards, lying on the knoll watching the stars come out, counting the falling ones as they shot across the sky, catching fireflies with Gray Horse's children, racing horses across the plains under a full moon, settling into bed, listening to the crickets and the soft laughter of her mother drifting up from the room below. There was no room for any of this in the schedule the sister had just given her. Where was the joy of childhood in this place? It suddenly dawned on Jenny that although she had seen children about, she hadn't heard one yet. The little girls who had been washing up while she had slept had talked in quiet whispers, and those she had seen around the place scurried about like scared rabbits. Come to think of it, the nuns acted timid, too, except for Sister Mary Frances, who was now sitting across from her with a serene expression on her lovely face. She was beautiful, Jenny realized, older than her mother, not quite as old as Elizabeth had been. Her face was worn but unlined. Jenny recognized something in her eyes, something she had seen recently in her own, but she wasn't sure what it was. She suddenly realized that she was very tired.

"Could I see Jamie again before I go to bed?" she asked meekly. The sister couldn't hide her surprise at receiving such a mild request from the brassy girl she had talked to earlier.

"Yes, that would be fine." She rose from the table. "We'll make sure to allow time for that in your schedule." Jenny smiled gratefully at the nun and followed her back to her brother's bed. He was still asleep, and she tenderly swept back his hair and kissed his forehead before making her way back to her cot in the girls' dormitory.

* * *

131

Jenny was awakened early the next morning by a gentle nudge on her shoulder. She heard a bell tolling, counted six peals of the giant instrument before it echoed off into silence. A nun was in the room supervising the smaller girls as they washed their faces, combed their hair and struggled into their clothing in the dimly lit room. Jenny quickly dressed in her customary uniform—Jamie's hand-me-down shirt and pants—and quickly brushed her hair into a single braid falling down her back. She splashed some cold water from the basin on her face and had started down the hall towards the wing Jamie was housed in when the nun grabbed her arm.

"Devotions are this way," she said quietly. The younger girls were lined up in the hallway, waiting to be led to the chapel, and Jenny had no choice but to fall into line and follow along. The way was dimly lit, and the only sound was the echo of footsteps in the early morning air. They soon came to a chapel, and Jenny slid into the end of the pew that was shown to her by a frowning nun. A number of boys came in behind the girls, ranging in age from around six to sixteen. They were seated opposite the aisle from the girls, and it didn't take Jenny long to realize that the sexes were always strictly segregated at the orphanage. There was a large boy sitting in the back and a small, wiry one next to him who seemed to be close to her age. She noticed the large boy giving her the once-over while the wiry one made comments into his ear. He was rewarded with a poke of a stick held by a nun, and they both turned their eyes forward, the large one rolling his eyes occasionally towards Jenny. She dismissed him from her mind and turned her attention to the goings-on in the front of the chapel.

Father Clarence entered through a side door and began a series of rising and kneeling with what Jenny assumed was prayer in between, but she really couldn't follow the sing-song sound of the words. All of the children quickly knelt and rose as if on cue, and Jenny's awkward attempts to follow were greeted by a snicker from the large boy and his wiry friend. After what seemed like an eternity, the devotional time was over. Father Clarence was making his way down the aisle towards the back with Sister Mary Frances following behind. He stopped short when he got to Jenny's pew, and a look of horror came over his face as he took in her clothing. The look of horror became one of rage, and Jenny actually felt herself shrinking in the man's presence. Sister Mary Frances laid her hand on the priest's arm and whispered in his ear, and the man turned on his heel and left. The sister held her hand out to Jenny and led her out of the chapel while the snickers of the two boys in the back rang in her ears.

"You must dress like a young lady now that you are here," the nun said to Jenny as they made their way down the hall.

Jenny looked down at the clothing she had worn most of her days. "This is all I really have, except for the dress I was wearing yesterday. What's wrong with what I have on? It's what I always wear."

"It is unsuitable for a young lady to show her figure in such an unbecoming way. It will lead to sinful thoughts."

"I always thought it was more practical to dress this way," Jenny retorted. The nun stopped and looked at her.

"You're not at home anymore; things are different here. You will have to learn to follow the rules if you are going to survive." Jenny looked at the nun and saw the very serious expression on her face.

"Survive what?" She couldn't believe what she was hearing.

"I'll let you see your brother for a few minutes while I find you some clothes," she said and took off down the hall. Jenny watched as she walked away, then fell into step behind her, determined that as soon as Jamie was better, they would be gone.

Jamie was awake when she reached his room. He was turned away from the door, the bandaged side of his face showing white against the russet of his hair. Jenny walked around to where she could see him face to face.

"Hey," she said softly.

"Hey," he answered, his eyes barely moving. Jenny knelt down and folded her arms on the side of the bed. Jamie rubbed the surface of her bandaged arm, wincing as the damaged skin on his arm stretched.

"Does it hurt much?" he asked.

"Sometimes. I haven't really thought about it."

"How did it happen?"

"I fell out of the loft."

He managed a small smile at the thought of her tumbling out of the loft. Jenny noticed it and felt a leap in her heart as she returned it.

"It seemed the quickest way down at the time," she added, her lips turning up into a grin. Jamie tried to grin back, but the movement was painful and it ended as quickly as it had appeared.

133

"I remember," he said after a while.

"What?"

"Being on fire."

Jenny closed her eyes as the memories of his screams once again rang in her ears. "Don't think about it. It's over now," she finally managed to say. She heard Sister Mary Frances enter the room and saw that she was holding up a skirt. "It seems that I don't have the proper wardrobe for mission life," she explained to Jamie as she took the skirt.

"So what else is new?" Jenny stuck her tongue out at her brother as she quickly shed her pants and stepped into the skirt. It was a bit big around the waist, and only hit her at mid-calf, but the nun decided it was more presentable than what she had been wearing.

"You must go on to breakfast and school," the nun instructed her. "You won't be assigned any chores until your arm has healed, so I have gotten permission to have you help here in the infirmary." Jenny smiled gratefully at the nun. "Go on now. Come back here as soon as you are done with school."

Jenny gave her brother a quick kiss and ran off to breakfast, slowing her pace to a walk when a nun chastised her for making too much noise.

Jenny ate a silent breakfast with the rest of the orphans, noticing that Father Clarence stared over his glasses at anyone who happened to make the slightest noise. Jenny wondered why the man had been put in charge of an orphanage when he so obviously hated children. She caught the large boy she'd noticed at devotions spying on her; and his wiry little friend was also looking her way. After breakfast she was led to a classroom where she was one of four students. The two who had been watching her were there along with another boy who was seated as far away from them as he could get.

When the teacher began, Jenny realized that her education was way beyond what the class was working on. She dutifully did her work and waited while the others struggled with theirs. One boy, Marcus, seemed to be bright and finished right behind Jenny. The other two seemed to be more interested in ways they could aggravate Marcus rather than learning anything. The sister just went on with her lesson plan; she was either unaware of the shenanigans of the two or unable to stop them, so she just ignored them. Jenny decided that ignoring them was her best defense also, even when she felt a wad of paper hit the back of her head, followed by a snicker.

"I hear you've got a brother in the infirmary," the large boy said as he came up behind her when they were going to the dining room. "I heard he was burned up and doesn't have any skin left on him." Jenny stopped and turned, her right hand balled into a fist. Surprised, the boy stopped so suddenly, the wiry one ran into him.

"It only shows your ignorance when you talk of something you know nothing about," Jenny hissed, her wide blue eyes mere slits in her face. The teacher, who had been walking in front of them, cleared her throat, stopping the large boy from pressing his attack. Jenny fell into step with Marcus as they made their way to the dining hall.

"That's the first time I've ever seen anyone stand up to Logan," Marcus whispered to her when they were a few steps ahead. He stole a look over his shoulder to make sure that the other two couldn't hear him.

"He's just a big bully."

"Yes, and he gets away with it, too."

"Jamie will fix that when he's better."

"Is he your brother?"

"Yes, he's my twin."

"I have a sister here. She's six. Our parents were killed in an Indian attack when she was just a baby. My dad was a doctor." Jenny looked at the boy as he gave her his entire history in one burst. He had sandy brown hair and kind brown eyes. She had seen a little girl who resembled him and decided to watch out for her.

"Do you ever get to talk to your sister?"

"I see her after school, and on Sundays we play together sometimes." His voice trailed off as they reached the dining hall. They all ate lunch as silently as breakfast, then were allowed to go outside for some exercise, as Father Clarence called it. A ball was found, and the smaller children went chasing after it. Logan and his wiry little friend, Joe, disappeared around a corner of the building. Jenny and Marcus sat down on the bench in the orchard, and Marcus told her about life in the mission, after Jenny briefly explained what had brought her there. A cute little girl with brown curls came running up, and Marcus introduced her as his sister Mary. He gave her a hug and she went back to her little group of friends. All too quickly they were summoned back to their classrooms.

After what seemed an eternity, class was dismissed for the day. Jenny flew out the door and arrived at the infirmary to find Jamie sitting up in bed. He had been bathed, his hair washed and the ragged, burned ends trimmed.

"We were waiting for you," Sister Mary Frances said. "Your brother needs some help with his meal." There was a tray holding a bowl of soup on the bedside table. Jenny sat down on the edge of the bed and placed the tray on her lap.

"I can't even manage a spoon right now." Jamie was clearly disappointed in himself.

"It's because you've been flat on your back for a week. You'll get your strength back soon enough, or at least you'd better."

"Why is that?" Jamie asked as Jenny raised the spoon to his mouth. Jenny looked around and saw that they had been left alone.

"There's someone here who needs to be taught a lesson, and you're the only one big enough to do it." She briefly told him about Logan, leaving out his remarks about Jamie.

"It will be a while before I'll be able to whip anything bigger than a kitten." Jenny set the spoon down at his remark.

"Oh, Jamie, I forgot about the kittens."

"What's happened to our home?"

"It's going up for auction. There was still a mortgage on the property—I guess Dad borrowed against the land to build the house and barn. Gray Horse has the stock. He's taking care of it until we can go back."

"Storm?"

"I don't know, he ran off. He went crazy when Dad was shot." Jamie stopped her hand, which held another spoonful of soup.

"Jen, tell me how . . . what happened to Dad and Momma."

Jenny set the tray back on the bedside table. She wrapped her arms around herself as she began to speak. "There was a man. It was so dark, I never saw his face."

"I remember seeing a man, too. He was laughing. I remember it gave me chills, it sounded so evil."

"He shot Dad, but one of the shots must have gone wild and hit the lantern. I didn't see Momma. Gray Horse wouldn't let me. He said she had hit her head on the hearth and the blow must have killed her instantly. Dad saw her when he was dying." Jenny wiped away the tears that had started streaming down her face as she remembered the look of wonder on her father's face as he took his last breath. "He said she was an angel and she was waiting for him." Jamie looked away, trying to hide the tears that had started in his own deep blue eyes.

"Why would anyone want to shoot Dad? I don't understand."

"I don't either, I told the marshal everything I knew. He said that all the tracks just disappeared into the traffic going into town. He was hoping someone had noticed a stranger around, but there just wasn't anything to go on."

"Could it have been the man who once wanted to marry Momma?" Jamie asked.

"I thought that too, but I couldn't remember his name. I told the marshal about him, but he thought it was a long shot, with all that happening so long ago."

"That woman who made Momma lose the baby could have told him where she was."

"I know, but without knowing his name, we have nothing to go on."

Jamie thought about that for a while, but he couldn't summon the name to his memory. "So now what happens?"

"You get better. Then we get out of here."

"And do what? Where would we go, how would we live?"

"Gray Horse could take care of us."

"Jen, I really don't think Momma would want us to go live like Indians. Besides, Gray Horse might not want us."

"I know—I just don't want to stay here, I hate it."

"It will take time to get used to it, I'm sure. I know I didn't want to wind up in a place like this, with burns all over my face." Jamie threw his hand up towards the bandages that still covered half of his face. Jenny grabbed the hand it and took into hers.

"The burns on your face don't have a thing to do with who you are, Jamie," she assured him.

"I know, but they'll have a lot to do with how people look at me. I heard some kids outside the window today. They were looking in and laughing at me." Jenny's mind flashed back to the earlier recess when Logan and Joe had taken off around a corner of the building.

"They are idiots. Don't worry about them."

"I guess I'll just have to get used to it. That's how it's going to be from now on."

"We don't even know what your face looks like under your bandages. How can you say that?" Jenny protested.

"I know what it feels like. I just know."

"Jamie—" Jenny began. He just pulled his hand from hers and turned away. Jenny got up from the bed and began puttering around the room, straightening the covers on the other bed, organizing instruments on the table.

"Would you like me to see if I can find some books?" she finally asked after an eternity of silence had passed.

"What I would really like is to get out of this bed for a while, maybe go outside, if there's nobody around."

"I'll have to ask Sister Mary Frances if that would be all right. The rules are pretty rigid here."

"They are? She's really nice, though."

"Yes, she's different from the rest of them. Father Clarence is a real tyrant. He's the one who runs the place, and the rest of the nuns are all scared to death of him. He doesn't seem to like children, that's for sure."

"Then why is he running an orphanage?"

"Funny, I've been thinking the same thing all day." Jenny sat back down on the bed and told Jamie about her day and all the things she had noticed. Jamie laughed when she told him about the morning devotions and how she hadn't known when to sit, kneel or stand. She was just telling him about her new friend Marcus when Sister Mary Frances came back into the room.

"I'm glad to see you're feeling better," she commented to Jamie. Jenny noticed Jamie's self conscious turning of his face so that his bandages were hidden from view. The sister noticed it also. "Do you think you feel well enough to get up, maybe take a walk?"

"No," Jamie answered curtly.

Jenny wanted to remind him that he had just mentioned going outside but stopped herself. "You need to eat some more. You hardly touched this soup." She pulled the tray back into her lap and began to stir the spoon around in the bowl. Jamie gave her a grateful look and obediently opened his mouth as she lifted the spoon to it. "You can't hide in here all your life. The sooner you get out, the sooner you get it over with," she whispered to him as the sister busied herself on the other side of the room.

"I know," he answered after he had swallowed. "I just need to think about it."

"Think about what?" The spoon went back into the bowl. "It's just children, and they can't hurt you," Jenny said.

Jamie halted the progress of the spoon with his hand. "Jen, please, I just need more time. I don't even think I can walk right now."

Jenny looked into his deep blue eyes and saw fear. He had always been the cautious one, while she barreled into things without thinking twice about it. He had saved her on more than one occasion from certain disaster. Maybe he did need more time. "How 'bout we just take a walk around this room to get your strength up?"

"I need to visit the chamber pot," he answered. "Can we start with that?"

Jenny looked at Sister Mary Frances, who pointed to a screen in the corner of the room that hid the necessary. Jamie slid over to the side of the bed and stood, with the help of his sister. The nun came to give support on the other side and looked up at his face in amusement.

"What?" he asked, a guarded look coming into his eyes.

"I didn't realize you were so tall," she answered.

"Our dad was tall . . ." Jamie's voice trailed off as he hesitantly took a step.

"Jamie is taller than our dad." Jenny looked up at her brother as he struggled to make his legs respond. "He's strong like him, too."

"Not right now," Jamie gritted out.

"Your strength will come back. You're just weak from the morphine," the nun assured him.

They reached the screen, and Jamie reached out a hand over the nun's head to steady himself on the wall.

"I can make it from here," he assured them. The pair stepped back and watched as he used the wall as a crutch and went around the screen. There was a moment of silence as he fumbled with the tail of his night shirt.

"I said I can make it," he declared. Jenny stepped away from the screen with a giggle. Sister Mary Frances folded her hands up into the sleeve of her habit and looked up towards the heavens. They heard his shuffling steps as he came back around. The nun went to lend assistance, but he held her off with an upraised hand. "I can make it on my own," he said proudly and made his way slowly back towards the bed. He sat down on the side and looked at the bowl of soup. "Do you think I can get something a little more solid to eat?" he asked the nun.

"That's a sure sign of recovery if I ever heard one." She smiled at him. "I'll see what I can do."

"What are you looking at?" Jamie asked his sister, who was leaning against the other bed with an amused expression on her face.

"Your legs," Jenny laughed. Jamie looked down at the long white legs sticking out from under his nightshirt.

"Do I have any clothes?"

"Yes, the marshal went back and packed our things for us." Jenny pulled a carpetbag out from under Jamie's bed. Jamie opened it and began to take inventory of the contents.

"It looks like he got everything," he said. His hand struck something hard at the bottom, and he pulled items of clothing out until he could see what it was. Jenny looked over his shoulder, and they both saw his revolver and holster lying next to the knife that had belonged to Ian. Two sets of deep blues eyes met. They would keep this a secret. Jenny helped him replace the clothes and set the bag back under the bed.

"I've got Momma's box," Jenny said.

"I want to see it."

"I'll bring it tomorrow."

"Where are they? I mean where did they—"

"In the cemetery at the church, next to our brothers that . . ." Jenny's voice trailed off, and Jamie nodded his head as if he could see the four graves in the yard next to the small white church they had attended. Jamie finally leaned wearily back against his pillow. Jenny was facing him, her upper arms pillowing her head atop her bent knees. They stayed that way for a while, lost in their memories of the life they had lost. Jamie reached up and wrapped a long finger around one of his sister's.

"Tomorrow I'll go outside."

"Okay."

They were silent again, their fingers still linked together when Sister Mary Frances returned to the room with a plate of scrambled eggs and a fresh-baked roll. Jamie flashed his grin as she set the tray down in his lap, and his hand automatically went to the bandages at the side of his face. Jenny handed him a fork, and he began to work on the eggs.

"It's time for you to go to dinner," the nun said to Jenny. "Come back tomorrow after school."

"And find me some books," Jamie said around a mouthful of eggs.

Jenny entered to the dining room just as the blessing was being said. She quietly went to her seat and bowed her head, saying a prayer for Jamie's recovery. After the Amen she raised her head to find Marcus staring at her. He inclined his head towards Logan and Joe, who had their heads together whispering. Jenny's eyes narrowed as she looked at them. Where those two went, trouble was sure to follow. She would be on her guard to protect Jamie. He wasn't ready for the terror they were sure to create, but when he was stronger, she was sure he would give them the thrashing they deserved.

The morning of the next day was much like the first. The residents of the mission moved from place to place at the sound of the bell tolling the hours. Jenny followed the schedule that had been set down for her, did her lessons, and ignored Logan and Joe when they pulled their sneaky little tricks in class. She told Marcus about Jamie when they took their short recess after lunch. Jenny was bored for the most part. She sought the plains to the west when she came outdoors like a thirsty man seeking water. She longed to be on horseback, Jamie at her side, the wind whipping her hair as they raced across the rolling land. She also understood that, as hard as this confinement was for her, it was even harder for Jamie. As least she had something to help her pass the day. He was still confined to the infirmary. She vowed to get him outside for at least a few minutes today. She needed him to get better so they could leave.

When her class was dismissed, Jenny raced to the infirmary, a book that she had borrowed from the teacher under her arm. She found Jamie sitting in a chair by the bed dressed in his clothes, a look of total disgust on his face.

"What's wrong?"

"She's going to take the bandages off."

"They have to come off sometime," Jenny said.

"That's what I told him," Sister Mary Frances said from the door. She was carrying a steaming pot of water. "We were waiting for

141

you." She quickly set Jenny to work soaking some cloths in the water. "We'll need to soak them off," she explained to the two of them. "Take your shirt off, young man."

Jamie unbuttoned his shirt and shrugged out of it, grimacing as the skin on his shoulder cracked and stretched with the movement. The nun took a pair of scissors and began to cut away the binding on the wraps. "We need to expose your skin to as much air as possible to help it heal. Before, we had to worry about infection," she explained as she worked on the bandages wrapped around his shoulder and chest. Jamie watched her hands as they worked the scissors, occasionally giving a little start when she came into contact with a tender area. The padding underneath the bandages was indeed stuck to the wound, and the nun had Jenny laid a steaming cloth on it to loosen the scabs. The sister next went to work on his neck, then finally pulled the top layer of bandages off his face, after instructing Jamie to lay his head back. Jenny applied a steaming towel to each area as the sister instructed her to. Jamie stared at the ceiling with his deep blue eyes full of apprehension. He was dreading this, Jenny knew, but it had to be done, and the sooner the better as far as she was concerned.

Sister Mary Frances tenderly pulled the padding back from the area on his chest. It revealed a red oozing area about the size of a fist. Removing the padding brought little rivers of blood, and Jenny quickly mopped them away as they trickled down onto his ridged stomach. Jamie kept his eyes on the ceiling. Jenny felt little quivers shoot through him as she wiped the blood away, and she began to pray to herself that he would be okay, that the rest wouldn't be that bad. She knew in her heart that it was bad, she would never forget how the blackened skin had looked on the day it happened.

The padding on the shoulder revealed several small burns, along with two cuts from the globe of the lantern. The cuts had scabbed over quite well, along with the smaller burns, but the larger areas were still oozing and dripping blood from where the padding had stuck. Jenny couldn't tell if his shirt had protected him or made the damage worse by catching fire from the oil.

The wound on his neck was long and narrow, as if the hot oil had slid down and then trailed onto his shoulder and chest. It ran parallel to the cords in his neck. Jenny watched the muscles in his neck work as he swallowed, his eyes still riveted to the ceiling.

Sister Mary Frances cast a prayer heavenward and crossed herself before she began on the padding that was still attached to the left side of Jamie's face. Jenny stood behind his chair, and caught his eyes with her own. She felt his terror at what was about to be revealed, felt the tugging of his skin as the nun gently worked the fibers of the cloth away from the wound. She heard once again his screams as he fell from the ladder; she smelled the burnt flesh again. She wanted to look away, but she was afraid that if she did, he would think she couldn't look at what the bandages had hidden. She kept her eyes locked on his as the nun pulled the padding away.

Jamie slowly lowered his head, and Jenny stepped around to the front of the chair as Sister Mary Frances examined the wound to make sure there were no threads remaining. Blood began to gush from the open areas, and Jenny placed a towel in the nun's out-stretched hand so she could stop the flow. She finally pulled her hand away to reveal the burn. It started right under his cheekbone at the corner of his eye and stretched back into his hairline, continuing all the way down the side of his face into his neck. The skin under his eye was perfect, but near his hairline it became a blistered, oozing mass. He would never be able to grow a beard or a sideburn there; the wound was that deep. He could grow his hair long and cover part of it, but it would always be visible from the front.

Jamie's eyes jumped from one face to the other as he waited for a reaction. Jenny felt tears well up in her eyes, but she couldn't tell if they were from pity or gratitude.

"Jen?" His voice broke on her name.

"It's not that bad," she answered. Jamie put his hand up to his face but stopped short of touching it.

"She's right; you could have lost an eye, an ear, even your nose, for that matter," the nun assured him.

"I want to see." His voice was strong now. Jenny felt a chill go down her spine at the words, because he sounded so much like Ian.

"I don't think you should right yet. The skin hasn't had a chance to heal," Sister Mary Frances said.

Jamie examined the wound on his chest and his shoulder. "Let me see it," he said. Jenny exchanged a look with the nun and nodded her head. The nun went over to her medicine cabinet and took a piece of silvered glass out of the drawer. She handed it to

Jenny, who in turn handed it to Jamie. Jamie took a deep breath and raised the glass to his face.

Wide, deep blue eyes full of fear stared back at him from the glass as he held it in his trembling hand. He willed his hand to be still, and focused on the side of his face. He turned his head to the right to better reveal the burn on his face and neck. They were right, it could have been worse. He was grateful for that, but still—"I'm a freak," he whispered.

"No!" Jenny cried. "No."

"It's okay, Jen, really. I'll deal with it." He handed the mirror back to his sister.

"Jamie, no." The look in his eyes made Jenny want to scream in frustration. He had always been the quiet one, who analyzed each situation thoroughly before making a decision, while she had just jumped in, come what may. Once he had made up his mind, however, there was no changing it. He stuck to his course with a fierce determination that had made their parents shake their heads on more than one occasion. She knew that he had made up his mind now. No matter what anyone said or did, he was convinced that people would look on him as something less than he was, that they would judge him as lacking because of the burns. It would take time to change his mind, she knew, and she wondered if she was strong enough to help him.

Sister Mary Frances had stood silent during the exchange between the twins, her lovely, serene face hearing the words and seeing what was left unsaid in each set of wide, deep blue eyes. She went to her work table as Jenny turned away from her brother in frustration. She found a jar of salve and handed it to Jenny, who had busied herself wringing out the bloody cloths.

"Put this on the wounds," she instructed the girl. "It will help protect them while they heal." The nun looked over at Jamie, who was still slumped in the chair. She squeezed Jenny's hand. "Go on, he needs you."

Jenny smiled gratefully at the woman. With her gentle squeeze she had imported a feeling of strength and calmness. It was the first time Jenny had felt safe since her parents had died.

Jamie sat as still as a stone while Jenny spread the salve over the open wounds. She knew it had to hurt when her fingers rubbed against the raw flesh, but he didn't flinch, just stared ahead, moving only when she instructed him to. When she was done, he got back on his bed, settled himself against the pillows and opened the book. Jenny looked at him for a short moment, her hands propped on her hips, then slapped the lid back on the jar of salve. Jamie's eyebrows twitched at her exaggerated motions, but he kept his eyes on the pages before him. Jenny began straightening the room, slamming cupboard doors, kicking chairs out of her way. Sister Mary Frances left the two to work it out for themselves.

Jenny finally had to leave the room. She was boiling over with frustration, and she knew that exploding would do more harm than good at the present time. Jamie had totally ignored her for the rest of the afternoon, giving all his attention to the book in front of him, as if he had never seen it before. She knew he had read *Oliver Twist* many times, could practically quote it by heart, so he wasn't fooling her with his act. She tore out of the mission as if chased by demons and headed towards the orchard at a full run. She ran into the stand of trees and didn't stop until she reached the end, where the trees gave way to a field that rolled down towards the buildings of St. Jo, just barely visible in the distance. Jenny threw her arms around a bud-laden tree and laid her forehead against the rough bark, willing her heart to slow down, the blood to stop rushing around in her head. She needed to be patient. Jamie's wounds were deeper than his skin. Jenny raised her head with a start and whirled away from the tree.

"He's blaming himself!" she said to no one in particular. Jamie had been charging down the ladder to help his father when the lantern exploded in his face. He hadn't been able to stop the murder of his parents; he probably would have died himself, and Jenny along with him, if he hadn't been stopped by the burning oil. Jenny's first impulse was to run back to the mission and knock some sense into her bull-headed brother, but for once she hesitated. "I need to give him time." She said it out loud, so that she could make better sense of the entire situation. "He'll realize it soon enough."

The decision made, she immediately felt better. Then the realization hit her that the words and tone she had used had sounded just like her mother. She grasped her upper arms in her hands and looked heavenward, trying to spot some blue sky between the white blossoms that waved so lightly in the fresh spring air. "Oh, Momma, help me to help him, please," she prayed. The branches sighed and swayed above her, the scent caressing her senses like the gentle touch of her mother's hand. Jenny inhaled deeply, taking the scents inside her to help her make it through the night in the dark rooms of the mission. She felt better, she felt refreshed, she was strengthened. She would tackle Jamie again tomorrow. She would bring him out here so he could find the same peace that she had. She started back to the mission with a determined step, but stopped short when she came upon Logan and Joe.

They were lounging against a tree, obviously hiding from their chores. She knew they had been spying on her by the smirks on their self-satisfied faces.

"Hey, Joe, maybe they should lock her up with her ugly brother," Logan said to his buddy, his eyes on Jenny.

"Why?" Joe looked at Jenny and gave a nervous little giggle.

"Cuz she's crazy. You saw how she was out here talkin' to the trees, thinkin' they were her dead mom."

"Maybe she'll think the barn is her dad," Joe added.

"Or maybe better, she'll think he's the jackass." Logan smiled evilly at her. Jenny balled her right hand into a fist and punched him in the nose, driving his head back into the tree he was lounging against. Blood began gushing out, and he grabbed his nose with both hands, trying to stop the flow trickling between his fingers.

"She broke my nose," he cried out. Joe nervously looked at Jenny, who was rubbing her fist, then back at his friend. He didn't seem to know what to say without his buddy standing solidly behind him. Jenny made sure he wasn't going to try anything, then stalked off, still rubbing her fist. She ran into Marcus at the edge of the orchard.

"Are you all right? I saw Logan and Joe follow you."

"I'm fine, but I can't say the same for Logan." Logan and Joe came out of the orchard, and Marcus grabbed Jenny, pulling her away from the two as they walked by, Logan stopping the flow of blood with his shirt. Marcus's eyes grew wide.

"Did you do that?" he asked.

"Someone had to do it," Jenny replied. "Come on, I want to make sure they don't go into the infirmary."

He shook his head as she began to run, and then followed behind her. Before they could enter the mission, Logan and Joe were stopped by a nun, who examined Logan's bloody nose in the courtyard while Joe hopped alongside, waving his arms and pointing towards the orchard. Jenny and Marcus ducked into the building and made their way to the infirmary at a fast walk, being warned to slow down by another frowning sister.

Sister Mary Frances was in the outer office when they came bursting in, and she rose from her desk at the interruption.

"You have a patient coming." Jenny was almost out of breath, but she managed to get the words out.

"Is it bad?" she asked, suddenly alarmed at the urgency in Jenny's face.

"No, I—"

"Go on in and shut the door," Sister Mary Frances said, understanding the situation when she heard the complaining Logan coming down the hall. Jenny dashed into Jamie's room with Marcus on her heels and firmly shut the door behind her.

Jamie greeted her with a look of horror when he realized that she was not alone. Marcus didn't hesitate. He walked over to the bed with his hand outstretched.

"Hi, I'm Marcus," he said with a friendly smile. Jamie looked at Marcus's hand, looked up at his friendly face, then looked past him to his sister, who shrugged and gave him an imploring look. Jamie took the outstretched hand and shook it, turning his face away to hide the burn.

"James Duncan," he said, and immediately began to fumble around, searching for his shirt. Jenny produced it from the back of the chair he had been sitting in earlier and held it up, hooked on the end of her finger, dangling just out of his reach. He leaned forward and jerked it out of her hand, giving her a murderous look as he pulled it on. Jenny gave him a sarcastic smile in return. Marcus decided to give the two of them some room and went over to the closed door, where he stuck his ear to the crack.

"What is going on?" Jamie asked, motioning towards the door with his chin. Marcus stuck his finger up to his lips, signaling Jamie to be quiet. Jamie started using the Indian sign language that Gray Horse had taught them to talk to Jenny. Marcus watched the exchange between the two with his ear still at the door.

"Uh-oh," he finally whispered, looking towards Jenny. "You're going to get in trouble."

"For what?" they both asked.

"Logan is telling the sisters that you went crazy and hit him for no reason."

"They won't believe that."

"Who is this guy?" Jamie asked.

"They're sending for Father Clarence right now," Marcus reported. Jamie got out of bed and went over to the door, leaning over Marcus so that he had his ear pressed to the crack above the smaller boy's. Marcus looked up, and Jamie flashed his grin. The salve that Jenny had rubbed on earlier had softened his skin so that he now could move about without feeling the pulling and tearing that he had experienced earlier. They both listened to the soothing tones of Sister Mary Frances as she ministered to Logan's nose. They also heard the angry accusations he was making, including several references to the freak hiding behind the door, in a voice loud enough for all to hear. Jamie stalked away from the door, the clear skin of his cheeks flushing red in anger.

"You punched this guy in the nose?" he asked his sister.

"He asked for it," Jenny declared.

"That's not all he's asking for." Jamie started pacing around the confines of his room, stopping only long enough to look out the window when his route took him past it. Jenny could hardly contain her joy at seeing him this way. He was ready to whip Logan but good, and he hadn't even met him yet. If anything would get him on the road to recovery it would be this. Jamie had always hated injustice of any kind; one time he had even fought an older boy at school when he caught him throwing rocks at a bird's nest. He would get strong again, just to keep this bully from picking on everyone else. Marcus saw the smile on her face and smiled back.

"Father Clarence is here," he whispered as he leaned back against the door. Jamie and Jenny joined him, each taking a station above or below. They listened as Logan angrily told his story, Joe interjecting his asides into the fabrication.

"Where is the girl now?" they heard Father Clarence ask. The three behind the door all looked at each other when they heard Joe announce that she had still been in the orchard with that punk Marcus when they came in. Sister Mary Frances never said a word as the priest instructed the other nun to find the missing girl immediately and bring her to his office. He then instructed Joe on the sins of name-calling, telling him not to refer to Marcus as a punk. Marcus put his hands over his mouth to cover his laughter as he listened to Joe being chastised for his "sin." The three of them scattered around the room, trying to look casual when they heard footsteps approaching the door.

"Father Clarence would like to have a talk with you," Sister Mary Frances told Jenny when she had the door closed firmly behind her. "Before he does, I would like to look at your hand." Jenny held her right hand out to the nun, who examined it closely, instructing her to make a fist, wiggle her fingers and flex her wrist. "I can't believe you didn't break anything on that hard head of his," she finally declared. Marcus began to laugh, and Jamie couldn't help grinning, his pride in his sister evident. Sister Mary Frances added her own sweet smile to the others and took Jenny's arm in hers.

"You'd best be off. Waiting will only make it worse."

"What's going to happen?"

"Nothing that can compare to what you've already been through," the nun assured her. She laid her hand along Jenny's cheek. "I'll say a prayer for you." Jenny nodded and took off down the hall.

"What will he do to her?" Jamie asked when she had disappeared from view.

"She's going to get a beating," Marcus declared and flopped down in the chair.

"Marcus, you don't know that," the nun answered.

"Everyone gets a beating, no matter how young or old. 'It drives the sin out, it helps to make us stronger in our war against the devil and his minions,' " Marcus quoted.

"Father Clarence will recognize the truth," Sister Mary Frances said, as much to herself as to the two boys with worried faces. Marcus threw his hands up in disgust as the nun left the room. Jamie went to the door and cautiously peered out into the office. He took a tentative step into the outer room, his hands braced against the door frame.

"You can't help her," Marcus said from the chair. "You will only make it worse for her and wind up getting in trouble yourself." Jamie looked over his shoulder at the younger boy, who sounded wiser than his years. "Besides, you know your sister would get really mad if you showed up," he added with a smile.

Jamie shook his head in wonder at the boy. "It didn't take you long to figure her out," he said, stepping back into the safety of his room. He hadn't realized how much he had been shaking until he reached the edge of his bed, where his legs suddenly gave out from under him.

"Are you all right?"

"I guess."

"Do you want me to leave?"

"No, stay, at least until Jenny gets back." Jamie surprised himself with the words. "It will make the time go quicker." He eased himself up on the bed and leaned back against the pillows. He suddenly felt weary, and very worried about his sister. As Marcus began to chatter about the mission, Jamie realized that he was the only one around to worry about Jenny, and the responsibility settled on him heavily. His heart began to ache for his mother and father and the peace that he had felt in their presence. They had made every day seem so easy, taking on the burdens of life and sharing them equally, giving Jamie and Jenny freedom from everything but the great joys that each day had to offer.

"What happened to your parents, Marcus?"

"Indians attacked our wagon. My father was going to set up a medical practice in Denver. We had an uncle but he said he didn't know how to care for my baby sister, so he just left us. That was four years ago. My sister Mary doesn't remember any of it. She was too little."

"Do you still think about them?"

"Every day. It's hardest at night when I'm falling asleep. That's when I miss them the most. Mary cries sometimes, but she doesn't really know what she's crying for."

"I wish I knew why my parents had to die," Jamie commented after a while.

"We were just in the wrong place at the wrong time," Marcus said. He wiped at some tears that had gathered at the corner of his eye.

"With my parents, it was deliberate, I know. I just wish I knew why."

"Sister Mary Frances said there are some things we'll never know the answers for. I guess this is one of them."

"I know, but I'm going to do my best to find out." Jamie closed his eyes. He really was tired. The ordeal of taking off the bandages had drained the little bit of strength he had built up since his injuries. Marcus settled into the chair, hoping that Jenny would be back soon.

*　　*　　*

Sister Mary Frances could not believe her eyes when she entered the office of Father Clarence. The priest looked as if he was ready to explode, his face a deep purple, his eyes bulging. He was standing at his desk, his arms planted rigidly on the surface, staring down at Jenny, who was calmly sitting before him.

"You will obey me!" the priest shouted. The girl did not flinch, just looked up at him with deep blue eyes full of rebellion.

"I will not let you touch me," she said calmly, as if she were speaking to a child that was having trouble understanding a difficult lesson.

"You have broken the rules and you must be punished!" The priest raised his voice again and slammed his fist against the desk top. "I will send for someone to hold you down if I must, but you will be punished!"

Sister Mary Frances loudly cleared her throat in hopes that the priest would notice her presence in the room. The priest turned to her, and she was momentarily taken aback by the venomous look in his eyes. "If I may have a word with you?"

The priest took his glasses off, then removed a white linen handkerchief from the pocket of his frock. He spent a few minutes cleaning and checking his glasses, then wiped his face with the cloth. As the nun approached the desk, Jenny rose from her chair. The nun shifted her eyes towards the door, and Jenny made good her escape before the priest had a chance to protest. His angry voice followed her down the hall as she made her way back to the infirmary.

She found Jamie and Marcus both half asleep in their places. Marcus jumped up when she entered the room, a questioning look on his face. She smiled at him, then took a place on the edge of Jamie's bed.

"Hey," she said, gently grabbing the arm of her sleeping brother.

"Hey, are you all right?" he asked sleepily. The bell began to toll, announcing the dinner hour.

"Fine, although Father Clarence is a bit out of sorts."

"Why is that?"

"He thought I needed a spanking. I disagreed."

"You what?" Marcus asked incredulously.

"I told him I wasn't going to let him punish me, that I didn't deserve to be punished." Jamie began to laugh. "It didn't set well with him. If Sister Mary Frances hadn't shown up, I believe he would have fallen over dead of heart failure."

Marcus looked at her with a delicious grin on his face. "I think I'm in love," he commented. Jamie tugged on his sister's braid, and she elbowed his side.

"We'd better go to supper before we get into any more trouble," she said as she got up from the bed.

"We?" Marcus asked as he followed her out of the room. "I'm staying far away from you, believe me." Jamie laughed as he heard their voices trailing off down the hall.

Jenny and Marcus took their seats at their respective tables and joined the rest of the children in the wait for Father Clarence to appear and bless the meal that was laid before them. Logan was sitting at his place, his nose swollen and his eyes ringed with black and blue circles. Joe was quiet for once. Apparently, Logan was not in the mood for Joe's snickering commentary. Marcus gave the two bullies a self satisfied grin and looked over at Jenny with a wink. Jenny just stared the two down, then turned her attention to Mary, who was seated across from her. The little girl seemed thrilled at the attention that Jenny gave her, and Jenny decided that she would take it upon herself to look out for her. The priest finally appeared, and quickly blessed the meal, but he still looked agitated.

Jenny knew she had not escaped when they gathered for chapel that evening. Father Clarence promptly began speaking on the wages of sin, and how sinners will be punished some day. He even quoted the scripture on vengeance, shaking his fist at the heavens. Marcus rolled his eyes at this, but Logan and Joe seemed to enjoy the passage, Logan staring down his swollen nose at Jenny as the priest expounded on the verse. Jenny let her mind drift back to the services she had attended with her family at the little white church in Council Bluffs and the loving fellowship that had existed among the congregation. She watched Mary, who was seated in front of her, struggle to stay awake as the priest went on past the nine o'clock hour when they were supposed to be dismissed to get ready for bed. Soon many of the smaller children were asleep, their heads tilted back, mouths open. Even Joe was snoring, the other boys giggling at the sounds he was making. The priest kept looking right at Jenny as he went on with his sermon, and she knew that he was making her the target of the other children, who anxiously wanted to leave and seek their beds. He finally closed the service, having exhausted his voice and the ears of the nuns, who had not dared even to move in the presence of his anger. The children shuffled sleepily from their pews, grumpy with each other and the nuns.

Jenny scooped Mary up, laying the child's curly head against her right shoulder so she wouldn't have to bear her weight on her broken arm. She helped Mary change into her nightgown, pulled the covers up under her chin, and turned to find Sister Mary Frances waiting to talk to her. She followed the nun to a small courtyard within the walls of the mission. There was a birdbath in the middle, circled with flowers that looked purple in the shadows cast by the half moon visible over head. Jenny was surprised at this oasis of color in the otherwise drab world of the mission. Once again, the nun showed Jenny a bench, then stood before her as she had that first day in the orchard.

"Do you think it was wise to defy Father Clarence today?" the sister asked after taking a moment to collect her thoughts.

"He expected me to bend over his desk and take a beating. I think I was wise to decline that offer."

"We have rules here, and he expects everyone to obey them."

"He didn't even ask me my side of the story, just told me to bend over and take my lickin'. My dad would kill anyone who laid a hand on me like that."

"Jenny, your dad is no longer here."

"I know." Jenny put her head down in her hands. Sister Mary Frances laid her hand on the girl's shoulders as the sobs began to rack her body. The nun sat down beside her and pulled her over so that her head was lying in her lap. She began to stroke her temple, smoothing the wayward strands that had escaped from the braid trailing down her back to her hips. The sobs soon gave way to a long sigh. "Every time I think I'm done crying, I start up again," Jenny said into the habit beneath her.

"There's nothing wrong with that. Sometimes you can go a lifetime and never finish crying for someone or something."

Jenny raised herself to a sitting position and looked at the nun as she wiped the tears away with the back of her hand. "Did you lose someone you were close to?" she asked.

Sister Mary Frances looked at her in surprise. "Yes, I did," she said after a while, a soft smile curving her lovely face. "I still grieve and pray every day." They sat in silence for a while, each lost in her own memories. Then Sister Mary Frances broke the silence.

"We still need to talk about you and Father Clarence."

"There's nothing to talk about. I won't just bend over so he can beat me, especially when I don't deserve it." Jenny jumped up from the bench and began pacing around the courtyard. "My dad taught me right from wrong, and how to stand up for myself when I've been wronged. No one has ever laid a hand on me that I didn't deserve, and I don't deserve anything from him." Jenny came to a stop and looked up at the half moon that was still shining above them. "Why is he here anyway? I can't imagine that he would ask to run an orphanage."

"It is not our place to question the wisdom of those who are in charge of such matters."

Jenny grinned at the nun, her teeth flashing white in the darkness. "You've wondered the same thing yourself, haven't you?" Sister Mary Frances crossed her arms, her hands disappearing into the sleeves of her habit. Jenny put her hands on her hips and looked at the nun, who sat piously on the bench before her. "I know you have, you can't help it. You're not like the others. They're scared of him, doing their best to stay out of his way and not make him mad, but you're different."

"I think it's time you went to bed. We have another busy day before us." Jenny dropped a quick kiss on the surprised nun's forehead. "Let's not discuss this with anyone else," the nun added.

"Okay, but I know Jamie has you figured out. Marcus too."

"Jenny." The nun stopped short at the door. "Let's make it our secret?"

"Who would I tell?"

Sister Mary Frances smiled as Jenny disappeared into the mission. For the first time in a long while, she felt as if she was not alone.

Chapter Fourteen

The next day passed in the same way as the one before. Jenny managed to avoid Father Clarence, and battle lines were drawn in the classroom, with Jenny and Marcus on one side, Logan and Joe on the other. Jenny and Marcus knew that when Jamie joined them the tide would turn in their favor, and Marcus looked forward to that day with great anticipation, glad that his torture would be finally over. Jenny was amused to find Mary following her as she made the rounds during the short recess allowed them after lunch. Marcus pretended to have hurt feelings, but he was actually very happy that Mary was getting some attention. When school let out for the day, Jenny hurried to the infirmary, anxious to get Jamie outside for a change. It was a beautiful day, almost summery, and she knew it would do him good to get outside in the fresh air. He was reading when she came into his room and seemed very glad for the company, even asking where Marcus was when he saw she was alone.

"Let's go for a walk," she said as he stretched on the bed, his muscles cramped from lying around all day. "You're getting lazy."

"Walk where?"

"Outside. There's an orchard. It's really nice."

"I don't think I'm ready for that yet," he said nervously, looking towards the window.

"When will you be ready? Tomorrow, next week, next month? Come on, Jamie, let's go outside. Everyone is busy with chores, no one will see you."

"Are you sure?"

"Would I lie to you?"

Jamie looked down at the face of his sister, who was trying her best to look innocent. "Yes, you would, if it would get you what you wanted."

"Jamie, I promise, to the best of my knowledge there is no one waiting outside these walls to look at you. Now, will you please go outside with me and walk around so you can get better? I miss you."

Jamie went over to the window and surveyed the area. In the distance he could see children working in a garden, and a little girl with curly brown hair handing laundry to a nun who was hanging it on a line. He could barely see the corner of a barn, and he was curious to know what kind of livestock was inside. The thought of an orchard sounded nice, too, although what he really longed for was the sight of the plains rolling out before him. He couldn't remember the last time he had felt the sun on his face, or the wind in his hair, and all he had to do was walk with his sister out through the door. It was the hardest thing he had ever had to do in his life.

Sister Mary Frances appeared at the door with a hat in her hand. "I thought you might need this. It will help shield your eyes from the sun," she explained as she handed the hat to Jamie.

He turned it in his hands, looking it over as if it were hiding some great secret. She didn't have to add that it would also shield his face from prying eyes, if any were about, and he was grateful for the offer. He pushed his hair back from his eyes and set the hat firmly on his head, cocking it a bit to the left and forward.

Jenny stood contemplating him for a minute, then held out her hand with a smile. "Let me show you around," she said as he took her hand. She led him past Sister Mary Frances and out into the halls of the mission. He tried to stop when he saw a nun coming towards them, but Jenny tugged on his hand and they passed the sister, who walked by with her eyes down, as if she never saw them. Jenny led him out into the bright sunshine, and on across the yard, never stopping until they reached the shelter of the orchard. He dropped her hand when they reached the bench and stood looking up at the limbs full of buds, swaying gently in the breeze.

"I told you it was nice out here," Jenny said. Jamie leaned back against the trunk of a tree and let the breeze wash over him.

"I feel like a baby," he finally said.

"Why?"

"I don't know. I guess I'm just weak. I feel like I can hardly walk back."

"You need to build your strength up."

Jamie stretched his arm out in front of him, made a fist, and began to flex his arm, watching the muscles move under his shirt.

"You still look the same. You haven't lost anything," Jenny assured him; then she waved her bandaged arm under his nose. "This, however, will probably look like a twig by the time I get out of these splints."

"You want to arm wrestle?" His grin flashed at her.

"Ha ha," she said, returning a grin of her own. "Come on, I want to show you something." She led him to the edge of the orchard where the rise fell away and tapered down to the town in the distance.

"Nice view," he agreed with her. "I wish Grandmother was still there."

"Yes, that would be nice." They stood for a while looking at the town, while the breeze scattered spent blossoms above them. Jamie put his arm around his sister's shoulders and soon was leaning on her.

"Let's go back and sit down for a while," she finally suggested when his weight became more than she could stand.

"Yeah, I don't want to go in yet." Jenny led him back to the bench where she had first talked to Sister Mary Frances, and he wearily sat down.

"We have to try a little more each day."

"Yeah." He leaned back against the armrest and stretched his legs out before him. Jenny sat down on the ground in front of the bench and busied herself with the spent blossoms littering the ground under the trees. She heard footsteps and looked up to see Mary coming towards them at a run. She glanced at Jamie, but he had his eyes closed. Mary was soon standing before her, out of breath from her run. Jenny saw that Jamie's eyes were open beneath the shadow of the brim of his hat, but he kept his breathing even as if he were asleep.

"Is this your brother?" the little girl asked, her eyes wide with curiosity.

"Yes, it is." Jenny laughed as she watched the brown eyes roam up and down Jamie's long frame.

"Wow, he is very tall."

"Yes, taller than anyone here, I'm sure."

Mary climbed up on the bench beside Jamie and peered up under the brim of the hat. "Are you asleep?"

He couldn't help it, he had to laugh. "No."

"What happened to your face?"

Jenny held her breath as she waited to see what Jamie would do. He froze for an instant, then slowly reached up and took off his hat. "I was burned," he said.

Mary carefully studied the side of his face, even reaching out her small hand to turn it just so, to see the wound better. She sat back down beside him and picked up his hand. "I got burned, too. Want to see?" she announced.

Jamie gave his sister a puzzled look, and she shrugged her shoulders in return. Mary was busy hiking up her dress tail and turned her hip around to show a crescent-shaped scar on her thigh. "See, I bumped into the stove door when we were living with our uncle. Marcus said I cried for a week. Our uncle sent us here after it happened. He said he didn't know how to take care of a little girl." Mary carefully rearranged her dress and settled back down beside Jamie. "Do you think you could ride me on your shoulders when you are feeling better? Then I would be bigger than everyone here instead of being the littlest."

Jamie looked down at the little hand that had managed to find its way into his. He looked down at his sister, who was smiling up at him, and he flashed his grin. "I think I could manage that, maybe in a week or two."

"Good, I can't wait to tell Rosy," Mary said with a smile of her own. She climbed down from her perch and took off towards the mission; apparently she was set on telling whoever Rosy was this very minute.

"That was Marcus's sister," Jenny explained as Jamie watched her go, shaking his head and grinning. "And I think she's in love with you." Jamie just kept on grinning as the little girl disappeared into the mission.

The days passed, one much like the other. Every day Jamie waited until Jenny was done with her schooling, then the two of them would wander around the grounds, Jamie growing stronger and more confident each day. They were careful to stay away from the others, especially Logan and Joe, who were constantly watching Jenny. Jenny didn't want anything to interfere with Jamie regaining his strength, or make him self-conscious about the way he looked. She was grateful for the way Mary had reacted, and included her and Marcus as often as possible in their walks around the grounds. Soon Jamie was able to do all the things he had done before the injury, and with the help of the hat that Sister Mary Frances had given him, he looked much the same. When he was inside, however, the hat had to come off, and the scabs that had formed over the wound were prominent. Jenny was not looking forward to the day when he would be pronounced well enough to join the rest of the orphans.

It was Father Clarence who made the decision for them. Jenny had managed to avoid the man altogether since her rebellion, and except for an occasional look at her over his glasses, he ignored her. She was surprised to find the priest in the infirmary looking at Jamie's face, his hand on Jamie's chin, tilting his head from one side to the other as if examining a rock. Jamie's eyes were turned to the ceiling, and Jenny could tell by the set of his jaw that he was raging inside. Sister Mary Frances was standing next to the bed, and she quickly motioned for Jenny to be still as she came into the room. The priest finished his examination and looked over his shoulder at Jenny, who had stationed herself against the wall at the foot of the bed.

"You say the other wounds have healed over like this one?" he asked the nun, disregarding Jamie, who was sitting between the two.

"Yes, Father, he is healing quite well. The worst wound is on his face."

"So there is nothing that will interfere with his going to school, or helping to earn his keep?"

"No, although I would like him to take it slow where the chores are concerned."

"Good. I'll expect to see him with the others tomorrow. You may move him into the dormitory today. We need someone to work in the barn." He finally looked at Jamie. "I believe you were raised on a farm and know how to handle livestock and such."

"Yes, sir."

"Good. Sister Alice will instruct you on your duties." He turned and looked at Jenny. "There will be no excuse for you not doing your share now that your brother has recovered. The cook—"

"Father, she has been helping me since the day she arrived," Sister Mary Frances interrupted. "There is always plenty of work here in the infirmary, and when we have a chance, we work on the mending. The girl has a fair hand with a needle and thread. It would be a shame to waste such a gift."

Father Clarence peered over his glasses at the nun, who turned her lovely face up to him with a hopeful smile.

"It is a shame to waste any gift that the Lord has given us. Let us hope that the girl will learn something from spending time with you." He gave Jenny an indecipherable look, then left, leaving all three of them to sigh in relief.

"I guess I should go meet Sister Alice," Jamie said. He looked rather nervous, and Jenny knew he was not looking forward to leaving the safety of the infirmary.

"Marcus should be in the barn also. Why don't you find him and have him show you where you can sleep?" the nun suggested. "Jenny, go with him and help him get settled." Jamie pushed his hair back and put his hat on. "You'll be fine," she assured him. He squared his shoulders and left the room, for the first time in the lead, Jenny following.

Jamie was genuinely excited to be in the barn among the livestock. There were some horses, a team for the wagon, and a pair of draft horses for plowing and heavy work. There were also some milk cows, one with a calf, and plenty of chickens underfoot. He stood in the aisle of the barn and breathed in the smells while Jenny poked around, trying to find Marcus. He was out behind the barn, shoveling the muck of the pigpen around while a sow protested angrily from a corner of the sty. Marcus was muttering to himself about how useless his chore was and how all his brain power was going to waste on such a stupid animal when Jenny interrupted him.

"What are you doing?" she asked with a laugh.

"What does it look like, I'm moving mud from one side of this stupid pen to the other. Anyone with half a brain can see that."

"Oh, I see it, I just don't understand why you're doing it."

"Because it needs to be done, because Sister Alice told me to do it, because she couldn't think of anything else for me to do and she knows I'd rather be inside reading a book than stomping around out here in the mud with this stupid pig."

Jamie appeared next to Jenny at the fence. "I've been sent to rescue you," he said to Marcus.

"What?"

"Father Clarence has decided that I'm cured and I am to report to Sister Alice right away for work."

Marcus looked up from his shoveling. "She's over there," he said with a jerk of his arm. Jamie went over to where a nun was struggling with a fence board. He took the hammer out of her hand and was soon pounding away, the nun standing at his side with a handful of nails.

Marcus watched him go to work, then turned to Jenny. "Are they moving him into the dormitory?" he asked.

"Yes. Sister Mary Frances wants you to help get him settled. He's supposed to go to school tomorrow."

"Do you think he's ready?"

"I hope so. He doesn't have much choice." Jenny watched her brother test the strength of the board he was working on. "Do you think he'll have any trouble?"

Marcus reached up to wipe sweat off his forehead and ended up smearing mud. "Yeah, he'll have trouble. The question is how much, and how much will he take before he breaks or pounds someone."

Jenny laid her head down on her arms, which were folded across the top of the fence. Marcus leaned next to her, turning his head so that he was looking into her deep blue eyes.

"What are you afraid of, Jenny?" His brown eyes were solemn, and Jenny had to remind herself that he was only a boy. "Are you afraid he'll fight, or are you afraid he won't fight?"

"I'm afraid he'll quit fighting, and I know he's going to have to fight for the rest of his life."

"And you'll be standing right next to him, no matter what he does."

Jenny looked at the grubby face on the rail next to hers. The face still had a lot of boy in it, but the features were starting to sharpen into manhood. She wondered briefly what his father had been like, what kind of doctor he had been, what it had been like to pack his family up to travel across a wilderness to start a new life in a new town. "How did you get to be so wise?" she finally asked, reaching a finger out to knock off a chunk of mud that was sticking to his cheek.

"I had to, to survive."

"I guess we'll have to, too."

Jamie was coming back, his stride long, his hat tilted at a jaunty angle. Jenny raised her head to watch him, and for a brief instant saw her father walking across the lawn with his self-confident step. She shook her head to clear it, then smiled when she realized once again how much Jamie was like their father. *He'll be okay*, she thought.

"Are you done playing in the mud?" Jamie asked Marcus as he approached the pen.

"Yeah, let me get cleaned up, and then we'll move your stuff."

"I'll see you at dinner, then," Jamie said to his sister.

"Are you sure?"

"About dinner?"

"No, about . . . you know. . . ."

"Go on, I'll be fine. I don't need you hanging around."

Jenny looked at Marcus, who nodded his head in agreement with Jamie. She looked back at her brother, but couldn't see his eyes beneath the wide brim of the hat.

"Okay, see you at dinner." She left slowly, hoping he would call her back, knowing he wouldn't. She knew he was right—whatever was going to happen would happen, and he didn't need to have her in the middle of it. Jenny's mother had always told her that the Duncan men were full of pride, and this was Jamie's way of showing it. As much as she wanted to follow along, she knew he needed her to stay away more. It was part of his healing, it was time for him to stand on his own. She went back to the infirmary. She knew he would have to show up there sooner or later to get his bag.

Jamie did show up at the infirmary. Jenny had just settled down with her needle and thread when she heard his long stride coming down the hall. She looked up expectantly and he came in, Marcus in tow, and grinned at her. He went into the room where he had slept, came out with his bag and tugged on her braid as he passed by. He stopped suddenly and came back to whisper in her ear.

"Don't worry about the gun and stuff. We found a place to hide it in the barn."

Jenny looked up in amazement, realizing that she had forgotten about the revolver altogether, with everything else that had been going on. Jamie went on his way, with Marcus chattering along beside him, his voice trailing off as they went down the hall.

Sister Mary Frances came in, having just passed them in the hall, with a smile on her face. "I believe those two will be good for each other," she commented.

Jenny was still amazed that Jamie had tackled the move with such good humor, but knew that, once he made a decision, he stuck to it. He couldn't change his scars, but he could change how he dealt with them.

The afternoon dragged on for Jenny. She was worried, but there was nothing she could do, and unless someone showed up at the infirmary with an injury, she had no way of knowing what was going on in the rest of the mission. Finally, after she had mended everything in sight, the dinner bell rang. She was out of the room like a shot, racing for the dining room. Sister Mary Frances shook her head behind her.

The group of older boys were conspicuously missing when everyone else had gathered for the evening meal. Jenny stood at her chair, her knuckles white from gripping the back, waiting for Jamie and Marcus to show up. A smile lit her face when she heard Jamie's long stride in the hall. He drew the immediate attention of everyone, but he ignored the stares, just flashing his grin at Jenny as he took a seat at the boys' table with Marcus to his left. Logan, Joe and a few more stragglers came in after them, the two bullies looking a bit out of sorts. Everyone remained standing for prayer, and then sat for the meal. Jamie and Marcus immediately put their heads together, and Jenny noticed that by sitting on his left, Marcus made sure that the healing wound was shielded from the prying looks that kept roaming their way. Jenny sent God a prayer, thanking Him for the presence of Marcus, then turned her attention to Mary, who was having trouble cutting her meat.

They caught up with each other on the way to chapel that night, Jenny wanting to hear everything that had happened. Jamie just shrugged his shoulders at her inquiry, and started talking to Mary, who was batting her big brown eyes at him. Marcus grabbed her arm and looked at her with a big grin on his face.

"You should have seen him," he whispered.

"What happened?"

"Logan and Joe came in while he was putting his things away and started in on him, calling him names and such. He just stood up, kind of towered over Logan and said, 'If I can survive this, I can survive anything you can throw my way.' He just stood there, daring them to say something or do something, and they were struck dumb. It was great." Marcus had obviously enjoyed the moment, he just kept grinning as he told the story. "I think they didn't realize how big he was until he was standing there looking down on them."

Jenny looked ahead at her brother, who was walking with his long index finger grasped in Mary's hand, her head barely coming to his waist. Being with him every day had made her forget about his great height, and since her father was also tall, she just took it for granted. A delicious smile hit her face as she imagined Logan and Joe staring up at Jamie's handsome features and every thought in their vacant heads scattering before his size.

"Do you think they'll leave him alone?" she asked.

"No, but they'll think long and hard before they do anything."

They went into the chapel, boys on one side, girls on the other. Jenny took Mary into the pew with her, Marcus slid in on Jamie's left, to help shield him once again. The service started, little heads began to nod, and Jamie looked over at Jenny and signed that he was bored, which made Jenny roll her eyes. Soon he was silently teaching Marcus Indian signs, and they began flashing messages back and forth, while Mary slept with her head on Jenny's shoulder.

The next day in class, the lines were drawn: Jamie, Jenny and Marcus on one side, Logan and Joe on the other. The nun who was their teacher looked from one armed camp to the other with an expression of bewilderment on her homely face. Once again, she decided that ignorance was bliss and began the first lessons of the day. Jamie caught up in no time, and the twins and Marcus sped through the lesson, then waited patiently for Logan and Joe to finish so they could move on to something else. Jamie perused the small selection of donated books, found a few he hadn't read and asked the sister for permission to read while he was waiting. The nun seemed astonished by his request but granted it and he settled down at his desk, his long legs stretched out before him, and began to read *David Copperfield*. Logan and Joe looked at him with something close to disgust on their faces and returned to their lesson, still struggling with the words. Jenny looked over at her brother, who had quickly lost himself in the book, and decided that he was going to be okay in spite of everything. Now she just had to talk him into leaving.

Talking to Jamie about leaving turned out to be harder than Jenny had first thought. He managed to evade the subject every time she brought it up by saying he hadn't healed enough to think about it. Sister Mary Frances had removed the splints from Jenny's arm and pronounced her fit, and Jamie's burns had healed over into raw, ridged skin. He wore the hat whenever he went out of the mission, and pretty much ignored the stares of those inside. His world consisted of the classroom and his duties in the barn, the rest of the time was just an inconvenience to be endured until he could get lost in his books, or lost in the gentle solace of the animals.

Jenny finally cornered him in the barn one day in late spring where he was brushing one of the huge draft horses, talking to him in the gentle tones their father had used when he had worked his magic with the animals. Jenny stood outside the stall and listened for a while, closing her eyes and letting her memories take her back to the days when she had lain in the straw and listened to her father speak in the same manner to Storm.

"What are you mooning over?" Jamie asked, tugging on her braid.

"Nothing. I was just remembering."

Jamie looked around the cool confines of the stall and at the huge brown horse, which was daintily nibbling on a straw. "Yeah, I know what you mean." He leaned over the stall door, letting his arms dangle down the front. Jenny leaned her back against the wall near the stall so she could see him.

"Let's leave now," she said.

"Why?"

"Why stay here?" she retorted.

"We have a roof over our head, and food in our bellies, that's why."

"I feel like I'm in prison."

"You'd feel worse out there on your own."

"How can you say that?"

"Jen, think about it. We have no place to go, no money, no way to make a living. No one would hire us, we're too young."

"Jamie—"

"*No*, I know I'm right. We have to stay here until we're old enough to make it on our own. It's not bad here. You just need to quit thinking about what we used to have."

"How can I, when every minute of the day I just want to jump on the back of a horse and go tearing out of here?"

Jamie looked out the door of the barn to the plains beyond. The sun was high in the afternoon sky and the heat of it rippled in the distance, creating the illusion that he was looking through a thick pane of glass. Occasionally, the warm breeze stirred the tufts of the long grass that covered the rolling land, turning the stems over so that the land looked like waves coming into shore, each one disappearing into itself.

"I know," he said simply, "but you can't, so get over it and get on with your life."

"Get on with my life?" Jenny could not believe her ears. "How am I supposed to get on with my life when I'm stuck here?"

"It won't be forever, Jen. I promise. We just have to wait until we're older. Then we'll go, we'll get jobs, and we'll get our own place."

Jenny tried to look into the deep blue eyes that were hidden within the shadows of the hat. She could not see them. He was good at hiding them from her now, and hiding all the things that were concealed in their depths. She wondered how much of what he said was coming from his practical nature, and how much was coming from his fear of rejection because of the scars. One thing she was sure of: he wasn't ready to leave. No matter what she said, she wouldn't change his mind.

He was back at work now, bent over the hooves of the giant horse, bracing his knee under a trunk-like leg that could snap his in an instant, confident in the knowledge that the horse would not harm him. *I wish I felt that safe,* she thought to herself as she watched him work. She felt as if she had been waiting on the edge of some precipice ever since she'd arrived at the mission, and she knew that someone was anxious to push her off and watch her tumble into space with nothing to hold on to. The feeling had been keeping her awake at night and followed her through her days as they melted into weeks and then months. But Jamie was content, and as long as he stayed, she would stay. She left him to his animals and went back to her mending.

Life at the mission soon became as routine as life at the ranch had been. Jenny still was restless, longing to leave, but not willing to go anywhere without Jamie, who managed to stay hidden in the deep recesses of the barn. Soon the long, hot, hazy days of summer were upon them and they found a small pond where they would sneak off on Sunday afternoons when they were supposed to be resting and studying God's word.

Jamie and Marcus would shed their clothes with great joy and splash around in the cool water while Jenny and Mary dangled their feet over the rocks and let the water wash the heat away. Jamie tried to get Jenny to join them in swimming, but she refused, now self-conscious about the differences in their bodies. After a while, Jamie and Marcus would come out and take Mary to sit under the nearby trees, allowing Jenny privacy to swim at her leisure. It seemed a lifetime since she had shed her clothes and swam, and she splashed around in the stream with joyous abandon. She submerged herself in the pond, the water coming up to her chin, and turned graceful circles, watching the murky water ripple away from her.

They had been sneaking out every Sunday since the end of June without being caught, but Jenny knew it was just a matter of time before this pleasure would be taken away from them, either by Father Clarence or the weather, as it was now coming to the end of August. She was determined to enjoy these outings while she could, so she closed her eyes and let her feet come to the top, the water carrying her up until she was floating on her back, little ripples breaking against her ears. She felt her hair fan out around her, the golden tendrils dancing around her fingertips and spreading out behind her like giant wings. Jenny lost herself in the sensation of floating, her body cooling until she didn't know where her skin ended and the water began. She cleared her mind of all the turmoil that was constantly nagging at her and concentrated on the moment, seeing nothing behind her closed lids but blue sky and cool water.

Something foreign caught her attention, the sound of a breeze rustling the branches of a tree, but when she opened her eyes, the leaves above her were motionless in the heat of the afternoon. She heard it again, so she planted her feet in the muddy bottom and ducked down until the water hit her chin.

"Jamie?" she called. There was no answer, so she turned slowly, thinking she would catch some animal that had come to the pond for a drink. Another rustle, low to the ground, behind her. "Marcus, you better come out!" Then she heard a snicker that could only have been made by Joe, and she knew that Logan had to be there, too. She heard Mary's laughter in the distance and felt a sinking feeling when she realized that Jamie was out of sight.

"I know you're watching me, Logan," she said to the bushes as she crossed her arms over her breasts. She heard a rustling again, then saw Logan stand, with Joe coming up behind him.

"Why don't you come on out?" Logan was holding her shirt in the crook of his finger; behind him Joe held up her skirt.

"Why don't you put my clothes down and leave before my brother kills you?" She hoped she looked confident, and she prayed that Jamie would get bored with waiting and come for her.

"I ain't afraid of your brother. He ain't gonna do nothin' to me."

"Yeah," Joe added.

"Come on out, or are you scared?"

"I'm not afraid of you, or your little weasel of a friend," Jenny retorted, hoping to buy time before the situation got out of control. She scanned the shoreline to identify the quickest escape route with the most cover available. Unfortunately, Logan and Joe were occupying the bank with the most shrubbery; the rest of the pond was surrounded by cattails which would do little to shield her from their avid eyes. The cattails would, however, offer minimum coverage until she could reach the trees beyond, and she was not above sacrificing her modesty to save her dignity.

She slowly began to move across the pond, feeling the bottom with her feet for any stout piece of wood that might have been blown in by a storm. All she felt was mud, and the occasional nibble of a fish tasting her toes. Logan stood before her, taunting her with her shirt. Joe, who had been scrambling around behind him, came up with her camisole and pantalets, waving a garment in each hand. He let out a whoop at his discovery, and Logan turned and began to curse him.

"Jenny?" Jamie called from the trees.

"Jamie, come quick!" she yelled. In the next instant she was

GET UP TO 5 FREE BOOKS!

Sign up for one of our book clubs today, and we'll send you
FREE* BOOKS
just for trying it out...**with no obligation to buy, ever!**

HISTORICAL ROMANCE BOOK CLUB

Travel from the Scottish Highlands to the American West, the decadent ballrooms of Regency England to Viking ships. Your shipments will include authors such as CONNIE MASON, CASSIE EDWARDS, LYNSAY SANDS, LEIGH GREENWOOD, and many, many more.

LOVE SPELL BOOK CLUB

Bring a little magic into your life with the romances of Love Spell—fun contemporaries, paranormals, time-travels, futuristics, and more. Your shipments will include authors such as KATIE MACALISTER, SUSAN GRANT, NINA BANGS, SANDRA HILL, and more.

As a book club member you also receive the following special benefits:

- **30% OFF all orders through our website & telecenter!**
  (Plus, you still get 1 book FREE for every 5 books you buy!)
- **Exclusive access to special discounts!**
- **Convenient home delivery and 10 days to return any books you don't want to keep.**

There is no minimum number of books to buy, and you may cancel membership at any time. See back to sign up!

*Please include $2.00 for shipping and handling.

YES! ☐

Sign me up for the **Historical Romance Book Club** and send my THREE FREE BOOKS! If I choose to stay in the club, I will pay only $13.50* each month, a savings of $6.47!

YES! ☐

Sign me up for the **Love Spell Book Club** and send my TWO FREE BOOKS! If I choose to stay in the club, I will pay only $8.50* each month, a savings of $5.48!

NAME: _____

ADDRESS: _____

_____

TELEPHONE: _____

E-MAIL: _____

☐ **I WANT TO PAY BY CREDIT CARD.**

☐ VISA   ☐ MasterCard   ☐ DISCOVER

ACCOUNT #: _____

EXPIRATION DATE: _____

SIGNATURE: _____

Send this card along with $2.00 shipping & handling for each club you wish to join, to:

**Romance Book Clubs
20 Academy Street
Norwalk, CT 06850-4032**

Or fax (must include credit card information!) to: 610.995.9274.
You can also sign up online at www.dorchesterpub.com.

*Plus $2.00 for shipping. Offer open to residents of the U.S. and Canada only.
Canadian residents please call 1.800.481.9191 for pricing information.
If under 18, a parent or guardian must sign. Terms, prices and conditions subject to change. Subscription subject
to acceptance. Dorchester Publishing reserves the right to reject any order or cancel any subscription.

JOIN NOW!

rewarded with the sight of his determined face scowling at Logan, who flipped her shirt up in the air and took off through the underbrush, with Joe on his heels. Jamie's long legs overtook the pair in seconds, and he shoved Joe out of the way before he brought Logan crashing down by diving and tackling him around the knees. Marcus was coming behind him and hauled the protesting Joe up by his collar. Jenny took advantage of the diversion and splashed out of the pond, gathering her clothes before disappearing behind a tree. Jamie hauled Logan to his feet and sent him sailing into the water head first. Marcus had Joe on the ground, and Jamie promptly picked him up and flung him squealing into the pond, too. Joe crashed into Logan, who had just come sputtering to the surface, and they both went under in a tangle of arms and legs. Jenny had scrambled into her clothes, and she joined the two on the bank as they dissolved into laughter at the sight of Logan and Joe spitting and cursing in the water. Jenny was wringing the water out of her hair as she watched them shake their fists and fill the air with empty threats. Mary joined them on the bank and began to giggle.

"We'd better get out of here," Jenny suggested and took Mary's hand. She led the little girl back towards the mission, and Jamie and Marcus joined up with them after they made sure the two bullies took an alternate route home. They knew that their wet shoes and clothes would slow them down, but the four hurried anyway, Jamie taking Mary on his broad shoulders and Jenny braiding her hair as they walked briskly towards the orchard. They came up on its back side and walked beneath the branches which were heavy with ripening fruit. When they reached the clearing that led to the mission, they separated, Jamie and Marcus heading towards the barn, Jenny taking Mary and hoping to reach the shelter of the dormitory before they were discovered.

Logan and Joe were not as lucky. The first person they ran into while trying to steal back into their dormitory was Father Clarence, who personally escorted the twosome to his office by grabbing on to their ears. He quickly sent for Jamie, Marcus and Jenny when Logan and Joe told how Jenny had tempted them with her body and her cohorts had then attacked them without mercy.

Jenny was made to wait in the hall while the boys were all taken in together, each one protesting at the lies the others told. Jamie finally threw his hands up in frustration and challenged the priest to do whatever he was going to do and quit wasting his time. Jenny cringed as she heard each lick being given by the priest's wooden paddle. The four soon came out, Logan giving her a look that would have caused trembling in a weaker person; it just made Jenny raise her chin a notch. Joe was sniveling behind him, rubbing his bruised posterior. Marcus rubbed his too, but he was smiling. Jamie just tugged on her braid and flashed his grin.

"I'll be close by," he whispered as Father Clarence summoned her in. She walked with what she hoped was a confident step into the dark confines of the office, but couldn't help shivering when she heard the click of the lock behind her.

Father Clarence sat down as his desk and indicated a chair. She sat with her arms resting on the arms of the chair, willing her pounding heart to slow down as the priest surveyed her over his steepled fingers.

"I knew you were full of sin from the first day I saw you," he began. "You have the body of a temptress and the soul of a whore."

Jenny could not believe the words that were coming out of his mouth.

"We must purge the evil from you."

"I didn't do anything," she protested weakly. The look in his eyes terrified her.

"You will not lead me into temptation, not this time." Jenny's eyes grew wide as she realized that he was confusing her with someone else. "I will be stronger than the evil that is within you."

She heard someone testing the latch of the door.

"Father Clarence?" It was Sister Mary Frances.

Jenny bolted to the door and fumbled with the lock. She heard the priest's footsteps behind her as he came around his desk. She finally turned the bolt and flung the door open, causing the nun to stumble back against Jamie, who was standing with fists clenched and a murderous look in his eyes. Jenny ran past them, and Jamie took off after her when he saw the fear in her eyes. Father Clarence watched the two disappear with a look on his face that caused the nun to cross herself and send a quick prayer up to heaven. Father Clarence went back into his office and bolted the door without saying a word to Sister Mary Frances.

"Jen, what happened?" Jamie asked when they had reached the safety of the courtyard. "When he locked the door, I panicked and went to find Sister Mary Frances."

Jenny began pacing around the birdbath in the center of the courtyard. "He thinks I'm someone else."

"What do you mean, someone else?"

"I don't know. He was talking crazy. He said I was a whore, and I wasn't going to tempt him again, that he needed to purge the evil from me."

"He's crazy!"

"He scares me. Oh, Jamie, can we please leave?"

Jamie ran his hands through his hair, pushing the growing mass back out of his eyes. "Jen, we'll tell Sister Mary Frances what he said. She'll know what to do."

"I want to go."

"We've no place to go. It's going to be autumn soon, then winter. There is no way we can survive by ourselves."

Jenny flopped down on the bench and crossed her arms in front of her. "I'm not sure I can survive him either." She said it so quietly that Jamie went and sat beside her. He gathered her slim hands into his big bronze ones and gently squeezed her fingers.

"We'll be careful. We'll watch out for you, me and Marcus. We'll make sure you're never alone where he can find you, I promise."

Jenny looked at the handsome face of her brother, at his deep blue eyes so like her own. She saw the depth of his concern, saw the fear for her, and the fear for himself. The ridges of the scar on the side of his face were pale, contrasting greatly with the deep bronze of his skin. His hair was longer than it had ever been, covering his ears and brushing against the collar of his shirt. The front continually flopped down over his eyes, and he was forever shoving it back and clamping his hat down to keep it in place. Jenny reached up and pushed the mass back, looping it over his ear in hopes that it would stay, but it wasn't long before it fell forward again. Jamie grinned at her attempt, and she threw her arms around his neck, burying her face under his chin. Jamie spread his arms out in surprise, but when he realized she was trembling, he wrapped his arms around her and pulled her close.

"Don't you know I'll always take care of you?" he said into the crown of golden blond hair. He felt her head go up and down in a nod under his chin. "You just have to try to stay out of trouble. Lord knows that will be a chore for you." Jenny punched the back of his shoulder with her fist.

"Was the lickin' worth it?" she finally asked when she felt she had her emotions under control.

"Oh, yeah." She felt his grin above her head. "It wasn't anything. He can't hurt me, and even if it did hurt, it was still worth it. It felt really good to throw those bullies in the water."

"This won't be the end of it, you know."

"I know. We'll just take it as it comes."

Chapter Fifteen

The long hot days of summer began to fade and the weather became cooler, the days shorter. Jenny stayed as close as possible to Sister Mary Frances, who had become pensive after the incident with the locked office door. Jamie and Marcus became a shield for Jenny also, each one making sure that one of them was within calling distance whenever they were about the grounds, or going to and fro in the halls.

Father Clarence began to take some of his meals in the privacy of his office and even missed several of the evening devotions, leaving the sisters to read some scripture, lead the group in a few songs and dismiss the happy children early. The sisters cared for their charges with puzzled looks on their faces, but beyond prayer, they didn't know what they could do. Most of them were relieved not to have to put up with the priest's oppressive company.

One afternoon the cook came and asked Jenny if she would be willing to go to the orchard and find what was left of the apples for some cobbler. She agreed, having seen Father Clarence depart the mission earlier in the buckboard to conduct some business in town. She went to see if Mary could join her, and the two went hand in hand to the orchard, anxious to be outside on such a beautiful day. They all knew that the mild days they were enjoying wouldn't last much longer, and Jenny looked at the task as a blessing. She was dreading the long winter and the confines of the orphanage walls.

When they reached the orchard, Jenny took off her shoes, tucked the tail of her skirt in her waistband and swung up into the branches to search the uppermost part of the tree. She smiled to herself when she remembered both her mother and father claiming to be the source of her talent for balance and climbing, then laughing as if sharing a secret joke. She had heard her mother say on more than one occasion that she was grateful for the oak tree that grew outside her bedroom window. Then her father would remark that he was going to make sure there was no such benefit for any suitor of his daughter.

She looked down below her at Mary, who was picking up apples off the ground, inspecting them, then heaving the discards with great relish into a pile, laughing with delight when a particularly rotten one spattered across the grass. Jenny laughed along with her as she made her way from branch to branch, finding a few good specimens to add to the bag looped over her shoulder. She made her way to the top of the tree and paused a moment to watch a few billowing clouds float across the deep blue sky. She sucked in the clear, cool air as she swayed on the thin branches at the top of the tree. She look down to see Mary scanning the branches, trying to find her.

"Jenny, I want to come up."

"No, you can't. You're too little."

"I'm always too little." Mary pouted, and Jenny watched her go scuffing off, kicking rotten apples out of her way.

She decided that she had picked this tree clean and made her way down to try another one, knowing she would need to fill the bag in order for everyone to get cobbler. The afternoon passed pleasantly enough, with Mary roaming around below, finding caterpillars and one time startling a small green snake which beat a hasty retreat from her squealing voice and stamping feet. The bag was so full that Jenny knew she'd have to drag it back, and debated whether she should send Mary for help. After testing the weight of the bag, she decided she could handle it, and the two of them started back for the mission, each one holding a corner of the bag, but Jenny doing all of the work.

They hadn't taken ten steps when they saw Logan and Joe coming their way, looks of pure glee on their faces at finding the girls away from their protectors. Jenny didn't even stop to think, she bent down and picked up an especially rotten apple and threw it with all her might at Logan's leering face. The apple hit him square in the forehead and exploded into a gooey mass that began to run down his face. She followed up with another bomb that smacked Joe in the chest, and with the help of Mary, whose throws mostly fell short of the target, continued the bombardment until the two turned tail and ran. Jenny laughed gleefully at the empty threats they hurled over their shoulders in their retreat, and Mary spun around for sheer joy after realizing that they had bested the bullies.

They continued on their way, with Mary giggling and chattering the entire trip, until they reached the huge kitchen that serviced the mission. The cook was nowhere to be seen, so Jenny emptied the bag of apples into the sink to be washed while Mary spun circles around the room, chanting a rhyme about the defeat of Logan and Joe. She spun so much that she became dizzy and crashed out of control into a wheeled cart that held the plates waiting to be set on the table for dinner. The cart tipped with the impact of her small body, and its contents went sliding onto the hard floor, shattering with a crash. The little girl looked up from the disaster with her mouth wide open, her hands flying up to her face. Jenny heard the scrape of a chair followed by a loud thump from the dining hall beyond, and she grabbed Mary to her.

"Run, go find Sister Mary Frances." She shoved Mary towards the back door and was kneeling among the broken plates when the door from the dining hall came crashing open. She looked up to find Father Clarence peering down at her over his glasses.

"What happened?" His voice was calm and flat.

"It was an accident. I tripped and crashed into the cart," Jenny said with a trembling voice.

"Do you expect me to believe that?"

"I swear it was an accident."

The priest came over and grabbed her arm, pulling her to her feet. "Look at what you've done," his voice hissed in her ear.

"I'll clean it up." Jenny couldn't help it, she sobbed on the words.

"Yes, you will, and then you will be punished." He pushed her down so hard that she lost her balance and fell, the shards from the dishes piercing her palms and knees when she landed. She caught a sob in her throat and gathered her feet beneath her, getting ready to run when the opportunity presented itself. "You need to be punished. I should have taken care of that long ago instead of letting the evil grow and fester inside of you."

He stepped away from the cart, and Jenny measured the distance to the door with a sideways glance. She saw that he was going for the broom in the corner and she slowly stood, thinking he was going to hand it to her to sweep up the mess. When he reached for it, she turned for the door, hoping that Sister Mary Frances was on the way and would calm the man.

She never saw the blow coming. She just felt the impact of the broom handle as it came down on her shoulder, sending her tumbling head first into the wall. She was dazed, but managed to turn and throw her arm up as another blow descended on her. She felt the bone in her arm snap, but raised it again as the handle came at her for the third time. The priest's face was a mass of purple in his rage, and Jenny felt as if the demons of hell must be standing beside her from the look in his eyes. A blow landed on her temple, and everything before her turned red before it all faded into blackness.

The priest looked at the crumpled body at his feet and then up at the broom, which was raised for another blow. He flung the weapon across the kitchen and left, making sure he didn't step in the trail of blood coming from the cuts on Jenny's hands.

Sister Mary Frances found her a few minutes later when she breathlessly followed Mary into the kitchen. She immediately sent the little girl to the barn for Jamie and then knelt beside Jenny's unconscious form. Jenny moaned when she touched the broken arm, and the sister sent a prayer of thanksgiving heavenward that the girl wasn't dead. She wrapped towels around her bleeding hands and knees and was wiping the trickle of blood from her temple when Jamie came bursting through the door. Marcus was right behind him.

"Jenny!" Jamie knelt beside Jenny. "Sister, what happened?"

"I don't know. It looks as if someone beat her."

Marcus gathered Mary up as she came in behind them. "Is she dead?" Mary asked with a trembling voice.

"No. Mary, did you see who did this?" the nun asked.

"No, I knocked the dishes over and Jenny told me to get you to

176

help." She was crying now and shaking her head. "There wasn't anyone else here but me and Jenny."

The nun stood and scanned the kitchen to see if there was some clue as to the identity of the attacker. Jamie gently slid his arms under Jenny and lifted her up, bringing another moan from her as her left arm flopped down. Sister Mary Frances tucked the arm up on Jenny's chest and led the way to the infirmary with Marcus and Mary bringing up the rear. Jamie placed her in the same bed that he had occupied upon his arrival at the mission and left without a word.

"You'd better go with him, Marcus, and see if you can keep him out of trouble until I find out what happened," Sister Mary Frances instructed him. "Mary, go see if you can find Sister Abigail."

Sister Mary Frances had the still unconscious Jenny bandaged up by the time the boys arrived back in the infirmary. Their search for Jenny's attacker had come to a dead end. Mary was perched on the other bed, sobbing occasionally as she sniffed back her tears and runny nose. Marcus pulled her onto his lap as Jamie took a seat on his sister's bed. Her arm was wrapped with a splint again, and her hands were bandaged along with her knees. Her right temple was sporting a large goose egg, and the side of her face had begun to turn black and blue. Her long golden braid was lying over her shoulder, and Jamie took the ends of it in his hands, stroking it with his lean bronze fingers.

"Has she said anything yet?" he asked the nun.

"No, she's still unconscious, poor thing. I hope she can tell us who did this to her."

"Me too."

The nun felt a shiver at the cold, flat tone of his words. She looked over at Marcus, and saw that he had felt it too. His eyes were wide as he looked at Jamie, who continued to stroke his sister's hair.

"Why don't you go on and eat," the nun suggested. "I'll let you know when she wakes up."

"No, I want to stay here." Jamie never looked up, just held the braid in his hand, rubbing the ends with his fingers.

"Marcus, you take Mary and go to dinner," the nun instructed the younger boy. He picked Mary up off the bed and left, giving both Jenny and Jamie a worried look on his way out. Sister Mary

Frances busied herself around the room, keeping an eye out for any stirring from Jenny. She saw her chest rise and fall steadily, but there was no other sign of life. "It could be a while before she wakes up," she informed Jamie.

"I know. I'll wait."

The nun saw that there was no reasoning with him at this point, so she just prayed that he would soon give in to exhaustion.

Jamie stayed by Jenny's bed throughout the night, finally moving to the chair and taking up a book. He fell asleep sometime after midnight, and Sister Mary Frances covered him with a blanket. She lay down on the other bed, hoping that if Jenny stirred, she would hear her before Jamie did. Sometime in the wee hours of the morning she heard a faint sound and looked over to see Jenny moving restlessly about in bed. She touched the girl gently on the shoulder and waited patiently as the deep blue eyes focused in the soft light of the lamp.

"What happened?" Jenny asked as she put a bandaged hand up to her throbbing temple. She examined the hand, then raised the other one, looking at the splint as if trying to figure out where it had come from.

"Don't you remember?" the nun asked quietly.

Jenny closed her eyes as if to help summon the incident from behind the wall of pain inside her head. "I was hit from behind," she finally said, her voice croaking on the words. Jamie began to stir in the chair.

"Jenny, I want you to think very carefully. Do you know who did this?" The nun touched Jenny's cheek, causing Jenny to look into her eyes. Jenny then looked beyond her at Jamie, who was now wide awake, sitting on the edge of the chair, his eyes shining silver in the dim light of the room. Something about the look in his eyes made Jenny hesitate as the attack began to play over in her mind.

"No," she said, the pain in her head making her nauseous. "I didn't see them."

"Them?" Jamie asked.

Jenny waved her bandaged hand in the air. "Them, they, he, she, whoever, struck me from behind while I was cleaning up the dishes." She turned her face towards the wall. "My head is killing me."

"Jen, are you sure?" Jamie was standing next to the bed.

"Yes, I'm sure. Now go away, it hurts to talk." She didn't turn to look at him. He stood there a minute, shoving his hair back as he waited for her to remember something, but she didn't speak, just closed her eyes as if his very presence pained her. He left with a promise to return first thing in the morning.

Sister Mary Frances sat down in the chair and waited for Jenny to say what was on her mind.

"You know who did this to me, don't you?" Jenny was still facing the wall.

"Do you?"

"Yes."

"Why did you lie to your brother?"

"Because he would kill him, and then they would hang him."

"What makes you say that?"

"Because it would be my word against his, and no one would believe me."

"I believe you, Jenny."

Jenny rolled over to look at the nun. "Sister, what am I going to do?" The nun sat on the bed and gathered the girl in her arms.

"I'm going to write a letter to the archbishop in Boston and ask for an investigation. Something is not right about Father Clarence. I know he was sent here as some sort of punishment, but I really don't know what happened. Until we find out, I'll keep you in here with me. I'll tell everyone your injuries are so bad that you can't be with the others."

"Why are you helping me?"

The nun smiled at Jenny and went back to the chair. She arranged her habit around herself and gathered her rosary beads into her hand. She counted down the beads, then placed them in her lap as if they were a string of precious pearls. "I had a brother at one time. He was the most beautiful boy, just a few years older than I. I adored him. When I was eighteen, I was being courted by one of his acquaintances, but my brother didn't like it, I finally figured out why when this boy took advantage of me. My brother found out and challenged him."

"What happened?"

"My brother was killed."

Jenny closed her eyes and let the impact of the words roll over her. She could only begin to imagine the devastating effect such a thing would have.

"It didn't solve anything. Not only was my reputation ruined, but I was also responsible for my brother's death. That was when I decided to devote my life to the church. I thought perhaps I could find some meaning in his death."

"Have you?"

"No. There's not a day that goes by when I don't think about it and pray for his soul. But now I hope that I can keep the same thing from happening to you and Jamie. I know you're right about what his response would be if he knew who attacked you."

"What about Father Clarence? What do you think he's going to do?"

"As far as I know, he's been locked in his office all evening. Let's just wait and see what he does tomorrow. No one knows what's happened except for a handful of people, and I'd like to keep it that way." Jenny nodded her head in ascent. "I'll give you something for the pain in your head. Then you try to get some sleep." Jenny knew that wouldn't be difficult. She felt as if she could sleep forever.

The next day dawned without a mention of Jenny's attack. Father Clarence acted as if he didn't know she existed. He accepted without argument Sister Mary Frances's plea that Jenny be released from school and chores because of an accident. In fact, he seemed relieved that the girl would be out of his sight for a time.

Jamie was livid when he found out that there was to be no investigation, but he silenced his ravings after Jenny came close to hysterics in the infirmary. He left the room with his mouth drawn in a tight line, the scar on his face a brilliant white against the angry flush of his sun-bronzed skin. He returned that afternoon with a new book, settled in the chair and began to read aloud from *The Arabian Nights*. Jenny closed her eyes and let the words carry her to a faraway place that had never existed for her before, not even in her imagination. Sister Mary Frances seemed caught up in the story also, and when the light of day faded, she went to place the lamp on the table next to the bed so Jamie could see to continue reading. Jenny caught Jamie shifting his chair away from the lamp as if the flame annoyed him. The days were by this time getting much shorter and lamps were now required for people to function in the dark confines of the mission. So far Jamie had been able to avoid being around them.

"My voice is getting tired. I think I'll stop for tonight," he finally said after struggling to see the pages in the dim light.

"That's fine. That way I can think about the story." Jenny had not missed the beads of sweat that had gathered at his temple and trickled down his face. He was terrified of the flame, and she couldn't say she blamed him.

Day after day passed in the same manner. Jenny remained within the infirmary, terrified to go out, and Jamie came and read to her in the evenings until he could no longer see the words in the coming darkness. Sister Mary Frances never offered to light the lamp until he had left to find his bed. They all had seen his fear, but left it to Jamie to work it out. Marcus and Mary came to visit also, but they never mentioned what had happened to Jenny. The nuns who lived and worked in the mission all went about their duties as if nothing had happened, but the older children saw the fear in their eyes, and noticed that they seemed to spend more time in prayer. Sister Mary Frances mailed her letter to Boston, voicing her concerns over Father Clarence and his unreasonable obsession with Jenny. There was nothing they could do now but wait.

Soon December was upon them. A few weeks before Christmas, Marcus and Mary were summoned to Father Clarence's office. It was a Sunday afternoon, and the little group had been gathered in the infirmary when Sister Abigail had come looking for Marcus and Mary with a special surprise. Jenny's hands had healed by this time, and she had gone back to her sewing. Sister Mary Frances had made good use of Jenny's talent with needle and thread, and Jenny filled her time with making shirts and dresses for the younger children.

Once Marcus and Mary had left, Jamie went back to reading the book and Jenny let the words carry her off to exotic places as she worked. After about an hour Marcus returned.

"My uncle has come for us!" he announced breathlessly as he entered the room. The twins dropped what they were doing as Sister Mary Frances said a prayer of thanksgiving.

"You're leaving?" Jenny asked.

"Yes, we're going to Denver with him and his wife. He's settled down, and said he felt bad about abandoning us, They brought us all kinds of gifts and stuff. He has a small ranch there and wants us to come be part of his family." His brown eyes were glowing with excitement as he went on about his uncle and his beautiful young wife.

"I am so happy for you, Marcus." Sister Mary Frances hugged him as Jamie and Jenny looked at each other in bewilderment.

"I came to say goodbye." He looked beyond the nun to his friends. "Mary is already in the wagon, she's so excited." The nun hugged him again and went out to say goodbye to Mary. Jamie shoved his hair back and extended his hand to Marcus, who returned his firm grip. "I'll write you when we get settled." Marcus looked at Jenny and shifted his feet uncomfortably. He seemed at a loss for words when suddenly Jamie's face split into his wide grin and he walked out of the room.

"I'm going to say goodbye to Mary. I'll see you outside," he tossed over his shoulder as he left. Jenny looked after her brother with a puzzled look. She was still reeling from Marcus's announcement and thought Jamie's leaving was a bit strange. The way Marcus was looking at her was strange, too, now that she had time to think about it.

"I'll never forget you, Jenny." Marcus was standing with his hands jammed in his pockets and was looking down at the floor.

"You've been a good friend to us. I won't forget you either."

"Would you mind . . . I mean, if I don't, I'll always wonder about . . ."

"What?" Jenny had to smile, he was acting so strangely.

Marcus took a deep breath. "I was wondering if I could kiss you."

Jenny suppressed the urge to giggle that suddenly came welling up from within. He was being so serious. "Yes, you may kiss me."

Marcus walked over to where she was standing. They were the same height, so that was not a problem, but he didn't seem to know what to do with his hands. Finally he placed them on her upper arms, and leaned forward. Their noses touched, and instinctively they both tilted their heads. Jenny shut her eyes and felt the cool touch of his lips gently brushing against hers, like a butterfly landing on her, its fragile wings moving slightly, like a whisper.

"Thank you," he said so softly that she almost didn't hear him. She opened her eyes and saw his brown eyes shining in his sweet face. She was suddenly overcome with the realization of how much she would miss him, and she threw her arms around his neck.

"Oh, Marcus, I'll miss you so much."

"I know, me too." He squeezed her to him. "I've got to go, they're waiting. Are you coming to see Mary?" He held out his hand.

Jenny took it and they went out to where the wagon was waiting. Mary was in Jamie's arms and raining sweet kisses on his cheek. He pretended to drop her, bringing squeals and giggles as he handed her up into the buckboard. Marcus hugged Sister Mary Frances again, then Jamie, then took a seat in the wagon. His uncle turned to say something to him, and their joy at being a family again was obvious to all who were around. The wagon pulled out to waves and promises to write and take care. Jenny had to wipe tears away as they faded out of sight so Jamie put his arm around her as they turned to go back inside.

Father Clarence was standing in the doorway, and he turned a look of pure hatred on Jenny as they made their way to the door. She felt the tightening of Jamie's arm against her shoulder as they approached the man, and she couldn't help the tremble that made its way through her body.

"It's such a wonderful blessing for those two children," Sister Mary Frances said to the priest as he watched the twins go by.

"Yes." He seemed distracted. "We should all rejoice and be glad for them."

"We will offer prayers of thanksgiving," the nun said as she watched the twins turn the corner that led back to the infirmary.

"Yes, prayers," the priest agreed. Sister Mary Frances followed her charges back, all the while hoping that her letter had made it safely to Boston.

They were quiet the rest of the afternoon, Jenny and Jamie giving in to the sadness of missing their friends. Jamie tried to read but his heart wasn't in it, so he went out to the barn, which had always been a balm for him. Jenny went back to her sewing, but she became restless and began to pace the confines of the room. She finally gave up and went to bed, leaving Sister Mary Frances to her private devotions.

Jenny tossed and turned, then let the events of the day replay in her head. She smiled to herself when she thought of how sweet Marcus had been and let her mind go over her first kiss. Suddenly she remembered a conversation she had had with her mother. "You'll know when you kiss him if you love him," her mother had said. Jenny went over the kiss in her mind and realized that although it was sweet, there hadn't been anything else to it. Her toes hadn't curled as her mother had said.

I guess you're not my true love, Marcus, Jenny thought. She went to sleep with visions of a dark-haired, dark-eyed prince from *The Arabian Nights* haunting her dreams.

Christmas was a somber affair for the Duncans that year. It was their first one without their parents, and with Jenny's seclusion they missed out on a lot of the festivities around the orphanage. Jenny presented Jamie with a new shirt she had made, and he gave her a fossil he had found that summer near the pond. Jenny added the polished stone to her mother's carved box, which led to the two of them going through the things it contained. They found the marriage certificate, along with the Bible. There was an envelope that contained a lock of golden hair and a soft red curl, both tied with a blue ribbon. There were also two tiny pearl-like baby teeth. They found their mother's silver wedding band, along with a feather and a few pressed flowers. They realized they would never know the story behind some of the things, but Jenny remembered how her father would sometimes surprise their mother with a bouquet of wildflowers and how her eyes would glow as she inhaled their sweet fragrance. Jamie opened the Bible and read the Christmas story aloud before the light of the day faded away. Sister Mary Frances presented them each with an orange and a small bag of sweets that had been delivered by a local Santa.

Before Jamie left for the night, Jenny gave him the box and asked him to hide it with the other things he had stashed away. He thought she was being silly at first and told her so, but the look of desperation in her deep blue eyes made him agree, and he took the box to the hiding place in the barn that contained his gun and his father's knife. He decided that night, as he made sure to cover his tracks, that as soon as the weather turned warm, they would be leaving. They would both be fifteen come the end of January, were both strong and willing to work. Anything that the world had to offer would be better than the fear Jenny lived with now.

Without Marcus to act as a buffer between him and the rest of the children, Jamie was lost. He hadn't realized how much he depended on the younger boy to shut out the rest of the world. As he went to class and sat in the dining hall, he felt the stares of the other children on him, and heard the gossip about him and his sister. Logan and Joe slowly gained more confidence around him because he was so unsettled. For the most part he ignored them, losing himself in his books and hiding in the barn with the animals whenever possible. Jenny saw how he was withdrawing from the world, but she was so unsettled herself that there was nothing she could do for him. Outside, winter had come with a vengeance, making the afternoons shorter that ever with the dreary, cloudy weather that had settled over the countryside. Sister Mary Frances anxiously waited for word from Boston, but with the weather being so bad, she was doubtful of hearing anything until spring.

Sometime soon after Jenny and Jamie's birthday, the sheriff showed up with a new resident for the orphanage. He had been found him lying in the snow beneath a small cliff where a flood had washed out a hillside. Above him on the rise was the body of a woman, riddled with arrows from an Indian attack. The sheriff didn't know what to make of it because the young man looked like an Indian but was dressed like a white man. He was unconscious and badly injured, so the man figured the best place for him was under the care of Sister Mary Frances until they could figure out who he was and what to do with him. Jamie was called to help carry the patient into the infirmary, and he was soon deposited on the bed where Sister Mary Frances could make an inventory of his injuries.

"Gosh, he's almost as big as me," Jamie commented as he helped Sister Mary Frances cut away the young man's clothing so they could get a better look at his injuries. He was indeed tall, with the same muscular build as Jamie, although he was a bit leaner. They found an arrow wound in his shoulder, the shaft still in the skin, and a leg that was broken so badly the bone protruded through the skin of his shin.

"I figure the impact of the arrow knocked him clean off his horse and into the gully," the sheriff volunteered.

"Any clue as to who he is?" Sister Mary Frances asked as she discreetly covered the young man's privates with a sheet. Jenny had been hovering in the outer office, waiting with the tray of instruments that the nun would need to treat the young man. She motioned for Jenny to enter when she was sure that the girl wouldn't see anything unseemly. Jamie grinned at her as she placed the tray on the bedside table.

"I think the woman was his mother, their hair was the same color. He might look Indian in the face, but his hair is not black like the rest of 'em," the sheriff pointed out.

Sister Mary Frances raised the lamp to get a better look at her patients face and hair color. His features, though lined with pain, were sharp, with a long straight nose, full mouth and high cheekbones. His skin had the same bronze hue that Jamie's had in the summer. His hair, which was matted with blood from hitting his head when he fell, was neatly cut. The color was a warm deep brown that glowed in the light of the lamp.

"Let me know when he comes 'round. I just didn't know what else to do with him," the sheriff said as he took his leave. The nun assured him that they would do what they could for the patient, and he left to consult with Father Clarence about the new arrival.

"Let's get that arrow out of him before we start on the leg," the nun said when she turned back to her patient. She held down the injured shoulder, instructed Jenny to take the other, while Jamie stood over him and pulled out the shaft, bringing the upper part of his body up as he extracted it. The patient fell back into the bed and moaned, then murmured a few words that no one could understand.

"It's not Lakota, I know that much," Jamie said.

"Save the arrow. It might help identify who attacked him," Jenny suggested. Jamie examined the feathers still attached to the end, then placed it on the table. Sister Mary Frances treated the wound after she had stopped the fresh flow of blood, then wrapped his shoulder tightly with a bandage. The patient occasionally spoke a few words, foreign to all of them, although Jenny swore she heard the word "mother" at one time.

"Now we need to set the leg," Sister Mary Frances announced after examining it from all angles. She instructed Jenny to get up on the bed and hold the patient down by his shoulders while Jamie pulled on his foot. The nun's task was to guide the bone back into place, all the time hoping that the fractured ends would come together without chipping. Jenny put all her weight against the patient's upper chest, but he still arched his back against the bed, grinding his teeth as he did so. His eyes flew open as the nun manipulated the bone, and Jenny found herself caught in the deep brown depths. She saw a spark deep within them for an instant, then they went blank as a wave of pain overcame him and he slid back into unconsciousness.

"How's he doing?" the nun asked.

"He woke up, but he's out again," Jenny answered.

"Poor thing. It's probably a blessing, the way this leg looks."

"Can you save it?" Jenny asked as she climbed down from her position.

Sister Mary Frances gave her a quizzical look as she measured the length of the patient's shin for a splint. "I hope so. It will take a lot of time, but it should heal."

"Good. I don't think he could go on if he lost it," Jenny said.

"Figured that out already, did ya?" Jamie grinned at her. Jenny realized that her eyes were roaming across the wide bare chest of the patient, and she suddenly flushed a bright crimson when she saw Jamie grinning at her from the other side of the bed. She decided to busy herself in the cabinet where the supply of bandages was kept and soon returned with enough to do the leg. Sister Mary Frances shared a smile with Jamie, then sent him out to find a way to suspend the leg from the ceiling. After what seemed like several hours, they were done, and Sister Mary Frances sent Jenny out so she could bathe the young man with the help of Jamie's strong arms to do the lifting and turning. They put one of Jamie's shirts on him and gently laid the still-unconscious patient back on the pillows.

"You can come in now. He's decent." Jamie grinned at his sister from the door, then ducked when she sent a missile of rolled bandages at his leering face. "Be nice to me or I won't read to you," he threatened.

"I can read to myself."

"Yeah, but I just got a new book, *Robinson Crusoe*, and I know you're going to love it." Jenny stuck her tongue out in annoyance at her brother, but asked him to come back when he was done with his chores. He tugged her braid as he left, and she turned to clean up the mess remaining from the earlier surgery. Sister Mary Frances went to give a report to Father Clarence, who was spending more and more time in his office. Occasionally, Jenny stuck her head through the door to see if the mysterious young man had awakened, but he lay as still as death.

Jamie came back later that afternoon and flashed a grin at Jenny when he asked about the patient. When she ignored him he sat down to read aloud. Jenny was trying to mend the young man's garments which had been cut from his body. Sister Mary Frances silently joined them. She had come to enjoy the quiet interludes the three shared, and marveled at how Jamie could make a story come alive with his voice. As the afternoon faded into evening Jenny looked up from her mending into the infirmary and thought she saw a flash of dark eyes, but when the nun went to check on her patient, she reported that he was still asleep. Jamie read until he could no longer see from the light that came through the window. Since Father Clarence had started spending all his time in his office, the three of them had been taking their meals in the infirmary, and they enjoyed supper together before Jamie went back to his dormitory.

As she climbed into her own bed, Jenny assured Sister Mary Frances that she would wake her if the young man came around in the night. She flipped through the pages of the book for a while, taking care not to read ahead. Once again, she felt a feeling of disquiet, but when she looked across the room to the other bed, all seemed still. She blew out the lamp and settled down under the blankets. Outside the wind began to pick up, reminding all inside that winter was still around, even though they had enjoyed a few days of mild weather. Jenny longed for springtime, her self-imposed imprisonment was beginning to wear her down. When she thought about it, she convinced herself that the reason she found the young man so interesting was because she was bored. She rolled over to face him, willing him to wake up, but all she heard was the sound of his steady breathing. She eventually fell asleep with the sound of his breathing in her ears, giving her a sense of comfort that she hadn't felt for a long time.

Sometime in the early morning hours she heard a curse that brought her quickly awake. She sat up and lit the lantern. The young man was sitting up, trying to figure out the brace that held his leg suspended from the rafter above. He scowled at her as she lit the lamp, shielding his eyes from the sudden brightness that filled the room. Jenny turned the lamp down and went over to his bedside.

"You can't move the leg; it's badly broken," she explained. The patient slumped back on the bed, throwing his arm over his eyes. Jenny investigated the contraption that Jamie had rigged to make sure it wouldn't come crashing down, causing further injury. "How do you feel? Do you need anything?" she asked.

There was no response, just a slight movement of the dark eyes that were shielded under his forearm. Jenny brought the lamp over to his bedside table and tried to peer up under the arm. The eyes followed her, but still he said nothing. His earlier struggles had knocked one of his pillows off, and Jenny bent to pick it up, tossing her hair over her shoulder so it cascaded down the front of her gown. She plumped the pillow and held it up hesitantly to the patient. He obliged her by leaning forward, and she placed it behind his back. He reclined on it, grimacing as the shoulder wound took the pressure of his weight. He looked over at the bandaged shoulder, then down at the strange shirt he was wearing.

"We took an arrow out of your shoulder, and set your leg. Your clothes are in there. We had to cut them off you." The dark eyes followed her, but he still didn't say a word. Jenny looked at him, tilting her head to the side.

She began to sign, "Do you need anything?" He looked at her hands in amazement, then up at her smiling blue eyes. "Would you like some water?" she continued signing. He nodded, and she went to pour him a glass from the pitcher. He drank thirstily, then held the glass out for more. He drained another glass and handed it back to Jenny, shaking his head when she held out the pitcher to see if he wanted more. "I guess I'll have to wake Jamie when you need to get rid of it," she said to herself.

"What is your name?" she signed. There was no response. "Your tribe?" He watched her hands, but if he understood, he gave no indication of it. He just watched her with his dark eyes. Jenny gave up and went back to her bed. She turned the lamp down low, so the light created soft glow around her bedside table. As she pulled the blankets up she saw that his eyes were turned on her. She lay facing him, but eventually her eyes grew heavy and she fell back asleep.

Jamie woke her the next morning by tickling her ear. "Wake up, sleepyhead," he said with a grin. She jumped up with a start, looking immediately at the other bed. Sister Mary Frances was checking on the rigging that held the patient's leg in the air. "He weighs a ton, I practically had to carry him to the chamber pot," Jamie said over his shoulder.

"Jamie!" Jenny smacked his shoulder, and he pretended that she had mortally wounded him.

"Can't get any words out of him so far."

"He understands sign," Jenny said, "At least he understood some of what I did last night." The patient's dark eyes met hers briefly.

"Why didn't you wake me?" the nun asked.

"I didn't think I needed to. I gave him some water and he went back to sleep."

"I'd love to know what his name is," the nun said as she rearranged the blankets around the patient.

"Do you speak Lakota?" Jamie asked in the language that Gray Horse had taught him. Once again the dark eyes showed surprise, but there was no response. Jamie picked the arrow up from the table where he had placed it the previous day. "Do you know who attacked you?" The eyes narrowed to slits, and he took the arrow from Jamie's hand, turning it over and over, examining the feathers attached to the end and the markings on the shaft. He gripped the arrow so tightly that his knuckles turned white, and finally the fine wood snapped in half, making the young man look down at the two pieces in wonder. Jamie reached out and took the arrow away, then casually sat down on the side of Jenny's bed. "Jen, why don't you go on and get dressed?" His wide blue eyes were serious, and Jenny immediately gathered her things and left. Sister Mary Frances said she would go find some breakfast for the group, and Jamie made himself comfortable after the nun left.

"The sheriff found you and your mother out on the plains. Your mother did not survive," Jamie began. The dark eyes closed as if in pain. "I know you can understand me, so you might as well talk to me."

"Where is my mother's body?" The words were precise and clear, the English perfect.

"I don't know. We'll have to ask the sheriff."

"I need to send her body to the spirit world so she can be with my father."

Jamie nodded his head as if in perfect agreement. "Your father was Indian?"

"Yes, Kiowa."

"Kiowa—then you're a long way from home."

"After his death, my mother wanted to return to her people. That's where we were going when we were attacked."

"Who attacked you?"

"Renegades, after our horses. We had no weapons, we left the tribe with nothing."

Jamie sat and digested this information while the young man lay back as if the conversation had drained him. "What is your name?" Jamie finally asked.

"My father called me Chase the Wind."

Jamie extended his hand. "My name is James Duncan, and my parents are gone, too. Everyone here has lost their parents." Chase the Wind looked at the outstretched hand and finally took it in his own, returning the firm handshake.

"I do not plan to stay here long," he said.

"Me either." Jamie grinned, causing the young man to grin in return. Jenny was standing in the doorway braiding her hair during this exchange and looked at her brother in amazement. "This is my sister, Jenny. I think you two have already met."

Jenny walked into the room and looked at the young man with a grin. "Did you enjoy making me go through all that signing last night?" she asked.

Chase the Wind gave her a sheepish look. "I thought it best to keep quiet until I knew where I was and what was going on. You would be surprised at what people will say when they don't think you can understand them."

"Did I say anything that surprised you?"

"No, but you did surprise me when you signed. Where did you learn that, and how do you know Lakota?"

"Our father had a friend who is Lakota," Jamie explained.

"I need to find out what happened to my mother."

Jamie and Jenny exchanged looks as Sister Mary Frances came in with a tray. She raised her eyebrows when she heard her patient speaking English.

"Chase the Wind would like to talk to the sheriff about his mother."

"But don't you know . . ."

Chase the Wind held up his hand to stop the nun from going further. "I know what happened to my mother; I saw the arrows bring her down. I just need to make sure she joins my father in the spirit world."

The nun looked aghast at what the young man had said. "I don't know about that." She looked in confusion at the twins, who seemed to be perfectly at home with this concept. "The sheriff said he would come back out sometime this morning to check on you."

"Please, it is very important." Chase the Wind looked around the room as if seeking an avenue of escape. Jamie saw that he was determined to take care of his mother's body, and he stepped up to his bed.

"Let's wait for the sheriff to find out what's going on. It's only been one day, and they're probably waiting to see if you have any family."

"There is none."

"But you said you were returning to be with your mother's people."

"Yes, people, not family." He became agitated as he sought to explain things to the group of strangers gathered around him. "After my father's death, we were not welcome with the tribe, so we were going to live among the white people, my mother's people."

"How come you were no longer welcome in the tribe?" Jenny asked, but Jamie held up his hand to stop her.

Chase the Wind looked at her with eyes full of pain. "It is not our way to speak of the dead. It keeps their spirits from finding peace." He turned away from the three standing near his bed.

Jenny walked away, a heavy feeling in her heart. Sister Mary Frances carried a plate to Chase the Wind, who took it with a murmured thanks and ate a little. Jamie attacked his own breakfast with his usual gusto, sitting cross-legged on Jenny's bed as he ate. Chase the Wind laid his plate aside when he was done and closed his eyes, as if to dismiss the group hovering around him. Jamie tugged his sister's braid as he went out to attend to his chores in the barn. He had stopped going to classes after Marcus left; he was just repeating what he already knew anyway.

Sister Mary Frances went to report to Father Clarence on her patient's condition. Jenny puttered about in the office, overcome with a restless feeling that she blamed on the changing weather conditions. It had started to sleet and a cold wind was coming in from the north, bringing the promise of snow before the day was over. She went back to the infirmary to make her bed, and noticed the steady rise and fall of Chase the Wind's chest. She wondered how he could sleep with his leg up in traction, but decided that his injuries, compiled with his loss, were enough to exhaust anyone. She picked up a piece of embroidery she had started and sat in front of the small stove that kept the room warm. She was working at the piece when Sister Mary Frances came back with the sheriff.

"It's getting fit to blow a big one," he said by way of a greeting. "I need to get back to town before the storm sets in."

Chase the Wind was wide awake when they entered the room and anxious to talk to the sheriff.

"What happened to you out there, boy?" the man asked.

"We were attacked by a small group, five of them. They were after our horses, and we had no weapons."

"What were you doing out there alone?"

"We were going east, to make a new home among my mother's people. Where is my mother now?"

"We buried her this morning—wanted to get her in the ground before it froze up again." Sister Mary Frances laid a hand on the sheriff's arm to still his callous words. "We'll put a name on a stone for her as soon as you tell us what it is." Jenny watched despair possess Chase the Wind as he realized he could not send his mother to the spirit world.

"Hannah. Her name was Hannah."

"Did she have a last name?" Jenny squeezed her eyes shut as she felt the sorrow that filled Chase the Wind, who looked at the sheriff with total disgust.

"I didn't know it if she did. She had no need of it with the Kiowa." The words were sharp, and the sheriff arched his eyebrows as if he had been insulted.

"Well, there's nothing else I can do here," he said to Sister Mary Frances. "I guess he's an orphan now, and this is an orphanage." The man left.

Chase the Wind closed his eyes, as if just looking around caused him pain. Sister Mary Frances laid a hand on his arm. "I'm sorry for your loss," she said, and there was no response. She left the room, and Jenny went back to her sewing, occasionally rising to check on the patient. He kept his face turned towards the wall, as if trying to shut out the world. Jenny felt for him, knowing that her frustration at being contained was nothing compared to his. He couldn't even rise from the bed without help from Jamie.

Jamie did not take long with his chores and returned in less than an hour. There wasn't much for him to do except make sure the animals were secure from the coming snow. He came stamping into the office, waving his arms like a windmill and shaking droplets of ice from his hair like a dog.

Chase the Wind opened his eyes as soon as Jamie stuck his head in the infirmary, and Jamie helped him up so he could relieve himself. The young man's face remained lined with pain, whether from his broken leg or grief they couldn't tell, but Jenny tried to be gentle as they replaced the rigging around the leg that kept it in traction. He settled back against the pillows when they were done. His eyes remained open this time, focusing on the window and the light pattering of sleet that was freezing on the pane and coming together to form large crystals. His dark eyes were filled with sadness as he watched the world ice over. He would be forced to remain where he was, in a strange bed, in a strange place, surrounded by strangers.

Jamie tugged Jenny's braid and led her into the office, where he picked up the book and flipped to the page where he had stopped the previous day. He pulled a chair close to the door of the infirmary and began to read. Jenny brought her chair over to face Jamie and see past him into the other room. She picked up her embroidery and went back to work, and when she felt that she had let enough time pass, she looked up to see glowing dark eyes watching her as Jamie read from the book.

The wind rattled the windows, the sleet turned to snow, and the drifts piled up against the walls of the mission. In the infirmary, however, three people were carried to a tropical island by the sound of a rich young voice that brought the words to life. Jenny and Jamie had been hardly aware that Sister Mary Frances had joined them, picking up her knitting and taking a chair by the small stove, which crackled and blazed against the creeping cold. The three blinked like owls when the bell rang, announcing the dinner hour, and the nun went out to bring back a tray for her growing family.

In his bed, Chase the Wind's eyes searched the room, as if he had just awakened from a dream. Jamie stood and stretched, reaching his fingertips to the ceiling, then bending at the waist to touch the floor. Jenny picked up the poker and jabbed at the embers in the stove, then threw another chunk of wood in. Jamie went in to see if Chase the Wind needed anything, but he declined and Jamie promised to attend to him again before he went to bed. Sister Mary Frances returned with their dinner, and she stayed with the patient to help him with his meal while the twins ate in the office. After they were finished, Jamie helped the nun settle the young man for the night, then went off to his own bed.

Sister Mary Frances left to take the dishes back to the kitchen. While she was gone, Jenny changed into her gown and stood in front of the stove, brushing out her hair while soaking up the heat before making a dash to her bed in the other room. She wondered if she should find another blanket for Chase the Wind and decided to mention it to Sister Mary Frances when she came back. She continued brushing out her hair, humming to herself all the while, until sparks flew from the ends when she pulled the brush through. She edged her backside as close to the heat as she dared, then made a run for her bed.

Jenny pulled up short when she realized that Chase the Wind was standing at the end of his bed, his splinted leg held out stiffly beside him. Somehow he had released his leg from the rigging. He appeared to be dizzy; his hands were clutching the bed frame so tightly that his knuckles were white, and his eyes were squeezed tightly shut.

"What are you doing?" Jenny asked.

"I have to go to my mother. I need to send her to the spirit world."

Jenny stepped closer, trying to determine if he was truly awake or perhaps caught up in a continuing nightmare from his attack.

"Your mother is already with your father," she said as she took another step closer to him. She caught a flash of silver in his eyes as he looked at her, a spark of some kindred understanding. "She was with him as soon as her spirit left her body," she said.

"How can you know this?"

Jenny stepped closer until she was standing right in front of him, and had to tilt her head up to see his face. She realized that he was the only person besides Jamie who was taller than she. "I know this because my father saw my mother's spirit waiting for him when he was dying. He told me that she was waiting for him to join her, and his spirit left his body so he could be with her."

"He told you this when he was dying?"

Jenny nodded, biting her lip to keep from crying at the memory of that awful day. She looked up into the dark eyes, which were suddenly filled with relief and gratitude, and saw the tense lines around the eyes fade. Suddenly he lost his balance, and tightened his grip on the bed frame. Jenny threw her arms around his waist, supporting him until he was able to back around and sit on the bed. She felt him trembling as he lowered himself, trying to keep the splinted leg from taking any of his weight. She waited until his body relaxed before she took her arms away. His own arm had become tangled in her hip-length hair, and as he tried to disentangle it, the ends flew up in all directions, still full of static from the brushing she had given it. Jenny finally just pulled it away with her hands, but some of it floated towards his arm, as if it didn't want to be separated from him. Jenny quickly smoothed it down, then tied a knot in the whole mass and flipped it over her shoulder.

"Are you all right?" she asked him when she finally felt that she had everything under control. He nodded. He seemed so weary he couldn't even speak. "Lie back and I'll fix your leg again," she instructed. He did as he was told, and Jenny gently placed his leg in the brace and pulled it back up into traction. He watched her with his dark eyes, followed her with them as she went to her own bed. She bundled up into a ball once she was under the blankets, tucking her feet up into the tail of her gown. "Are you cold?" she asked.

"I'm used to it."

"Good night"

"Jenny?"

"Yes?"

"Thank you."

Sister Mary Frances returned to find both of them asleep. She placed extra blankets on both beds before she retired to her own small chamber. Outside, the wind continued to beat against the windows, and the snow piled up, drifting where the wind blew it until there was barely a dusting in some areas and the drifts were waist-high in others. Those travelers that had taken advantage of the few warm days just past regretted their foolishness as they looked for shelter from the elements. Those lucky enough to be inside snuggled deeper under their blankets and came closer to their fires, grateful for the comfort of those simple blessings.

Jenny was dreaming. She knew she had to be because she saw her mother and father. The weather was warm, the sky blue, and she was in the middle of a beautiful pond, swimming without a stitch of clothing on. On the bank she could see Jamie, Sister Mary Frances, Marcus, Mary and Chase the Wind, all enjoying what seemed to be a picnic. They were all smiling, and occasionally one of them would wave to her. Above them in the branches of a tree sat her parents. They were happy, wrapped in each other's arms and looking down on the group below. They looked over at Jenny and waved to her, and Jenny waved back. She felt her arm move against the weight of the water, but she couldn't lift it up where they could see it. Her father began to motion for her to come to shore, and Jamie stood up and waved for her to come in. She started to swim towards them, but something held her back. She felt as if her hair was snagged on something. She turned and saw Logan and Joe both holding on to long tendrils of her hair, and they were laughing at her. She pulled her hair away from their grasp and turned to go in to shore, but before she could move, her head was shoved under. She fought her way to the surface, and tried to draw a breath, but before she could, she was pushed under again. She reached her hands up and felt a hand on her head, holding her down as she struggled in the water. Her hair was floating all around her and she fought against it, pulling it out of her eyes as she tried to surface. Above her she could see where the water ended and the air began, but it was just out of her reach. Her fingertips just broke the surface, sending ripples in all directions. She could still see everyone on the shore, standing now, looking down at her, telling her to come in, to quit fooling around, they were waiting for her. She tried to scream for help, but all that came out of her mouth was a trail of bubbles that skipped to the surface and exploded, each one carrying the sound of the different voices on the shore. The hand holding her would not let go, and she felt her lungs burn, desperate for air. She knew she had just seconds left, and she fought with all her might against the pressure on top of her head.

Jenny woke with a start, drawing air in with a hoarse gasp as she sat up in bed. Father Clarence was standing before her, peering at her over his half glasses as he leaned heavily on a stout stick that had been polished to a high sheen.

"You seem to have recovered from your injuries," he said. He raised the stick and began to poke at the mattress where her feet had been. "It will do you no good to hide from me. I can feel your evil all around this place."

Jenny retreated against the headboard of the bed and searched the area for a weapon. She remembered well the damage the broomstick had done; there was no doubt in her mind that the stout stick he now carried was more dangerous. Behind the priest, Chase the Wind was sitting up, his hands braced around the upper thigh of his broken leg to swing it out of traction if need be. His eyes narrowed at the back of Father Clarence's head as the priest continued to poke at the mattress, coming closer and closer to

Jenny's retreating feet. There was a pitcher of water on the bedside table, and Chase the Wind reached out and sent it flying to the floor with a crash, drawing the attention of Father Clarence.

"I knew I never should have allowed that heathen in here. They don't know how to act in civilization," the priest said to Jenny.

Sister Mary Frances came rushing in, pulling a robe around her gown, her short hair spiked out in all directions.

"Sister!" he exclaimed. "You are not properly dressed."

The nun smoothed her hand over her hair as she quickly took in the situation. "It's the middle of the night, Father. I thought perhaps there was an emergency and my patient needed some assistance."

"Except for being incredibly clumsy, he seems to be all right," the priest said, waving his cane in the direction of Chase the Wind. The nun began to pick up pieces of the pitcher from the floor.

"Was there something you needed, Father, that brought you to the infirmary at this time of night?" she asked as she carefully placed the shards in what was left of the pitcher. She looked at Jenny as she talked, and Jenny silently made her way down to the foot of her bed, where she could leap through the door if need be.

"I came to check on our new resident. The sheriff left him in my care, and I realized I don't even know what his name is."

"His name is Chase the Wind. He is part Kiowa Indian," the nun replied. Finished with the pitcher, she rose, taking a position between the two beds. Father Clarence stuck his cane out in the direction of Chase the Wind's bed.

"I know he is a heathen, that much is obvious." Chase the Wind jerked his head, his eyes narrowing again. "We shall have to save his soul and baptize him with a Christian name. I will not have any heathens in residence here."

"I plan to leave as soon as possible," Chase the Wind ground out between clenched teeth.

Father Clarence poked at the youth's bed with the cane. "How old are you, boy?"

"I have just passed my seventeenth winter," came the answer.

Father Clarence leaned on his cane and peered at him over his glasses. "It might be too late to undo the damage done by all the years he's spent among the savages. I will have to consult with my peers to learn the best way to help him. We may have to scourge the evil from him . . ." He left the room, still muttering to himself.

Sister Mary Frances crossed herself as he left. Jenny melted into a heap on the bed, pulling the covers around her as she began to tremble. The nun put her arms around her and smoothed her hair, which was in wild disarray from her nightmare. Jenny sat up and wrapped her arms around her knees, placing her forehead against them. Chase the Wind was slumped back against his pillows, his eyes shut, his full mouth a thin line as he clenched the blankets in hands that were curled into fists.

"Who was that man?" he finally asked when his rage was under control.

"Father Clarence—he runs the mission," Sister Mary Frances explained.

Chase the Wind looked over at Jenny, who was still sitting up in the bed, her hair falling around her shoulders and covering her knees. "He hates Jenny?" he asked.

Jenny raised her head and looked at him with wide blue eyes that held fear in their depths. "Yes," she said.

"We don't know that," Sister Mary Frances said, laying her hand on Jenny's arm.

"I know it. He hates me. I don't know why, but he does. I'm afraid he's going to kill me," She whispered.

"Jenny, you know I will never let that happen. I'm sure we will hear something from the bishop soon."

Jenny jumped from her bed and went over to the window, where the first glimmer of dawn was lighting the cluster of snowflakes that had gathered like lace on the pane. "How will we hear anything? No one can travel in this, and you know the storm is moving east. It might be months before you hear anything, and even then, they might think that you are the one who is crazy, not him."

She whirled back around, her hair swinging out about her. She gathered the mass in her hands and knotted it again, flipping it back over her shoulder as she began to pace the small confines of the room. Chase watched her, while she prowled about like a mountain cat, her movements graceful as she made her way around the chair, kicking a missed shard under the bed. "I have got to get out of here before something happens to me, or worse, to Jamie." She was talking to herself as she paced from bed to window, window to bed. "As soon as the weather breaks, we have to leave. He'll have to go with me."

Sister Mary Frances stopped the pacing by placing her hands on

Jenny's shoulders. "You can't go anyplace until spring gets here. You know that." She looked up into Jenny's eyes, forcing the girl to focus on her words. "We'll move Jamie in here until then. He can sleep in the office, and if something else happens, he'll be here to stop it. I think Father Clarence is afraid of him, or else Jamie wouldn't be getting away with cutting class and eating in here with us."

Jenny looked at the nun and then over at Chase the Wind. He smiled at her, an encouraging smile, showing perfect white teeth in his bronze face. There was a dimple there also, and it looked so out of place in his regal face that she smiled back.

"Okay," Jenny said to the nun. "Can we move him in today?"

"I'll take care of it," Sister Mary Frances assured her. "Why don't you try to get some more sleep?"

Jenny nodded as she suddenly realized that she was shivering, whether from the cold or the shock of the morning's events she could not tell. She climbed back into bed and pulled the blankets up under her chin. In the other room, she could hear Sister Mary Frances stirring up the fire in the office. Then all was quiet as she went to prepare for the day.

"What injuries?" Chase the Wind asked after they heard the door close behind the nun.

"I don't know what you mean." Jenny closed her eyes, hoping to discourage any more conversation.

"The priest said you have recovered from your injuries. I was wondering what they were."

Jenny held a palm out towards the other bed so Chase the Wind could see the scattering of small scars there.

"What happened?"

"I fell on some broken dishes."

"Is that all?"

Jenny sat up and looked over at the other bed. Chase the Wind had turned his upper body so that he was lying on his side, the leg turned slightly in the sling.

"Yes, that's all. I fell and cut my hands and knees on some broken china."

"It doesn't seem like that would be serious enough to confine you to the infirmary for so long." Chase the Wind was tracing patterns with his long bronze finger on the sheets in front of him, but he looked up as he talked to her. Jenny felt as if her very soul was laid open to him as he looked at her, his eyes like a hawk's that could see everything as it flew over the plains, searching for food.

"I broke my arm, too," she said.

"Oh, I see." He propped himself up on his elbow and pushed the blankets down around his waist; the heat from the stove was beginning to drift into the room. He grimaced as he put weight on the injured shoulder, but decided he could bear it for a while. "How did you fall? You don't seem like the clumsy type."

"Why are you suddenly so interested in what happened to me several weeks ago?" Jenny demanded. She began to rearrange her blankets with exaggerated motions, folding the sheet over the blankets and creasing it until it suited her.

"I was curious, that's all. I thought maybe . . ."

"Maybe what?"

"I want to know if Father Clarence had anything to do with your injuries."

Jenny looked at him in horror, then looked out into the office to make sure no one was around. "Please, don't mention that to anyone. Don't even suggest it."

"Why?"

"Because I'm afraid of what might happen."

"To Jamie?"

"Yes."

"But it's his duty to protect you and avenge you."

"I don't want him to avenge me. I just want to leave."

"So your brother does not know that the priest attacked you."

"No." Jenny felt she was going to cry, and struggled to keep the tears at bay.

"The nun knows."

"Yes. She's doing her best to protect me until we can leave."

"Why does Father Clarence hate you?"

"I don't know. I think he has me confused with someone else, someone he used to know. He talks crazy sometimes when he's around me. Sister Mary Frances wrote a letter hoping to find something out, but it's been months since she sent it."

"You won't hear anything until spring."

"I just hope I survive that long." Much to her amazement, Chase the Wind was smiling at her. "You think I'm kidding?"

"No, but you are being a little melodramatic."

Jenny flung a pillow at him, which he deflected with his arm. His eyes were dancing with laughter, and she realized that he was trying to lighten her mood. "Melodramatic—how did you learn a word like that, growing up in a Kiowa village?"

"You'd be surprised to know what I know. What makes you think you know more than me anyway?"

Jenny could not find an answer that would not sound condescending, so she just did what worked with Jamie. She stuck her tongue out at him. Chase the Wind fell back on his pillow and started to laugh. Jenny was surprised at how nice it sounded. It had been a long time since she had laughed from the heart. She grinned at him, flashing white teeth while he enjoyed his moment of having her at a loss for words. His laughter finally trailed off, and in the quiet they heard the sounds of the mission coming to life.

"Were your parents killed in a fire?" he asked after a few minutes.

"No. Oh, you mean because of Jamie?" She motioned down the side of her face, and he nodded. "No, they were murdered. We don't know who, or why. Jamie's burns came from a stray bullet that day; it hit a lantern, and the oil and flames went over him." She shuddered at the memory.

"I'm sorry."

"What happened to yours? I mean your father." Jenny looked at him with tenderness in her deep blue eyes. "I know you don't want to discuss him, because of your beliefs, but I was just wondering. You said you had to leave the village . . ."

"My father was killed by white soldiers who were coming to rescue white captives. They didn't know that some of them did not want to be rescued. The tribe blamed my mother because she was white. Many warriors were killed that day, so the tribe made us leave."

"But you're part Kiowa."

"They never saw that part. They only saw the white blood in me."

"Then your mother was killed by Indians."

"Yes, Pawnee."

"So you have reason to hate the whites and hate the Indians."

Chase the Wind looked at her as if she had made a great revelation. His eyes narrowed as his head filled with memories of torment from childhood, when the other children had made fun of him because he was different. Then came the banishment from the village immediately following the death of his father, the strangeness of the fort and the white soldiers who had been responsible for his father's death, and his mother wanting to get as far away from the memories as soon as possible, without regard for the weather or their safety. It had all happened so fast, he had hardly had time to deal with it all. He had not even given a thought to where he would go after he left the mission. Jenny had laid it all out before him with one simple statement. Now the question looming before him was where *did* he belong?

Jenny watched as a variety of emotions made their way across his regal face. She knew she had struck a nerve somewhere, but didn't know if that was good or bad. She knew his mind was elsewhere, lost in some memory, but she was also curious. She had assumed that his mother had been captured by the Kiowa, but he'd said she didn't want to leave. "Tell me about your mother and father. How did they meet?"

Chase the Wind blinked his eyes as if he were waking up.

"My mother lived with her mother and stepfather at a mine. They were isolated from the other workers, and she said her stepfather was always worried about claim jumpers. He would beat her mother, and my mother would run and hide when he did. She was afraid of what he would do to her. He was an evil man, and he drank a lot, which made it worse. My father would see her hiding in the woods when he was out hunting, and he became curious about her, so he started to watch her. He spent days just watching her family work the mine; then the man would get drunk and start in on his wife. One day he just walked up to my mother when she was crying. She wasn't afraid. She said later that she figured an Indian couldn't be any worse than what she was living with every day, and it wouldn't have bothered her a bit if he had killed her. My father knew a little English, so they managed to communicate. One day she just got on his horse behind him, and he took her to his village. The tribe was not happy, because he was a great warrior and they wanted him to make a good marriage, but he said he loved my mother and that was the end of it. The tribe never accepted her, but my parents were so much in love that they didn't care. She taught me how to read and write English from her Bible and made sure that I spoke it well. I think her mother must have been a teacher before she married the miner. My mother barely remembered her real father. She said that life was hard after he died and they couldn't make ends meet, so that was why her mother remarried. She said the man changed after they came west. My father took her back to the mine one time, but all they found was a deserted cabin and a grave. They believed that he had finally killed her."

"So your mother and father were very much in love?"

"Yes. When the soldiers came, my mother fought them, but one of them hit her, knocking her unconscious, then threw her on the back of a horse. My father went after them in a rage. He shot the soldier so my mother could escape, but then he was killed."

"Where were you?"

"I was out of the village, chasing wild horses. When I came back, the entire village was in mourning, and they told us we had to leave, that we had brought the white soldiers down on them."

"Were there any other whites in the village?"

"There were some; they all went back."

"But they still blamed you?"

"Yes."

"I'm sorry. This must all be so strange for you."

They sat in silence for a while, both thinking about what had happened to the young half-breed.

"What about you—how long has it been?" Chase the Wind asked.

"A year this spring. One minute we were a family, and the next we were orphans."

"Then your family was happy. You were happy?"

"Yes, but I didn't realize it until it was gone. I mean, I never knew anything else; we never needed anyone else; we were complete." Jenny placed her chin on her knees, which were tucked up under her. "I wonder if I'll ever know happiness like that again, the innocence that we lost."

"You've lost the innocence forever, but you can find the happiness. At least I hope you can. I don't know really, because I never had that kind of happiness. I was never accepted into the tribe, so I knew bad as well as good when I was with my mother and father." Chase the Wind captured her again with those dark eyes that showed the pain of his isolation. "At least you're not alone."

"I'm grateful for that. I don't know what I would do if I didn't have Jamie."

"I'm glad to know I'm so appreciated," Jamie said as he came strolling into the room, grinning widely. "Have you been waiting for me?" he asked Chase the Wind while winking at his sister.

"Forever," Chase the Wind answered as he shifted uncomfortably in bed. Jamie helped him up, and they disappeared behind the screen. Jenny discreetly slipped out of her bed as they went.

"You know, Chase, we've got to find an easier way to do this," Jamie said as he helped him back to the bed. "I don't plan on being your crutch for the rest of my life."

"Chase?"

"Yeah, Chase. It's easier than Chase the Wind, you know. Just like I'm James Duncan, but my friends call me Jamie.

"Friends."

"Well, I should hope so. We've been up close and personal, if you know what I mean, and I'd hate to think I'm doing all this for someone who isn't my friend." Jamie grinned as he arranged the leg back in the sling, then moved it into the raised position. "I'm pretty handy to have around, too," he said as he admired the contraption. Chase couldn't help laughing, and when Jamie extended his hand to him, he took it. In that firm exchange they took full measure of each other and found a kinship.

"Jamie," Chase began, once the formalities were out of the way. "The priest was here this morning."

"What happened?" Jamie's face went from its usual open friendliness to wariness.

"Nothing, but he scared your sister. The nun wants you to move in here with Jenny for her protection."

Jamie began to pace, much as Jenny had earlier, but where she had moved gracefully around the room, Jamie prowled like a tiger in a cage.

"What did Jenny tell you?"

"She's afraid for herself and for you."

"For me? Why should she be afraid for me?" Jamie stopped his prowling and stood in the middle of the floor.

"She's afraid you might seek revenge and get hurt in the process."

"Revenge for what?" A sudden realization came over Jamie's face as the events of the past month came together. "Damn!"

The instant he spoke, a mug went sailing past his head and crashed into the wall above Chase's head, making him jump, then look over his shoulder at the milk running down the wall. Jenny was standing in the doorway, hands on her hips, her eyes narrowed into slits.

"I trusted you," she snarled from between clenched teeth. "You had no right."

"Your brother needs to know what's happening."

"It's none of your business!" Jenny was shouting now.

"Yes, it is. You should have told me," Jamie said.

"Why? So you could go out and get killed, or worse?" Jenny came stomping into the room, and Jamie met her halfway.

"It's my job to take care of you." He stuck his nose inches from hers, leaning over her.

"And it's mine to take care of you."

"No, it's not. I'm the man of the family now, you are my responsibility and if something is going on, I should know about it."

"Not if I don't want you to."

Chase watched as they stood toe to toe, nose to nose.

"Jenny, he could have killed you." Jamie shoved his hair back, his frustration growing at his sister's unreasonable stand.

"Yes, and if you go after him, who would stop him from killing you?"

"He's not going to kill me. He can't hurt me."

"No, but he could have you arrested, and then who's going to stand up for you and take your side?"

"I think you're being ridiculous."

"Ridiculous! I'm not the one who goes off half-cocked all the time."

"Yes, you are."

"What?"

"You're the one who goes off half-cocked. I'm the sensible one." Jamie gave her a smirk that sent her temper flaring. Jenny whirled around, searching for a weapon of some sort to use against his hard head. Chase was sitting up, watching the proceedings with rapt attention. "See, you're looking for something to throw, aren't you? Admit it, you don't think things through. I, at least, listen to reason." Jenny opened her mouth to answer his latest challenge, then snapped it shut. She turned, her skirt flaring out, and left the room, slamming the door as she stormed out.

"I guess that shut her up," Jamie said to Chase as the sound of the door slamming echoed in the tiny room.

"You'd better go after her before she gets into trouble—or, worse, runs into Father Clarence."

"You just hope I can get her calmed down before she starts in on *you*." Jamie grinned at him.

Chase looked down at the shattered pieces of mug. "I guess it's a good thing I can't walk. It looks pretty dangerous out there."

Chapter Sixteen

Jamie didn't have any trouble following Jenny; she had left clear tracks through the snow. The air was frigid, the sky still overcast. He hoped she hadn't gone far. She wasn't wearing a coat, and he pulled his ragged one closer about him as the full force of the wind hit him. The wind was so strong he had to hold his hat down on his head. "Now is not the time for you to be so stubborn," he mumbled as he made his way through the snow, his long legs breaking through the crusty top layer.

He caught up with her in the orchard. She was leaning against a tree, her arms wrapped around it as if she were afraid the wind would take her away. Jamie took his coat off and draped it around her shoulders.

"I guess you're pretty mad at me," he said. She wouldn't answer him. "Jenny, come on, its freezing out here." He cocked his head so she would have to look at him, but she turned the opposite way. "Jen," he begged. "Come on, you have to go back and yell at Chase. You can't do that if you're frozen to a tree." Jamie grinned when he saw her shoulders shake; he knew she was trying not to laugh. Jamie began to jump up and down, waving his arms against the chill. "Come on, I'm freezing."

She turned and looked at him. "Serves you right."

"Can we please finish this inside?"

Jenny reluctantly let go of the tree, and Jamie turned to go back to the mission, jogging in place as he waited for his sister to fall in step with him. Jenny scooped up a handful of snow and dropped it down the back of his shirt, taking off like a shot after she did so. Jamie let out a whoop and set out after her. Jenny's shoes were old and worn, and she hadn't gone far when the slick soles gave out and she went sliding into a drift, landing face first, her skirt flying up over her backside. Jamie came upon her and doubled over in laughter as she came blinking and dripping out of the snow. He finally stopped laughing long enough to help her up, and the two of them slipped and slid all the way back to the mission. Jenny finally joined his laughter when his legs went in two separate directions, causing him to land in a split position in the snow.

When they got back to the infirmary, Sister Mary Frances was using a broom and dustpan to clean up the mess while Chase watched with a contrite look on his face. Jenny walked to his bed, her head humbly bowed as if she were going to apologize, and promptly deposited a snowball down the front of his shirt, bringing him up with a howl. He whipped the shirt off and picked up the snowball to return fire. Jenny hastily placed herself behind the shelter of Sister Mary Frances, daring him to throw. Chase held the weapon in his hand while mopping his chest with his shirt, trying to decide if he should or shouldn't. The nun silently held out her hand to take the snowball away. He placed it there and she carried it off, her hand still outstretched as if the snow were contaminated.

Chase narrowed his dark eyes at Jenny, and she danced away in case he had something else ready to throw. He held his wet shirt out to her and pulled the blankets up over the wide expanse of his bare chest as she took the garment away to dry near the stove. Jamie had removed his own shirt and held it out to Jenny as she went by, looking like a cat who had just been at the cream. After she had draped the shirts, she stood with her backside to the stove, pulling her skirt up to help dry her pantalets. She moved over to make room for Jamie, who was briskly rubbing his arms, but he declined with a shake of his head and she did not push him. He managed to avoid anything that produced a flame of any kind, not minding the cold as long as he didn't have to confront his fear. He went into the infirmary and came back with a blanket wrapped around his shoulders, then sat down to breakfast with his usual hearty appetite.

That afternoon after they had moved a cot into the office for Jamie, the snow started again. Jamie brought Chase out into the office and they put him in a chair next to the stove, propping his leg up on another chair. Jenny and Sister Mary Frances took seats close to the stove, and Jamie read to them as the snow blew and drifted outside, building up against the walls of the mission, sealing in the warmth. When it got too dark for Jamie to see the words, he began to fashion a crutch for Chase to use, and Jenny wrapped the top with padding and a soft cloth. They helped him try it out, and he was soon able to move around, although with difficulty. The effort soon wore him out and he gratefully sought his bed, his entire leg throbbing.

Jenny soon climbed into her own bed and settled back with a sigh after turning down the lamp.

"I'm sorry I made you so mad today," Chase said in the darkness.

"It's okay. I actually feel relieved now that Jamie knows everything."

"I'm glad."

"Yeah, me too." Jenny said with a yawn. "Good night."

That night Jenny dreamed of a dark-eyed man with long, dark, flowing hair. She was older, a woman full grown, and she was running from the man, all the time hoping he would catch her. She saw everything as if she were on a soft cloud floating above the scene. She saw herself running across the plains, looking back to see how close he was, and she saw the man running, his dark eyes intense, his long hair flowing behind him as he effortlessly covered the terrain. Jenny was laughing, running for pure joy, exhilarated at her freedom. She knew the man with the dark eyes could catch her whenever he wanted, but he was enjoying the chase, pacing himself to stay right behind her. She felt the air pumping through her lungs, felt the motion of her legs and arms, felt the man's breath on the back of her neck as she slowed. She watched from above as he reached out his arm, wrapping it around her waist, pulling her off her feet and swinging her around to face him. She looked up into dark brown eyes obscured by the long hair that swirled around his face. She watched as he lowered his face to hers, reaching a hand up to pull the wind-blown locks away, and then he mumbled.

Jenny's eyes flew open with a start as she heard the muffled sounds coming from the other room. Jamie was talking in his sleep, something he had done his entire life. Jenny had quickly stopped noticing it when they were young, but it had been nearly a year since she had slept near him and the sounds had penetrated her dream. She closed her eyes to recapture the dream, but it had faded, blown away like the cloud she had been floating on. Across the room she heard the steady sound of Chase's breathing, and once again it lulled her to sleep.

The next morning they woke to sunshine so bright that the reflection off the snow was blinding. Everything was covered with crystals of ice that gave the appearance of a fairyland to the drab brown of the mission and outbuildings. The small group housed in the infirmary were in high spirits as they started their day. Jenny was relieved that her secret was out in the open so they could start making plans for the future. Jamie now knew who the enemy was, and he was ready to leave; the only thing holding them up was the weather. Chase was happy to be mobile again; the necessity of relying on others for the simplest need had chafed at his proud spirit. He made his way from one room to the other on his crutch, occasionally giving them a scare as he teetered precariously. Somehow, he always recovered his balance and went on his way, smiling and shaking his head as he did so.

As they days passed, the snow began to melt and they began to look anxiously for signs of spring, hoping that it was here to stay as the days of March began. Jamie did not want to risk setting out with the chance of another storm coming in, especially since they did not have any supplies and would have to live off the land until an opportunity for employment presented itself. Sister Mary Frances began to check the mail, and soon began making trips into town when the weather was nice. After she took off in the wagon, Jamie and Jenny would help Chase go outside to the orchard and spend the afternoon soaking up the weak rays of the sun. Chase seemed to be more at home under the trees than he ever was in the confines of the infirmary, and every day he would test his strength, placing a small bit of pressure on his broken leg until he could set it on the ground without any pain.

After one of her excursions to St. Jo, Sister Mary Frances came into the office with a glow on her lovely face.

"You got the letter?" Jenny asked as the nun removed her cloak.

"No, better," she said as she took Jenny's hands and led her to the table. Jamie came up behind Jenny and placed his hands on the back of her straight-backed chair, waiting for the news. The nun looked up at Jamie and smiled. "I've found a place for the two of you."

"You have?"

"What? Where?"

Sister Mary Frances held up her hand to silence the barrage of questions as Chase thumped into the office with the aid of his crutch. "There's an older couple on the other side of town—their last daughter has married and gone west. They had a bad winter and need someone to help with the farm and help around the house. I'm going to take you—" she looked at Jamie—"to meet them tomorrow. They didn't quite believe me when I told them how big you are. Jenny, you'll stay here in case Chase needs any help. If they agree, you can both move in on Sunday afternoon."

Jamie and Jenny exchanged happy grins at the news. It seemed to be an answer to a prayer for both of them. "What about Chase?" Jamie asked.

"I'm leaving as soon as my leg heals up. Don't worry about me, I'll be fine," Chase said from the door jamb he was leaning on.

"Where will you go?" Jenny asked.

Chase waved in the general direction of the west. "Out there somewhere. I'll know it when I get there."

"Maybe you could come with us," Jenny suggested.

Sister Mary Frances opened her mouth to speak, then thought better of it. Chase looked around the room at the three people who had cared for him during the past few weeks and knew that the mission had sheltered them from the real world. Sister Mary Frances was looking down at the table, her hands folded gracefully. Jenny and Jamie were looking at Chase expectantly, waiting for him to complete their happiness by agreeing.

"No, I don't think a farm is the place for me. I'll go west again." He knew in his heart that the couple who were being so generous to Jamie and Jenny would never accept a half-breed; there weren't many people who would. He was grateful for the three in the room who had taken him in and nursed him, but he knew there weren't many more like them in the world. He would make his way west, maybe even go back to his tribe and claim his birthright, as soon as he was able. He smiled reassuringly at the group, but the expression didn't quite reach his eyes, and he knew that Jamie and Jenny saw the doubt.

Sister Mary Frances continued telling her plans. She wanted to get Jamie some new boots before they went to the farm, his own being worn to nothing. He needed a coat also; since he was the biggest one at the mission, there were no hand-me-downs to choose from. The nun assured him that she had her own money that she kept for her own good works, and getting the two of them started was the best thing she could do at the present. She promised Jenny a shopping trip on Saturday to replenish her wardrobe also. Father Clarence was to know nothing of the plans beyond the fact that Jamie was going shopping with her. The nun hoped she could get the two of them off without the priest knowing until the deed was done.

Jamie assured everyone that he would charm the elderly couple into turning over the operation of the farm to the two of them, and the couple could sit out the days on their porch while Jenny and he turned the farm into the best place in Iowa territory.

Chase was silent during this exchange and took to his bed, only giving Jenny a quick good night when she turned down the lamp.

The next morning Jamie and Sister Mary Frances left right after breakfast. She had explained Jamie's need for new boots, and the priest had sent them off with his blessing, making the nun feel comfortable about leaving Chase and Jenny in each other's care. Sister Abigail promised to bring a tray to them at lunchtime, and Jenny locked the door to the office as the two departed, happy to know that her imprisonment was soon to come to an end. She promised Chase a visit to the orchard after lunch if he was good, and he waggled his eyebrows at her as if planning some mischief. Jenny laughed and began to spin around the room just for the pure joy of it, her golden hair flying around her as she twirled, her deep blue eyes sparkling as they caught Chase's dark ones with each spin. She finally fell laughing into a chair, placing her fingertips against her temples to keep the room from cartwheeling away as Chase joined her laughter from his place on his bed.

Beyond the laughter they heard a pounding on the door, and Jenny went to open it, thinking Sister Abigail had brought their lunch tray early so she could go about her duties. She gasped when she pulled the door open to find Father Clarence and a strange man standing in the hall. The man smiled when he saw her, taking in her flushed cheeks and disheveled hair; then his eyes narrowed as he surveyed her tall, slim figure. She stood with her mouth half open, feeling as if she had just been put on the auction block. Father Clarence stepped in, pushing her away from the door, and the strange man followed, closing the door behind him.

"I have some good new for you, my dear," Father Clarence began. "You've been adopted."

"Adopted?" Jenny backed up to the table, her hands behind her back searching the surface for a weapon.

"Yes. Mr. Miller and his wife have adopted you. They're going to take you to California to live."

"I can't leave," Jenny said, sidling away from the table.

"Oh, but you don't understand. The Millers have made you a very generous offer. You see, Mrs. Miller is with child, so the trip will be difficult for her. In exchange for your help with the chores and the baby, they'll provide you with a home. It's really a wonderful opportunity for you." The priest was talking to her as he would to a wild animal he was trying to tame. Jenny looked beyond him at the worn, dusty clothes that Mr. Miller was wearing and wondered how the priest could use the terms *generous* and *opportunity*.

"Take someone else," Jenny said as she wrapped her fingers around the back of a chair. Chase had silently made his way to the doorway of the infirmary, his eyes narrowing at the two men as he saw the fear on Jenny's face.

"As you well know, there aren't any other girls here even close to your age. There are none that could handle the tasks the Millers would need you to do. You are the logical choice."

"I won't go. You can't make me."

Father Clarence took off his glasses and rubbed his eyes, his stout stick tucked under his arm as he massaged the bridge of his nose, as if talking to Jenny was tasking him beyond his limits. He carefully replaced the glasses and put the stick out in front of him, placing both hands squarely on it. "Now is not the time to be difficult. You'll give these nice people the wrong impression."

"Where is his wife?" Jenny asked. She was trying to buy time for Chase, who was making his way quietly up behind the priest, hobbling on his broken leg, his crutch held like a club before him.

214

"You told me she was feisty," Miller said. "I reckon she's worth every penny I paid ya."

Jenny looked in amazement at the weak eyes, the greasy, thinning hair, then saw the man lick his lips as he returned her look. Jenny shuddered, then saw Chase balancing himself on his good leg, his eyes lethal as he nodded at Jenny, encouraging her to fight.

"We're going to have to force her. She won't go any other way," the priest said with a sigh.

Jenny shoved the chair at them, then ran around the table, placing her hands on it to give it a shove. Miller and the priest split up, one coming around each side of the table.

"Watch out!" Miller yelled.

Father Clarence turned in time to see Chase raise the crutch over his head. He swung his stick like a club and caught Chase's splint, sending him down with a cry of anguish as he clutched his leg.

"Chase!" Jenny screamed as Miller grabbed her around the waist from behind. Jenny began fighting, scratching at his arms, kicking out as she bucked against the hold he had on her. The table went flying as she caught it with her feet, knocking Father Clarence in the stomach. He doubled over as she continued to fight. Then the priest straightened up and hit Jenny in the jaw with his fist. Stars exploded in her head as a red haze filled her eyes, and she slumped over. The only thing that kept her from hitting the ground was Miller's arms wrapped securely around her waist.

"I told you not to mark her," she heard Miller protest through the ringing in her ears.

"She'll have plenty of time to heal before you reach California," the priest hissed.

Miller leaned Jenny's limp body back against one arm, turning her face with his hand, checking the bruise already rising on her delicate cheek before running his hand down over her breast. "Yep, worth every penny." He nodded at the priest, who looked at him with bored contempt.

Chase managed to climb up on his hands and knees, his stomach rebelling at the pressure the floor was putting against his leg. Miller threw Jenny over his shoulder, her hair trailing down over her head and dragging on the floor as he made his way out. Chase lunged for Miller's knees as he went by, grabbing only a handful of Jenny's hair for his effort. Father Clarence swung his club down on Chase's back, and his face hit the floor as the breath was knocked from his body. The priest locked the door on his way out, taking the key with him. Chase heard the delicate ping of metal hitting the floor outside the door as he tried with all his might to draw air back into his body.

"Jenny," he was finally able to gasp. "Jenny?" Chase crawled to the door, reaching up to try the knob. The chair Jenny had flung was close by, and he pulled himself up, waves of nausea washing over him as the room spun out of control. He closed his eyes, forcing his rebellious body to respond, to move forward to the window. He finally reached it, and caught sight of a covered wagon parked in front of the mission. Miller threw Jenny into the back of it, then turned to talk to the priest. The wagon began to bounce as if it housed a wildcat, and Jenny's head poked out the back only to be met by the back of Miller's hand, knocking her back inside. Then all was still.

Father Clarence looked around to see if anyone was watching, then stepped back as the wagon began to move away, even waving when it made the turn onto the road to St. Jo.

"Jenny . . ." Chase whispered as a single tear tracked down his cheek. He turned away from the window, his leg catching in the chair as he turned, causing him to lose his balance. He went down, hitting his head on the table; he was unconscious before he hit the floor.

Chapter Seventeen

Jamie was whistling as he drove the buckboard back to the mission. The team of horses bobbed their heads as they plodded along, keeping time in their own way to the tune of "Good King Wenceslas." Sister Mary Frances began to hum along, enjoying the warmth of the sunshine, the sound of the birds singing, the sight of the spring flowers bobbing in the breeze along the road as if they too were keeping time with the tune.

"Why are you whistling a carol in the springtime?" the nun asked.

"I don't know. It's one my father always whistled and I guess it just stuck with me," Jamie answered. The hat was pulled low over his face to keep the curiosity of the townspeople they passed at bay, but he sat tall and proud on the bench, his hands sure on the reins as they made the return trip from the farm they had just visited.

The elderly couple had been so amazed at his size that they didn't even question his scars as they interviewed Jamie about his skills. He admitted to being more at home with animals than plants, but he was willing to work, as was his sister, and under the gentleman's fine tutelage they would soon become experts, he was sure. The lady had beamed at him, then fixed him a plate of sugar cookies with a glass of milk. Jamie grinned at her with delight as he bit into one, his hair falling over his eyes as he devoured the feast placed before him. The woman had cooed over him, promising to fatten him up and even offering to give him a much-needed haircut. Jamie promised to get one before they returned on Sunday, and they left, anxious to return to the mission and share the news with Jenny. Jamie continually checked his new boots as they rode, making sure the fine black leather had not gotten scuffed on his tour of the farm. He had his pants legs tucked into the calf-high boots, showing off the expanse of them to any who cared to see, and Sister Mary Frances smiled to herself at his obvious joy and pride.

They arrived at the mission, and the nun waited while he took care of the team, not wanting to ruin the surprise for him when he told Jenny of their good fortune. She noticed that he had a cocky jaunt to his walk as they entered the mission. The boots were sure to make Logan and Joe envious, he knew. They found the office door locked, which did not surprise them, but repeated knocking brought no response.

"Do you suppose they could be in the orchard?" Sister Mary Frances asked.

"No, I checked when we rode by. Besides, it's suppertime." The bell was indeed tolling in the tower above, and the nun smiled at Jamie's tendency to put mealtime above all else. They heard footsteps and looked up to see Sister Abigail coming down the hall.

"Sister, I'm sorry I didn't know that Jenny and Chase had gone with you. Father Clarence was quite upset at the waste when I carried the lunch tray down," the young novice said.

"They didn't go with us," Jamie said as he pounded on the door. "Jenny, Chase, open up!" he shouted against the stout wood.

Sister Mary Frances placed her hand over her heart as the realization of what Sister Abigail had said sank in. They saw the knob rattle as if someone had grabbed it from the other side.

"Jenny!" Jamie shouted. "Open up!"

"I don't have the key," Chase's voice responded.

"Chase, where's Jenny?"

"The key is out there somewhere. I heard it hit the floor."

Jamie felt his heart fall when the weakly spoken words came through the door. He stepped back and began searching the floor, finally catching the gleam of brass next to the baseboard. His hand trembled as he tried to insert the key, and Sister Mary Frances finally placed her own delicate hand over his large one and guided the key into the lock. She helped him turn it, and they found Chase sitting next to the door, his back against the wall. Jamie immediately searched the infirmary, calling out for Jenny.

"She's gone," Chase gasped as Sister Mary Frances ran her hand down his leg. His eyes were huge in his pale face as he looked up at Jamie. "The priest sold her to a man named Miller. He's taking her to California."

"How long?" Jamie's voice was steely, his eyes dark with anger. His face had turned bright red, the scar a vivid white as rage settled over him.

"This morning . . . I don't know, I've been unconscious. I tried to stop them, but the priest hit me with his cane."

Sister Mary Frances went to place her hand on Jamie's arm, but he stepped past her as if she weren't even there.

"Jamie, wait," she called after him as he took off down the hall towards Father Clarence's office. She gathered up the skirt of her habit and ran after him.

"I've waited too long already," he spat over his shoulder as his long strides ate up the distance. He kicked open the door to the priest's office, causing it to bounce against the wall before it swung back. Jamie halted the backswing with an outstretched hand and stepped in.

Father Clarence calmly looked up from the cup of coffee he was sipping as Jamie stepped around the desk and pulled him to his feet, his hands about the priest's neck. The cup of coffee hit the floor with a crash.

"Where is she?" Jamie hissed between clenched teeth as his strong hands tightened around the white collar. The priests hands scrabbled uselessly against the iron muscles in the arms that held him. His face turned purple, his eyes bulging as he tried to draw a breath. Sister Mary Frances burst in, panic-stricken as she watched the priest fight the stranglehold that Jamie had on him.

"Jamie, no!" she cried, then watched as the sheriff, who had been drinking coffee with the priest, raised his gun and brought the handle down against the back of Jamie's head. Jamie jerked, his hands still tight around the priest's neck. The sheriff raised the gun again, striking harder, against the temple this time, and Jamie slid to the floor.

Jamie Duncan took a thorough inventory of all his parts as he lay on a hard cot in a jail cell in St. Jo. His head was pounding, and each beat of his heart seemed to echo through his body in a torturous rhythm. He considered the pain and decided he could live with it. He swung his long legs over the cot and sat up. The small confines of the cell swam before him as all of his internal organs settled back into place. He put his head in his hands, and groaned as he touched the goose egg on his temple.

"Oh, so you've decided to wake up," the sheriff said. He was leaning back in his chair, his boots propped up on the desk.

Jamie ran his hands through his hair, trying to get his wandering brain to settle on something. He was in jail and he had received a blow to the head: Those two facts were painfully obvious. He held his hands out in front of him, looking at them as if they held the answers. Suddenly an image formed in his mind of his long, lean fingers closing around a white-collared neck. Jenny . . . Jenny was gone. He jumped to his feet and staggered to the bars, wrapping his hands around them.

"My sister's been kidnapped."

"No, she's been adopted. I saw the records," the sheriff said.

"You don't understand. She didn't want to go. Father Clarence sold her, and they're taking her to California against her will."

"Father Clarence said that your sister went willingly after Mr. Miller made a generous donation to the orphanage."

"She didn't go willingly. They beat her up. Ask Chase—they beat him up, too."

"Now, who do you expect me to believe, a priest or a half-breed?" The sheriff's booted heels hit the floor as he sat up straight. "If I were you, I'd be worried about the predicament I was in instead of my sister."

"What predicament?" Jamie couldn't believe the sheriff's casual attitude. "My sister has been kidnapped, and you need to go after the people who did it."

The sheriff pointed a finger at Jamie. "No, you need to sit down and shut up. You're gonna be here for a while, and you need to stay on my good side."

"Be here, for what?" Jamie was quickly losing patience with the man.

"Attempted murder, that's what. You're gonna stay here until the circuit judge shows up and decides what to do with you."

"Attempted murder . . . who? Father Clarence?' Jamie began to pace the small cell, barely taking three steps before he had to turn and go the other way. "He tried to kill my sister, several times, then he sells her off to God knows who, and you've got *me* in jail?" He kicked the three-legged stool and it bounced around in a corner before it finally settled, upended.

"Don't have witnesses to any of that."

"What about Sister Mary Frances?"

"She told me some stuff about the girl fallin' and breakin' her arm and such, but she never saw any of it. Father Clarence said the girl was always lying and sneakin' around, causin' trouble."

"He's the one who's lying. He's hated Jenny since the day we arrived."

"You can explain it all to the judge, but I'll tell you right now, boy, I saw you chokin' him. I'm the one that busted your head to get you to stop. You was plain loco, and that's what I'm going to tell the judge."

"How long until he gets here?'

"Oh, probably a couple of weeks."

"And I've got to stay here until he comes?"

"Yep."

Jamie rattled the bars in frustration. He needed to go after Jenny now. By the time two weeks were up, all trace of her would be gone. He went back to his cot and sat against the wall, his head in his hands as he willed the throbbing to go away so he could think. "I need to see Sister Mary Frances," he groaned.

"I expect she'll be 'round sometime tomorrow." The sheriff stood and hitched his pants up, then rearranged his gun belt. "Time for my rounds. Don't you go nowhere." He laughed at his own joke on the way out the door.

Jamie looked after him, wondering how such an idiot could hold such an important position. He realized that he was starving. Since it was dark, he knew it had been hours since he had eaten, if it was indeed the same day. He wondered about Chase. He had not looked well when Jamie had last seen him.

"Oh, Jen," Jamie sighed to himself, the thought of her too painful for consideration. "Where are you? Oh, God . . ." Jamie put his head in his hands and wept, the pain of separation more than he could bear. His heart felt as if there were a hole in it, a hole so huge and empty that it would never fill up again. He looked up through russet hair that had fallen across his eyes to the west, where he knew his sister was headed. The way to California was long, the area so vast there was no way he could find her, no way at all. He lay down on the cot and wrapped his arms around himself, tucking his legs up under his chin, and cried until he went to sleep.

Chase had felt alone his entire life, always the outsider in the village where he grew up, never accepted, always wearing the label of half-breed. It hadn't been any easier in the world of the whites. The brief time he and his mother had spent at the fort before they started on their doomed trip east had been filled with hostile looks and insults. When he was in the village he had fought the boys who taunted him, at first coming away bloody and bruised, but gradually emerging the victor more and more often, until the vicious insults stopped, at least in his presence. He knew people made fun of him when he wasn't around, and they never accepted him. He was never invited to join in any play, or later any hunts; that was something he only experienced in the company of his father. At the fort, he had challenged the first soldier who whispered "whore" as his mother walked by, but he learned quickly that he was no match for the three or four who joined in for the pure joy of beating up an Indian.

He realized now that he hadn't known what true loneliness was before. Now he desperately missed the companionship of Jamie and Jenny. He had grown accustomed to their easy banter, to seeing Jenny stretching like a cat before she got out of bed each morning. He missed listening to Jamie read each afternoon, or relate the events of his day, finding humor in the smallest incident. He missed watching Jenny brush her hair every night until the golden mass was blindingly bright. He pictured the graceful way she moved, making the smallest task seem like a dance . . . He shut his eyes as if he could shut out the memories. The rooms were so empty now, where before they had been so full of life, even when they were all sitting quietly listening to Jamie read. He held the unfinished *Robinson Crusoe* in his lap. The words were easy enough, but reading it to himself wasn't the same as when Jamie read. Jamie made the words come to life, transporting all who were listening into the world of the book.

Time seemed to stretch out endlessly before him. Sister Mary Frances had confined him to bed again, only letting him get up to relieve himself. She wanted to make sure that his leg was not broken again. She had removed his splint to find his entire shin black and blue, along with his back, where he had been struck with the cane. She felt sure that he now had some broken ribs to go with the injured leg.

Sister Mary Frances had been beside herself with worry, she blamed herself for the entire incident. She had begged Father Clarence to let Jamie go, hoping to send him on to catch up with Jenny, but the priest had been unreasonable, saying the guilty must be punished and the Lord's will must be done. The nun had returned to the infirmary in tears, going to her knees in anguished prayer only after she had seen to Chase. Sister Mary Frances had prayed through the long night and was now on her way to town to see Jamie, leaving Chase with the book until she returned.

He flipped through the pages to where Jamie had left off and began reading, but instead of words all he could see was Jenny, sitting in front of the stove with some sewing in her lap, the light turning her golden as she listened to the tale. Chase slammed the book shut in frustration and let out a snarl, daring anyone to cross his path, but all was silent, the entire mission in a state of shock over the events of the previous day.

The crutch Jamie had made was leaning against the wall within reach if Chase needed it. He looked at it, then down at his heavily bandaged leg. He lifted the leg, the muscles in his thigh tightening as he held the leg rigid above the mattress. He moved his ankle, making circles with his foot, then flexing, pulling the toes back, then pointing them towards the opposite wall. The front of his shin was tender from the bruises, but there was nothing more than a slight ache deep in the bone. He looked at the knot that kept the bandages in place. Then, his mind made up, he began to undo them, unwinding the length until he reached the two stout boards that held his leg straight. He pulled them away, then went through the whole process again, lifting and flexing, moving the foot in every possible direction, watching it respond to the commands he gave it.

He moved over to the side of the bed and gingerly touched the

223

floor, bearing down with the ball of his foot until he could feel real pressure. Once again he felt nothing but tenderness and a slight ache. He stood, his bruised back protesting at the movement, but once he was up, everything supported him well. He took a tentative step, wincing as the unused muscles protested, but he was standing, so he took another, then another, until he had crossed the room to Jenny's bed. He turned and walked back, growing more confident with each step.

He spied his pants in the outer office and decided to venture there. The pants' leg had been split to allow him to wear them with the splint, and he took them back into the infirmary, where Jenny's sewing basket was sitting on her bedside table. He knew that Jenny and Jamie would have been consumed with laughter over his attempts to run the thread through the eye of the needle, but he finally mastered the task and went to work on the seam, imitating the sewing he had watched his mother and then Jenny do for hours on end. He finally had the seam closed and held it up for inspection, knowing that his stitches were not as neat as Jenny's but also knowing that the pants were now wearable.

After he had pulled them on, he searched for his boot, having worn only one since his arrival. He finally located it on top of the cabinet where Sister Mary Frances stored her medicines. He shook his head at the thought of Jamie thinking that was a logical place to put it. Pulling the boot on turned out to be harder than he'd thought; his shin was so tender that even the touch of his fingers made his stomach turn, but once the boot was up over it, the pressure from the leather seemed to be a comfort instead of a nuisance. Chase once again placed his injured leg solidly on the ground, testing its strength. When he was satisfied, he went out into the halls, limping noticeably, but walking all the same.

Chapter Eighteen

Chase and Sister Mary Frances had reached an impasse where his leg was concerned. When she had returned that first morning from visiting Jamie, she had been horrified to find him out walking the grounds. The nun had begged him to come in, but he had refused, sticking to the course he had laid out around the various buildings, limping badly but walking with determination. The leg was supporting him, and that was all he needed to know at the present time. Chase let the nun examine him when he finally came in that afternoon, but beyond some sore muscles, there was no further damage. She was not happy about his plan, but he stuck to his routine every day until he was able to jog a bit, then move up to a run. At the end of the second week he was running at full speed, and the smaller children would watch him fly by, their mouths wide open as he ran, his face set, his arms pumping, his eyes intently focused on something far before him that only he could see.

While Chase was regaining his strength, Jamie was losing his, sinking further and further into a deep depression, until Sister Mary Frances began to fear for his life. Every morning the nun faithfully visited the jail cell where he was kept, and every morning without fail he asked for news of Jenny. He showed no concern about his own predicament, shrugging it off as if it were nothing. Finally a letter arrived from Boston, and her hands shook as she opened it, praying that it held a miracle. Chase was sitting across from her at the table in the office, waiting to rip the letter from her hands if she couldn't get it open.

"Dear Sister Mary Frances," she began to read. "It was with great concern that I read your letter regarding our mutual acquaintance Father Clarence O'Malley. You were right in your assumption that he had been sent to St. Jo to remove him from a difficult situation in his own parish. It is with heavy heart that I share these difficulties with you, because after reading your letter I realize that we were wrong about where we placed the blame for the problems Father Clarence experienced. It was brought to our attention that Father Clarence had become infatuated with the daughter of one of his flock, a beautiful young girl with golden hair and blue eyes, if memory serves me, a lovely, graceful, refined lady on the verge of becoming a beautiful woman. It seems that she had become engaged to a young man that her father did not approve of and confessed the fact to Father Clarence, who began to counsel her. Somewhere in the counseling sessions a line was crossed. We were led to believe that the young woman was a temptress of some kind, bent on destroying Father Clarence and his good name. The young woman was sent to Europe to remove her from any gossip, and Father Clarence was sent to St. Jo, where we hoped being around the children would help restore his faith and good works. Now that I have read about the problems your young friend Jenny has experienced, I realize that Father Clarence has an illness of the mind, one that we overlooked in our haste to save face. Please show this letter to anyone necessary in order to ensure the safety of Jenny and any other orphan who may suffer at his hands. We are sending someone to relieve Father Clarence of his responsibilities and escort him back to Boston for a hearing. Until that time, keep the faith and know that I am praying for you and your charges. Your brother in Christ our Lord, Father Timothy Wyndham." Sister Mary Frances folded the letter and replaced it in the envelope.

"It's a little late for it to do Jenny any good," Chase remarked.

"Yes, but it might save Jamie." The nun stood up. "Let's go to town."

"You're taking me?"

"Yes. Jamie needs to see you."

While Chase went to ready the wagon, Sister Mary Frances showed the letter to Sister Abigail, who cried in relief, promising to share the news with the other sisters, who had been living in tight-lipped apprehension since before Christmas. Sister Mary Frances soon joined Chase on the wagon and they drove to St. Jo. Chase was anxious to see Jamie; it would be the first time in two weeks. He sat proud and tall on the bench, enduring the second glances of the civilized folk who were not used to seeing an Indian in the middle of town.

"The two of you together will attract a lot of attention, that's for sure," Sister Mary Frances commented as they tied the horses to the rail outside the sheriff's office.

"Jamie would say it's because of our good looks." Chase was clearly excited, and she did not want him to be disappointed by what he saw when he went inside.

"Jamie's not saying much these days, but I hope he will soon enough."

Chase stopped short, then nodded in understanding when he saw the look in the sister's eyes.

When the two entered the office, Jamie was in his usual position, curled up on his bunk, but upon seeing Chase he jumped to his feet and ran to the bars, sticking his hand through to touch Chase as if he were a mirage. Chase was momentarily taken aback by Jamie's pale face and unkempt hair, but he took Jamie's arm and squeezed his hand in greeting.

"Chase, you're walking!" Jamie exclaimed.

"Have been all my life," Chase replied with a cheeky grin. Jamie flashed his own grin at his friend's dry humor and felt an immense sense of relief wash over him as he saw the confident look on Sister Mary Frances's face.

"Wait just a minute!" the sheriff protested. "I didn't say you could bring that half-breed in here."

"You didn't say I couldn't, either," Sister Mary Frances pointed out as she turned her lovely smile on the sheriff. "I have received a letter that may have bearing on this young man's case; may I show it to you?" The sheriff held out his hand to take the letter and read it loud enough that Jamie could hear. Chase held on to Jamie's arm as he read to keep him from exploding in a fit of temper that would keep him locked in the cell.

"So, what you're telling me is that this letter verifies all the claims you and this boy have been making against the priest?" the sheriff asked as he leaned back in his chair.

"Yes, it proves that Father Clarence was out to hurt Jenny. Wouldn't you react the same way if it had been your sister?"

"Shoot, ma'am, I woulda horsewhipped him if it had been me." His boots hit the floor with a thud as he opened the desk drawer and pulled out the keys. "Boy, I'm gonna let you go. Do I need to tell you to stay away from that priest?"

"No, sir, I'm leaving here as soon as you open this door."

"Going after your sister, then?"

"Yes, sir."

"They got a two-week start on you, you know."

"Yes, sir, but I've still got to find her."

The sheriff swung the cell door open. "Don't let me catch you round these parts again. You too," he added to Chase. "I don't know what it is about you, but you seem like you'd be trouble."

Jamie blinked as he walked out into the bright sunshine, standing on the porch of the office as if to orient himself to the outside world again. He shoved his shaggy hair back and looked around for his hat, as if he expected it to magically appear in his hands. Sister Mary Frances pointed him in the direction of the buckboard, and he helped her up before climbing aboard himself.

"Any word?" he asked as he settled onto the wagon.

"No," Sister Mary Frances answered. "I'm so sorry. I feel as if this has all been my fault."

Jamie squeezed the nun's arm as she picked up the reins. "It's not your fault. I should have got her out of there when she asked me to. I was just afraid."

"Afraid of what?" she asked, concerned.

"This," Jamie said, motioning with his hand all around as the wagon began to move and the people began to stare, at the scarred boy who had been locked up, and at the half-breed sitting in the wagon bed behind him. "I can't hide from it anymore. Jenny's out there somewhere, and I've got to find her."

"*We've* got to find her," Chase corrected him.

"You're coming with me?"

"Yes. I haven't got anything else to do right now, and besides, you need me."

Jamie flashed his grin. "I need you?"

"Yes, you do," Sister Mary Frances answered for Chase.

"All right then, we'll leave as soon as we get back."

"No, you'll leave as soon as you take a bath," Sister Mary Frances declared. "You are absolutely rank."

"You ought to try being downwind of him," Chase said from the back of the wagon.

"It's not like I've been staying in a luxury hotel."

"You can get cleaned up, and we can see what kind of provisions we can put together for you." The nun began to make a mental list. "I wish we could come up with some horses for you."

"I have horses," Jamie declared. "I just have to go get them."

Early the next morning the two set out on the road to Council Bluffs. They had let Sister Mary Frances fuss over them the night before, and she had prepared them for their departure as best she could, giving them blankets, a bit of money and a sack of food. Jamie had risen early and gone to the barn, where he removed his gun, his father's knife and the carved angel box from the hiding place and wrapped the items carefully in his jacket before rolling the lot up in his blanket. The blanket was now slung over his back, both ends tied with rope to keep the contents from spilling out.

"What's the big secret?" Chase asked after they had said their goodbyes to Sister Mary Frances, who had made them promise to write as soon as they found Jenny, then had burst into tears after hugging them both.

"I'll show you after we get to Council Bluffs," Jamie promised. They were soon picked up by a wagon, where they rode in back, their long legs dangling over the road as Jamie told Chase about Gray Horse and where they might possibly find him.

Instead of going into town, they left the wagon and circled west on foot; Jamie was not ready to deal with the townfolk and their questions. Memories came rushing back as the landscape became familiar, and he set a course to the north, between the town and what had been his family's land. They made camp close to the glade where Ian had first met Gray Horse.

After they ate, Jamie carefully unrolled his blanket and the treasures it held. Chase looked on with amazement as Jamie examined the pistol that had been a gift to him from his father the last Christmas they had spent together. He carefully cleaned it and loaded it before strapping the holster on. He lined some rocks up on a fallen log, then took aim and shot. He missed the first, but hit the second and the third. He returned the gun to its place, turned away, then whirled back and drew at the same time, hitting the next three rocks in quick succession.

"Where did you learn to do that?" Chase asked when the last whine of the bullets had died away.

"I taught myself, mostly—just practiced a lot, that's all." Jamie shrugged indifferently at the display he had put on.

"Have you ever shot at anything besides targets?"

"You mean have I ever shot anyone?"

"Yes, that's what I mean."

"No, but I would have if this hadn't happened." Jamie motioned down the side of his scarred face. "And if I ever meet up with the man who did this, I won't even think about it. I'll just shoot." Jamie reloaded the gun and replaced it at his side. "What about you, you ever shoot at anyone?"

"Yes," Chase stirred the fire as he drifted back to his life before the mission. "We had to protect ourselves from raids from other villages, from the white settlers, who couldn't tell one Indian from another, from the horse soldiers who didn't care. The threat of attack was something we lived with every day."

"Did you ever kill anyone?" Jamie moved further back as the flames from the fire flared up. Night was settling over them, closing around the glade like a blanket.

Chase's eyes gleamed silver in the firelight as memories came rushing back, as a face flashed before him, a knife held above his heart, a struggle in the dirt, a fight for life, his or that of this man who was trying to kill him. "I did what I had to do to survive."

Jamie nodded, hoping that he, too, would have the determination to survive when he needed it. He picked up the knife that was still in its sheath and held it out to Chase. "This was my father's. I want you to have it."

Chase took the knife and pulled it from the sheath, watching as the light from the fire danced on its shiny surface. He ran his thumb down the blade and pricked it on the end, sticking the injured surface in his mouth to suck off the blood. "It's a fine weapon. I'm honored that you would give it to me."

A few moments passed as they contemplated what they had told each other, both wondering if they would need the weapons they had just strapped on. Jamie's eyes searched the heavens above, Chase stared into the fire. Finally Chase broke the silence as a crescent moon rose above the treetops. "Tell me about your father. I've never heard you talk about him."

Jamie closed his eyes and leaned back against a tree. "My father . . ." He didn't know where to begin. "I guess I look like him. I'm a bit taller, and I have my mother's chin, but the rest, it's all him. His name was Ian, and he had this . . . I guess you would call it magic, with horses. They just responded to him like nothing you've ever seen."

"I've seen it."

"You have?"

"Yes. I've seen it with you, with those big plowhorses at the mission, they worshiped you."

Jamie grinned at the thought. "My mother always said I had the same touch. I haven't thought about it since we left our stock. We had the best horses west of the Mississippi on our ranch. My father had a reputation for having only the best, and we were starting to do a really great business when they were killed." He paused for a moment, to get past that day and back to happier times. "Dad was funny, too. He was always telling some simple story but turning it into a great adventure. Even if it was just the cat getting stuck in the woodpile, he made it wonderful. We were always laughing and carrying on over something. And he loved my mother. She was so beautiful. She was smaller than Jenny, and more silver. Where Jenny is all golden, like sunshine, my mother was more like the moon." Jamie picked up the wooden box and ran his fingers over the carved angel. "He always said she was his angel."

"Was that box hers?"

"Yes. As long as I can remember, it sat on the table next to their bed." Jamie handed the box to Chase, who held it carefully as he examined the carving.

"Jenny said that your father saw your mother when he was dying, that she was waiting for him."

"She told you that?" Jamie closed his eyes and pictured his father's death from what Jenny had told him.

"I think the only reason she told me was to stop me from doing something crazy."

"Like what?"

"Walk through a blizzard with a broken leg and dig up my mother's body so I could send it to the spirit world."

"Yeah, that would have been crazy." Jamie flashed his grin, then became serious. "Chase, do you believe in heaven?"

"Yes. My mother taught me about heaven and hell, you can't have one without the other. The Kiowa have the same thing, just called something else, so I believe it's all the same."

"We were brought up the same way. I hope there's a heaven. I know that if there is, my parents are there, watching over us. I hope they are watching over Jenny right now."

"Me too." Chase lay back on his blanket, placing his arm under his head so he could look up at the stars popping out in the night sky. "She's looking at the same sky whereever she is."

"She's probably madder than a wet hen, too."

Chase laughed at the vision of Jenny that filled his head at that comment. "Yeah, I bet she hasn't been the easiest thing to get along with."

"I bet they wanted to return her as soon as she woke up," Jamie added. "I've seen her mad, and it's not a pretty sight."

"I've seen it, too. Remember when she threw that mug at my head?" The two of them collapsed in laughter as they compared ideas on what Jenny's kidnappers were going through at the mercy of her temper. They finally settled down, quieting as they both thought of Jenny alone. Eventually they slept.

A few mornings later Jamie cautiously stretched his abused muscles as the first sounds of dawn woke him. He was sore, unaccustomed to sleeping on the hard ground, and his legs were cramping from the hard exercise after weeks of inactivity. He could hear Chase stirring under his blanket, and he wondered if his friend was also suffering. At least having horses would make the travel easier, and he hoped they would find Gray Horse soon.

"Jamie," Chase called out.

"What?" Jamie bit the word out as he squinted against the bright sunshine.

"We have company."

Jamie sat up instantly, bringing his revolver level with his waist. Gray Horse was sitting between their blankets, sizing up Chase, who was still under his blanket.

"Hello, young Duncan," the Indian said without looking at Jamie.

Jamie laid his gun down and shoved his hair back. "Chase, this is my father's friend Gray Horse. Gray Horse, my friend Chase the

232

Wind." Chase kicked his blanket off, standing before Gray Horse, who had also stood. The Indian turned to Jamie and extended his hand, helping him to his feet. He carefully scrutinized the scar on Jamie's face as he held on to his arm.

"I am glad the white doctors were able to help you," he commented.

Jamie turned his cheek away from the Indian's dark eyes. "We've been looking for you."

"I saw that I was being followed, so I waited. It is good to see you."

"I need some horses." Behind Gray Horse, Jamie saw Chase shake his head as if in warning. Jamie looked into the eyes of his father's friend and apologized. "I'm sorry. A lot has happened, and I haven't even thanked you for what you did for Jenny and me after our parents died." Jamie began to pace, shoving his hair back.

"You are much like your father, young Duncan. Come, let us go to my camp and you can tell me your story."

Jamie and Chase gathered up their things and followed the Indian to where his horse was waiting with two other riders, both boys a few years younger than Jamie. He recognized them as Gray Horse's sons, whom Jamie had shared many adventures with, and they smiled when they saw him. Jamie and Chase swung up behind the boys and they took off for the village.

Jamie's thick russet hair drew more attention than his scars as they rode in. After he dismounted, several children gathered round his knees, chattering like little birds as they pointed up at his hair which the sun had turned to molten copper. Jamie grinned at them and knelt, waiting patiently as they took turns touching the top of his head, some of them jumping back as if they had been burned by the heat. One little girl tentatively touched his scar and he jerked self-consciously, accidentally scaring the child.

Gray Horse touched Jamie's shoulder and led him to his tent, with Chase following. Gray Horse's wife shooed the children away as the men stepped inside, each taking a seat on the ground. They sat patiently while the woman prepared them a meal. Jamie carefully copied Chase's eating manners so as not to insult his host.

"Now, tell me your story, young Duncan," Gray Horse said when the remains of the meal had been taken away.

Jamie looked at Chase, who gave him an encouraging look. As succinctly as possible he told Gray Horse everything that had happened since they had left the ranch. Gray Horse listened carefully, asking a few questions about the things he didn't understand, nodding at the things he did. When Jamie was finished with his tale, Gray Horse left, stopping to speak to someone outside.

"He's sending someone to get us horses," Chase whispered to Jamie. Jamie shoved his hair back and looked up anxiously when Gray Horse came back in.

"Come with me," he said, holding the flap open so they could follow him out. They followed him to another tent, where several men of the village were holding council. Jamie and Chase were led to places away from the main group and sat waiting while Gray Horse conferred with the men seated around a small fire. Chase listened intently to the conversation, and Jamie followed as best he could, not being fluent in the language. Gray Horse motioned for them to join the circle, and they complied, Jamie edging as far away from the small fire as he could without seeming rude.

"You must consult the spirits before you begin your journey," Gray Horse explained. Chase sat stone-faced in front of the fire as Jamie looked questioningly at his father's friend. "The spirits will give you a sign to guide you." Jamie heard the undercurrent of conversation going on around the circle, but he still did not understand what was happening. Chase seemed to turn in on himself, leaving Jamie feeling very alone and vulnerable as a bowl of liquid was passed around the circle. He watched Chase take the bowl and drink from it, then pass it on to Gray Horse, who drank also. "Let the spirits guide you, young Duncan," Gray Horse said as he handed the bowl to Jamie, who quickly examined the contents before taking a sip. Gray Horse tipped the bowl up to Jamie's mouth with his finger, making him swallow more of the bitter mixture than he intended to. Jamie's eyes grew wide with surprise as the mixture began to take effect, then they lost focus, and he felt his limbs go numb. The small fire flickered in front of him, and against his will he felt himself being pulled closer and closer to the flames. He began to tremble as he felt the heat, and he could feel himself screaming, although he didn't make a sound. The fire surrounded him until he shot up out of the top of the flames, floating above like an ash, then drifting up through the smoke hole in the tent until he was suspended in the air above.

Jamie looked down and saw his body sitting inside the tent, his shoulders slumped, his chin resting on his chest. He saw Chase also, only his head was thrown back as if he was looking up at him. *Come with me*, he wanted to say, but no words formed. He heard someone calling his name and he looked out of the village and saw the plains beyond. His body followed where his eyes went, soaring above the ground like a hawk. Horses were running below, a huge herd, and at their lead he saw Storm, flying over the ground like the wind. Jamie willed his body to go down, until he was hovering right over the gray's back as he ran, his head even with the horse's, so close that he could feel Storm's mane beating against his face. He stayed with him until the mountains rose up before him, stopping the horse's mad flight. Jamie continued on, following the voice that was still calling to him.

He looked down and saw a lake, the center of it full of churning waves. In the midst of them he saw Jenny thrashing about in the water, her hair swirling around her. She was calling his name, begging him to help her, so he willed his body down, reaching his hands out to Jenny's outstretched one, but she was out of reach. The water was pulling her away, spinning her round and round until a whirlpool formed in the lake. Jenny was flying around in the water, her body tumbling out of control. As the whirlpool grew stronger, the bottom of the lake became visible where the water had pulled away. Jamie looked down, but instead of seeing sand or mud, he saw green grass, and Chase. His long hair was blowing in the whirlwind, and he was just standing there looking up, his eyes shaded with his hand as if he was looking into the sun. Jamie knew that Chase could help him rescue Jenny, so he willed his body to go to him, and as he passed through the whirlpool, he caught Jenny's hand and pulled her through, so that she landed next to Chase on the grass. He could see them standing there together, but he could not stop his flight.

He continued on, flying away from them until they were so small he couldn't see them. He kept on going, desperate to go back but having no control over his direction. He finally came to a stop in a small glade. He was so tired from his journey that he lay down in the cool grass and rested, totally alone except for a red fox that walked out and sat before him, watching him curiously as he lay there. He closed his eyes and slept.

Gray Horse gently lowered Jamie so that he was on a blanket beside the small fire. On the other side of him was Chase, who was still deep in the spirit world.

Chase had heard Jamie calling to him from above and he had followed, soaring with him over the plains, feeling the excitement of the horses as they ran, until they stopped short of the mountains. He went on, following Jamie, until he heard Jenny's voice calling to him. She was swimming in a beautiful pool of clear water, and she called to him to join her. He felt himself pulling off his clothes, and his body slicing through the water as he joined her, taking her in his arms, and feeling her skin, slick with the water, press against his own. He held her, and as he looked into her deep blue eyes, he felt her golden hair float around him, entwining with his own long, dark hair, until the only way he could tell where her hair ended and his began was by the color. The water was warm and comforting, and he felt as if he could stay there forever, even when he looked up and saw that a pack of growling, snapping wolves had surrounded them, the only thing holding them back their fear of the water. Through his dream, he felt himself being lowered onto a blanket, and he smiled, content to stay where he was for the time being.

Jamie felt too warm, and a frown creased his face as he struggled against the discomfort. He knew that it was early summer, so he should be a little hot, but this was not right, and as he tried to surface through the many layers of fog that surrounded him, he came to the realization that he was lying next to a fire. He sat upright with a start, and slid away from the flames as he looked around to see if anyone was watching. He was alone, and he took a minute to collect his thoughts as he scrubbed his hands through his hair. He could hear the soft murmur of voices from outside and he staggered to his feet, grabbing a tent pole as his head began to spin. He could see through the opening that the sun was going down and the men who had earlier been drinking the potion with him were all seated outside, talking among themselves. Chase was in the middle of the group, speaking Lakota and signing the words that he didn't know.

Gray Horse saw Jamie and came to him, a smile on his face.

"The spirits spoke to you, young Duncan?"

"I guess you could say that," Jamie answered. His mouth felt like cotton, and he was having a hard time orienting himself as he took a trembling step forward. He managed to make it to the circle under his own steam and gratefully accepted a drink from one of the men at the fire. Chase was grinning at him, his own cobwebs already gone, and Jamie fought down the urge to punch him. Strangely enough, the drink refreshed him and he began to feel like himself again after a few minutes.

"Tell us of your dream," Gray Horse said when he saw that Jamie had recovered.

Jamie looked around at the concerned faces and began to speak, haltingly of what he remembered about the strange vision he had experienced. When he was done, there was a flurry of conversation, all in Lakota, as the men in the circle compared opinions on what they had heard. Jamie looked over at Chase, who just shrugged but continued to pay rapt attention to the words flying around him.

"You and your friend are on the same quest," Gray Horse began to translate. That wasn't news to Jamie, but he let him go on. "You will take the same path, but it will become difficult when you come to the mountains. Your sister will go through many raging waters before you are reunited with her, but her path lies with you." Gray Horse looked at Chase as he spoke. "There are many who will try to separate you, but you must trust in each other."

Jamie looked around the men of the circle, who were all nodding in agreement with the words Gray Horse had spoken. He hadn't learned anything new. He had known when he started out that it was not going to be easy to find Jenny, and his so-called vision hadn't given him any revelations on how to find her. It had only added to his confusion. Why did he go on away from Jenny and Chase if their paths were all together, and what was the meaning of the fox?

"Tomorrow you shall begin your journey with the horses that I have been keeping for you," Gray Horse said. "Tonight you will be our guests." Jamie felt immense relief at Gray Horse's announcement. Tomorrow they would be under way. With good horses, they should be able to catch up with the wagon that was carrying Jenny in just a few weeks. He stood, following the lead of the others, and when he saw they were all wandering off, he turned towards the west where the last rays of the sun were showing on the horizon.

"There's a lot of country out there," Chase said as he stepped up next to him.

"Yeah."

"Don't worry, we're going to find her."

"We are?"

"Yes. That's what the spirits told us. You found her, and I found her."

"You did?"

"Yes, I did."

"Was I there?"

Chase puzzled over the question. "No, not when I saw her. I was following you, and then you were just gone."

Jamie wrapped his arms around himself as he looked off towards the west. "That's what I was afraid of."

"Jamie, don't worry about it. We both found her. We just found her in different ways, that's all. You're not supposed to take these things so seriously."

"I'm sorry, Chase. It's my first vision. I didn't know what to expect." Jamie stalked away.

Chase was shocked by his friend's vehemence, and decided to give him some time to work it out. After all, Jamie did not have much experience with Indian ways.

The next morning Gray Horse presented Jamie with two saddled horses. Jamie knew them, and as he began to whistle, they turned towards him, their ears pricked forward in recognition. There was a tall black with white stockings and a white blaze that he had ridden many times, so he chose that one, leaving Chase the buckskin. He didn't want to know where the saddles had come from, he was just happy to have them, along with the food Gray Horse had packed for them.

Gray Horse promised to continue to care for the remaining stock until Jamie could come back, and wished them well on their journey.

"There's one thing I've been meaning to ask you," Jamie said as he mounted. "Do you ever see Storm?"

"Your father's horse?" Gray Horse asked. Jamie nodded. "He is out there, running wild. He steals the mares, but we will take their foals when they are ready. No one can get close to him."

"Perhaps I'll give it a try, after I find Jenny."

"It should be you. You are like your father."

Jamie flashed his grin, then shoved his hair back before putting his hat on. He and Chase rode out of the village and headed west.

Part Three
Wyoming Territory, 1860

Chapter Nineteen

"Don't know what they're so happy about," Jamie grumbled and tossed his chin towards the whooping cowboys on the other side of the herd. Chase's dark eyes peered through the dust kicked up by the cattle and watched as one of the hands chased down a steer that had wandered off. "They act like finding one stray is equal to rescuing the entire herd."

Chase shook his head at his friend's complaints. As soon as they got the herd in, the two of them would have to head back out again to do the job that had been theirs since they had arrived at the Lynch ranch three years earlier. Chase was one of the best trackers around and could find most of the hiding places the other cowboys missed. The only time his tracking skills had failed him in the years since they'd left the orphanage had been during the search for Jenny. Her trail had ended in the mountains west of Denver that autumn after she disappeared, and there had been no sign of her since.

Chase and Jamie had wandered back to St. Jo after wintering with the Kiowa. No one had seen her. They were heading west again when they had come across Cat Lynch and rescued her from a stagecoach robbery. She had suggested that they come to the

Lynch ranch in the southeastern corner of Wyoming. They had told her about Jenny, and she'd assured them that her father could help.

Jason Lynch and his daughter Cat were waiting on a knoll for Jamie and Chase to catch up with them. They could see Cat scanning the riders, looking for Ty. The judge had hired Tyler Kincaid the spring after Jamie and Chase had arrived, and Cat had been head over heels for him since day one. Ty had left his home in North Carolina and gone west after a nearly fatal fight with his older brother; the strife that was threatening to tear the nation apart had already worked its poison in his family, setting brother against brother. The judge had known his grandfather in law school, and had taken the soft-spoken, well-educated young man in. Ty had quickly shown his worth, pulling his weight, not giving anyone a chance to accuse him of being soft from the affluent childhood he had known. Cat had taken one look at his sandy brown hair, serious blue eyes and long, lean frame and decided that he was the man for her; she just had to convince Ty of it.

Cat was used to getting what she wanted, although she was not the spoiled brat she was reputed to be. She was the only daughter of a man who had married late in life, more to carry on his name than for love. Jason Lynch had loved once, but the girl had disappeared from his life without a trace, much the same way Jenny had from Jamie's, which made Jason feel a special bond with Jamie that he did not share with the rest of the so-called orphans he took in and put to work. When he had heard the story of Jenny's disappearance and the fruitless search for her, he had hired detectives to track her down, and put up fliers with her likeness in every town between Denver and St. Jo, but there had been no news. They had found no trace of her. Jamie didn't mention her much anymore, but he still felt a constant ache, like a wound that would not heal. Chase talked of her at times, and Jamie knew he dreamed of her; he heard his friend say her name in his sleep sometimes. Jamie never dreamed of Jenny, but he still had terrifying nightmares about being on fire, and kept his distance from flames of any sort.

Jamie and Chase urged their horses up the knoll to where Jason and Cat waited. "Did you get them all?" the judge asked. He was tall and slim for a man over sixty; his face was lined and bronzed, his full head of hair more silver than the golden brown it had been. His blue eyes were still sharp and missed nothing, much to Cat's dismay. He had encouraged her many times to be patient where Ty was concerned, but she was more inclined to charge in, full speed ahead.

"I'm sure you'll let us know," Jamie said, flashing his grin. He took his hat off and shoved back the mass of hair that fell over his eyes, then wiped some of the dust away with his bandanna.

"I'm not worried. Chase will find them no matter where they are," Jason said. Cat was moving restlessly in her saddle, still scanning the herd and the riders around it.

"He's riding drag," Chase said, and she took off towards the back of the herd.

Jason opened his mouth to stop her but thought better of it and let her go. "If she wants him bad enough to eat dust all the way home, then I'll let her get a taste of it," he said.

Chase and Jamie grinned. The romance between Cat and Ty had provided a lot of entertainment for the hands on the Lynch ranch, and this latest episode would provide more fuel for the teasing the group heaped upon Ty when Cat was not around. They heard a whoop from the other side of the herd and saw Zane waving his hat in the air at Cat's fading figure. Zane would be sure to bring up the fact that Cat had ridden drag with Ty, and his cheeky comments would keep them laughing through the evening.

Zane was a charmer who loved hard work but constantly complained about doing it, usually making whatever woman who happened to be around feel sorry for him. He had a wide grin, hazel eyes, straight light brown hair and a way with women that amazed those around him. He was constantly finding willing companions, sometimes in the most obscure places, and his sexual exploits were a legend among the female residents of Fort Laramie. Cat and Grace, who cooked for the hands, had proven themselves immune to his charm, and he treated them with the respect due to a sister or aunt.

Jake was riding behind Zane and looked up to see what the noise was about. Jake was the most dangerous one of the group, he was deadly with the two guns he wore on his hips. He was quiet and brooding, but also sensitive and caring with those he felt close to. He was slowly opening up to the men who lived and worked with him, but there were times when something would come over him, and then they knew to leave him alone. He had finally told them about the repeated beatings his father had given him and his mother, which explained a lot. His reputation with his guns had become a problem for him. Gunslingers were always wanting to prove they were faster than Jake, but so far no one had been. He had pale blond hair that he wore long, like Chase's, and light blue eyes that could turn to ice with a blink. He considered the group that lived at the Lynch ranch to be his family now and would defend any one of them to the death.

The rider at point was Caleb. Caleb was the quiet one, always listening intently to the goings-on around him. Caleb was devoted to his fellow hands and supported them all; he also had an amazing talent for drawing. He had drawn the likeness of Jenny from Jamie's description, and her brother was amazed at how true to her it was, even though Caleb had never seen her. He would sit and sketch people as they talked and worked. Many times Jason had told him he was wasting his talent working the ranch, but Caleb swore he didn't want to be anywhere else.

The ranch was over the next rise, and Grace would have supper ready for them. Jason would count the herd, and the next day Jamie and Chase would go for the stragglers while the rest worked the stock, branding the calves, cutting out the ones that would go to market after growing fat on the summer grass. Tonight, however, they would rest and talk and eat, and maybe Jamie would not wonder about Jenny and where she was and what she was doing. And later, when everyone was asleep, he would sneak into Grace's cabin and lie in her arms after they had exhausted themselves making love.

Grace took the pan of biscuits out of the oven at the same time that the herd came over the long ridge to the north. She heard the whooping and hollering as the hands urged the cattle on into the huge pen beside one of the many outbuildings that made up the Lynch spread. She walked out onto the porch of the small cabin that served as the dining hall and her home, placing a hand over her eyes to shield herself from the sun that hung low in the sky. Her brown eyes scanned the multitude of cows, horses and riders rolling down the hill and spotted a flash of copper in the dust surrounding them. She smiled to herself, looking forward to the night ahead and the secret romance she was having with young James Duncan.

Grace had been born onto a rich plantation on the banks of the

Mississippi thirty-odd years before. Her grandfather had been alive and had ruled the place with an iron hand, doling out a small allowance to his irresponsible son, Grace's father. Her mother had died in childbirth, and her father had brought her to the plantation to be raised by his own nanny. When her grandfather had died, her father had quickly gambled away his inheritance, leaving the plantation and all his other properties to be auctioned off to pay his debts. Grace and her father had wound up on the street. He had taken to the riverboats, dragging his teenage daughter along. Grace quickly learned the card games he played, helping her father cheat others to support themselves.

Her father had lost his life over a card game, leaving Grace to pick up the deck and make her own way, using her natural beauty and feminine wiles to win whenever possible, and cheating when necessary. She had done well—well enough to begin saving money to buy her own place. She had known that her beauty would soon fade and she would need another way to live. Then she had met a gambler, an attractive man whose background was similar to hers and who had fallen on hard times for the same reasons. She had thought herself in love with the man, but soon found that he had a violent temper when crossed. She had tried to leave him, but he'd found her and left her beaten and scarred for life. He had slashed both of her high, classic cheekbones with his knife, leaving scars that marred her smooth skin from her temples to the corners of her mouth. He'd also taken her savings and disappeared into Texas, leaving Grace alone and unable to support herself.

Jason Lynch had found Grace on a visit to New Orleans, working as a maid in the hotel where he was staying. He looked beyond the scars, saw the educated, refined lady and brought her to Wyoming to take care of his hands. He found her to be an interesting opponent in chess and enjoyed her talent for cards and conversation. For her part, Grace was grateful that he required nothing more of her. She knew her choices were few, and some men would not let her scars keep them from enjoying her womanly attributes. She was still a beautiful woman, her features elegant, her dark brown hair abundantly curly and bright, but the scars were there, and she was always conscious of them, until Jamie showed up.

Chase had remarked soon after they began working at the ranch that he knew he would never starve with Jamie around. His friend had a way of charming every cook west of the Mississippi. Jamie had sat down at the table, shoved his unruly mass of hair back off his head and dived into a plate of beef stew and homemade bread, grinning at Grace the entire time he was eating. She had an uncontrollable urge to run her fingers through the mass of russet hair that kept falling over his eyes, and felt absolutely giddy inside when he complimented her on the meal. She had a long talk with herself that night about acting foolish and being practically old enough to be his mother, but she still felt flustered every time he flashed his grin at her.

Then one day, some weeks later when they happened to be alone, he had asked her about her face, and she had asked him about his, and they had wound up in each other's arms. She knew it wouldn't last, was surprised their affair had gone on so long, and was determined to enjoy it while she could. Jamie was a sensitive lover, giving, she felt, more than he got, and Grace was happier than she had ever been in her entire life. She suspected that Jason knew, realized that everyone else did, but nothing was ever said except for an occasional nudge or wink, so she didn't worry about it. The men were discreet, and everyone seemed to be happy for them, so it went on.

The hands came stomping up the steps, slapping dirt off, trying to edge each other out of position at the washstand as they splashed off the dust from the trail. The smell of fried chicken and biscuits was making each and every mouth water as the men made themselves presentable for dinner. Cat elbowed her way to the table, sliding onto the bench between Ty and Caleb, her green eyes sparkling in her smudged face.

"Will you join us?" Grace asked Jason as he stood on the porch, his hat in hand.

Jason looked in at the wild group busily passing bowls and slopping servings onto plates. "No, I think I'll take my meal up at the house." He put his hat on and stepped off the porch. "I don't suppose you'll be up for a game of chess later?"

"No, it will take me a while to clean up after this bunch." Grace leaned against the post as Jason mounted his horse for the ride up to the main house. It had been built on a ridge to the south, facing away from the outbuildings hidden in the small valley. He tipped his hat and rode off, and Grace went in to tend to her brood.

They were all attacking the meal, an indication that the food was good. They were too busy eating to make conversation, until Zane looked up from his plate at Cat, who was sitting across from him at the long table.

"I'm surprised you can eat anything tonight, Cat," he commented with a smirk.

"Whyzat?" Cat said around a biscuit that she had smothered in honey.

Jamie and Chase grinned as they waited for Zane's retort.

"All that dust you was eating today, riding drag with Ty." Elbows nudged stomachs as the group waited for Cat to explode, but she just tilted her nose up and gave Zane a look that said she would remember she owed him one.

"I don't know why anyone would ride drag on purpose, unless they were blind or stupid or . . ." Zane raised his eyebrows quizzically at Cat.

"Or what?" Cat asked, "If you've got something to say, then say it."

Ty put his fork down and looked at Zane. "You got something to say, Zane?" he asked. Ty was tired of the jokes and tired of holding Cat at arm's length all the time.

Zane grinned around his food. "Nope, I was just wondering."

"Wonder all you want to, just leave me out of it," Ty said.

"Me, too," Jake added. "I'm tired of hearing your mouth runnin' all the time."

"What did I do?" Zane began, but Grace put an end to the debate by placing a pan of blackberry cobbler in the middle of the table. They attacked it with their usual gusto, and the conversation turned away from Ty and Cat.

"Hey, Grace, did you know that Chase has an Indian name?" Caleb said.

"Why, no, I never really thought about it." Grace looked at Chase, who was sitting in his usual place next to Jamie. "What is it?"

"Chase the Wind. Jamie shortened it to Chase. He said it was more practical."

"Yeah, I can see why," Jake snorted.

"That's an interesting name. How did you come by it?" Grace asked, ignoring Jake. The others all leaned forward to listen. Chase didn't talk about his past much, and they knew that it had to be different from their own upbringing, so they were attentive to his every word.

"I think it sounds romantic, especially since you have been following the wind, trying to find Jamie's sister and all," Cat said.

Zane batted his eyes at Cat, who threw a biscuit at him. Ty frowned at the two of them and turned to Chase. "What would our names be if we were Kiowa?" he asked Chase.

Chase leaned back on the bench and folded his arms, studying his companions. "I don't know, some of you are easy, some are hard."

"Do Jamie," Cat said.

"That's easy. Grinning Fox."

Jamie grinned and shoved his hair back.

"How about Caleb?"

Chase raised his head to study the dark-haired, dark-eyed artist. "Eyes Like A Hawk because he sees everything."

They all expressed their approval. Somebody suggested Jake.

"I would just call him Wolf."

Jake smiled, something he did not do much, to show his approval. "Do Zane," he said.

Chase had to think about that one for a while. "Whines Like A Dog."

"I do not," Zane protested as they all erupted into laughter. "Come on, you can do better than that."

"Give me some time," Chase laughed. "Cat is easy. She has cat eyes, so she already has her Kiowa name. Cat."

Cat curled her hand up like a claw and hissed at Zane. "Watch out, Dog, I'll get you." Zane acted afraid as Cat turned to Chase. "How about Ty?"

"I don't know. I really need to think about that one."

"What about Grace?" Jamie said, his dark blue eyes smiling on her as she cleared the table.

"White Swan," Chase said, and Grace smiled at him. Jamie nudged his friend under the table to say thank you, but Chase didn't feel it because suddenly Jenny was floating through his mind.

What name would you give me? she asked inside his head, and names started pouring into his mind.

"I'll talk to you all later," Chase said and suddenly rose from the table, trying not to place his hands over his ears as the words tumbled around in his mind. *Beloved,* he thought. *Soul mate. Lover.* Chase walked to the corral and leaned across the fence. The moon was climbing in the night sky, and he wondered if Jenny was looking up at the same golden orb above. "I know you are out there," he said to the moon. "I know we are meant to be together." Up in the hills the mournful cry of a coyote rang out, bringing the ranch dogs awake to join in the chorus. He heard the sounds of the men washing up. Zane, Jake, Ty and Caleb were all heading to town for some female companionship; Jamie was getting ready for his rendezvous with Grace. He could hear Cat muttering to herself as she went to the main house; Ty had sent her on her way, frustrated as usual.

"Hey, Chase, care to join us?" Zane hollered as they mounted up.

"No, thanks."

"Suit yourself." The coyote continued to howl. Chase knew just how he felt.

Chapter Twenty

"Caleb, I swear that whore you were with was so fat you probably had to throw a saddle on her just to keep from falling off." As usual, Caleb ignored Zane's ribbing.

"Well, at least she had all her teeth," Jake put in. "That one you were with looked like a busted-up piano."

"She has other qualities that make a few missing teeth desirable." Zane waggled his eyebrows in an innuendo that brought a snort from Ty. They were all stretching the truth just a bit—the whores in town weren't fat or ugly, they were just well used.

The boys were late getting back from town and had decided to shorten the trip by cutting cross-country instead of staying on the road. They rode up on a small ridge and were brought up short. A vision had surfaced in the pond below them, throwing her long blond hair back in an arc as she came out of the water. The four cowboys quietly dismounted and sent their horses back down the ridge.

"Did you see that?" Zane jabbed Jake with his elbow as they lay on the hillside above, watching the vision squeeze water from her hair.

"How could I miss it?" Jake grunted in return. Caleb just grinned at them, then turned back to watch.

"She is beautiful," Zane said as the woman leisurely scrubbed the soap down a long thigh. Her back was to them, and each one wished with all his might that she would turn around. "Hey, Caleb, do you think you could draw her?"

"I have"—Caleb smiled at him—"in my dreams." Zane put his head down as he was overcome with laughter.

"Will you shut up? She might hear us," Jake hissed.

"We shouldn't be doing this," Ty whispered.

"Then don't, nobody's making you," Zane whispered back. "How many opportunities do you get to see something like this?"

"What do you mean? You saw the same thing last night," Ty retorted.

"Yeah, but this is different."

"How is it different?"

"She's not a whore."

"How can you tell?"

Zane pointed down to the prominent bulge in his pants. Ty shook his head in disgust, and Jake started to laugh.

"You are the only man I know who can wake up from a night of lovin' with your weapon cocked," he said.

"He hasn't failed me yet," Zane said proudly.

Ty began to slide back down the hill. "Come on, Caleb, let's go home." Caleb looked down the hill towards the beauty, then followed Ty.

"Caleb, come back here," Zane whispered after him, but the two mounted and headed around the hill away from the pond. Jake and Zane looked back down the hill towards the pond. The woman was walking out, and Zane grabbed Jake's arm as he got the full impact of her beauty.

The woman's horse tossed his head as she came out of the pond, and she immediately became wary. She picked up her gun and held it ready as she pulled on her shirt. Then she grabbed the reins and scanned the hill above. She cocked the gun, holding it easily in her hand. The horse looked towards the hill, then snorted as he went back to his browsing. The girl relaxed with the horse, and went to put on her clothes.

"I am in love!" Zane exclaimed as they mounted their horses. "Did you see her? Did you see how long her legs were and her . . ."

Zane's hand circled his chest as he tried to find the words to describe what he had seen.

"Yeah, I saw her. I saw her first."

"Don't start that. You know I did."

"I'll draw you for her."

"No way, I'm not falling for that." The two rode off, arguing over the girl without even knowing her name.

"You boys are in a heap of trouble with Jason," Grace declared as the four entered her cabin looking for lunch.

"Why?" Zane asked as he took the lid off a bubbling pot to smell the contents.

"Because he expected you to start cutting the herd this morning instead of laying about town all day."

"You know we aren't going to do any cutting until Jamie gets back."

"That's not what Jason said. He wants you to start cutting today, immediately." The boys ignored Grace as Caleb took out his pad and began to draw. "Caleb, what are you drawing?" she asked.

"An absolute vision," Zane answered for him. Jake and Zane were looking over his shoulder while Ty sat beside him, offering help where he thought it was needed. A pool of water began to form, with an image of a tall, slender woman's back, and arms holding a mass of hair up on top of her head.

"Who is that?" Grace asked as she peered over Caleb's shoulder.

"We saw her this morning down at the spring," Jake said.

"You were spying on her?"

"I guess you could say that." Zane grinned.

"I wonder who she is and what she's doing out here," Grace said as she began to take dishes off the shelf.

"She's looking for me, that's what she's doing," Zane commented.

"Will you shut up! I'm sick of hearing you go on about her like she's one of your conquests," Ty snapped.

Zane rolled his eyes. "Sound's like you fell for her yourself."

"No, I'm just tired of the way you talk about women."

"So, Grace, you say Jason was pretty mad at us." Zane couldn't help grinning as he set Ty up.

"Yes, he was."

"I bet he wasn't as mad as Cat."

Ty sighed in frustration as Zane began to laugh.

"Yeah, she was here this morning and she rode away like a bat out of hell." Grace ladled the bowls full of stew and set them down on the table. "Now you boys eat so you can get to work before Jason runs us all off." Conversation ended as they dug into the bowls and passed the sketch around, each agreeing that it was a good likeness of the goddess they had seen, with Zane adding that he would like to see the view from the other side.

"I could do it," Caleb said, and they all urged him on, even after Grace smacked him with a towel. The noise was soon interrupted by a knocking at the door, and Grace shushed them as she opened the portal.

"Excuse me. I wonder if you could help me—I'm looking for someone." Four mouths at the table dropped open. The beauty they'd spied on that morning was standing in the doorway, her golden hair tumbling around her shoulders, her blue eyes wide with apprehension.

"Who are you looking for?" Grace asked, wondering if this was the woman they had been talking about.

"James Duncan. Jamie. He's my brother."

Grace put her hand to her mouth as realization sank in. "Oh, my God, you are his sister. You're Jenny? Your eyes—they are just like his."

"He's here?"

"Yes. I mean no. I mean not right now. Oh, God, please come in." Grace realized she was babbling as she pulled Jenny into the cabin. "He lives here on this ranch, but he's out with Chase hunting strays. He'll probably be gone a couple of days."

Jenny blinked back tears as she realized that she had at last found her brother. She looked around the room as if in a daze, and Ty, seeing her condition, leaped into action, sweeping a chair out to her just as her knees collapsed.

"I'm sorry. It's just that it's been so long," Jenny apologized as her head began to swim. She heard paper rustling and saw the pages in a sketchbook being flipped back until suddenly everyone was staring at one of the pages.

"She looks just like that, Caleb," Zane commented as they looked between Jenny and the page. Caleb turned the pad around so Jenny could see the likeness he had drawn from Jamie and Chase's description.

253

"I drew this so they could put up posters to find you. I guess it didn't work."

"No, it didn't." Jenny looked in amazement at the drawing. "Do you have any of Jamie?"

"Sure, look through the book. There are lots."

Jenny began to flip the pages and saw her brother—looking so much like their father—on horseback, standing, sitting, in a group, by himself, amid drawings of others. Then she saw a drawing of Chase, his body poised, waiting, his shoulder-length hair blowing out behind him.

"Chase," she said almost to herself.

"Those two are inseparable—they have been ever since they arrived," Grace said.

"Inseparable—that's how they used to describe me and Jamie." She had to wipe the tears away again, and she noticed the man they called Ty watching her closely. "How long have they been here?"

"A couple of years—three, I think," Grace answered.

"Three. I was with Gray Horse three years ago."

"Gray Horse—I've heard Jamie mention him."

"Yes, he was a friend of our father's. Jamie had been in Gray Horse's village before me, and I guess he never thought to go back."

Grace sat down next to Jenny and took her hand. "He looked for you, I promise. He never gave up, Jamie and Chase both were determined to find you, but you just disappeared." Jenny looked into the soft brown eyes above the scarred cheeks of the woman who sat beside her and saw her sincerity.

"I know. I made myself disappear for a while, actually."

"You two will have a lot of catching up to do, I know."

They were interrupted by the sound of clattering hooves outside. Cat came bursting through the door, her curiosity piqued by the strange horse outside. She pulled up short at the sight of Ty hovering close to a strange woman sitting at the table.

"Cat, guess who this is." Grace said excitedly. The other faces were grinning as Cat narrowed her eyes.

"She looks familiar," Cat said, her manner reserved as she sized up this new threat.

"It's Jenny."

"Jenny? Oh my gosh, you mean Jamie's Jenny?" She was excited and disappointed together, happy that Jenny was found but worried because she was here, and she was beautiful. Cat stalked around the table to get a better look.

"This is Cat Lynch. Her father owns this ranch."

"I ran into Jamie and Chase out in Nebraska. They saved my life," Cat said.

"That's Jamie, all right. Always around when you need him." Jenny started flipping pages again, the images before her now having names and faces attached to them. She stopped when she came to the last drawing. She looked up into a trio of red faces across from her; Ty was conveniently looking out the window. Cat came around and saw the drawing, her green-gold eyes narrowing to slits as she perused the back of Ty's head.

Caleb tentatively reached out for the sketchbook, his dark eyes avoiding Jenny's wide blue ones. She let it go, and he slid the book back across the table as Jake turned and walked away. Zane looked down at the drawing and grinned at Jenny. "You are talented, Caleb. No one can deny that."

"Indeed," Grace said, breaking the awkward silence that followed.

"We'd better get back to work, fellas," Ty said from his place near the window. There was a shuffling of boots and a scraping of chairs as the boys filed out, each of them giving Jenny a second glance, much to Cat's annoyance.

"So, what are your plans?" Cat asked when the men were gone.

"Cat, where are your manners? She just got here."

"No, that's okay," Jenny said. "I realize I'm intruding. If you can tell me where to find Jamie, I'll go on, and after we're together again we can decide."

"Don't be ridiculous." Grace gave Cat a look that immediately made her feel guilty, but Cat had her own interests to protect, and Jenny was much too beautiful to remain here where Ty could see her every day. She hadn't missed the looks Ty, along with the others, had given Jenny. While Jamie was a valuable employee, he wasn't worth her own happiness. "We have no way of knowing where Jamie and Chase are, you'll just have to wait here until they get back. As a matter of fact, I'm sure Jason will want you to stay in the main house while you're visiting. Cat, go find your father and tell him who's here."

Cat rolled her eyes but left to obey, hoping to explain her point of view before Grace had a chance to influence her father.

"I couldn't do that. Maybe there's a place I could camp until Jamie gets back." Jenny was looking down at the table, trying to hide the pain that Cat's obvious dislike had caused her.

Grace sat down next to Jenny and took her hands. "You are most welcome here. I consider this place my home, and the people here are my family. I can't even begin to explain right now what Jason Lynch has done for me, but I can tell you that he saved my life when he brought me here, much as he has done for everyone else on this ranch. When Jamie told us about you, Jason did everything he could to find you: he hired detectives, he posted fliers, he advertised in every newspaper, but we never heard a word. Still, I know that they never gave up. Believe me when I tell you that Jason will be thrilled you are here, just as I am. Even all those dirty-minded cowhands are thrilled, because they have shared Jamie's pain for the past few years."

Jenny had to laugh when Grace mentioned the hands, but Cat's words still hung over her.

Grace put her finger under Jenny's chin and lifted it a notch. "Don't worry about Cat. She's obsessed with Ty, who so far hasn't given her the time of day. She'll come around. She's just worried about the competition, that's all. If it wasn't you it would be someone else, believe me."

"Tell her I'm not interested. I'm not interested in any man."

Grace looked down into Jenny's deep blue eyes and saw the fear hidden there. "You've had a rough time, haven't you?"

"It could have been worse."

"It's hard for a girl out on her own, I know. I lost my daddy when I was seventeen, and I was all alone."

Grace got up to fix Jenny a plate. "Of course, from what I've heard of your family, your loss was greater than mine. My father was a bum."

"Our father was wonderful. Jamie looks just like him."

"And your mother? Do you look like her?"

"No. My mother was beautiful, like an angel. I don't look anything like her."

Grace looked down at the perfectly oval face, the straight nose dusted with freckles from the sun, the clear golden skin, the wide blue eyes that could drown a man in their depths, the golden hair that waved and curled down around her shoulders. The woman sitting before her was tall, with long legs, a flat stomach and ample curves. And she had no idea that she was beautiful. Grace's heart went out to her, but she fought the impulse to comfort the girl. Jenny had the look of a skittish colt that would run at the first sign of trouble, and Grace hoped that Jamie would return soon, before Cat had a chance to run her off.

"What was Jamie like when he was young?" Grace hoped that getting her to talk would help relax her.

Jenny had to gather herself to answer the question. It had been so long since they had been children, running wild across the plains without a care in the world, knowing that their parents would be there to take care of them. What had Jamie been like as a child?

"He was more serious than I. I was pretty wild, now that I think about it." Grace sat down, anxious to hear. "He was steady, and I was impetuous. I guess that's the best way to describe us, but he had a great sense of humor, and always had us laughing at something."

"He still does." The comment shocked Jenny as she realized that Jamie might have changed in the five years since she had last seen him. Her thoughts scattered as she began to turn the five years back.

Seeing a wild look come into Jenny's great blue eyes, Grace grabbed her arm. "What else?"

"He loved to read aloud. He would read to us every night. He could make the stories come alive. I would rather listen to him read than read myself. I will never forget when he read *The Arabian Nights*, but that was later, when we were at the mission."

"That's where you met Chase?"

"Yes, Chase came right before I was. . . ." Jenny's words trailed off as she remembered that fateful day when Thad Miller had dragged her away. "I guess he's all right, then? He was unconscious the last time I saw him, he was trying to help me."

"He's fine. You know he's been with Jamie ever since you were taken. They are like brothers. Chase even goes by the last name of Duncan now."

"Really? That's strange, but maybe not. Jamie was always practical. He's the one who started calling him Chase instead of Chase the Wind."

"How did you know to come here?" Grace suddenly asked as she recalled how isolated the ranch was.

"I've been searching for years. But yesterday I overheard a man

257

talking about someone that could make a horse dance, and his description of the man fit Jamie. I knew it had to be him. There's not many who look like him."

"There's not many who can work a horse like him."

"My father was like that, and his father before him. My mother called it the Duncan magic. Oh my gosh, Storm! Jamie doesn't know I have our father's horse. Is there someplace I can put him?"

The sound of riders approaching stopped Grace's answer. They heard the long stride of boots on the porch, and Jason Lynch burst through the door. All the color drained from his bronzed face at the sight of the girl standing before him.

"My God—Jenny?" he asked.

"Yes." Jenny looked at Grace, who was looking at Jason quizzically. He put his hands up to rub his eyes and looked at her again. His face looked shocked, but he regained his composure.

"I am so glad to finally meet you." He extended his hand and Jenny gave him hers, unsure of what she was supposed to do. Cat was behind him, looking unhappy, and Grace knew that her father had set her back on her heels. "Jamie rode out this morning with Chase to look for strays. There's no telling when he'll be back. You must stay with us at the main house."

"I really—"

"No, I insist. Cat, help her get her things, and I'll make sure that Bill takes care of your horse." Jason Lynch was a man accustomed to having his orders obeyed, and Jenny didn't have the energy to fight him.

"I don't have much," was all she could say, and she went out to get her saddlebags off Storm. An older man appeared and took the horse up to the barn.

"That's a fine-looking animal," Jason commented as Storm was led away.

"He belonged to our father."

Jason watched as the gray walked away, his neck still proudly arched, his tail high behind him as he stepped lightly after the man. Behind them was the sound of bawling cattle where the boys were hard at work cutting the herd. Jason led Jenny up the hill to the main house. She was nearly overwhelmed by the luxuriousness of it when Jason opened the door and she stepped into the cool interior onto finely polished wood floors. Jason had to take her arm and lead her into the hallway, where a white-trimmed staircase led to the second floor.

"I built it for Cat's mother, but she didn't live long enough to enjoy it," Jason explained, almost apologizing for the grandeur. "I used to live in a cabin down in the valley when it was just me, but that was a long time ago." His mind seemed to drift off with the words.

"It's lovely," Jenny murmured as she looked around at the rich furnishings.

"I hardly notice it," Jason admitted.

"Daddy pays more attention to the cows than to his chairs," Cat added.

"Those cows pay your bills," Jason said sternly. Cat just smiled sweetly and flopped into a chair. "You'll have your choice of several rooms," he said as he started up the staircase. "We have a house-keeper, Agnes. If you let her know what you need, she'll take care of you."

"I really don't need anything," Jenny said as she followed Jason up the steps. She felt dirty and out of place amidst this luxury, and she longed to take Storm and leave. Jason led her to a bedroom with a wide high bed and a window that overlooked the valley. Jenny was overwhelmed as she turned around, not knowing what to do next.

"I can have Agnes fix you a bath if you like," Jason suggested.

"No, really, I'm fine."

"Dinner is around six."

"Thank you."

Jason stood, just looking at her, which made Jenny feel more nervous. He finally turned and left, reminding her to make herself at home.

Jenny dropped her bag and went to the window, taking in the many buildings below. She recognized the cabin where she had met Grace and the boys; next to that must be the bunkhouse. There were a few barns and smaller outbuildings that held a forge and tack, and beyond a small smokehouse. There were several corrals as well as the huge pen where the cattle were being separated into groups by the cowboys she had met earlier. She saw Cat going back down the hill, no doubt to protect her interest in Ty. Jenny shook her head as she dismissed the jealousy the young woman had shown. The last thing Jenny wanted was a relationship with a man—any man.

Her visual tour of the valley over, she turned to investigate the room she was in. There was a washstand, a wingback chair covered with a soft rose fabric, a huge wardrobe that was empty when she opened the doors. A flash caught her eye as she was about to shut the doors, and she realized there was a mirror attached to the inside. She stared at the reflection before her. Deep, wide blue eyes looked back at her, full of fear. Her knees trembled as she took inventory of what she saw.

"Jamie, will you recognize me?" she asked staring at the reflection. Faces flashed before her: Thad Miller, the man who had taken her from the orphanage, his wife Millie, then Wade Bishop, the man who had found her on the trail after her escape from the Millers. They were the faces of the people who had used her before she had learned self-preservation. Others were the faces of the ones who had been kind, but there weren't many of those, her wall of reserve had kept out many who would have helped her. "Jamie, will you still love me?" she asked. There was no answer.

Jenny went down to dinner promptly at six, and immediately felt embarrassed to still be wearing the clothes she had arrived in when she saw Cat in a lovely dress. Jenny apologized for her attire, but it was all she had. Jason did his best to make her feel comfortable, and even Cat could find no fault with her manners, for which Jenny said a thanksgiving prayer to her mother, who had always insisted that they learn proper etiquette. Grace came up after she was done feeding the hands and contributed to the polite conversation in the salon after dinner. Jenny excused herself early and made her way to her room, the strain wearing her out. It had been a long time since she had tried to make conversation, and she wasn't sure enough of herself or the company to keep it up for long. When she went to her room, she opened the window, wanting the chill of the spring evening to make the bed more warm and inviting. She heard the sound of the back door opening below and heard Jason and Grace on the porch off the kitchen.

"Poor thing, she's had it rough," Grace commented.

"I know, and Cat is determined not to make it any easier for her. I wanted to wring her neck when she came down all dressed up, knowing Jenny didn't have a stitch with her."

"Maybe we should get her some things."

"I don't think she'd accept them," Jason said. "She's got a lot of pride—that much is obvious. Has she said anything to you about what she's been doing or where she's been?"

"No, just that she was trying to find Jamie. What do you think he'll do, now that she's here?"

"I don't know. I hope he'll stay on, but a lot of it depends on her, I guess, and if Jamie goes, that means Chase will go, too. I know that much." They stepped off the porch and Jenny leaned back so they wouldn't see her spying on them. "They'll be back soon I guess, and everything will work itself out."

"There's something I wanted to ask you, Jason, about Jenny,"

"What is it?"

"When you first saw her, it was like you knew her. Your face went white as if you were in shock. Have you seen her before?"

"No, but when I first saw her, I thought she was someone else, someone I knew a long time ago." Silence followed as Grace looked up into his eyes, but the darkness kept the secret hidden, and she knew Jason well enough not to pry.

"Why don't you let her spend her time with me, instead of sitting in this big old house waiting around?"

"I'll suggest that to her in the morning."

Jenny saw Grace take off down the hill towards her cabin. Jason stood and watched her go before he turned into the house. Jenny watched as the lights went out in the bunkhouse, then at Grace's, then heard the sounds of the main house settling for the night. The moon was full and its light shone over the hills beyond, giving them a silver glow before they faded into the dark purple of the mountains that rose up behind. She wondered which of the canyons was sheltering Jamie and Chase for the night, and envied the peace that being here had evidently given them. Grace had said they were like a family, and Jenny had seen for herself the genuine concern that Jason had for his employees.

As she climbed into the big bed, she began to wonder what they would do now. Finding Jamie had been a priority for so long that she had not given any thought to what would happen once they were together. It had never occurred to her that he might have a life without her, but obviously he did, and she had no clue where she was to fit in. Jenny finally fell asleep, feeling very alone and lost in the big, comfortable bed.

The next morning she awoke to the sounds of cattle bawling in the valley below. She went to the window, trailing the sheet that she had wrapped around her nude body. The hands were busy at work cutting the herd, and she could see Cat watching it all from atop the high fence of the pen. She noticed that Jason was there also, working alongside the rest of them, and the sight increased her respect for the man. She hastily dressed, embarrassed that she had slept so late, and made the bed, leaving the room much the way she had found it. She went down the back stairs to the kitchen, intending to head straight to Grace's cabin, but Agnes stopped her and insisted that she eat the breakfast she had kept warm for her.

After breakfast, Jenny found Grace busy working on lunch for the boys, who had been hard at work since sunup. Grace gave her a quick smile and instructed her to start peeling potatoes, hoping to keep her busy while they waited for Jamie. Jenny gratefully attacked the pile before her, and before she realized it she was chattering away, Grace's easy manner overcoming her reserve.

The sound of stomping boots interrupted their conversation, and the cowboys came in, looking for lunch. They gathered around the table, Jason and Cat joining them, and Jenny helped to serve, enjoying the flow of conversation, most of it either started by Zane or directed at him. He gave Jenny a wounded look, trying to gain her sympathy when Ty shot him down, but she just laughed with the rest of them, then was surprised at how easily it had come. When lunch was over, Jason asked if he could get a closer look at Storm, and she went with him to the stable, beginning to feel comfortable in his presence.

They turned the gray out into a small corral and he began to trot around, his tail waving like a flag around him as he inspected his new domain. There were some mares in another pen, and Storm stood with his head high as he looked them over, whinnying deep in his throat.

"How old is he?" Jason asked. Jenny was sitting on the fence rail and he was leaning beside her, admiring the stallion's lines.

"I think around twenty-five. Our father raised him from a colt and used him as stud to start our ranch. Storm ran off the night my parents were killed. He ran wild until I found him, or rather he found me, out on the plains. I probably would be dead now if it weren't for him." Jason raised his eyebrows in surprise at Jenny's comment, then watched in amazement as she whistled "Good King

262

Wenceslas" and the horse came to her, putting his head in her lap with a contented sigh. "I think he misses my father," she said as she rubbed under the dark forelock.

Jason reached out and stroked the finely arched neck. "Do you mind if we turn him out with some mares?"

"No, go ahead. I'm sure he'd love it." Jenny grinned as Storm began to swing his head up and down as if agreeing with her. Jason laughed, glad to see that she was something like Jamie.

"I've had my eye on a mare I want to buy. I've been waiting for a chance to send Jamie down to look at her," Jason said as they walked back to Grace's. "I think she and Storm could have some fine foals, given a chance."

"I'd love to see that," Jenny said, surprising herself again at making a commitment. Jason left her at the cabin where Grace had just finished the dishes. Jenny immediately felt guilty about leaving her with the mess, but Grace said she was used to it and began to sweeping the floor. There was a pile of clothing stacked in the corner, and something in it caught Jenny's attention. She pulled a shirt out of the stack and held it up. It was well worn and had a tear in the side.

"That belongs to Chase," Grace said. "It needs mending, and as you can see, the pile gets ahead of me."

"I made it for Jamie a long time ago," Jenny said as she held it to her breast.

Grace came over and took the shirt, admiring the fine stitches. "It's a fine shirt, and I know the only reason Jamie gave it up is because he outgrew it."

"He's even bigger now?"

"He's pretty big." Grace smiled at the thought of him.

Jenny shook her head as she tried to envision what he must be like now. "Would you mind if I worked on the mending?" she asked as Grace refolded the shirt. "That is the one thing I know I can do best."

"Honey, you just help yourself," Grace said as she handed her the sewing basket. Jenny carried the basket and clothing outside to the porch swing and began mending, content to have work to keep her busy, and knowing she was giving something back to the people who were being so generous to her.

The next few days passed in much the same way. Jenny slept in the big house but spent her days with Grace, helping her with the meals and the laundry, then working on the mending. When she had worked her way through the stack, Grace brought out a length of soft blue calico and asked Jenny's advice on making a dress out of it. They went through some patterns, and Grace selected the one that Jenny kept going back to. She soon had Jenny cutting away, thinking she was making the dress for Grace, who intended it to be for Jenny. They were similar in build, with Grace a bit fuller in the bust, but Jenny needed extra length, which Grace made sure she provided for when she cut out the skirt. Jason had conspired with her to get the fabric, making a special trip to town to pick it out, and choosing a shade that matched the blue of Jenny's eyes.

The boys became accustomed to seeing Jenny sitting in the swing, sewing away, and she soon settled into the routine of the ranch, each day bringing her closer to her reunion with Jamie.

Sunday soon came, and with it rain and a day of rest for the hands. Jason and Cat went to church, along with Ty and Caleb. Grace stayed behind, self-conscious of her scars when she went out in public. Zane and Jake chose to spend the day sleeping after spending Saturday evening at the saloon in town. Jenny became sleepy as she sewed in the cabin with Grace and decided to take the laundry over to the bunkhouse, hoping the quick dash through the rain would wake her up.

Zane and Jake were lying in their bunks, involved in a never-ending argument about something, when she came in. It was her first time in the bunkhouse, and she was amazed at how cozy it was, with its pot-bellied stove and beds stacked one above the other. One in particular drew her attention, it was a top bunk, with an extension on the end.

"His feet were always sticking out, so we put him up top and added on," Zane explained.

Jenny climbed up and looked at the blanket, which had been pieced at the bottom to give her tall brother extra coverage. She lay down on the bunk, surrounding herself with the scent of her brother, and her mind wandered back to the days of sharing the loft at home, and their whispered conversations after they'd been tucked in for the night. The rain was pounding on the roof overhead and she soon drifted off to sleep. She rolled over facing the wall, and her braid hung over the side of the bunk, shining brightly in the dim light that came in from the window.

Caleb noticed her when he came in from church and he took

out his sketchpad, his imagination transforming her surroundings to something more luxurious, as Zane added his own ideas in Caleb's ear. Ty looked on in disgust as he read in his bunk, and Jake went back to his own slumber.

Chapter Twenty-one

The rain was pouring off their slickers as Jamie and Chase herded the last of the strays into the pen. They had been struggling to make it home before the rain came, but a rock slide had turned them around, causing them to lose time. They stabled their horses and slopped through the deserted yard, knowing everyone else was warm and dry. They were both starved, so they went to Grace's cabin first, hoping to find a bite to tide them over until dinner was ready. Grace met them at the door with a dazzling smile.

"Where have you been?" she asked as they stood dripping on the porch.

"Doing our job, and now we're hungry. Let us in, Grace," Jamie begged. His hair was soaking and rivers were running down his neck.

"Oh, no, you are not coming in here until you get out of those wet clothes."

"Grace, we are starved. Give us a biscuit or something," Chase begged.

Grace shook her head, afraid to say anything more. Jamie looked at her as if she had lost her mind, but she just slammed the door in their faces. They stood looking at the closed portal in shock, then turned to go to the bunkhouse. Grace cracked the door when they had got off the porch, then quietly followed, pulling a shawl over her head to protect herself from the rain. Zane pulled open the door to the bunkhouse before they even got to the porch and put his finger over his mouth to hush Jamie and Chase's grumbling that had started as soon as they stepped off Grace's porch.

"Has everyone around here lost their minds?" Jamie whispered angrily at Zane as he pulled off his slicker. The rest of the boys were looking at him with big grins on their faces, and Jamie turned to Chase, who was looking at Jamie's bunk.

A golden braid was dangling over the edge of the bunk, and above it was a gracefully curved back, and long, lean legs. Jamie took a step towards the bunk, his eyes wide and staring. Chase caught the eyes of the boys, who all nodded, and he looked toward the bunk in eager anticipation.

Jamie reached out and took the braid in his hand, rubbing the silken strands between his fingers before he gave it a gentle tug. A hand reached back to grab the braid, and he jerked on it harder, pulling the head around so that he was looking into a pair of deep blue eyes. Recognition hit her like a shot, and Jenny propelled herself out of the bunk, launching herself into Jamie's arms with such force that they hit the floor with a crash, becoming a tangled pile of long leg and arms and flying hair. Grace came through the door and looked on in tearful joy as the rest of the boys laughed at the whirling mass before them.

Jenny and Jamie were both talking at once as they untangled themselves and stood. Both were wiping tears away, from themselves and each other. "When?" one said, "Where?" the other asked, and both of them were saying, "I looked for you."

"Both of you, sit down," Grace finally said as the confusion went on. They looked at her; then Jamie led Jenny to the table and they sat, still holding on to each other's hands. "Everyone else, out!" Grace commanded, and the boys filed out, slapping Jamie on the back, wanting to share in his joy.

"Chase, wait," Jamie said as Chase started out the door.

"No, I'll catch you later." Jenny looked up into Chase's dark eyes and saw that they were shining as if he, too, had been crying. His face held a sweet smile as he looked at her. That last morning they had been together, when she had spun around the room in joy, flashed through her mind.

"Chase, thank you," she said softly.

"For what?"

"Being there for Jamie."

Jamie grinned at his friend.

"It wasn't easy, believe me." Chase grinned back and left.

"Oh, Jamie, you look just like Dad," Jenny cried when they were alone.

Jamie smoothed back the wild hairs that had escaped her braid. "And you are so beautiful."

"I am?"

"Jenny where did you go? We followed your trail up into the mountains. We found a burned-out wagon and the bodies of the folks that took you, but there was no sign of you. I was so afraid you were dead, too."

"The Millers—they're dead?"

"Yes, we found them in Indian territory. Looked like they'd been attacked. I didn't know where to look after that."

"I was in Texas."

"Texas! How in the world did you get to Texas?"

"I was picked up by a fellow who thought I'd make a nice addition to his whorehouse," Jenny explained with a hard look in her eye. "I didn't hang around there too long, I can tell you. Once I escaped, I started making my way back to St. Jo."

"If only I had gone back to St. Jo," Jamie said. "But when the trail turned cold, we kept looking further west."

"There is no way you could have known, and you still might have missed me. I don't know how long I was wandering before Storm found me."

"Storm?"

"Yes, Storm found me, out on the plains. I'd been shot—it's a long story—and I'd lost a lot of blood. I got on his back, and he took me to Gray Horse."

"Chase and I went to him, too, but that was at the beginning of our search." He put his arm around her. "God, I hate to think what you've been through just to survive. It isn't easy, being on your own, and I know it had to be harder for you than for Chase and me because you're a woman."

"That's why I cut my hair, so I could pass as a boy. It seems every man I came across wanted to make me into a whore."

"But they didn't."

"No, I managed to survive intact, if that's what you mean."

"That's not what I mean, and you know it. I knew you would find a way to get away from the Millers, but I never dreamed that someone else would be waiting there to snatch you up."

"You and Chase have been together the entire time?"

Jamie showed her the faint scar across his palm. "We're blood brothers. He is the one who kept me going; he knew we were going to see you again when I thought you were dead. He never gave up on you, and he was always there for me. I don't know what I would have done without him."

"I'm glad he was there for you."

"You should tell him that."

"I will." The sound of Jamie's stomach growling brought them back to the present.

"I am starving," he said as he rubbed the sound away.

"I'm glad to see that hasn't changed any."

He grinned at her and shoved his hair back off his forehead.

"Let's go get something to eat, if there's anything left over there." He stood up and held out his hand. Jenny stood, and looked up, grinning. She had always been a few inches shorter than he, but now the difference was greater.

"I don't think I can wear your hand-me-downs anymore."

"I gave them all to Chase anyway. By the way, what happened to Storm?"

"Go out to the stable and see for yourself."

"He's here?"

"Yep, and Jason already wants to use him for stud." Jamie's face nearly split as he grinned at that prospect, and the two of them made their way to Grace's cabin.

Several sets of curious, smiling faces greeted them, and Chase moved down so Jamie could take his customary place next to him on the bench. Jamie made room for Jenny to slide between them, and she suddenly felt very safe with the two sets of broad shoulders on either side of her. She gave Chase a quick glance, then looked back when she saw that his hair was the same length as hers.

"You've changed a bit since the last time I saw you," she said as his dark eyes caught her look.

"You have become more beautiful."

Jenny blushed at the softly spoken words.

Grace hastily set a heaping plate before Jamie, who dug in with •

his usual gusto, and Jenny joined him, until the questions from the others became more than they could handle while eating.

"Will you guys let me eat in peace!" Jamie finally exclaimed.

"Yeah, we know better than to get between you and food," Zane said.

"Everyone run along and leave these two alone," Grace commanded, and chairs began to scrape the floor as the gang dispersed to their favorite Sunday afternoon pursuits. The rain had finally stopped, and a glimmer of sun was breaking through the clouds as they went outside. Jenny got up to follow Chase out to the porch.

Chase was standing with his arm wrapped around the corner post, leaning out to see what the skies had in store for the rest of the day. He had wanted to take a long nap, but the excitement of Jenny's return had put an end to that. He knew he could use a bath, and had decided to walk to the shed they used for a bathhouse when he heard Jenny call his name.

"I never forgot what you did for me the day the Millers took me away."

Chase leaned back against the post as Jenny sat down in the nearby swing. She had changed since he had last seen her. The girl she had been was gone, replaced by a woman who held all the grace that the girl had promised. She was long and lean, her limbs straight and strong, but her eyes held a hint of sadness that was buried deeper now than when she was fifteen. Chase remembered the morning when she had danced around the room with joy, until she was so dizzy that she had fallen against the bed, drunk with happiness. He had tried to save her, had come after the two men who were taking her away from the brother she loved, but his broken leg and youthful inexperience had failed him.

"I should have killed them," he said, his dark eyes flashing as he remember her anguished cries and struggles.

Jenny shivered when she saw the look in his eyes, and did not doubt that if it happened again, he would. "You did all you could," she said simply, her deep blue eyes looking up at him, assuring him that she did not blame him.

"It wasn't enough." He shrugged, as if dismissing his efforts as feeble at best, then turned to look once more at the sky. "Look, there's a rainbow." He pointed towards the east.

Jenny walked over to stand next to him and saw the arc of color coming down into the hills beyond. "They say there's a pot of gold at the end."

"There's treasure there, but no gold."

"Then what is it?'

"Land—the most beautiful land you've ever seen. Crystal lakes set in green valleys, with mountains rising up around them. It almost takes your breath away." Chase spoke passionately, and his passion made Jenny want to go there.

"I can show it to you." It was almost as if he read her mind, and she gazed up into his dark eyes, seeing a longing there that she had never seen before.

"Hey, Jenny, want to see the new foal?" Zane called from the barn, waving to get her attention. Chase stepped off the porch when she turned to wave back.

"Let me tell Jamie where I'm going," she called back as she watched Chase walk away. Jenny opened the door to Grace's cabin and stopped dead in her tracks. She backed out, softly closing the door as her cheeks flushed a dark pink.

There was no mistaking the kiss that Jamie was giving Grace, and the older woman was sitting in his lap as if he had pulled her off her feet. They were lovers—they had to be; there was nothing casual about what she had just seen. Jenny felt her stomach heave as she walked towards Zane, who was waiting for her with a cocky grin on his face.

"You look like you've just seen a ghost," he said as she came into the barn.

"Just too much excitement," she answered. Zane led her to a stall where a newborn foal stood on wobbly legs as his mother nuzzled him. By the time Jamie caught up with her, Jenny was in the stall with her arms around the foal.

"I wondered where you ran off to."

"Oh, don't worry about Jenny." Zane grinned. "We'll take care of her."

"That's what I'm afraid of."

Zane threw up his arms as if to ward off a blow, but Jamie ignored him and went down the row of stalls until he came to Storm. Jamie stood at the stall door, tears welling in his eyes as he looked at the magnificent animal that had belonged to his father. Jenny walked up behind him as he began to whistle "Good King Wenceslas." Storm came to him, sucking in air as he drank in the

271

scent of Jamie, who was so like his father. Jamie rubbed the noble forehead and gazed into the dark eyes of the horse, whispering long-forgotten secrets into ears that stood at attention, catching his every word.

"I can't believe you found him."

"Like I said, he found me. It was as if he was done with his wild ways and wanted to come back home, but he didn't know where home was."

"I know how you felt, believe me," Jamie murmured into the pricked ear. "Now I need to show you something," he said to his sister.

Jenny looked up at the wide blue eyes that held many secrets now, the price they had paid for growing up apart from each other. She was still reeling from her discovery of the relationship between Jamie and Grace, and wasn't sure how to act, but he was her brother, so she let him take her hand and lead her back to the bunkhouse.

Jake was napping again while Caleb and Ty were sitting at the table, drawing and reading, each pursing his favorite pastime. Jamie made a production of sitting Jenny down on the lower bunk while he reached beneath and pulled out a small trunk. He opened the lid and took out a cloth-wrapped package. Jenny's eyes opened wide when he laid their mother's angel box in her lap.

"Oh, Jamie, I thought it was gone forever!" Jenny exclaimed as she reverently ran her fingers over the carving of the angel. She slowly opened the lid, afraid to look, sure the contents would be gone, but they were all there as she remembered, with one addition, a drawing of Jenny, with the offer of a cash reward for anyone knowing her whereabouts.

"I took care of the box for you. Now you need to take it back." Jamie was on his knees beside her, a soft smile on his usually animated face. Jenny hugged the box to her breast, the memories of her mother strong as she felt the smooth surface of the wood.

"Do you remember Momma's quilt?" Jenny asked as the image of her parents' bed came into her mind.

"Yes, I remember. I wish we had it."

"So do I."

Their reminiscing was interrupted when Chase came in, dressed in a clean pair of pants, his hair dripping from the bath he had just had. Jenny jumped up from his bunk as he reached underneath to pull a clean shirt from his box of clothing. It happened to be the one Jenny had mended, and he looked at it in surprise as he pulled it on.

"I see Grace finally got to the mending," Chase commented as he buttoned it up over the wide expanse of his smooth chest.

"Actually, Jenny has been doing the mending," Ty said, looking up from his book. Jenny gave him a dazzling smile, and he read the same line three times before he was able to move on.

"You must be tired, too," Jenny said to her brother as Chase stretched out on his bunk and closed his eyes.

"I could use a bath." Jamie ran his hand through his hair, and instead of flopping over, the mass stuck straight up. Jenny laughed, a light sound in the room that drew everyone's attention; she reached up to pat the stray hairs down. "I'll let you get cleaned up."

"I'll catch up with you in a bit."

They walked out together, Jenny still holding on to the box. She hesitated when she walked by Grace's cabin after Jamie went off to the bathhouse. She wasn't ready to deal with the affair between the two of them, so she went on up to the house. She knew that Jason and Cat had missed the reunion and expected them to be pleased to hear about it.

Jamie joined them after he had cleaned up, and the four of them sat on the wide front porch, rocking and talking into the evening hours. Jason and Jamie talked of the ranch, and Jenny marveled at the weight Jason gave to Jamie's opinion. She felt pride in her brother growing inside her as the gray head leaned close to the russet one while they talked about Storm and the potential for breeding him. Cat eventually wandered off, feeling that she had punished Ty enough for one day, and went down to see what was brewing in the bunkhouse. Soon enough the three on the porch were yawning, and since the next morning was the start of a work week, they said their good nights.

Jenny went straight up to her room and to the window, where she could watch her brother walk down the gentle slope to the bunkhouse in the moonlight. He passed Cat, who was on her way up, and said something to her, causing her to swing at him playfully. Jenny smiled to herself, remembering the easy way Jamie always had with people. When he got to the bottom of the hill, he stepped up on the porch to Grace's cabin, which was dark except for a light in the side window. Jenny waited, and never saw him come out the other side. Eventually the light went out, and she realized that he was not coming out, that he had sought the company of Grace, no doubt sharing with her the secrets he used to share with her when they were children.

"He's twenty years old, Jenny. What did you expect, that he was a monk?" Jenny grumbled to herself as she stripped off the only clothes she owned and slid beneath the smooth sheets of the big bed. "Just because you've avoided men doesn't mean that he feels the same about women," she went on. A mental picture filled her mind, of her brother's long body entwined with Grace's generous curves, of her hair spread in wild abandon, of Jamie's hair falling over his face as they made love. "Stop it!" She spat the words out to get control of her imagination. "You're acting jealous, and it's ridiculous." Jenny sat up in bed and turned the lamp up. The earlier rain had brought a warm westerly breeze that gently caressed the curtains at the window. Jenny flung the covers back and went to the wardrobe, opening the door so she could look in the mirror.

She stood before the mirror, taking time to study her body in the dim light of the lamp. The darkness softened her figure until she appeared luminous in the wavy glass. She could find no fault with what she saw. She had seen the way the boys in the bunkhouse looked at her, had seen the sketches that Caleb had made, and realized that perhaps she was beautiful, as they said. She lifted the waves of golden hair up, turned her neck gracefully to examine the angles, and then dropped the mass with a sigh. "Oh, Momma, am I pretty? Will a man ever love me, instead of wanting to use me for profit, or beat me because I remind him of someone else?" She looked in the mirror again and summoned Cat's image to mind, her petite frame, her slanted eyes with the golden glow, the glorious curls that tumbled around her heart-shaped face. Then there was Grace, who seemed to be the image of her name, refined and elegant even with her arms buried in bread dough, her brown eyes wise and serene, her curves generous enough to make any man want her, even with her scars.

"The scars," Jenny said in surprise. "That's what brought them together." That realization brought sudden peace to the turmoil that Jenny had experienced since that afternoon. She hadn't even thought about Jamie's scars—they were so much a part of him—but they must be a burden to him, always obvious to those who saw him for the first time, and it was probably the same for Grace.

Jenny crawled back into the big bed again, feeling relaxed for the first time in years. She had found her brother, he was well and happy, and whatever happened next, they would be together. Maybe she could even find someone to love her. Her mind settled on Ty, whose glances she had noticed since she had arrived. She closed her eyes and summoned up an image of sandy hair and blue eyes set in a serious, handsome face. "Maybe Cat should be worried, after all," she said to herself as she fell asleep.

The warm breeze that danced through the open window gently caressed the golden wisps of hair that curled around a perfectly oval face. Like the touch of a lover's hand, the air moved over the long expanse of well-toned leg that had found its way out from under the sheets. It brought forth a sigh from full lips that longed for more, just one more kiss, but the wind teased and was gone. In the dream, however, the lover remained, running sure, strong hands over a body brimming with desire, surrounding the two of them with dark hair that tickled and teased at the bare breasts below, mingling with the golden strands until the two bodies were joined together in a dance that had been going on since the beginning of time.

Jenny woke with a start, kicking the clinging sheets away from her tingling skin. She felt an ache inside, every nerve was on fire from the dream which had stopped just short of consummation. She had not been able to see the face of her lover, but she could still feel his presence in every part of her. The bed felt suffocating, so she walked to the window to let the breeze dry her sweaty skin and calm her frazzled nerves. The valley below was quiet; there was nothing to be heard but the creatures of the night singing their songs in full chorus, secure in the darkness. Jenny knelt before the window and laid her head on the sill, not anxious to return to the comfort of the big bed and the demons in her dreams.

A slight movement caught her eye and in the shadows below she could see someone standing on the porch of the bunkhouse, leaning against the corner column, facing up towards the main house. A hand went up and smoothed back hair that was lost in the shadows, and the way the hand trailed down over the shoulder, she knew it had to be Chase, even though Jake wore his hair long also. She briefly wondered what was keeping him up late, knowing he must be exhausted from his time on the trail, and she attributed his sleeplessness to the heat. Something caught his attention, and Jamie appeared in the opening between Grace's cabin and the bunkhouse. She could see Jamie talking to Chase, then watched as Jamie went inside the bunkhouse. The next thing she knew, there was the sound of a huge crash, followed by Jamie's angry voice.

"Damn it, Caleb, that's my sister you're drawing pictures of!" There was another crash, as if a mad scramble was taking place, and Zane and Caleb came flying out into the yard, followed by the irate Jamie. Jenny saw Chase hanging on to the column to keep from falling down laughing.

"Don't pretend to be innocent, Zane. You might not be able to draw, but your hand was in on this, too."

Jenny heard Zane's pleas of innocence and smiled to herself, feeling that her modesty had been protected. Caleb and Zane made their way sleepily to the barn, and the light went out in the bunkhouse. Chase remained on the porch, looking up towards the main house.

Jenny was stiff and sore the next morning when she finally woke up. She had fallen asleep at the window, and a cramp in her neck finally drove her to her bed, where she remained far longer than usual. The restless night combined with the excitement of the day before had drained her, leaving her exhausted when she rose and dressed in her usual uniform. The house was empty when she went down, so she made her way to the corral, where the cowboys had congregated.

Everyone was gathered around or sitting on fence rails as they watched Jamie work a horse. The horse stood alert in the center of the corral, his ears pricked, his nostrils quivering, waiting in silent anticipation for the commands that were unknown to everyone but the horse and rider. Jenny detected a slight tightening of the long muscles in Jamie's lean thigh that would send the horse whirling in one direction or another. Jamie put the horse through a series of exercises that left the watchers brimming with awe and excitement, but to Jenny it was just like watching her father. He had used the tricks and techniques that had been handed down to him, and he had passed them on to his own eager pupils, Jamie and Jenny. Jamie grinned at her when he concluded the display, knowing that she understood his secret.

"You do it," he said to her as he rode the horse over to the rail she was sitting on.

"It's been a while."

"This horse practically reads my mind. Go ahead, give it a try," he urged her as he dismounted.

Jenny slid her leg over the saddle from the rail and lightly took up the reins, stationing the horse in the middle of the corral. She whirled him through his paces, and the cowboys applauded, amazed to find that the sister was as good as the brother. Jenny smiled shyly at the applause, embarrassed by all the whistling and shouting that Zane was directing her way. She saw Chase out of the corner of her eye as he watched her with a slight smile on his face.

When she had finished her paces, Jason walked to her and took a rein as he patted the horse.

"I think it's time I added you to the payroll," he said as Jenny dismounted.

"What?"

"I want you to work for me. I've seen for myself what you can do."

Jenny looked over at Jamie, who was grinning at her encouragingly. A thousand thoughts poured into her head, the foremost of which was whether she really wanted to stay. Everyone seemed to be waiting for her answer. "What exactly do you want me to do?" she asked Jason.

"Whatever you do best," he answered, "and whatever you feel best about doing."

No help there, she thought to herself as she looked up into his kind eyes. Jenny took a deep breath. "Okay," she said and extended her hand to Jason, who took it into his own strong grip. A collective sign of relief went up, but Jenny wasn't sure if it was because she was staying or because Jamie wasn't leaving. She went over to the rail, not sure of what to do next.

"Zane, go help Jenny pick out a mount. We need to get these yearlings out to the summer pasture." Jason, as usual, was in control.

Jenny followed Zane to the pen behind the stable, where several fine horses were milling about. Jenny pointed out a tall bay with white stockings and a long blaze, and Zane smiled in approval as he threw a rope over the horse. They led him into the stable, and

Zane followed Jenny into the tack room, where her rig was stored.

Jenny was gathering her things when Zane came up behind her. She felt awkward at his closeness, and was unable to turn in the narrow space with her arms full of saddle. She stood for a moment, and Zane began to massage her upper arms.

"What are you doing?" she asked, her voice filled with apprehension.

"Relax," he said soothingly, as if she were a skittish colt. He reached around her, took the saddle out of her hands and dropped it, leaving his arms locked around her. Jenny turned, intending to shove him away, but before she had a chance, his mouth moved down on hers, grinding her lips in a kiss. His arms were locked behind her, and she tried to pull hers up to get leverage, but he was holding her too tight. She went limp in his arms, and he relaxed his hold, moving one arm down into the arch of her back to bend her backwards. "Oh, Jenny," he whispered as his lips began to move down her neck. Her knee came up, and with all her might she brought it up into the delicate region between his legs.

Zane groaned deep in his throat and doubled over, which brought his face into just the right range for a ringing slap to the ears. He fell over into a rack of saddles and became entangled in the stirrups and girths. "What did you do that for?"

"What did I do that for?" Jenny spat out despite the merriment that had threatened to consume her at Zane's predicament. "What gives you the right to kiss me like that?"

"Oh, come on. I was just trying to get my dibs in first, that's all."

"Dibs? On me?"

"Yes, dibs. I wanted to get you before anyone else had a chance to."

"Get me for what?"

"To be my girl, that's all. Oh, come on, Jenny, don't pretend you didn't like it." He was standing now, smiling at her, trying to look guilty but failing miserably.

"I'm not pretending at all." Jenny made a great show of wiping her mouth off.

Zane saw that his attempt had failed and decided to try another approach. "You're not going to tell Jamie about this, are you? Or anyone else. I mean, after all, I have my reputation to protect, and it wouldn't do me any good for everyone to know how you shot me down, and, er, injured my, er, privates." He made a production of rubbing the offended area. "I would hate to have to get rough with Jamie, you know." His hazel eyes sparkled with a mischievous glint, and his smile was so charming that Jenny thought he probably had a lot of success with women. He was actually doing a pretty good job of charming her, now that she thought about it. The idea of him getting rough with Jamie was actually pretty funny, since he was only a few inches taller than she was, and a little on the skinny side compared to Jamie and Chase.

"No, I won't tell anyone, provided it doesn't happen again," she finally agreed, making sure she kept her grin from showing. "Now see if you can find my rig in all this mess." She walked out, leaving him shaking his head.

"Geez, Zane, why are you walkin' so funny?" Jake asked when he rejoined the cowboys.

"What makes you think I'm walkin' funny?" Zane retorted as he unhitched his horse from the rail.

Jenny moved her mount to where Jamie was waiting for her, and he flashed his grin when he saw the cocky set of her hat.

"Something happen that I need to know about?" he asked, making sure no one else could hear.

"Nope."

Behind her, Chase began to laugh as he saw Zane gingerly lower himself into his saddle, taking time to arrange his injured parts just so as he settled into the seat. "She's the one who should have the red hair," Chase commented to no one in particular as the group set off for the day.

As Jenny rode beside her brother, a memory teased in her mind, that of a young girl with her hair in pigtails talking to her mother about love, and the sight of her mother's toes curling against the rough wood of the porch as her father leaned over to kiss her. She sighed as she thought of the sloppy kiss Zane had given her. "No love there," she thought to herself. A rider came up on her other side. It was Ty.

The group returned dirty and weary from the day's work but happy to have it done, except for Cat, who had looked daggers at Jenny throughout the day. Ty had managed to stay casually close to her, offering companionship but nothing more, sensing her skittish mood and avoidance of Zane, who whined and complained the entire day. They all hit the dinner table with a vengeance, and as soon as she was done eating, Jenny left to seek the comforts of the bathhouse.

There was a makeshift shower set up behind it that they all used in warm weather. A bucket tipped water into a half barrel that had holes punched in the bottom, allowing the water to trickle through. Jenny stepped inside the stall and threw her clothes over the side, taking time to examine the worn seat of her pants. *I hope these will last till payday*, she thought, knowing her meager wardrobe would not see her through the hard work that she was now expected to do. She went about her bath, wanting to finish before the sun set and the chilly spring evening set in. She lathered her hair and was scrubbing her face when she heard a commotion from behind the bunkhouse. She wiped the soap from her eyes to see Zane dangling some six inches off the ground, the collar of his shirt held in Jamie's strong grip, which held him pinned against the bunkhouse wall. Zane's legs kicked the air as he tried to draw breath, and Jenny watched as his face turned red, then purple as Jamie calmly talked to him. Finally Jamie released him and he slid down the wall until he was sitting in the dirt, his legs sprawled out before him.

"Yeah, look at you run," he hollered as Jamie strode away. "It won't be so easy next time, believe me," he muttered. He stood up and dusted himself off, then looked somewhat embarrassed when he saw Jenny peeping over the wall of the shower. "We were just talking," he said, motioning towards the vanishing Jamie.

Jenny just shook her head and went back to her shower, a huge smile on her face as another of her burdens fell away. Jamie would take care of her, and though she knew she could make it on her own, she didn't have to anymore. She began to sing a foolish tune, knowing she was getting carried away but not caring, just happy to be alive.

She finished her shower, quickly dried off, wrapped her hair in a towel and turned to pick up her shirt, but it was not hanging where she'd left it. A quick scan of the four walls showed the absence of all her clothes. Frustration and anger overcame her recent silliness as she ducked her head to look under the walls to see if they clothes were lying on the ground. She saw nothing. Biting her lip and threatening dire consequences to the thief, she wrapped the towel around her body and inched the door open. To her amazement, a set of neatly folded clothes was lying on the chair next to the door, including a sturdy camisole and pantalets. Jenny knew they were a contribution from Grace, but the shirt must have come from Chase, because it was the one she had made for Jamie and mended just the week past. She figured the tan pants had been his also, because the length was enough to cover her long legs, with a small cuff left over. Pulling on the pants she stuffed the cuffs down into the tops of her boots and cinched in the waist with a leather belt that was hanging on the chair back.

Chase was sitting on the porch of the bunkhouse reading when Jenny came around. He looked at her over the top of the book and smiled when she twirled in front of him, her hands out and open as if she was modeling an expensive gown. "Just wanted to say thanks," she offered with a smile. "I fear I was close to embarrassing everyone around here with those other clothes."

"I don't think there are many around here that would mind," Chase replied casually.

Jenny's good mood had come back with the discovery of the clothes, along with her naturally teasing nature.

"Would *you* mind?"

Chase set the book down and looked at her smiling face; her wide blue eyes held a mischievous glint that was captured by the last rays of the setting sun. He leaned forward with an intent look on his face. "You forget, Jenny, I've already seen what you have to offer." Jenny looked at him with mouth agape. "We slept together—don't tell me you've forgotten." He went on in mock seriousness, "I am a very light sleeper, the slightest noise will wake me up for instance, I remember many nights when I was lying in bed unable to move because my leg was strung up, and this young lady who was sharing my room would come in and try to sneak into her gown in the corner of the room without waking me."

"You were awake all those nights?" Jenny said indignantly.

"Not all of them, but often enough." Jenny's face began to flush, but Chase continued. "The best part was early in the morning when you would kick off your blankets and your gown would be all tucked up underneath you and your legs were bare. That was the sight I liked best."

"You are no gentleman." Jenny raised her nose in the air as Chase began to laugh.

"No, I'm not, and most people can tell that by looking at me."

Jenny tilted her head to get a better look as he pushed his long hair behind his ears and closed his book. "I think you are just teasing me, so I'll let it go this time. Just don't let it happen again."

Chase threw his hands up as if seeking protection. "Thanks, ma'am, I'd hate to end up gimping around here like Zane." He got up from his chair and limped away, his legs spread apart in mock pain, turning once to look at Jenny, who stuck her tongue out at him. Chase stopped at the door and watched her walk away, her stride strong and sure as she went up the porch into Grace's cabin.

Chapter Twenty-two

The weeks passed quickly, filled with work, play and talk until the past became like a bad dream, banished to the back of Jenny's mind, only to come out and haunt her in the fleeting moments before she fell asleep at night, or right before she woke up in the morning. She felt uncomfortable sleeping in the big house with Jason and Cat, then working with the hands during the day, but there was no place else for her to go unless she moved in with Grace, and though no one mentioned it, everyone knew it would make things uncomfortable for Jamie and Grace. So Jenny kept on sleeping in the big bed, and kept her distance from Cat, who was growing ever more concerned at the attention that Ty was paying to Jenny.

Ty's courtship of Jenny was nothing like the full-speed-ahead onslaught of Zane's. He was very casual, always working his way around to where Jenny happened to be, just talking to her, behaving like the Southern gentleman he was brought up to be. Ty was always ready to open a door or pull out a chair, which the boys found amusing, since Jenny had demonstrated that she could ride, rope and shoot as well as any of them. As time passed, Jenny and Ty wound up together more and more, which led to Cat spending more time complaining to her father and Grace. Concurrently, Chase began to spend more time alone, away from the main group. Jamie noticed his absences but could not figure out the reason why, and Chase refused to talk to him about it. Jenny, meanwhile, began to blossom under Ty's steady attention, the lines of worry and fatigue fading as she grew more comfortable with each passing day.

Talk around the bunkhouse turned to the spring dance to be held in town at the end of the month. The cowboys all pulled out their suits and dress shirts so Grace could freshen them up, and Cat began to go through her wardrobe to find just the right gown to bring Ty's attention back where it belonged. Grace made Jenny try on the dress she had been stitching and convinced her that it had been intended for her all along. Jenny's pride made her want to argue the point, but the sight of the soft blue calico swirling around her legs, and the glow of pride on Jamie's face, won out. Her bare toes sticking out from under the unfinished hem brought up another point, however, and Jamie declared that they were going shopping for shoes on the following Saturday so his sister would no longer be an embarrassment to him. Jenny responded by throwing a tin mug at his head, but agreed that he was right, and he owed her a pair of shoes anyway for the way she had to put up with him.

The day of the dance soon was upon them, and Jason, knowing he wouldn't get any work out of them, gave everyone a half day off to prepare for the festivities that night. Grace did Jenny's hair up for her. Jenny's wide blue eyes shone with excitement in the mirror as Grace pinned and wrapped until an elegant cascade of golden curls was dangling against her swan-like neck. Grace then tried to soften Jenny's work-hardened hands by soaking them in a special concoction she had made up while Jenny squirmed impatiently in her chair.

"Hold still so I can work on your nails," Grace said impatiently as Jenny tried to get up.

"Grace, you're spending so much time with me that you're not going to have time to get yourself ready."

"I'm not going."

"Why?"

"Jenny, young men and young women go to dances to meet each other, and I am not a young woman anymore."

"You're still young, and attractive. Why don't you go?"

Grace smiled sweetly at Jenny, the scars almost disappearing into the laugh lines that rimmed her eyes and mouth. "My time for dances is over. This is your time, so don't worry about me. I'll be fine."

Jenny looked intently at the head that was bent over her nails, shaping and polishing. "Jamie's not going either."

Grace looked up, her face going pale as she realized that it was a statement more than a question. "No, he said he would like to stay here and keep me company tonight."

"I know it's been hard on him, with the scars and all, hard for him to meet a girl who would be special to him." Grace started to interrupt, but Jenny went on. "I'm glad he has someone to talk to, someone who knows how he feels. He said I would never know how it was, and he's right. The truth of the matter is, I don't even think about his scars any more than I think about him having a nose or a mouth or eyes, but sometimes I remember his screams and the pain he was in and I can't stand it . . ." Jenny's voice trailed off as her emotions threatened to overcome her. Grace gripped the hand she had been working on.

"Tell me, Jenny. When it happened—was it bad? He just skims over it like it was nothing, but you were there."

"I think the worst part for Jamie is thinking that if he had not gotten burned, he could have saved our parents. I just remember his screams, and the smell of burned flesh, and seeing my father lying in a pool of his own blood. Jamie was unconscious for a week after it happened, they kept him that way because of the pain. I know he dreamed horrible dreams, but he never talked about them. When they took the bandages off, he decided that he was a freak and that his life was pretty much over. He was all right with the people he knew and trusted, but if anyone else came along, he would hide under his hat or in the barn. It's nice to see him so free and easy here."

"It's his home, Jenny, and he knows we don't judge him for what he looks like. I feel the same way."

"I know, and I'm glad he's found someone who understands how he feels." The women smiled at each other through tear-filled eyes.

"Oh, my goodness, look at the time. We've got to get you ready," Grace exclaimed and went back to work on Jenny's hands. She soon pronounced them adequate, which brought a rueful grin from

Jenny, who realized that she was a far cry from the lady her parents had wanted her to be, but it couldn't be helped. Fate had made her who she was.

The soft blue dress was put on. Grace wished it were fancier, but to Jenny it was just fine. She found it hard to believe that the tall young woman in the mirror with the done-up hair and the pink cheeks was she.

"He won't be able to take his eyes off you," Grace said softly as she came up behind Jenny.

"Who?"

"Does it matter?"

Jenny thought about it, tried to picture the dance and a crowd of young men standing around, fighting for her attention. Something was missing from the vision, so she closed her eyes, drawing images of Ty, Caleb, Jake and Zane along with faceless others into a circle in her mind, but beyond, in the shadows, there was another man standing, watching, waiting, patiently giving her every opportunity to choose.

"Jenny?"

Jenny shook her head as Grace called her back to the present, scattering the images like droplets of water.

"Where did you go, girl?"

"I guess I was at the dance."

There was a great banging of boots on the steps and then a thundering at the door.

"Are you about ready? Jason is bringing the buggy down." It was Jamie beating on the door. Grace made a huge ceremony of presenting Jenny in her new dress, and Jamie beamed proudly at her as she twirled gracefully before him. He handed her a flower he had found along the trail and she tucked it into her hair. "You look beautiful," he said, grinning. "Maybe I need to come along to keep you from being carried off."

"I might want to be carried off, thank you very much," Jenny sniffed daintily at him.

"And if you don't, I'm sure you'll let them know with your usual good humor," Jamie added, playfully tweaking a curl that was lying on her shoulder. Grace handed her a shawl, and Jenny stepped out onto the porch.

The cowboys were all combed and polished, and mounted on horseback, teasing each other about the coming festivities. When she appeared, they went slack-jawed, overcome by the change in her. They had become used to Jenny working alongside them, giving back what they dished out, but now she looked and moved like a lady, and they didn't quite know how to act.

"Where's Chase?" she asked.

"He's not going," Jamie answered.

"Why not?"

"I don't know. Go ask him yourself—he's in the barn." Jenny was confused by Jamie's brusque tone, but decided he must have argued the point with Chase and grown exasperated with him. She gathered her skirt and made her way to the barn, stepping into the dim light to find Chase saddling his horse.

"Jamie said you're not going to the dance."

"No, I'm not." He didn't look up, just continued at his task.

"Why?"

Chase stopped and looked at her over the back of his horse. "It's not a place where I feel especially welcome."

Jenny drew her brows together and stepped into the stall. "Chase, you'll be surrounded by friends. Why wouldn't you feel welcome?"

"I'm a half-breed, Jenny. I'm not welcome anywhere."

"That's not true." Chase went back to saddling his horse. "I wish you would come."

"You don't need me there. You'll have plenty of men who will want to dance with you, and none of them would like seeing you dance with me."

"I wouldn't care if they liked it or not."

"Go to the dance, Jenny. Have a wonderful time with Ty, or any other fellow you want to be with."

"What makes you think I want to be with someone?"

"Isn't that what everyone wants, to be with someone special, someone you are meant to be with for all time, for eternity, from this life to the next?" His dark eyes were piercing, looking down into her soul, tugging at her heart, while her mind was whirling, screaming in protest, afraid of what his eyes might see in the inner recesses she had kept hidden for so long.

"Jenny? Jason is here with the buggy." It was Ty, dressed in a suit, his hair combed back. Chase angrily slapped the stirrup down as Ty entered the stall. "Sure you don't want to go, Chase? It's not too late," Ty said.

"No, go on, have fun. Don't worry about me."

Ty held out his arm to Jenny, who placed her arm in the crook of his elbow, turning to look at Chase as Ty led her out. He gave her a half smile that didn't reach his eyes, and she almost turned to go back. Ty put his hand over hers firmly, as if he could sense her hesitance, and she went on to the buggy, where Jason and Cat were waiting.

"I forgot to tell you how beautiful you look," Chase said when she was gone, but no one heard except the horse.

The dance started out well enough. The music drifted towards them on the cool evening air as they approached town, bringing with it a sense of excitement and promise that nearly lifted Jenny out of her seat in the rear of the buggy. She enjoyed the aimless chatter of the boys who rode alongside, Zane's endless monologue making Jake roll his eyes in disgust while Caleb laughed at his every word. Ty carried on polite conversation with Jason, who was sitting next to a strangely quiet Cat. She had exchanged a few words with everyone, even acknowledging Jenny's new dress, then sat quietly on the seat, her shawl pulled around her intricately upswept hair, and watched the countryside roll by in the twilight. When they arrived at the dance, Cat waited for her father to help her down, then took his arm after he helped Jenny from the buggy.

The father and daughter entered like royalty, the others trailing behind but still catching the full effect that Cat's appearance had on the numerous soldiers and cowboys already present. Her gown was more suited for a big city like New York or Chicago than a small town in Wyoming Territory, but the Lynches were part of the local aristocracy and Cat carried it off with all the grace and sophistication that went with her position. The dress was a soft green silk, low cut with a square neckline and just a touch of lace hiding the curves that threatened to burst forth over the top. The skirt accented her small waist before belling out over a multitude of crinolines that swayed gently when she walked. The dress color made her up-tilted eyes all the more green, the flecks of gold sparkling as she surveyed the group of eligible young men who were now making their way towards her. She tossed her cascade of golden brown curls as a tall-lieutenant bowed before her, taking her away from Jason. Ty asked a suddenly shy Jenny to dance, and the other cowboys drifted off to their own pursuits while Jason took the opportunity to talk with other leaders of the community.

Jenny felt as if she were dancing on Ty's feet more than her own, but soon enough her natural grace took over and she became more confident as she followed his lead. Even though Ty was dressed like a common ranch hand, his formal training was obvious to all who saw him, and the other boys imitated his ways. He swept Jenny through a reel until she was laughing breathlessly, her eyes dancing too as she gave herself over to the pure joy of the moment. When they stopped, Zane was there to partner her in the next dance, and she couldn't help noticing that Cat had moved on to a new partner, too. Next Jake whirled Jenny onto the floor, then Caleb, and even Jason took his turn with her, while Cat was working her way through the soldiers, who were all anxiously awaiting their turn. Not once did Cat give Ty a glance, which was strange. At the ranch, she was always watching him, always placing herself in his path. But now Cat laughed and talked and charmed every other man present and acted as if Ty did not exist.

Jenny finally begged the soldier she was dancing with to let her rest, and promised to wait while he went to get her a cup of punch. They were standing together drinking their punch and talking when Cat came floating towards them, her crinolines swaying, a sweet smile on her face.

"Jenny, I feel near to fainting. I wonder if you would let your gentleman friend go and get me a cup of punch also." Cat smiled up at the soldier while she briskly fanned her flushed cheeks.

"It would be my pleasure," the soldier replied and turned briskly on his heel to attend to the matter.

"Jenny, I really need to talk to you for a minute," Cat whispered urgently when the soldier was gone. Jenny was shocked. Cat had hardly given her the time of day lately, but she let the other girl pull her into a hallway. Cat faced the dance floor, and Jenny stood with her back to the room, her cup of punch in her hand.

"I'm sure you know I want to talk to you about Ty," Cat began, her eyes focusing on his handsome face as he made his way towards them.

"What about Ty?" Jenny asked, curious but cautious. The next thing she knew, Cat grabbed her hand and dumped her cup of punch down the front of the soft green gown.

"Oh, Jenny, how could you?" Cat wailed as the punch stained the silk and ran down into the folds of the skirt.

"What happened?" Ty was there, concern written on his face as he looked questioning at Jenny, then at Cat, who had tears running down her cheeks as she tried to blot the spreading stain.

"After all we've done for you, I can't believe you could be so vindictive, so mean." Cat dissolved into sobs as Jenny stood there, her mind spinning, trying to make sense of what had happened. "Oh, Ty, please take me home. Please, before somebody sees me like this."

"I'll get your father."

"*No*, please, just take me home. Please don't tell him about this. I would hate for Jamie to get in trouble for something his sister did. Just take me home, now, please." The words were barely distinguishable through the sobs, and Jenny quickly realized that they were all being manipulated.

"I'm sorry, Cat, I don't know what came over me," Jenny said, reciting the words as if reading lines that Cat had written for her. Ty looked questioningly at Jenny who just shook her head. "Go on. I'll tell the others that you took the buggy. I'm sure I can get a ride with someone."

"What about Jason?"

"He can ride your horse," Cat said as she picked at the fabric and shivered in horror at the mess. Ty took off his jacket and put it over her shoulders, Cat pulling it around to cover the damp stain. They went out through the hall, Cat still sniffing and quivering as if her world had come to an end.

An hour later Jenny was riding behind Jason on the back of Ty's horse, desperately trying to keep her balance without touching the man who rode stiffly before her. Riding double on a skittish horse was not easy, especially when dealing with petticoats and shawls.

"Damn it, Jenny, quit your squirming," Jason barked as the horse danced around in the darkness.

"I'm sorry." Jenny bit her lip to stop herself from crying, and marveled again at how quickly Cat had brought on the tears. Jenny had told Jason that she had accidentally spilled her punch on Cat, knowing that Cat would call her a liar if she said any different. Jason had become sternly quiet after the tale and said they might as well go home, so now they were together, and Jenny fervently prayed for an end to this ride that seemed to be going on forever.

"I didn't mean that," Jason said, suddenly realizing how upset

Jenny was. He reached around and pulled her hand around his waist. "Just hold on. We'll be home soon enough." He patted her hand reassuringly, and Jenny relaxed a bit against his solid frame.

"I'm sorry if I ruined Cat's dress. I'll pay to have it cleaned, or replaced—"

"I'm not worried about the dress. She has a hundred of them. Actually, I hope it is ruined. It was a bit too revealing, if you ask me."

"I know how much she was looking forward to the dance. I guess I ruined it for everyone." Jenny sighed. She knew she should keep quiet, but she was still reeling from Cat's trickery.

"You didn't ruin anything for anybody," Jason assured her, but Jenny thought he was just being a gentleman so she fell back into uncomfortable silence.

Jason, meanwhile, had some thoughts of his own on the subject, and though he had always been one to let things work themselves out naturally, he began to wonder if maybe it was time for him to become involved in the personal lives of the people who lived at his ranch.

Jenny went straight to her room, noticing the quiet that had settled over the ranch. The only sound to be heard was the soft murmur of Jason and Cat's voices coming from Cat's room. Jenny lay in the big bed until she heard Jason's footsteps in the hall, then the sound of Cat crying. She would bet they were real tears this time. Jenny became restless. She kicked off the covers and went to the window. She looked out on a night that was so still you could hear the crickets moving in the grass; the moon was just a sliver in the sky. "God's thumbnail," her mother used to say when they were young and safe in the loving arms of their parents, watching the moon climb up in the sky on many a night such as this one.

She looked down at Grace's cabin, where she knew Jamie would be. Was he wrapped in Grace's arms, or was he wondering about the evening's events? Surely he'd guessed when Ty and Cat came back early that something had happened, but more than likely he was enjoying his time with Grace.

A frown creased Jenny's forehead as she thought about the coming day. Everyone would now think she was ungrateful and mean, if Cat had her way. And how could she live and work here without the respect of the others? Also, there was Jamie to consider, he was happy here, but she had put him in a tenuous position just because Ty had paid attention to her and Cat was jealous.

"Ty." Jenny said his name softly as she leaned her forehead against the cool glass of the windowpane. The name brought a face to mind, nothing more. Was there some connection between them? Was she an intruder in a relationship that seemed to exist only in Cat's mind? The boys had all said that Cat had pursued Ty since the day he had arrived at the ranch. Ty had been polite, they said, but he but did not feel right having a relationship with his employer's daughter. It would complicate things, and that was the last thing he wanted. Of course, Cat had risen to the challenge and set out to prove him wrong, and Jenny had walked right into the middle of it. Jenny shook her head. She hadn't even had a chance to find out how she really felt about Ty.

In the distance, a wolf began to howl, a lonely, mournful wail, the sound trailing away into the stillness before starting again. Jenny remembered a night long ago when she had been lying in bed, comforted by the sound of her brother snoring across the room and her parents talking on the porch under the open window. It had been a still night, not unlike this one, and the sound of a wolf's howl had come to them, carrying for miles in the quiet.

"He's calling to his mate," Ian had said.

"How do you know?" Faith had asked.

"Gray Horse told me. Wolves mate for life, and if I couldn't find you, that's what I would do, howl at the moon until I found you."

"Oh, so you'd miss me, then, if I was gone?" Faith had asked teasingly.

Jenny had heard the creak of the porch boards as her father rose and leaned over her mother. "If you were gone, I would stop living. There would be no reason for me to go on." The words had been said so quietly that the young girl lying safe in her bed barely heard them.

A single tear slid down Jenny's cheek as she listened to the howl. "Where is your mate?" she asked the wolf. The reflection in the window had no answer.

Chapter Twenty-three

There was no use dreading it. The sooner she faced the day, the sooner it would be over with. Jenny kicked the blankets off and dressed, looking out the window to see if anyone was out and about. Smoke was pouring from the chimney at Grace's cabin, so Jenny made her way down there to talk to Jamie about the happenings of last night. She wanted to talk to Grace, too, perhaps the older woman could give her some insight as to how to handle the ever worsening situation with Cat.

An awkward silence greeted her when she entered the cabin. Zane, Caleb and Jake seemed a little the worse for wear after their night of revelry in town, their eyes were swollen and bloodshot, and they reeked of cheap perfume and liquor. All they would be good for this day was lying in their bunks, and Jenny couldn't say she blamed them, as long as they would make use of the bathhouse first. Ty looked the most uncomfortable. His head had been close to Jamie's when she came in, and she guessed they had been talking about the events of last evening. Grace handed her a plate of eggs, and she sat down at the end of the table.

"How did you get home last night?" Jamie asked as she picked up a fork.

"I rode with Jason on the back of Ty's horse."

A leering grin lit Zane's face as he began to picture that.

"Aren't you boys about done?" Jamie looked at Zane, Caleb and Jake until they put down their forks and shuffled away, taking most of their smell with them. Ty got up to leave also, but Jenny stopped him with a word.

"Things aren't always the way them seem, Ty." It was the most she could say without sounding petty, and she didn't feel she should have to defend herself when she had done nothing wrong.

"I'm sorry I dragged you into this mess, Jenny," Ty said, but his eyes were still doubtful as he left.

"Whatever possessed you to dump a cup of punch down Cat's dress?" Jamie asked, a grin on his face.

"Oh, so just like that, you think I did it?"

Jamie threw his hands up defensively. He had expected a scathing retort that Cat deserved it, not a quick declaration of innocence. "It wouldn't be the first time you'd done something like that."

Jenny shoved her plate away from her. "Oh, and I suppose Cat is innocent of any wrongdoings in her lifetime?"

"Hey, all I know is what I heard. Ty said that Cat was devastated because you dumped a cup of punch down the front of her dress. He said she was more upset about the fact that *you* did it than missing the dance, or messing up her dress, or anything else. Ty said she was shocked that you would do such a thing after she and her father have been so good to you."

"Yeah, that's me, ungrateful Jenny. I just take and take, then throw it back in their faces." Jenny folded her arms, and Jamie quickly recognized the stubborn set of her shoulders.

"Wait a minute, you haven't given Jenny a chance to tell her side of the story," Grace said calmly as she saw the storm rising before her.

"Okay, Jen, what happened last night?"

"You wouldn't believe me if I told you."

"Try me."

"Cat dumped the punch on herself and blamed it on me."

"Why would she do something like that?"

"Ty, that's why. She wants him and he doesn't want her and she couldn't stand it."

Jamie shook his head, not understanding the complicated logic of the female mind. "That doesn't make any sense."

"I knew you wouldn't believe me."

"Actually, it makes sense to me," Grace put in. "Have you ever known Cat to let anything stand in the way of something she wants?" she asked Jamie. "She got Ty away from Jenny last night, that's for certain, and now he's not so sure about her, which has got to be in Cat's favor. She's just trying to eliminate the competition."

"Well, I'll make it easy on her," Jenny declared.

"How's that?" Jamie asked.

"I'm leaving."

"You are not, you're staying right here."

Jenny got up and started out the door. "I don't need you to tell me what to do."

"Yes, you do. I'm your brother, and it's my responsibility to take care of you." Jamie followed her out the door.

"Oh, yeah? well, you've done a fine job of it for the last five years."

"Hey, you can't blame that on me. It wasn't my fault you were taken away. I was out trying to find us a place when that happened."

"If we had left the mission when I begged you to go, none of that would have happened, now would it?"

They were standing toe to toe, nose to nose in the middle of the yard. Their voices had risen with each statement until they were fairly shouting at each other, bringing three sleepyheads out of the bunkhouse and Ty out of the barn. Grace had followed the two out of her cabin.

"That's what it all goes back to, isn't it? You have never forgiven me for staying at the mission," Jamie said.

"Hiding there, you mean, just like you are hiding here."

"Jenny, I was fifteen years old. What was I supposed to do?"

"Come with me now."

"Where?"

"I don't care, anywhere. Let's just go."

"I'm not leaving. This is my home—it's our home."

"It's not mine, it's yours."

They were so loud now that they didn't hear Chase ride up, his eyes wide and concerned as he heard the words spewing forth.

"You would spend your whole life running if you had your way," Jamie spat, hurting deeply from her words.

"And you would spend yours hiding." Jenny kicked dirt on the toes of his boots.

Jamie's cheeks flushed, anger now over taking reason, his face the deep russet of his hair, which was hanging down over eyes that had turned dark and cold. He found that his rage was so deep, he couldn't speak, so he scooped Jenny up and threw her over his shoulder. He dropped her unceremoniously, backside first, into the trough. Jenny came up spewing water, splashing, clawing, and he shoved her back under until he saw her eyes go wide with panic. He let her up and she sucked in great breaths of air.

"This is our home now, so get used to it." He slowly enunciated every word. "We are staying here as long as Jason wants us to. I will let you know when it is time for us to leave. Meanwhile, you need to settle down and quit your whining. The past is over, so get on with your life. I have." He turned and left her sitting in the trough, soaking wet and shivering.

Everyone stood with mouths agape. Jenny sat in the trough, willing the tears back but unable to control the trembling of her chin. As Chase walked over to the trough the others went inside, shaking their heads, graciously sparing Jenny more embarrassment. Chase extended his hand to her, and she stood with his help, the water running off her in great sheets, her hair plastered down around her face and neck, her clothes soaked through, clinging to her long lines like a second skin.

"Are you all right?" Chase asked gently, breaking through the red haze of anger that still possessed her. She looked up into his dark eyes, blinking droplets of water off her eyelashes, her deep blue eyes full of shock and disbelief.

"What did I say? What did I do?" she whispered to Chase. Chase looked over his shoulder at the departing Jamie, who was riding hard, away from the ranch.

"Made up for lost time, I'd say." He steadied her arm as she stepped out of the trough, a puddle forming around her on the ground.

"I've got to talk to him."

"Later. Give him time to cool off."

"What if he won't forgive me?" Jenny looked at Chase in panic.

"He loves you." The look he gave her was tender, his eyes deep and shining, making Jenny's heart melt. "He will forgive you."

Grace came out with a blanket and threw it over Jenny's shoulders. "Let's get you out of these wet clothes."

Jenny didn't know what to do or where to go, so she let Grace lead her into the cabin, water sloshing over the sides of her boots as she went. Chase watched as the two women went inside, Grace speaking soothing words the whole time, then he went into the bunkhouse, anxious to find out exactly what had happened the night before.

Grace got Jenny out of her wet clothes and sat her down at the table with a steaming mug of coffee. "Now why don't you tell me exactly what happened last night, in your words, not Cat's."

"Cat pulled me into a hallway, I had a cup of punch in my hand, and she grabbed my arm so that the punch spilled down the front of her dress."

"And where was Ty when all this happened?"

"I don't know, my back was to the room, but he must have been close, because he was there right after it happened."

Grace perused her own cup of coffee as she replayed the incident in her mind. "It sounds to me like Cat hoped to eliminate her competition while bringing Ty over to her side all in one night."

"Well, she got what she wanted."

"Don't be so sure of that, Jen." Grace gently placed her hand on Jenny's forearm. "She'll never get Ty by trickery. He's too much of a gentleman for that. The thing I want to know is, how do you feel about Ty?"

"I don't know. I guess I really haven't thought about it that much. So much has happened since I got here." Jenny pulled the blanket tighter around her shoulders and leaned back in the chair. "I used to think that when I found Jamie life would be perfect again, but I guess all I found was another set of problems. Please don't think I'm sorry I found him, I thank God every day for that. It's just that I had this vision of us going back home and working our ranch again with Dad and Momma looking down on us, while we lived happily ever after." Jenny got up and walked over to the window. "Jamie is right, the past is behind us, and things will never be the same again, so I just need to get over it and get on with my life, like he has." Jenny's voice trailed off as she leaned her head against the windowpane.

"But?" Grace asked from the table.

"But something is missing inside of me. I always thought it was Jamie, but it's not."

"Maybe it's Ty?"

Jenny turned around. "Maybe it is, maybe it isn't. I just don't know." Jenny's face tightened as a thought flashed before her. "I guess it isn't. I mean, if Ty was for me, wouldn't I feel as passionately about him as Cat does?"

"Cat has been passionate about that boy since she first laid eyes on him, that's for sure."

"Do you believe in true love? I mean one man for one woman for all eternity?"

"I can't say. If there is one man for me, I've missed him somehow."

"Not even Jamie?"

Grace had the decency to blush. "Jamie doesn't love me. He just loves being with me. I know he'll leave me when he does fall in love, and until then, I'll treasure him."

"And when he does leave?"

"I'll miss him desperately."

"I believe that my parents were destined for one another. They lived for each other."

"Jason told me that he loved a woman like that but he lost her, couldn't find her, and he never loved another."

"That is so sad, to love someone who is gone."

"I know. I couldn't believe it when he told me, but we had had a few brandies and he was feeling melancholy."

Jenny came back to the table and sat down. "Sometimes I have dreams about a man." Grace arched a delicate brow as Jenny continued. "I used to think they were just fantasies, like when Jamie read *Arabian Nights* and I dreamed about a handsome prince with dark hair and dark eyes, but the dreams just kept on coming."

"Tell me about this handsome prince." Grace had a delicious grin on her face that made Jenny laugh.

"Well, there's not much to tell. I've never seen his face, but I know he's there, close by. All I can ever remember is dark hair and dark eyes—long dark hair, come to think of it—"

They were interrupted by Chase bursting through the door. "Jamie's horse just came back without him," he announced.

Jenny jumped from her chair and grabbed her clothes, which were drying by the stove. She turned her back and dropped the blanket as she whipped her shirt on. Grace was panicked by his words, but not enough to miss the spark that lit Chase's eyes when they caught the graceful length of Jenny's legs as she pulled on her pants.

Long dark hair, dark eyes, close by . . . Jenny's words whirled through Grace's mind as she imagined all the calamities that might have befallen Jamie. *He might be closer than you think*, she thought as Chase and Jenny ran to mount their horses.

Chapter Twenty-four

"Have you ever not found anything you were tracking?" Jenny asked Chase a half hour later. He was on the ground, running his hand over some long grass.

"Just once," he replied. He looked at the earth beneath the grass and then swung back up on his horse.

"Once?"

"Yes, once,"

"What were you tracking?"

"You." Chase took off across the grassy field, leaving Jenny stunned by his announcement as she followed him. In another moment they heard a shot echoing before them. Chase pulled his gun out and answered by shooting into the air. Moments later they came across Jamie sitting in the middle of an ocean of grass.

"Damn horse stepped in a gopher hole and rolled over on me. My leg is broken," he said as he looked up at the two of them. Jenny couldn't help it—she took one look at his leg and started to cry. Jamie rolled his eyes at her, and Chase dismounted and ran his hands down the outstretched leg. "Watch it," Jamie howled. "Like I said, it's broken and I don't need you grabbing it to tell me so." Jenny laughed through her tears at the look of pure aggravation he bestowed upon Chase. "I don't suppose you two brought a wagon with you?"

Jenny shook her head as she tried to compose herself. She dismounted and went to her brother, who was sitting on the ground with his hands propped behind him. "Jamie, I'm so sorry for everything I said this morning. Will you forgive me?" Her chin trembled as she looked down at the ground beside him. Jamie reached up and tugged on the braid that was still damp from the dunking he had given her. He flashed his grin, and Jenny flew into his wide chest, throwing her arms around him and knocking him onto his back with a grunt.

"I forgive you! Now get off me before I break something else."

"I'm sorry. Oh my gosh, I'm such an idiot." Jamie rolled his eyes again as Jenny started gushing all over him, and he finally put his finger to her mouth to stop her tide of apologies and self-incrimination.

"I just want to say one thing," he said when she stopped. "I reserve the right to dump you in the trough any time you act as foolish as you did this morning."

"Considering how big you are, I won't have a lot of say in the matter anyway." Jenny sighed.

Jamie pulled her close and kissed her forehead. "Now will you two get me up out of here?"

Chase got under one arm while Jenny got under the other and they pulled him up. Jamie teetered precariously above them, then dropped his head and threw up, splattering the ground in front of them with his breakfast. Jenny and Chase both turned their heads away while they held him until the heaving and gagging had stopped. Jenny went for her horse while he leaned on Chase.

"This is going to be the real trick," Chase commented when Jamie leaned against Jenny's saddle, his face pale from his endeavors. The only thing they could think of was for Chase to shove while Jenny helped swing the leg over the saddle.

"Just leave me out here to starve, why don't ya? I'd be better off," Jamie groaned when they finally had him settled on the back of the saddle. Jenny managed to squeeze in front of him, and he leaned heavily against her when she took up the reins. The horse snorted in protest at Jamie's added weight but turned when Jenny told him to and began to walk towards home. The motion promptly set Jamie's stomach off again, and he leaned over to the side and brought up more of the contents.

Chase arched an eyebrow at the mess. "The way he eats, this could take all day."

"Don't say a word," Jamie warned Jenny, "or the next load is going straight down your back." He wrapped his arms around her waist, and Jenny felt the shudder of his stomach down her spine as he swallowed back bile that had risen in his throat. He managed the rest of the ride without incident, much to Jenny's relief.

The three of them arrived to find a concerned group ready to go out in search of their fallen comrade. Jamie was greeted with several teasing comments until his friends realized that he was hurt and reached up to help him into Grace's cabin. The boys carried him in, only hitting his leg once on the door jamb and another time on the bed frame before they deposited him in the big bed in the room that Grace slept in.

"Geez, Jamie, you look right at home there," Zane commented as Grace bent over to pull a boot off the uninjured leg.

"Zane, will you shut up?" Grace snapped at him. "Chase, hold his leg so I can get this other boot off."

"Zane, go to town and fetch the doctor," Jason commanded. "The rest of you, get out of here and give Jamie some air." The men filed out, leaving Grace, Jason, Jenny and Chase, who was helping Grace strip Jamie of his clothes.

"I guess we've come full circle now," Chase commented as he held his friend up while his pants were pulled off.

"Don't even think about trussing me up with my leg hanging from the rafters," Jamie ground out between clenched teeth. "Why don't you just smack me upside the head with something and be done with it." Grace shook her head as she realized how difficult a patient he was going to be.

"Go ahead, Chase, do it. You'd be doing all of us a favor," Jenny said.

"That's it. As soon as I can walk, you are going back in the trough."

"You might want to think about that," Jenny said as she squeezed a toe on his healthy foot. "You might be lying in this bed a long time, wanting food, water, company, a trip to the outhouse. . . ." She smiled sweetly at him as Jamie flopped his head back on the pillow and groaned.

After many complaints and much moaning and groaning, the doctor arrived and announced that, just as Jamie had said, his leg was broken. Jamie took some satisfaction in knowing that he was right, but turned grouchy again when his leg was put in a splint and firmly bandaged, and he was given instructions not to walk on it for at least a week. The tide of sympathy began to turn towards Grace as the list of her patient's requests became long and tedious. The rest of them decided to leave before Jamie demanded something of them. They escaped to the crisp air of the front porch, where Grace soon joined them.

"Jenny, I'm going to need you to fill in for Jamie this week," Jason said.

Jenny was almost jumping at the chance to get away from her brother's whining, but she knew she was no physical match for Jamie. "I'll do whatever you need me to if I can," she said.

Jason laughed at the look on Jenny's face. "I need you to go down to Denver and pick up some mares for me. Jamie knows the blood lines better than anyone, so I'd planned to send him. Since he's laid up, you're the next logical choice."

"You need these mares for breeding?"

"Yes, there's a breeder down there who has some good stock. I was hoping to breed the mares with Storm—that is, if you think they would be worth it."

Jenny felt overwhelmed by the responsibility, but also honored to be asked to undertake it. "I'll do the best I can for you," she said.

"I don't doubt it for a minute." Jason smiled kindly at her. "Oh, by the way, I'm going to send Ty with you. You'll need some help bringing them mares back, and it doesn't hurt to have an extra gun on the trail. You can leave first thing in the morning. Maybe by the time you get back, your brother will be in a better mood."

Taken aback by the announcement that Ty would be accompanying her, Jenny didn't know what to say. Grace, however, caught the flare of pain that showed in Chase's eyes before he stepped wordlessly off the porch and went towards the barn. "I guess I'd better get ready to go," Jenny said, almost to herself, and went to gather the supplies she would need for a week on the trail.

"Jason, do you think that's a good idea, throwing them together like that?" Grace asked when Jenny was gone.

"I think it will get things settled one way or another, and that's what we all need around here. I'm not blind to what's going on, no matter what my daughter thinks. If Ty and Jenny belong together, then so be it, and now is as good a time as any to find out. And it's also a good time for Cat to realize that she can't always get what she wants."

"There are more people involved here than just Cat," Grace commented.

Jason walked over and put his arm around Grace's shoulder. "I know. I haven't missed that either." He gave her shoulder a squeeze. "It's funny how sometimes people don't appreciate what's right in front of them." He stepped off the porch and headed to the bunkhouse. "Be ready for the screams when Cat finds out what I've done," he said as he walked off.

Grace shook her head at Jason's meddling and went in to find out if Jamie needed anything.

Jenny was amazed at how easy the trip had been. The first morning on the trail had been uncomfortable as both Ty and Jenny were nervous about being together, but they soon settled into easy conversation, talking about their lives and what had led them to Wyoming Territory. Ty told Jenny about growing up in eastern North Carolina on a plantation where it took a day's ride to go from border to border. He talked about how his father had controlled every detail of the family's life as he controlled the plantation, about his mother, who retreated into her bedroom, the only place his father never went. He talked about his frustration with his older brother's cruel treatment of the slaves after the death of his father had left his brother in charge. Finally he told of the fight he had had with his brother after his brother had beaten a slave to death. When he'd had his hands wrapped around his brother's throat, he'd realized that he was no better than the man he was trying to kill. So he had left, making his way west and finding Jason Lynch, who had gone to school with Ty's grandfather. Ty missed his home, but he hated the institution of slavery and did not know how to change it. The news of the strife in the South did not escape him, even in Wyoming Territory, and he felt that the nation was headed for a war that would tear the country apart. Jenny listened to his story, and missed once again the loving childhood she had shared with her brother.

After spending several days together in easy companionship, each contributing to making camp at night, spreading their blankets on either side of the fire, each content and comfortable, it dawned upon Jenny that somehow, some way, the conversation always turned to the subject of Cat. They were a day away from home, returning with six mares that Jenny had purchased with the bank draft Jason had given her, and had made camp beside a wide stream. In the past few days she had heard about all of Cat's likes and dislikes, how well she could ride, what a sweet singing voice she had, and how nice the yellow dress they had seen in the window of a dress shop would look on her. Jenny felt that if she heard Cat's name mentioned one more time, she would scream, so she walked downstream a bit to wash up.

The water was running crisp and clear over several flat rocks that lined the stream bed, and beneath the surface the moonlight glinted occasionally on the trout coming up to feed. Jenny took off her boots and rolled her pants up before jumping from stone to stone until she was in the middle of the wide rush of water. She sat down on a boulder and dangled her feet into the water, wanting desperately to immerse her entire body and wash off the dust and grime of the trail.

She let her mind wander back over the happenings of the last few weeks, especially the night of the dance and the day after. She let her thoughts dwell on the conversation she'd had with Grace when the older woman had asked about her feelings for Ty. Jenny had just spent a week in his company, totally alone, and while she could now say that she knew him well, respected him, admired him, she still couldn't say if she loved him, and surely didn't know how he felt about her. The water had taken away the stress of the day and left her feet chilled, so she pulled them out and sat with her chin resting in her hand. She heard the snap of a branch and looked up to see Ty walking towards her, a smile on his handsome face as he spotted her in the middle of the stream. Jenny noticed the ends of his sandy hair curling up and thought about how far he'd strayed from the polished Southern gentleman he had been raised to be.

"Catching anything?" he asked when he stood opposite her on the stream bank.

"Probably a cold," she answered.

Ty picked up her boots and socks and waved them at her. "Then you might need these."

Jenny stood up, dusted off the back of her pants and began to hop and skip over the slick rocks that would take her back to shore. At the last jump, she miscalculated and teetered precariously, swinging her arms out to regain her balance. She was sure she was going in until Ty swept her to the bank on his arm. She landed solidly against his chest, and he backpedalled, not wanting to get wet any more than she did. He finally regained his balance, and relaxed his hold a bit, his arm coming down around her waist. Her eyes were even with the tip of his nose, and she moved her head back a bit, placing her hands on his chest, noticing that his eyes had turned gray in the dusk.

"I think we're safe now," she said.

"I know." He didn't seem inclined to move his arm, but instead moved the other one around her waist also. A question formed in his eyes; he tilted his head, then brought his mouth down on hers in a tentative kiss.

Jenny willed her lips to relax, moved her head a bit to accommodate his, then felt the increased pressure as he realized her acceptance. His lips moved over hers gently but firmly, asking a question. The kiss ended and he moved his head back. Jenny looked up at him, not knowing what to say or what to do until Ty finally dropped his arms.

"That was nice, wasn't it?" he asked, as if he, too, were a bit confused.

"Yes."

"But that's not enough."

"Ty, I—"

"No, don't say it. I know what you're thinking."

"What am I thinking?" Jenny hoped he would explain it to her, because she didn't have a clue.

"All I've done this whole trip is go on about Cat, and then I kiss you and you've got to be thinking, how come he's talking about Cat and he's out here kissing me?"

"Okay, how come you talk about Cat so much if you don't feel anything for her?"

"I never said I didn't feel anything for her."

"Well, you sure act like it. Every time she comes around, you run in the opposite direction."

"I just don't want anyone thinking I'm courting her to keep my job or anything like that."

"Who's going to think that?"

"I don't know. It's just that she's so different from all the girls I've known. She's just so . . . I don't know . . . aggressive I guess is the word." Ty ran his hands through his hair, making the curls stand up on end. He sat down on a boulder and put his head in his hands, as if he could magically transfer all his confusion into his hands and throw it away.

"Cat just knows how she feels about you, that's all. I wish someone felt that way about me." Jenny placed her hand on his shoulder, offering comfort and companionship.

"What are you talking about?"

"I wish someone loved me the way Cat loves you."

"Are you blind?"

"What do you mean?" Jenny suddenly became defensive at the tone of Ty's voice.

Ty started to laugh, folding his arms over his stomach as he realized how ridiculous they both had been.

"Chase is madly in love with you," he finally said through the laughter. "He has been ever since I've known him. Jamie hardly ever talked about you, but Chase does all the time. He remembers everything you ever said or did. Haven't you seen the way he looks at you?"

Jenny felt her world begin to spin around her. *Chase is in love with you, Chase is in love with you* became a chant that echoed through her head. Images flashed in her mind, memories from the mission, combined with her dreams of the lover with the long dark hair, and dark eyes. At last he had a face. She felt her heart explode in her chest, the fragments scattering into thousands of pieces like droplets of water, then coming back together in a rush, but now whole where before something had been missing. "Chase is in love with me," she said to herself.

"Jenny, are you all right?" Ty was standing before her, concern written on his face. "You look like you've seen a ghost."

"Chase is in love with me?" she asked, her voice a mere squeak.

"Yes, he is, and I think you're in love with him, too." Ty took her upper arms in his hands. "I don't know about you, but I feel like a complete idiot. I mean, Cat loves me, and that's not something you throw away. Starting as soon as we get back, I'm going to make it up to her."

"The sooner we go to sleep, the sooner we can get going in the morning." Jenny turned to walk back to the camp.

"Jenny, wait." Ty stopped her, concern showing on his handsome face. "I hope you don't think I was just using you. It's just that . . ."

"When you kissed me you realized that there was nothing between us," Jenny finished for him. "Don't worry Ty, I felt it too, or I guess I didn't feel it. My momma told me that I would know the man for me when he kissed me. Now I'm just as anxious as you are to get back and find out for myself if what you say is true."

"Let's get some sleep," Ty said as he wrapped a brotherly arm around her shoulders and they made their way back to camp.

Chapter Twenty-five

Ty and Jenny were up at the crack of dawn, clearing their camp in record time, leading the mares at a quick pace, their joy at going home soon infecting the horses and keeping them at a trot. They sang and laughed and acted foolishly, both of them grinning from ear to ear as the miles faded behind them. They crested the ridge above the ranch when the workday was over, dinner had been eaten and the ranch folk were all relaxing. The boys saw them coming and swung open the gate to the corral, slapping and whistling so that the mares kicked up their heels and put on a show for Storm, who was watching from his pen with head held high, his nostrils quivering in excitement. Cat was sitting on the rail, studying the mares and ignoring the riders, but she turned when Ty rode up to her and dismounted, taking his hat in his hand as he leaned against the fence to talk to her. She looked up as Jenny rode by, her slanted green eyes wide with shock as Jenny flashed a Duncan grin at her.

Jamie was sitting on the porch of Grace's cabin, his bandaged leg propped up on a chair by pillows and quilts, scowling at the proceedings that he was missing in the corral.

"How'd you do?" he asked Jenny when she stopped in front of him.

"See for yourself."

"I wish I could."

Jenny refused to feel sorry for him, knowing that he had probably run Grace ragged during the week. "Where's Chase?" she asked.

Jamie gave her a puzzled look as he turned his head away from the corral and the exclamations over the mares. "I don't know, check the bathhouse." He watched her with growing curiosity as she swung off her mount, setting out with determined steps.

Chase was walking towards the bunkhouse, his hair wet and slicked back from his face, his white shirt unbuttoned, revealing a wide expanse of smoothly tanned skin. He smiled when he saw her, then caught himself, his eyes becoming guarded as she walked directly to him.

"You're back," he said, wondering why she seemed to be so fascinated with the middle of his chest.

Jenny stood before him, her eyes concentrating on the valley between the muscles of his chest, where she could almost believe she had seen a flutter of movement, as if his heart had suddenly accelerated. Her hands itched to reach out and touch the hardness of him, to feel the smoothness of his skin, to compare her golden color to his bronze. She shook her head as she realized he was talking to her.

"What?"

"I said, you're back."

"Yes," she said with a grin. "I am."

"And?"

"I wanted to ask a favor of you," she said as she looked up into his dark eyes, her deep blue ones sparkling with joy, anticipation and mischief.

"What?" Chase became guarded, puzzled by the way she was acting, and wary of being hurt by any revelations she was going to make about her and Ty.

"I want you to kiss me."

Chase looked around to see if anyone was watching. "You want me to what?"

"I want you to kiss me. Is that a problem for you?"

"Jenny, what are you up to?"

"Nothing. It's a simple request—I want you to kiss me."

Chase stepped around her and started for the bunkhouse. "Find somebody else. I'm sure Zane is up to the task if Ty isn't."

Jenny grabbed his arm, pulling him to a stop. "I've already kissed Ty, and Zane tried to kiss me, but I didn't like it much."

Chase smiled briefly as he remembered Zane's limping walk a few weeks past. "I don't like to play those kind of games, Jenny," he said intently, looking down into her shining eyes.

"It's not a game, Chase. I'm dead serious. I need you to kiss me."

Chase grabbed her arms and pulled her behind the bunkhouse. "I am serious too, I am not like Zane or any of the other ones who mess around for the fun of it. When I kiss you, you will know it."

"Then kiss me now."

"You don't know what you're saying."

"Yes, I do." Jenny smiled at him, her eyes deep and moist as she gazed up into his handsome face, the face that had haunted her dreams, regal and fierce with eyes that glinted with silver and pierced her soul. She stood there before him, his hands gripping her arms, knowing that he could snap the bones if he wanted to, and she just looked at him, sweetly smiling, inviting him to do something he had only dreamed of.

I'm damned, he thought to himself as he brought his mouth down on hers. He felt her sharp intake of breath as her lips parted slightly. Her arms moved up, wrapping around his neck, her hands tangling in his hair, and he pulled her to him, one hand on the back of her head, the other moving down her waist, pressing her close as he poured his soul into hers. Their lips moved in a dance that was slow, tantalizing, pulling at the core of each until neither one could breathe. They finally broke apart, each dragging in air as Jenny leaned heavily against Chase, who was using the wall behind him to stay on his own two feet.

"Momma, you were right," she whispered against his chest, feeling once again the flutter of his heart.

"What?" he murmured against the top of her head.

Jenny pulled her hand around, moving it under the tail of his shirt and trailing it lightly across his chest, causing his loins to tighten in agony. She stopped when she felt the thud of his heart and left her hand there, raising her eyes to look into his. "I said I love you."

Chase closed his eyes to hide the longing, the joy that threatened to pour forth. He felt he must be dreaming, and tried to make sense of the last few minutes. Her hand was still there, he felt his heart pounding against it; his own hands were still pressing her against the hardness that she had to feel, and she was still there. He opened his eyes, his entire being hanging over a precipice as he looked down at her.

"Chase, I love you."

He hesitated for a second, then brought his mouth down again, finding hers willing and open, taking everything he poured out and giving back herself.

"Jenny . . . how . . . why . . . oh, God, I love you, I have since the first time I saw you," he said into her ear when he could finally tear himself away from her mouth. "I thought I had lost you. I was going to leave. I couldn't stay here watching you and Ty together."

Jenny brought her fingers to his lips to stop the tide of words pouring forth. "If you leave, I'm going with you."

"I'm not going anywhere."

"I just want to know one thing." She was serious, her eyes dark as she looked into his. "Why didn't you ever say anything?"

"It wouldn't have worked that way. You wouldn't have believed me. So I had to just wait for you to figure it out for yourself."

"Actually, you have Ty to thank for that."

"Why?"

"I told him that I wished someone loved me the way Cat loves him, and he said that somebody already did. Chase, all those years I was searching for Jamie, I didn't realize that I was really searching for you. I dreamed about you but never saw your face, and then suddenly all the pieces fell together and I realized that you were the one I was missing. Even after I found Jamie, I was still looking for you." Jenny brought her hand back to his heart and tucked her head under his chin. "This is where I belong, and this is the only place I ever want to be."

Chase began to laugh, joy erupting from his soul as he realized that Jenny was indeed in his arms instead of in his dreams. He picked her up off her feet, swinging her around as she began to laugh also, their happiness overwhelming, their world centered on the two of them, so that nothing else mattered.

A cough brought them back to earth, and Jenny hung against Chase's chest, her head still spinning as Jason rounded the corner of the bunkhouse.

"I'm sorry to interrupt," he began, a smile suddenly lighting his face. Jenny managed to straighten up while Chase began buttoning his shirt. "I just wanted to let you know what a fine job you did with those mares." His eyes glowed as he looked at the two standing red-faced before him. "They were more than I expected. I hope this will be the beginning of a fine partnership between the Duncans and the Lynches."

"I hope so, too," Jenny managed to say. She felt the rock-hard presence of Chase behind her and took the hand that Jason extended.

"It looks like you had a good trip," Jason commented.

"It was an eye-opening experience," Jenny admitted with a sheepish look on her face. Jason laughed and slapped Chase on the back.

"I think your brother is wondering where you wandered off to. He hasn't been the best company this week, that's for sure."

"Maybe we should go talk to him."

"That might be a good idea." Jason turned to go back towards Grace's cabin, but before Jenny could follow, Chase pulled her back for another mind-numbing kiss that left her breathless and weak.

"It's going to be hard to get any work done around here now, that's for sure," he said against her ear when they finally came up for air.

"We might need to go in opposite directions."

"No, that won't work." Chase lifted her chin so he could look into her sapphire blue eyes. "Because now that I've got you, I'm never going to let you go."

"I guess we'll think of something, then."

They were interrupted by Jamie, whom they could hear hollering for Jenny from the porch. "Let's go see what he wants before he drives Grace crazy," Chase said and took her hand as they went around the bunkhouse.

"What is going on?" Jamie demanded as soon as they came into view. He noticed their hands and looked again, his eyes opening wide in amazement and the Duncan grin swelling on his face. He shook his head as they came onto the porch. "It's about time," he said. "I was beginning to think I'd have to knock some sense into both of you."

"What do you mean?" Chase asked as he leaned against the porch rail and crossed his arms.

Cindy Holby

"You've been mooning over my sister for years, and she didn't have enough brains to see it."

Jenny hooked the toe of her boot under his chair. "I've got enough brains to knock you flat on your backside," she threatened. "Let's see how long it will take you to get up with that broken leg."

"Did you hear that? I get no sympathy from her. Here I am all busted up and it's practically her fault, and all she's does is make threats."

"My fault? I didn't make you go riding across a field of gopher holes like a maniac."

"See, Chase? Are you sure this is what you want in a woman?" Jamie threw his arm up to block the half-hearted blow that landed on his head.

"I'm positive," Chase answered from his perch on the porch rail, his eyes glowing as Jamie tugged Jenny's braid.

"Now tell me about those mares you brought in. I want to make sure you did it right."

Jenny rolled her eyes. "Why don't we just show you? You know you won't be happy until you see them." She and Chase each got under a shoulder and propped Jamie up, his leg sticking out before him. "Can you make it?'

"Yeah, anything for a change of scenery."

They made their way to the corral that held the mares and sat him down on a barrel so he could look them over. Storm, penned on the other side, was doing the same, alternating between watching with his ears pricked and showing off, dancing around with his tail slashing the air. The mares milled around before him, each one jostling for position in the corral, showing off in their own way.

"They're perfect," Jamie said, his eyes shining as he watched the dance going on before him. Jenny was reminded again of how much like their father he was. Ian Duncan had watched his own stock many years earlier with the same look of wonder and anticipation of the future on his face.

It wasn't long before Ty and Cat joined them at the rail, neither of them talking, each one appreciating the promise that was before them.

Chase and Ty helped Jamie back to Grace's, and Cat fell into step with Jenny as they followed. Jenny could sense Cat's hesitance but didn't say anything, deciding it was best to let Cat take the lead. When they got Jamie settled, Ty and Jenny sat down to eat the supper leftovers.

"I was wondering . . ." Cat began, then cleared her throat. "Jenny, I was wondering if you would like to go to church with us tomorrow."

Jenny stopped her fork in midair and looked over at Chase. *Anything as long as we're together,* his eyes said.

"Yes, that would be nice. It's been a long time since I've been to church, and I have just recently found out that I have a lot to be thankful for." She smiled at Chase, who was sitting across from her, then looked at Ty, who winked behind Cat. Jenny suddenly felt as if the weight of the world was off her shoulders. She was home, she was safe, and she was loved. And Cat was being nice to her. If Jamie would just quit complaining, life would be perfect.

Chapter Twenty-six

There were only two people missing when the group from the Lynch ranch attended church the next morning: Jamie, who was propped up in bed with a book, and Jake, who refused to go and wouldn't change his mind for anything. He promised to look after Jamie, and also threatened to shoot him if he didn't stop whining. Grace had decided to join the church goers; the week of waiting on Jamie hand and foot had left her much in need of a break. She was dressed elegantly in a dress and matching bonnet that shadowed her face so that the scars were barely visible. Cat was wearing one of the many creations she had brought back from her last trip East to visit her aunt. Jenny had only the blue calico, but she didn't mind. She was amazed to see Chase in a coat and tie, his long hair thrown back over his shoulders, defiantly showing his heritage. He handed her up into the carriage with the same gentlemanly manners as Ty, making Jenny wonder what type of woman his mother had been.

Cat had decided to make Ty pay for his earlier disdain of her and kept him at a distance, making him pursue her instead of the other way around. Ty knew it was his penalty for treating her so callously before and bore it with good grace, playing the consid-

316

erate suitor. Chase and Ty had sat up half the night talking, and Chase knew that Ty would play Cat's game for a while before laying down the law, which was what Cat wanted anyway.

Chase was just happy to have Jenny at his side in the carriage, to know that later, when they were alone, he would have her in his arms, and he was anxiously awaiting that moment so he could talk with her about his dreams for their future. He held her hand, her skin glowing golden against the dark bronze of his, her fingers delicate in his work-hardened ones. He felt the calluses in her hand rubbing against his own, felt the strength of her easy grip, and was proud of her, knowing she would not be afraid to stand beside him and carry her own weight. But then, all he wanted to do was protect her and provide for her, and he knew it wouldn't be easy. There weren't many men around like Jason Lynch who judged you by who you were instead of what you were. It was not an easy life being a half-breed, and it would be harder still on the woman who chose to marry one, especially if she had golden blond hair and deep sapphire blue eyes like the ones gazing at him now. His smile did not reveal any of his turbulent thoughts, and the one she gave him drove them all away.

Jenny was amazed at how much her life had changed in the past twenty-four hours. She felt as if she had been asleep all those years that she had spent wandering, and had just been awakened by the kiss of a prince, as in the stories her mother used to tell her. The sky seemed bluer, the grass greener, the wildflowers waving alongside the road brighter. Even Zane and Caleb, who were riding by the carriage, seemed merrier. Caleb was grinning at Zane's endless monologue, which held many innuendoes about the outbreak of spring fever that had overcome the locals.

The townsfolk were gathered in the churchyard when the ranch party rode in. Zane and Caleb made their way to the gathering of young ladies, pursuing interests that had developed at the dance. Jason joined the gossip of the men. Then the entire congregation filed in to the ringing of the bell. Chase and Jenny slid into the back pew, along with Zane and Caleb, while the rest of the party went to their customary place in the third pew on the left. A few heads were turned, a few frowns directed at the long hair on the half-breed in the back, but all that faded into the background as their discovery of each other overshadowed everything else.

Chase and Jenny sat hip to hip, thigh to thigh, the blue calico overflowing onto the dark of his neatly pressed pants, the white cuffs of his shirt gleaming brightly against the bronze of his skin. The muscles in his thighs flexed as he tried to find room for his long legs in the tight confines of the pew. The morning light streaming through the row of windows turned Jenny's hair to gold, and Chase had to fight the urge to pick up the curl that lay on her breast. *Later,* he said to himself, *when we're alone, when we have all the time in the world.*

They stood together, sharing a hymnal, Jenny's clear soprano blending in with Caleb's tenor. Zane's voice was a monotone, and Chase just followed the words, listening. When the sermon began, Zane fell asleep, Caleb began sketching on a scrap of paper, and Jenny opened her mother's Bible to follow the scripture. The minister started in, his topic addressing the strife that was threatening to divide the country, comparing the slavery in the South to the slavery of the chosen people in Egypt. He started in on the plagues, and Chase reached down and flipped the pages from Exodus to the Song of Solomon, placing a long index finger on chapter two. Jenny's eyes followed his finger and she began to read, a soft blush coloring her cheeks as she did so. "Did you forget that my mother taught me to read from her Bible?" he whispered in her ear.

She grabbed his hand and dug her nails into the palm. "No, I didn't forget," she mouthed. He squeezed her fingers, then both hands relaxed, the fingers weaving together and then resting on his leg. She felt a twitch in his thigh as her hand settled against it, but his face was set, giving no indication of the turmoil that her touch caused within. Jenny looked at his profile as he attempted to concentrate on the sermon. She tried to imagine what he would be like if he hadn't been driven from his tribe. *He would be a great warrior,* she thought to herself. *He's so steady, so steadfast in his resolve, he would have to be.* She pictured the regal face covered with war paint, feathers and beads braided into his long hair, and covered her mouth with her other hand to hide the smile that had come forth unbidden.

He looked down at her out of the corner of his eye, and drew his eyebrows down in a frown, as if she were an unruly child disturbing his meditation. She batted her eyes innocently at him, and he pulled her hand up against his chest, holding it tightly to discourage her from causing any more trouble. An elderly lady across the aisle gave them a disapproving look, but Jenny smiled sweetly at her and even gave her a little wave. Caleb snorted into his paper, which disturbed Zane's nap and he sat up and began to blink like an owl, trying to figure out what he had missed.

Jenny couldn't stand it any longer—she was too full of joy, and the sermon was suffocating her. Her legs, which wanted to spin and dance and fly across the ground, began to bounce, her feet tapping against the floor. The man in front of them cleared his throat noisily, and the muscles in Chase's cheek worked to hold back the laughter that threatened to spill forth.

Miraculously, Jenny and Chase made it through the service, even managing to give the benediction its proper respect. The minister shook their hands, trying to figure out who they were and where they came from. He relaxed when Jason pointed them out as his employees. Cat was clinging tightly to Ty's arm, wanting all the other single ladies to see that she was now with him; she was in no hurry to leave. Chase and Jenny, on the other hand, couldn't wait to get back to the ranch and fly away, so they waited by the carriage and made their plans for the day, wishing the gossip would run out so they could be on their way.

An hour later, they were on horseback, a cold lunch in their saddlebags, on their way to the place that Chase had claimed as his own even though it was part of the Lynch property. It was the place he went to when he needed to be alone, the place where he had dreamed of Jenny and which he dreamed of sharing with Jenny.

It took her breath away. A crystal lake was sitting before a ridge of mountains that rose higher and higher until they disappeared into the clouds. The land rolled softly down, an ocean of sweet grass that was already knee deep in the early summer. A grove of trees stood off to the side, offering shelter to the deer that came down to drink at the lake.

Chase watched her face as she looked, trying to see it all but too overwhelmed by the beauty of it to absorb everything.

"It's so beautiful, I can't understand why Jason didn't build here," she said finally.

"The snow gets pretty deep here in the winter," Chase explained. "Probably because of the mountains."

"You come here in the winter?"

"I come here whenever I can. This is where I was the night of the dance. I camp down there, between the trees and the lake."

"Show me."

Chase led the way down to the lake and around to the place where the ring of stones still sat from his last fire. They dismounted, turned the horses out to graze, and spread a blanket for their lunch. They listened to the sounds of the horses browsing, the gentle laps of the waves against the shore, the scream of a hawk that circled above. Then all those sounds faded into the beating of their hearts.

Chase laid his hand against Jenny's cheek and gently kissed her, their lips barely touching as they began to explore the newfound feelings inside. Her hand once again found its way inside his shirt and lay against his chest, feeling the beat of his heart. He kissed her eyelids, enjoying their flutter against his lips; his mouth moved to her temple, where wisps of baby-fine hair curled against her skin. He watched while her eyes deepened in color as his mouth moved down to take hers again, only this time he was more insistent, demanding, and she returned his kiss and gave him more. Her lips parted, and he took full possession of her mouth, plundering with his tongue, his arms wrapped around her, crushing her to his chest.

They finally broke apart, panting for breath, drawing in reserves for the next kiss, and soon they were lying on the blanket, their legs tangled together, their hair wild around them. Chase couldn't get enough of her, and Jenny couldn't drink her fill of him. She had unbuttoned his shirt and spread it open to give her better access to the skin that she wanted to taste with her mouth; her trail of kisses was driving him wild, driving all logical thought from his mind. He rolled over on top of her, catching her arms underneath his, and he captured her face in his hands, stopping her innocent pursuit.

"I want you, Jenny, but I won't take you here. I want you for a lifetime."

"Chase," she began, her eyes dark with desire, but he stopped her with a quick kiss.

"I want us to marry, but we're not going to rush it. I want you to be sure."

"I am sure."

"I want you to be sure tomorrow when you wake up and aren't caught up in the moment. I want to give you time to think about us like I have, I want to know that you have no doubts, because it won't be easy for us. There won't be many that approve."

"I don't care what people say, and besides, the people we care about do approve."

"I know they do, but I want you to be sure, because I couldn't stand it if you looked at me one day in the future and said that you were wrong."

The dark eyes above hers showed his pain and his weakness, and Jenny's heart skipped a beat when she realized that she held his heart in her hand.

"Chase, I know without a doubt that I love you, and I would marry you today if I could, but I'll wait if that's what you want, because I want you to be sure about me." She moved beneath him to escape a rock pressing into her back, and he groaned in agony, dropping his forehead down to touch hers, his hair falling around them like a curtain.

"Move like that again and I'll change my mind," he said between clenched teeth. Jenny actually considered it for a moment, then he moved off her and pulled her to her feet. "I need to cool off, and the lake is the perfect place to do it." Jenny gave him a lecherous look. "Keep your hands to yourself," he added.

"The same goes for you, if you can." She stood there looking at him, her hands on her hips, her hair wild around her, and he couldn't help himself, he pulled her to him for another devouring kiss that left her weak in the knees and leaning against him as his hands roamed over everything within reach.

"I can't," he admitted when he stopped. He stood her upright and dropped his shirt on the blanket. "I've got to cool down." He took off at a run down to the lake, pulling his boots off and dropping his pants on the shore. Jenny was treated to the curve of his backside before he hit the water with a slicing dive that took him out into the deep before he broke the surface again with a splash. The water slid down his chest in sheets as he popped up from below, then settled, his arms slowly moving to keep him afloat as he faced the shore where Jenny stood on the blanket.

"I can't either," she said to no one in particular and sat down to pull off her boots.

"Jenny, what are you doing?" Chase asked from the lake.

"Going swimming."

"You can't."

"Why?"

"Because I'm out here."

Jenny stood and unbuckled her belt. "It's a big lake, Chase. There's plenty of room." Her pants fell to the blanket and she kicked them off.

"Jenny, you're making things difficult."

She started walking towards the water, her shirt tail billowing out in the quick breeze that skimmed the lake surface. "No, I'm not. I need to cool off, too."

"Jenny, this lake will boil if you come any closer." Jenny started to unbutton her shirt. "I mean it, Jenny, I can't be responsible for anything that happens if you don't stop."

"What are you going to do, beat me?"

He took a few steps towards her, then stopped when he realized that coming any closer would reveal more than he wanted. Jenny tilted her head to get a better look as the water lapped under his navel, and then the wind blew the tail of her shirt up, puffing it around her face like a sack. She threw her arms up and wrapped them around herself to keep from flying off like a kite. When she looked again, he was gone. The lake was smooth except for the gentle ripples that broke the surface from the breeze.

"Chase?" she called out, concerned that he had been under too long. She waded out into the shallows, placing her hand over her brow to shield her eyes from the sun. "Chase, where are you? This isn't funny anymore."

The next thing she knew, she was flying through the air out into the water, where she landed with a big splash. She came up coughing and spitting, with her hair heavy in her face. She shoved it back and saw Chase standing on the bank with his pants back on, his legs set wide apart and his arms crossed across his wide bare chest, looking down on her like he was a king and she a disloyal subject.

"It wasn't a beating but it will do for now," he said as he perused her dripping features.

Jenny sank back under the water to straighten her hair, then made her way towards the bank. When she came out of the water, Chase decided that dunking her hadn't been such a good idea because her shirt had become transparent and clung to her curves, revealing more than it covered. He couldn't tear his eyes away, and Jenny took some pleasure in knowing that he was pretty much in the same condition that he had been in before his swim.

Chase picked up the blanket and wrapped it around her, then handed her his shirt so she could change out of hers. She pulled her hair up on top of her head and tied it with a piece of rawhide string, then spread the blanket back out on the ground. She tucked the shirt tail under her as she sat after spreading her own shirt out on the grass to dry in the sun. She patted the blanket next to her invitingly, and he sat down, his eyes wary, watching for her to seek some revenge.

"Why is it," she started, "that you and Jamie have this need to throw me into whatever water is available?"

Chase laughed and stuck a blade of grass in his mouth. "Maybe it has something to do with our visions."

"What visions?"

"We went to Gray Horse after we left the mission, and he wanted us to have visions to guide us in our quest. It's the way of most Indians—we have spirit guides—and Gray Horse wanted us to find ours before we set out. So we performed the ceremony and we both had visions, and we both saw lakes in our visions."

"Tell me about your vision."

Chase stretched out on the blanket and laid his head in her lap, taking the blade of grass out of his mouth and twirling it between his fingers. "I followed Jamie. He was flying across the plains like a hawk, and I was behind him. I could hear you calling to us, so we went towards the sound. I saw you swimming in a lake, so I stopped, but Jamie went on."

"Then what happened?"

"I joined you—we were together." He drew the blade of grass across her cheek. "Really together, in the lake. It was like we were one. That's how I knew we would find you, because we were one. There were wolves around us, too, but they would not attack. They were afraid of the water."

"I had a dream about wolves, too. You were fighting them, protecting me from them."

"I guess that just goes to show that the heart knows before the head," he said, his eyes dark. Jenny ran her fingers through the drying strands of his silky hair and bent over to kiss him gently.

"But what about Jamie's vision? You said he saw a lake, too."

"He saw you drowning in a whirlpool and pulled you through and then left you with me. He never would really say much about it, except that he wished he could be as sure as I was that we would all be together again someday."

"Maybe it's because he is white and isn't conditioned to believe in those things."

"It came true for me—except for the wolves, that is."

"That could still happen."

"And I will protect you from them." He pulled her head down and felt her shiver from the cool breeze that had kicked up with the setting sun. "We'd better be heading back."

"I don't want to leave."

"We'll come back again." They gathered their belongings and mounted up to head back to the ranch, letting the horses set their own pace as they rode side by side.

The days of summer began to fly by, but time was split into just two segments for Chase and Jenny: the time they could be alone together and the time they were apart. Jenny would go to bed at night dreaming of the day they would be married. She began to make plans for their life together, as her mind roamed back to the home she had grown up in. The thing she most regretted losing was her mother's quilt. It had been in her life as long as she could remember. Whether spread on the ground for a picnic or folded at the foot of her parents' bed, it had always been there, a symbol of their family. Her mother had told her that her own mother had made it in anticipation of her own marriage, so Jenny went about gathering scraps to start on a quilt herself. During the long summer evenings they would sit on the porch of Grace's cabin, Chase and Jenny in the swing with Jenny sewing pieces of fabric together, Jamie in a chair with his leg propped up and a book in his lap, reading aloud as he used to. Grace would sit on the steps and listen to his voice, and the cowboys would often come around and listen, or talk, or have Caleb draw illustrations to the story. Jake had never learned how to read and would let Jamie work with him some, until he could pick up a newspaper and proudly show off his new-found skill.

Jake began to open up to the group, sharing some of his troubled past as they talked long into the warm summer nights. His father had been a preacher, who would talk of forgiveness in his sermons, then go home and beat his wife and son for imagined transgressions. His sisters would try to hide Jake from his father's anger, but the preacher always found him. His father said he had the devil in him, and the only way to get rid of it was to beat it out of him, until one day Jake left without a word, determined that no one would ever beat him again. He taught himself how to shoot and made himself fast on the trigger, so fast that no one would want to come up against him, but a few foolish ones had tried. Jason had found him trying to hide from his reputation and brought him to the ranch, seeing a sensitive soul underneath the brash exterior. Jake would gladly give up his life for any one of his friends, but they still treaded lightly around his quick temper.

Towards the end of summer, Jake's temper was wearing thin after a week of hard rain had kept the hands confined, except for the necessary chores that always needed tending. As soon as the weather cleared they were going to drive the cattle to market in Independence. Everyone would be going except for Grace and Caleb, who drew the short straw this year. Jamie was on his feet again, his broken leg nothing but a memory now, except for teasing reminders about what a difficult patient he had been. He was anxious, like everyone else, for the adventure of the drive and paced the confines of the cabin like a caged tiger.

Zane, Jake, Caleb and Ty were playing cards while Cat watched, her chair drawn up next to Ty's. They were in Grace's cabin, gathered around the table, trying to pass the rainy day the best way they could. Chase and Jenny missed being able to go to the lake but were surviving somehow, passing the time with the rest of them.

"Jamie, would you sit down? You are driving me crazy," Grace finally said after he walked the length of the cabin for the hundredth time.

Jamie shoved his hair back and stopped in the middle of the floor. "A month ago you were begging me to get up and walk."

"A month ago you were lying in the bed complaining."

Jamie walked over and leaned over her chair, bringing his mouth next to her ear. "I never complained when I was in your bed," he whispered, and she blushed, shoving his head away. He grinned at the boys, who hadn't missed the comment. His gaze settled on Jenny and Chase, who had their heads together at the end of the table. He walked over and propped his leg in an empty chair, leaning over the table.

"Jen, make me some cookies," he said.

"Cookies?" Zane's head came up from the other end of the table.

"Remember those sugar cookies you used to make? I haven't had one of those in years. Please make me some."

"Yeah, Jen, make us some cookies," came a chorus from the end of the table.

"Cookies sound all right to me," Chase added.

Jamie looked at her like a whipped dog, then flashed his grin at her. Jenny got up and went to the cupboard and began to pull out the ingredients for the cookie recipe that her mother had taught her. Cat joined her, and soon they were mixing dough and laughing with their heads together. They had started to roll the dough out into little balls the size of walnuts when Jamie decided to come over and stick his finger into the bowl. Jenny smacked his hand, and he jerked back, bumping into Jake's chair.

"Watch it," Jake snarled as his poker hand was given away to Zane, who gleefully raked in the pile of money.

"I knew you were bluffing," Zane said as he made a production out of arranging his winnings.

Jamie ignored the card game and circled again, trying to sneak some dough. Jenny knew her brother well, and threw her elbow into his stomach as he came in again. He rubbed his side and decided to work on Cat, who was a smaller target. He snatched the ball of dough out of her hand and popped it in his mouth with a satisfied sigh.

"Eat all the dough and we won't have any cookies," Jenny warned him.

"Blu is shoo goo," he said around the blob in his mouth.

"Hey, let me have some of that," Ty called from the table. Cat turned with a ball of dough in her hand and Ty opened his mouth, challenging her to hit the target. She tossed the ball just as Jake rose from his chair, and it landed on the back of his head, clinging to the blond strands of his hair. His chair hit the floor with a thud, and silence filled the cabin.

"Damn it!" Jake exclaimed as he reached around his head. Jenny and Cat exchanged glances and moved towards the door as one, slamming it behind them just as Jake lunged for them. He snatched the door open, bouncing it off the wall, and ran through the opening. He became airborne when his foot hit a leg that was stretched across the doorway, and he flew out into the yard and landed face first in a puddle. Jenny and Cat fell into each other's arms, laughing hysterically as the rest of the group came to see what had happened.

The rain had just let up as Jake raised himself from the puddle, his light blue eyes resembling chipped ice as they landed on Jenny and Cat, who had to sit down they were laughing so hard. They heard the slamming of the door behind them, and realized they were in trouble when they saw Zane's face pressed against the window.

"Open the door," Jenny yelled as Jake took a step. Cat was behind her, beating on the locked portal. Inside, they could hear voices being raised as Chase and Jamie started in on each other.

"Jamie, open the door now."

"Sorry, I can't do that."

"Jamie, get away from that door," Chase yelled from inside the cabin. Jenny picked up a stool and jabbed it at Jake as he came up the steps, while Cat continued her pounding.

"Ty, let me in!" she screamed.

"I can't move him," Ty groaned from the other side.

Jake grabbed the stool from Jenny's hand and flung it out into the yard.

"Damn it, Jamie, will you move?" Chase hollered.

"Dang, look at that, he's got both of them," Zane said, and faces crowded into the window around him.

Jake had Cat under one arm where she was trying to land blows but was mostly hitting air. He was dragging Jenny with his other arm, her legs too long for him to pick her up the same way he had Cat. Jenny had her heels dug in and was trying to break his hold, but he was determined and pulled her down the steps, where he flung her into the mud. Then he dropped Cat beside her, face first. Jenny came up swinging and managed to land a blow before he pushed her down again, all the while holding a snarling Cat down with his boot.

"I think we're even now," he said after he had made sure they were covered with mud. The group inside had spilled out onto the porch and were laughing hysterically at the three muddy people before them. Jenny flung the mud out of her eyes and scooped up a handful. Jake had turned towards the porch and was in the process of bowing when she let go of her bomb. It hit Jamie square in the face. He jerked his head back, then blinked a few times, while Zane fell to the floor of the porch, holding his stomach in painful laughter. Jamie reached down and picked him up by his belt loops and flung him out into the mud hole, where he landed beside

Jenny. Cat had scrambled out of the way and began scooping up mud to throw at Jake. Jamie let out a whoop and pitched Jake back into the mud, followed by Caleb. Ty bailed out over one porch rail and Chase wisely took the other. Jenny had decided that Chase looked entirely too clean and tackled him as he came around the side of the porch. Soon everyone was rolling in the mud, except for Grace, who had wisely gone back in and locked the door.

The rain started up again, a downpour so intense that it blinded them as it washed the mud away. Chase pulled Jenny over to the side of the porch, where the water drained off like a heavy waterfall. She stuck her head under the flow, running her hands through her hair to wash out the mud that clung to the heavy strands. Chase helped her by combing his fingers through the mass that reached halfway down her back. She tilted her head back, letting the water wash over her face and down her neck. Mud began to accumulate inside her shirt, so she pulled it out and unbuttoned it. Chase ducked his head under, clearing his hair and face, and pulled his shirt off.

Everyone else had taken shelter, Jake, Caleb and Zane dashing for the bunkhouse, Ty and Cat heading into the barn. Jamie had begged at the door for Grace to let him in, and she finally did, after throwing a towel at him to clean up with. The water washed over Chase in sheets as he turned Jenny against the house, shielding her from any prying eyes with his body. She pulled her shirt off and plucked her camisole away from her skin so the water could wash away the mud that had accumulated.

Chase leaned an arm against the wall and looked down at the cleavage revealed beneath him, watching the water sluice down the valley between her breasts. He slowly raised his eyes and saw Jenny's parted lips, her eyes the deep blue of sapphire as he bent to kiss her. Her arms twined around his neck, and he pulled her close, the heat of their skin burning against the cool water. He felt the softness of her breasts against the smooth hardness of his chest, and it started a fire deep inside him that threatened to consume them both in the midst of the shower. He couldn't stop; she begged him not to as his mouth claimed hers, pulling at the depths of her soul.

"Ahem."

Chase raised his head, blindly, looking towards the noise. Jason was standing on the porch, covered with a rain slicker, water dripping off the brim of his hat. Chase turned towards him, and Jenny peered over his shoulder at the interruption.

"Perhaps I should send for the minister."

"Actually, I was hoping you would do the service for us," Chase replied.

Jason raised his eyebrows in surprise. "I would be honored. So you've set a date?"

Chase looked over his shoulder at Jenny, who was looking a bit surprised herself. "I was thinking maybe as soon as we get back from the drive?"

Jenny wrapped her arms around him from behind. "Just give me time to find a dress."

"I think that can be arranged." Jason smiled at them. "If you don't die of pneumonia first." He shook his head at their foolishness and knocked at Grace's door before going into the cabin.

Chase turned around into Jenny's arms. "Will you marry me when we get back?"

"I'd marry you now, soaking wet, covered with mud."

"While the thought is enjoyable"—he moved his hands over her bare shoulders—"I don't really want to share you with the brutes that hang around this place, so we'll wait." He pulled her dripping shirt off the porch rail and wrapped it around her shoulders. "Go on into the cabin, I'll get you some dry clothes from the bunkhouse." Chase kissed the tip of her nose and took off through the rain. Jenny watched him run from the porch and wrapped her arms around herself.

"We'll be married in just a few weeks," she sang to herself. "I can hardly wait."

Chapter Twenty-seven

The long days of the drive were over, the herd had been sold, Jason had given everyone a well-deserved bonus, and they were heading home. Chase and Jenny were anxiously looking forward to their wedding day. Jason had presented them with the cabin that had been his first home when settling the ranch, and Chase had many busy nights ahead of him to restore it to livable condition.

There was only one thing left to do before they started on the wedding plans. Jenny and Jamie needed to go home one last time to see their parents' graves and close that chapter of their lives. They turned north when they came out of Independence, promising to catch up with their friends in a few days. Chase did not go with them. He felt that it would be better for just the two of them to go so they would have the time to grieve and talk and put all the pain of the past behind them. They said their goodbyes and looked forward to being together again in a few short days.

The town had grown in the years they had left, so much that the cemetery that used to be on the outskirts of town was now almost in the middle. The place was still well tended, and they easily found the stones that marked the last resting places of Ian Duncan and his beloved wife, Faith, and the smallest ones that belonged to the two baby brothers. They stood in silence, gazing down at the chiseled stones and at the grass that had been clipped short within the confines of the white picket fence.

"Dad's not here," Jamie finally said. He shoved his hair back and plopped his hat on his head. "He's out there somewhere, standing on a ridge watching the horses run."

"And Momma is right beside him."

"Yes, she is."

"When he died, he saw her," Jamie nodded his head, remembering the story. "He said she was an angel," she said.

"I guess they both are."

"Do you think they're watching us?"

"Every day."

"At least they can be with the babies now."

"They have more family up there than they do down here." Jamie looked around restlessly, the town now suffocating him, and his scar making him self-conscious. "Let's go by the ranch. I never got a chance to say goodbye to it, either."

"Maybe someone is living there," Jenny warned him.

"It's okay, we'll just tell them who we are and we wanted one last look."

"I would like to find out if anyone has Momma's quilt."

"If they do, I'm sure they'll give it to us. Come on, let's go."

The Duncan ranch was still a good ways from town, and it surprised the two of them that there weren't more homesteads out that way. Jenny wanted to go in by way of the ridge, to see the lay of the land first, but Jamie insisted that they had nothing to hide, so they rode down the drive, circling the rise and coming up into the yard in front of the house.

The place had run down in the years since they had been gone, the well-tended gardens nothing but a memory. The porch was missing some boards, and the window in the loft was broken. A bunkhouse had been added out beyond the barn, and the area around it looked like a pigsty, littered with broken bottles and busted pieces of furniture. The farm animals were missing; not even a dog barked to announce their presence.

"Should we see if anyone is home?" Jamie asked after they had sat a minute, trying to take in the sad state of affairs. His horse stomped and shook, trying to free itself of a fly buzzing around his head.

"I don't think so. Let's just go on."

"No, I want to find out about Momma's quilt."

"I doubt if it's survived this." Jenny swung her arm out to encompass the mess.

"Come on, Jen, have a little faith." He grinned at her as he swung off his horse. Jenny took his reins and decided to keep her distance from whatever was living in the house.

Jamie tested the rotting boards of the porch before he stepped up and knocked on the door. There was no answer, so he went to the window of what had been their sitting room and tried to peer in through the grime.

"Come on, let's go," Jenny called. Jamie rolled his eyes at her and went to the end of the porch and leaned out over the rail to see if there were any signs of life at the back of the house. "Jamie, please." Jenny could feel the hair standing up on the back of her neck.

"Don't move." The voice came from the loft in the barn, and Jenny heard the sound of a rifle being cocked as she slowly raised her hands. In the blink of an eye, Jamie had turned with his gun drawn, and was leaning sideways against the post of the porch, the thin column offering little protection to his wide frame.

"Drop that gun, or your girlfriend is history."

Two sets of sapphire-blue eyes exchanged looks. *Don't worry*, Jamie's said, *we'll talk our way out of this*. He flashed his grin towards the loft and twirled his gun around so he was holding it by the barrel, his arms held out in surrender.

"We didn't mean to trespass. We used to live here and came to look around, that's all." His arms were held out in innocent supplication, proving that they didn't mean any harm.

"Drop that gun."

The next thing they knew, the yard was full of riders, close to a dozen in all, the horses milling around Jenny as a horrid stench filled the air. Jenny's eyes widened as she recognized Logan and Joe in the group, and she ducked her head, hoping they wouldn't notice who she was.

A bulky man on a huge horse rode up to the porch where Jamie was standing, his arms still spread wide. "Well, I'll be damned," he said. "You look just like the bastard." He pulled his gun out of his monogrammed holster. "Now drop that piece." Jamie's fingers released his gun as the man leveled his own pistol at his head. "Push that hat back, boy, so I can get a better look at you." Jamie's eyes narrowed, but the gun cocked so he pushed his hat back off his forehead. The man rode closer to get a better look, then turned his huge head towards the barn and returned it to Jamie with an evil grin on his face. "I know who you are. I heard your screams that night."

Realization hit three people at the same time. Jenny and Jamie knew in a flash that this was the man who had murdered their parents. Logan realized that his longtime enemies were before him. He reached up and knocked Jenny's hat back at the same time that Jamie dove off the porch, aiming for the huge man's neck with his arms outstretched, determined to choke the very life from his body as he knocked him off his horse and wrapped his hands around his beefy neck.

Jenny hauled on the reins of her horse and pulled her gun. Her horse reared, pawing the air, just as arms from all directions reached out, clawing at her. She shot at the first face she saw, Joe's, his eyes opening wide as the blood spread on his chest. He hit the ground dead, just as she was swept off her horse and pulled to her feet by Logan, who ran his hands over her breasts as he jerked her from the ground, her fists managing to land a few blows before he wrapped his arms around her from behind.

"Let me go, you son of a bitch," she snarled. "I'll kill you just like I killed your sneaky little friend," Jenny hissed, desperate to get away from him. She kicked the air as he swung her around in time to see Jamie dragged off of their boss by six men, three on each arm, using all their strength to hold him back.

Randolph Mason raised his huge bulk out of the dust and slowly cleaned himself off. Unlike his companions, a ragtag bunch who seemed to have an aversion to bathing, he wore stylish clothing, cut from fine cloth and embellished with initials on everything. The fine cut of his clothes could not disguise what years of eating rich foods and drinking fine liquors had done to his body. Where once he had had the build of a strong bull, he was now soft in the paunch and around his jaw. His eyes were lost in the folds of his face, and his mouth was nothing but a narrow slash in his flesh.

One thing that had not changed through the years was his hatred of Ian Duncan. Though his rival was long dead, Mason was still haunted by the knowledge that Ian Duncan had beaten him and humiliated him by stealing Faith away the night before their wedding. Killing them had not been revenge enough, he had realized: not even taking over the land that had been their dream was enough to dampen the hatred that still burned within him. And now, before him stood their children, the son the image of the father, the daughter strong and glorious in her anger. He almost laughed in glee as he approached the snarling Jamie, who stood red-faced with rage, almost knocking the men who held him off their feet as he tried to jerk his arms from their hold.

"So you are the son," Mason said as he stood before him. "Randolph Mason, at your service," he sneered. He grabbed Jamie's jaw and tilted it to get a better look at the scar that gleamed white against the flush of his skin. "I guess I got you good that night and didn't even know it." Jamie jerked his jaw out of the fleshy fingers. "How 'bout that boys? I got me two Duncans with one shot, and this one squealed like a pig." The group guffawed.

"You bastard," Jenny screamed. "He was just a boy!"

Mason turned his attention to Jenny, who was struggling in Logan's hold, wrestling her way off the ground, only to have her legs slammed down as she pushed against his arms. Mason reached out and picked up the braid of golden hair that had fallen over her shoulder as she fought against Logan. "And the daughter," he mused as he rubbed the silky strands between his fingers. "You look a bit like her, I suppose, around the mouth, but you're taller, bigger, I guess you get that from your father. It's a pity, you know, because I was supposed to be your father, not that Scottish stable boy." Jenny landed a kick in the soft paunch of his belly.

"Hold her!" he shouted after he had caught his breath. Logan brought his hands up under her arms and firmly placed his palms on either side of her face, wedging her so she could not turn her head. She stood with clenched jaw, seething as Mason stood before her, his dark eyes roaming over her body. "We called your mother the Ice Princess." He reached out his hand and cupped her breast, Logan firmly placing his booted heel on top of her foot to keep her from kicking again. She could feel Logan's hot breath against her neck as he laughed. Lower, pressing into the small of her back, was his erection. Jenny fought the urge to vomit as Mason squeezed her breast. "I believe you've got more spirit than your mother. Like a wild thoroughbred, isn't she, fellows?" The gang in the yard agreed wholeheartedly, some of them even licking their lips. "Have you ever been broken?" he said into her ear.

Jamie's rage reached a new level as he watched Mason running his hands over his sister's body. He managed to break an arm free, throwing his guards to the ground as he turned towards the others holding him. One of them had the presence of mind to strike him in the back of the head with the butt of his gun, and Jamie fell to one knee. The mob was upon him again, driving him to the ground, where they kicked him repeatedly in the head, back and side.

"Stop it!" Jenny screamed, choking on a sob as Jamie tried to protect himself from the barrage of blows. Mason held up a hand and the men stopped instantly, leaving Jamie curled on his side as he tried to draw a breath. At Mason's signal, Jamie was hauled to his feet, this time needing the support of three men. Mason grabbed the hair that had fallen over Jamie's face and pulled his head up. To his surprise, the boy's blue eyes were flashing with rage.

"I burned you, didn't I, boy, in that barn right over there?" Jamie's eyes darkened; his hands ached to close once again around Mason's stout neck. "Dick, go fix me a torch," Mason commanded, and one of the men took off to follow his orders. Jamie and Jenny locked eyes as the group waited in nervous anticipation for what was going to happen next, the day's excitement a high spot in their dreary, worthless lives. Mason stood patiently waiting, slapping his gloves against his thigh as he looked between the two Duncan offspring, wondering what he had done to earn such a glorious reward.

The one called Dick returned, carrying a flaming torch before him like a trophy as he breathlessly skidded to a halt before his employer, handing him the torch as if it were a great treasure.

"Have you ever seen anyone burn?" Mason asked as he held the torch up for all to see. Jenny felt her stomach turn and the earth drop beneath her as she saw the color drain from Jamie's face. The torch danced before him, Mason jabbing it in the air like a sword, the flame hypnotizing the group as they yearned for what was sure to happen next. Logan giggled in Jenny's ear, and she jerked her head back hard, hitting it against his jaw and shutting him up for the moment.

Surely he's not that evil, Jenny prayed as Mason played with the torch, bringing it closer and closer to Jamie. Then in her mind she saw her father lying in a pool of blood. She was standing almost in the exact spot, and she knew that this man was capable of anything. "Wait! Stop!" she screamed, her voice rising above the nervous laughter of the watching men. Mason turned to her, one eyebrow raised, enjoying the moment and the power it offered him. "Take me and let him go!" Jenny yelled.

"Jenny, *no!*" Jamie cried.

"Oh, I plan to take you, have no doubt in your mind about that."

"You plan to take me, yes—" the wheels began to turn in Jenny's mind as she remembered everything her father had told her about Randolph Mason. "But how would you like to have me, willing, in your bed? Wouldn't that be sweet revenge? To have me, Ian Duncan's daughter, as your whore?" Jenny gave what she hoped was an encouraging smile as Jamie began to curse. "Let him go and I'll be everything you wanted my mother to be and more. As you said, I'm no Ice Princess. I'm my father's daughter." Jenny prayed she was hitting the right note as she went on, her voice growing silky and seductive.

Mason threw his head back and laughed. The sound of it sent a chill down Jenny's spine as it awoke the demons of her past. She kept her eyes focused on Jamie, who was desperately fighting the men who held him. "Duncan's daughter my whore? Oh, that is too sweet." He laughed some more, finally letting his mirth die into a few grunts as he contemplated the situation. Logan, behind her, was shaking his head. He had a stake in this, too. He wanted to see Jamie burn, wanted his turn at taking revenge on Jenny for killing Joe, but he saw the peculiar light that was burning in Mason's beady eyes and knew that Jenny was winning the day.

Mason walked up to her and grabbed her breast again, pinching it painfully in his fingers, Jenny's face remained frozen in a half smile the whole time. She knew that if she flinched, Jamie was done for. Mason brought his hand up, under her neck, and she raised her head to give him better access. He hooked his hand in the front of her shirt and jerked it down, ripping the buttons off. The sides of her shirt gaped open so the tops of her breasts were revealed by the camisole underneath. He ran his hands over the curves, testing the softness of her skin as he kept his eyes on her face, waiting for the sign that would consign her brother to a painful death. She didn't bat an eye. "You're his daughter, all right." He sighed as if a heavy load had been lifted from his shoulders. "Let him go!"

Jamie fell snarling to the ground as the three released their hold on him. He quickly jumped to his feet. "Jenny, I won't let you do this."

"You don't have a choice," Jenny said. She made her eyes soft as she looked at Mason. "Let me talk to Jamie, please." Mason jerked his head at Logan, who begrudgingly let her go. Jenny ran to Jamie, who was trembling with rage or fear, she could not tell which. "Jamie, please, they will kill you."

"I won't let you do this." His voice was low, their heads together.

"You can't fight them. There are too many."

"I won't leave you here."

"Go, get the others. It will only take a few days." They were whispering, their heads turned away from the men who watched. They heard Mason impatiently clear his throat. "I can hold on that long. He won't kill me." Jenny took his face between her hands. "It's the only way. If you don't leave, he'll kill you and then let all of them have me. At least this way, it won't be so bad." Her eyes begged him, the depths of her love for him spilling over into tears.

Jamie punched the porch post in rage. He knew Jenny was right. There were too many—he couldn't fight them all, and they would both surely die, horribly, at the hands of this man.

"I'll be back. I swear it on my life, I'll be back." He pulled her to him and hugged her desperately, his eyes burning as he fought back the sob that threatened to wrench forth from his gut.

"I'll be here," she whispered. "Tell Chase . . ." She didn't dare cry or he wouldn't go.

Jamie nodded, picked up his gun, jerked it into his holster and went to his horse. The gang of men fell back as he went by, so powerful was the rage radiating from his body. Jenny wrapped her arms around the post as he took off. It was the only way she could keep from collapsing into a sobbing heap in the dirt. She had to stay strong until he was out of sight, she had to keep her end of the bargain until she knew he was safe.

"You know he'll be back," Logan said as Jamie disappeared around the bend.

"Oh, yes, I know, and when he comes back, we'll torch him, but in the meantime, I'll be enjoying myself with the daughter. I never dreamed my revenge would be so complete. This is much better

337

than anything I could have thought of. I hope that Scottish bastard is spinning in his grave."

They watched as Jenny slid down the post, hanging on to it for dear life as she landed on the step. Mason walked over to where she sat, still watching the bend in the road, scarcely believing that they hadn't gone after him with guns blazing. She looked up at Mason in a daze, blinking at the afternoon sun shining directly behind his head. He didn't say a word, just reached down and wrapped his fingers into her hair, then pulled her behind him as he made his way across the porch. Jenny wrapped her hands around his to keep her hair from being pulled from its roots and willed her body to relax as he dragged her through the front door, kicking it shut behind him.

Chapter Twenty-eight

Jason scrutinized the group ranged on the ridge on either side of him, overlooking the ranch where Jamie and Jenny had been raised. Two days had passed since Jamie had caught up with them, his rage still wild as he kicked them awake, ranting about Jenny and Randolph Mason. It had taken him two days of hard riding to find them, and another two days for them to return, and Chase had not spoken a word since Jamie had told them the story, nearly choking on the words. No one faulted him, they all knew that he and Jenny had done the only thing that would save them, but Jason knew it was eating Jamie up that he had deserted his sister, even if it was to go for her only hope of rescue.

The Chase that they knew had disappeared with the telling, replaced by a savage whose only thoughts were of taking revenge on the men who held his love prisoner. Jason shuddered as he imagined the lengths Chase would go to to make them pay.

They had come up behind the ridge, leaving their horses hidden in the brush below, all of them crawling up on their bellies. Ty, Cat and Jake were on Jason's right, Jamie, Zane and Chase on his left, all with jaws set and death in their eyes as they surveyed the scene before them.

It was late afternoon, and obvious that the chores were done for the day. There was smoke coming from the chimney of the main house, and the sound of muted laughter could be heard from the bunkhouse. In the loft of the barn, they caught the occasional glint of sunlight on a gun barrel and assumed that a guard was posted there to watch for Jamie's return.

"Where do you think she is?" Jason asked Jamie, who was lying beside him.

"Probably in my parents' room, to the right of the door," Jamie replied, never taking his eyes off the house. A sound caught their ears, and they all held their breath as the front door opened and Randolph Mason stepped out onto the porch, yawning and stretching, his shirt tail hanging out and his suspenders dangling around his knees. There was a sharp intake of breath as Jamie's hand curled into a claw against the ground, grinding dirt into his palm. Chase's eyes focused on the man, imprinting his face and the approaching moment of his death into his brain.

"Ty, you and Cat circle around the back and see if you can find Jenny," Jason said. "The rest of us will split up and come at them from both sides. Jake, can you take out that rifle in the loft?"

"Yes." There was no doubt there, just the look of death in Jake's light blue eyes. They snaked back down the hill and checked their guns, making sure once again that they were loaded and ready.

"Okay, fifteen minutes and I'll start shooting," Jason reminded them as they mounted up. He grabbed Ty's arm before they rode off. "Take care of my daughter."

"I will," Ty assured him, his face set as he took off with Cat, swinging out and around behind the trees. Jake, Zane and Jason went around by the road, while Chase and Jamie came up by the stream, waiting for Ty and Cat to get into place, waiting for Jason's signal.

Jenny tried to bring the walls into focus as she leaned against the corner beside the bed in what had once been her parents' bedroom. Her left eye was swollen shut, the skin around it cut and bruised from the fist Mason had used on her. He had an awesome right, she had thought at the time, but couldn't follow through with his left and just settled for backhanding her, which stung like crazy but didn't leave much of a mark. Her right ankle was swollen where it had been twisted in one of her attempts to escape, foolish attempts really, because she couldn't go far. Her other ankle was chained to the bed post. What pained her most however, even more than the cuts that his knife had made on her breast, or the constant ache between her legs, was her shoulder, which she had dislocated when she had tried to escape the knife he held to her breast as he sat across her stomach. She had twisted away, but he had grabbed her arm and forced her back, until the shoulder had popped out of joint and she had screamed in agony as he carved his initials into the soft skin over her heart, branding her, he said, so everyone would know whom she belonged to. "Nobody takes what's mine!" he had said over and over again, pounding it into her brain the same way he was pounding into her body. Her shoulder now hung at an odd angle, the whole left side of her body lower than the right. The pressure from the dislocation or some broken ribs, she wasn't sure which, made it hard for her to breath.

She had lost track of time, the days and nights fading into a never-ending hell, but it was better than death, she tried to convince herself, better than watching them burn Jamie alive. She knew she would not have been able to bear the screams, would have sought death herself in the fire rather than watch it. The irony was that she hadn't even had to act the whore. Mason had simply dragged her in the house and raped her, ripping her clothes off, throwing them in a corner where they still lay in a heap and taking her trembling body beneath his without a thought in the world beyond the pleasure it gave him to know that he had Ian Duncan's daughter in his bed. In Ian's bed, actually, and that thought gave him more satisfaction than the actual deed.

She laid her head against the wall, her nude and bruised body shivering, but still having enough fight in her to prefer the cold to the stinking blankets on the bed. A touch of color caught her eye in the dust under the bed, and she tilted her head, bringing her right eye around to see better. She moved a bit, biting back the pain, and reached under with her right hand. She pulled out her mother's quilt, stained and filthy but still whole, having been carelessly kicked under the bed many years ago and forgotten. Jenny pulled it around her body, sobs overcoming her. Grief only added to her pain as sobs shook her injured shoulder, but she was unable to stop the tide. "Oh, Momma," she cried into the quilt, wrapping her arm around it, holding it up to her face. The sound of a gunshot rent the air, but she ignored it. They were always hollering and shooting after a few drinks, but then she heard a barrage of bullets and she raised her head, watching the shadows that flitted across the window, hearing the sounds of hoofbeats, the sounds of men dying.

She heard running feet, heard Cat calling her name, then heard the sharp intake of breath as Cat caught sight of her and skidded to a halt.

"Don't let Chase see me, Cat," Jenny whispered between her split lips. Cat held out her hand to stop Ty, who came flying in, his gun drawn. "Please, don't let him see me like this."

Cat holstered her gun and knelt in front of Jenny. "Ty, keep Chase out of here," she said as she reached out to pull the quilt away.

Jenny looked down, her shame unbearable as she heard Cat's choking sob as she saw the bent shoulder, the bruises, and the bloody R and M carved on her breast. Jenny pulled the quilt back up, and Cat helped her put it in place.

The shooting died down as Zane and Jake gave chase to the few who had managed to get away, Logan among them. Chase stood over Randolph Mason, who looked up at him with beady eyes, his brain still in shock from the attack, wondering at the identity of this half-breed who was looking down on him with such contempt. The breed had been ruthless, he thought to himself, cutting a swath through his men as if they were nothing, intent on destroying them and all for a girl who had turned out to be as cold as her mother. Chase turned on his heel and went up the steps, Jamie falling in behind him as he holstered his gun. Jamie didn't even give Mason a look.

Ty was standing by the door, and the look on his face made Chase's heart stop beating.

"Where is she?"

"She doesn't want you to see her."

Chase stepped toward the door, and Ty grabbed him. They swung around and slammed into the wall, Ty holding Chase against it with all his strength. "Jenny?" Chase called. "*Jenny?*" he screamed.

Jenny sobbed as she heard his voice, heard the struggle going on in the other room. Jamie dashed by the two and into the room as Cat ran out to stop Chase.

"Chase, listen to me . . . she's alive, and she doesn't want you to see her now. Please, leave her her pride . . . please," Cat implored.

Chase stopped his struggling and stood panting against the wall. They heard the sound of a fist hitting the wall inside, three times in quick succession, then Jamie's hoarse croak as he cried out her name. Chase shook off the hands that were holding him and walked out the front door, his eyes black and empty.

"Oh, Jenny, I'm so sorry, I'm so sorry," Jamie cried as he gathered her into his arms. The chain around her ankle stopped him, so he pulled out his gun and shot the chain off. She didn't flinch, but the pain when he picked her up made her dizzy, and she almost fainted as he carried her out of the room and into the kitchen at the back of the house, the quilt still wrapped around her.

Outside, Chase hauled a bleeding Mason to his feet. "You can't hurt me," Mason spat out, "I'm dying." The dark eyes, however, said otherwise, and for the second time in his life, Randolph Mason felt real fear. Chase dragged him to the corral and tied his arms, stretched out on either side, to the rail. Jake watched as Chase pulled out his knife, the knife that had once belonged to Ian Duncan.

Jason was examining Jenny's shoulder when a high-pitched scream rent the air. Ty, Cat and Jason exchanged scared looks as Zane went to see what was causing the noise. Jamie seemed to already know, and he didn't take his eyes off Jenny's face as her eyes suddenly focused on his.

"Your shoulder is dislocated," Jason said. "I'm going to try to put it back into place."

Jenny nodded weakly and Jason grabbed her arm, pulling it straight and bracing his hand against her other shoulder as he pulled and pushed, until the shoulder went back in with a pop. Jenny fainted, her head falling back against Jamie's arm and the quilt sliding out of her grasp, baring her breast to Jason's eyes.

"Son of a bitch," Jason gasped as he saw the deep cuts over her heart. Jamie blinked back tears as Jason pulled the quilt up. Jamie pulled her close and sobbed into her hair. "Cat, see if you can find her clothes. We've got to get her cleaned up and get out of here. I don't want to have to explain this to the local sheriff if I can help it. Ty, see if you can do anything with Chase." They scattered to do Jason's commands, and he went to fetch a pail of water and a towel. He stopped at the window, startled to see Zane retching in the side yard. Jason put it down to seeing too much death and reminded himself to have a talk with the boy on the way home. Cat returned with Jenny's clothes, torn but pretty much wearable except for the shirt. Zane came up the back steps, his face pale, his mouth green around the edges, but they didn't notice as they sent him out to get another shirt for Jenny to wear from the spares they had all brought.

Jamie held Jenny in his arms as Cat gently wiped her skin under the quilt, trying to preserve her dignity, at least. Even in her unconscious state, Jenny flinched as Cat wiped the dried blood from between her legs; she moaned when they pulled a sock over her swollen ankle. Jason pressed a wet towel to her eyes and she came around, blinking and startled, but relieved when she saw the faces of people who cared for her, when she realized that Jamie's arms were supporting her instead of holding her down, as Mason did.

She couldn't walk, so Jamie wrapped the quilt around her and picked her up, carrying her through the sitting room and out on the porch. Chase was there in the yard, on his horse, waiting. Jenny buried her head under Jamie's chin when she saw him. "No," she whispered into his neck.

"This is one argument you are not going to win," Jamie said and handed her over the rail into Chase's waiting arms. Her dislocated shoulder had been wrapped tightly against her body, and it now rested against Chase's chest as he adjusted her over his legs, her head falling into place on his shoulder, her nose tucked up under his chin, her cheek lying against the silky hair that fell over his shoulders. His arms trembled as he resisted the urge to squeeze her to him, to never let her go. Instead, he just held her, his arms loose and relaxed until he felt her body ease against him. The others were waiting. They were all mounted except Jamie, who still stood on the porch.

Cat let out a gasp as she turned her horse towards the fence.

"Don't look," Ty said, but it was too late. Ty reached out and grabbed Cat's rein and led her towards the drive, Zane and Jake following with Jenny's horse, which they had found in the barn.

"My God," Jason said and turned to look back at Chase, who had his head down over Jenny's, and at Jamie, whose face showed no emotion at all. Jason followed the others.

Jamie and Chase looked at each other, their faces in complete agreement. Chase turned his horse and directed it towards the fence where Randolph Mason was tied, his body slumped against his restraints, his pants down around his ankles, and nothing but a bloody mess left between his legs. The part of him that had been removed lay in the dirt before him.

"Look at him, Jenny. He can't hurt you or your family anymore," Chase said gently.

Mason raised his head and saw her eyes on him beneath the shadow of Chase's chin.

"Is this what you want?" His words were slurred. "A half-breed? Is this the man whose name you called?" Mason tried to laugh, but all that came out was a gurgling sound as his lungs filled with blood. "Just remember one thing, half-breed." He was dying and he knew it, but he could still hurt them. "When she closes her eyes, it will be my face she sees, not yours."

Jenny trembled at the words, and Chase felt it.

"But you'll be dead," Chase said simply. Jenny turned her face into the steel cords of Chase's neck, and he reined the horse away. Behind him, Mason's head lolled to the side as his last breath was drowned in blood. Chase rode to where the others were waiting and he felt his heart leap in his chest as he felt Jenny's hand, beneath the quilt, make its way between the buttons of his shirt, coming to rest against his pounding heart.

While the others waited at the curve in the drive, Jamie went back into the house and returned with a lamp. He carefully lit the wick and watched as the flame jumped to life. Jamie stepped off the porch and stood with the lamp in his hand, looking up at the broken window in the loft, turning his head to look down the stream and up to the other side where his mother had grown flowers along the porch. He took another step back and flung the lantern against the front wall, where it shattered. The oil inside ran down the planks of the wall, the flames giving chase and soon licking up the door frame. The wood was dry and the flames were strong; he took another step back as the fire roared to life. Jamie's horse danced nervously as the fire grew, and the heat drove Jamie into the saddle. He looked at the barn, turned the horse in a slow circle as his mind's eye saw what had once been, and then he joined the group that was waiting at the curve in the drive. He didn't look back.

Chapter Twenty-nine

Chase felt as if the pounding of his heart would dislodge the frail hold that Jenny had on his chest. He felt the weak touch of her hand, held in place by the strength of the buttons on his shirt instead of any desire that might have been there at one time. She had not spoken a word since Jamie had laid her in his arms, just softly cried out in pain whenever he adjusted her into a more comfortable position. She was sleeping restlessly, the movement of the horse occasionally penetrating into her unhappy dreams. He barely felt her breath against his neck, and actually had a few moments of panic when he thought that she had ceased breathing altogether. But then she would stir against him, not having the strength to do much else, and his heart would resume pounding in his chest.

Chase fought to control the anger that threatened to boil up from within. He had been like a madman since the night Jamie had come barreling into camp and kicked him awake, his face white, his voice grim, the words "Jenny's being held prisoner" like a knife in his heart. Jason had asked all the questions while Chase went to saddle his horse, not speaking a word, afraid that if he opened his mouth his very soul would pour out in a painful wail. The ride to find her had been agony, his mind going over every possible alternative from finding her alive and well to finding her dead and gone, and he planned, in great detail, the painful deaths that would come to those who had harmed her.

The battle was over, Randolph Mason was dead, his multitude of sins sending his spirit to the worst kind of hell for the pain he had inflicted upon the Duncans, but still Chase was angry. He had heard Jenny's weak pleas when he had come into the house. He did not have to look beneath the quilt to know that her body was bruised and damaged, her face gave enough evidence of that. It was her spirit he was afraid for, afraid that this time her spirit would not be able to recover from the blows that life had dealt her. Chase looked over at Jamie, who was riding next to him, his head bobbing in exhaustion. The only sleep he had gotten in the past few days had come on the back of a horse. His face was streaked with dirt, soot and blood, so that the only way you could tell he was scarred was by the uneven texture of skin between the eye and hairline. Chase mused to himself, *Jamie's scars are on the outside, Jenny's on the inside.* He felt a soft sigh against his neck. He wondered which were worse.

Jason called a halt to the weary group's travel when the sun was setting. Jamie was ready to fall from his saddle, Jason wasn't sure if Jenny was up to traveling with her injuries, and the rest of the group seemed in a state of shock over what they had seen Chase to be capable of. Jake was the only one who seemed to treat Mason's fate as a normal state of affairs. To his mind, justice had been served, and that was the end of it.

While Chase held Jenny in his arms, Cat and Jamie made a pallet for her on the ground, making her as comfortable as possible under the conditions. When Jamie saw that she was settled, he spread his blanket next to her and fell asleep instantly, not even bothering to wash off the grime. The rest of the group made an attempt to eat, except for Chase, who disappeared into the darkness, much to the relief of everyone else. They were still in shock over his actions, although when they thought about it, they couldn't really blame him.

Cat finally excused herself and disappeared into the darkness, where they soon heard the sounds of muffled sobs. Ty and Jason exchanged looks, then Ty got up to go after her, wrapping his arms around her in the darkness and pulling her onto his lap as he sat down with his back against a tree, whispering words of comfort into her ear.

Zane and Jake took to their blankets, Zane for once speechless, and left Jason to tend the fire until the others made their way back. Cat and Ty soon appeared, and Cat sat next to her father, leaning heavily against him when he put his arm around her.

"Is she going to be okay?" Cat asked as they watched the slight rise and fall of Jenny's chest.

"I don't know. Physically, I think she'll heal, but we don't know about the rest."

"You mean her mind?"

"I mean her spirit. She's been through a lot in her lifetime, and up till now managed to cope pretty well, but we just can't know about this."

"But this time she has people around her who love her."

"You're right." Jason squeezed his daughter to him just as Chase materialized without a sound into the ring of light around the fire. His hair was wet, his face and hands cleaned, and he resembled again the man they had known and worked with for the past few years. When he sat down at the fire, Cat and Ty excused themselves and spread their blankets next to each other. They lay down, their hands touching in between.

"I feel like you need to talk to me about today," Chase said as the fire crackled before him and Jason. The firelight cast an eerie reflection in his dark eyes as he raised them to look at Jason.

"I really don't know what to say."

"I know you think what I did today was savage, brutal, but it was the way I was raised, and my honor would not permit anything else. If you want me to leave, I will, just as soon as Jenny is well enough to go with me."

"Chase, I am not going to judge you for anything you did today. You did what you had to do to protect the woman you love, and I can't say I would have done anything differently if it had been me. I never had a chance to." Chase looked at Jason, curiosity evident on his face. "Many years ago, I loved a woman. I loved her with every fiber of my being, but I lost her."

"What happened?"

"My parents did not approve of her. They thought I was marrying beneath my station. They thought she was a phase I would outgrow, a foolish whim, so they arranged to have me drugged and placed on a ship to England. By the time I got back, she was gone, married to another man a month after I had left, moved off to God knows where, and I had no way to find her because her family had all been killed in a flood." Jason shook his head as the memory filled his mind. "Her name was Jenny also, and the funny thing is, your Jenny reminds me of her. The first time I saw her, I thought I had seen a ghost, but it was just my mind playing tricks." The fire crackled and popped between them. "If I had the chance to do it over, nothing on earth would have kept me from her, and I would have killed anyone who tried. I should have just taken her and eloped instead of hoping everything would work out with my family. After I found she was gone, I left home, came west. I never saw my family again." Jenny shifted in her sleep, a slight groan coming weakly from her split lips. "We might need to see if we can get her to eat something. Not that this trail food will do her much good, but we need to get her strength up. It's a long way to home."

Chase knelt beside the pallet and laid his hand on Jenny's cheek. Her eyelids fluttered open, the sapphire-blue eyes full of fear before they focused on Chase. "Am I dreaming?" she asked hesitantly.

"No, you're safe." The words sounded real, but she had heard them before and then had realized they were lies when she saw the gentle, regal face of Chase dissolve into the harsh countenance of Mason as he pounded and pawed her body until she had wished desperately for death to take her away. Maybe if she slipped back into sleep, she would once again be held tightly in Chase's arms, her hand feeling the pounding of his heart beneath the smooth skin of his chest. She closed her eyes, willing the bliss to overcome her again. "Jenny." The voice was insistent but soft. "Jenny, you need to eat something."

Stay in your dreams where it's safe, the voice inside her said, and she obeyed.

It was the quiet that finally woke her. The peaceful stillness of the night had settled over the campsite, giving all who were in their bedrolls around the fire the rest they needed. Jenny's eyes flew open, her brain trying desperately to orient itself. She became conscious of a wall to her left, but her arm was strapped down to her chest so she could not reach out and touch it. She shifted her head and saw that the wall was Jamie, lying on his side, facing her. Her eyes had become accustomed to the soft glow of the fire, and she realized that his face was covered with grime and soot, with a bit of blood mixed in. She wondered briefly where the blood had come from, he didn't seem to be wounded anywhere. A slight movement caught her attention, and she turned the other way to find Chase facing her, his body lying between her and the fire. His face was a sharp contrast of light and dark, his high cheekbones catching the firelight. She was safe, she realized, away from the ranch and the horror that it had held for her. "Thank you, God," she repeated over and over, grateful that she was alive. She tried to remember what had happened. She remembered the shots being fired, the look on Cat's face, then Jamie's when they found her. She looked at Chase, remembering his agonized calls as he was held away from her. "I couldn't stand to see the look in your eyes," she whispered.

Jason had fixed her arm—she remembered the pain as he maneuvered it into place. Blessedly, that pain was gone, except for a dull ache. Her ankle was throbbing, and she wondered where her boots were. She knew she couldn't walk, so it really didn't matter except that they were comfortable and she hated to lose them. The pain between her legs had diminished, just leaving her feeling raw; she didn't want to think about that.

Jamie had placed her in Chase's arms. She remembered the trembling she'd felt when he had hugged her, as if he was afraid she would break. Then the sight of Randolph Mason loomed up before her, his bleeding body exposed to all. *You deserve worse*, she had thought as she looked at him, and then his words had hit her.

"It will be my face she sees when she closes her eyes." Jenny shut her eyes, hoping to shut him out.

And it will be his brand Chase sees when he looks at me, she realized. She squeezed her lids tightly, knowing she didn't have the strength to cry. *How can he love me when he'll know, every time he looks at me, that Mason had me, that he had me first.* Her mind was racing as she imagined the rejection, the hurt in his beautiful dark eyes. Jenny brought her clenched fist up to her mouth, biting it to keep from crying out and disturbing the sleep of the two who protected her.

Chase stirred, disturbed by a dream. He rolled on his back and began talking in his sleep, the words slurred and running together, his face agitated, his brow drawn down in a frown. Jenny ran her hand across his forehead, and he quieted instantly, his face clear

350

and peaceful once again. His blanket had fallen away, and she reached to pull it up, but a spark caught her eye.

Beside him on his pallet was his knife—her father's knife; he always slept with it next to him, relying more on it than the gun he wore. Jenny eased it off the blanket, holding her breath as she pulled it away from his side. When she had it in her hand, she sat up, using her left hand, which was strapped to her chest, to pull the knife out of its sheath. She looked at the fire. It was well banked, more coals than flames, ready to be blown into life again when morning came.

If only I could walk, she thought, knowing there was no way she could raise herself up with only one arm and one leg functioning. She eased down her blanket, scooting along on her bottom, awkwardly unbalanced, checking after each movement to make sure she hadn't woken Chase or Jamie, who was now on his back snoring away. The sound he was making would either cover her movements or wake the dead, she wasn't sure which. When she reached the end of Chase's long legs, she managed to get up on her knees and crawled with the knife held tightly in her hand. She needed to get the blade into the fire, it was just ahead, and she shifted the knife to her good hand and reached out to lay it on the coals.

Before she could do so, the knife went flying out of her hand, landing behind her, point stuck in the earth, the blade quivering. Her hand stung from the impact, and she pulled it to her, rubbing it with the bound hand as she slumped into a sitting position. She looked up to see Chase kneeling before her, his eyes shooting silver sparks as he looked down at her shocked face.

"What are you doing?" His voice was low and even, as if talking to a wild animal. Jenny pushed her untidy braid over her shoulder as she looked at him with wide, scared eyes. She looked over at the knife that was planted in the ground, the blade taking on a copper cast from the glow of the coals. Chase reached around her and returned the blade to its sheath, firmly, daring her to try to take it again. He turned where he knelt and placed it under his blanket and then turned back to Jenny. Chase saw Jason's eyes on them from across the fire, but luckily no one else was awake. Chase placed his hands on Jenny's arms and pulled her to him. "I love you," he whispered against her hair. Jenny nodded and let him hold her, to drained to do anything else. She felt like a rag doll in his arms, and just rested there, accepting his arms around her but

351

not responding in any way. Chase slid his arms under her and laid her on his blanket, then wrapped his arms tightly around her as he pulled the filthy quilt over them. Jenny shut her eyes and fell into a troubled sleep, but it was a long time before Chase slept, the image of her leaning over the fire with the knife in her hand still haunted him.

Chase said nothing about the incident with the knife when they awakened the next morning. Jenny did as she was told, letting Jamie carry her to a private place where Cat could help her with her morning routine. Cat was sympathetic without being morose and even managed to get a smile out of Jenny, which quickly ended when her lip split and started bleeding. Jamie handed her over to Chase when they were ready to leave. Jenny knew better than to argue by the look on Chase's face, so she just laid her head on his shoulder and relaxed for the ride.

Later that morning a fever overtook her and they debated whether they should search the nearest town for a doctor, but Jenny roused enough to say she wanted to go home, so they pressed on. Her temperature continued to rise, eventually soaking the two of them with her sweat. The night was spent trying to cool her down while listening to her ravings about Mason, which sent Jamie off into the darkness, unable to stand it any longer. She quieted towards morning and settled down into a deep sleep; she didn't even stir when they broke camp in the morning.

Chase had spent the night sitting by her side and making a sled for her to ride in behind her horse. He placed her on it, wrapped in the quilt when it was time to leave. Except for a few soft murmurs, she could have been dead. They hoped to make it home by nightfall, so Zane and Jake were sent ahead to prepare Grace and have the doctor waiting when they arrived. It was a haggard group that rode into the yard late that night, their worry over Jenny showing clearly on their faces.

Grace was waiting, a bed ready in her cabin where Jenny was placed by Chase, who looked at the doctor with a face full of worry, great dark circles under his eyes.

"I don't think she moved all day," he said as the doctor bent to examine her.

"She's feverish," the doctor said, and the group watching from the doorway rolled their eyes at that revelation. The doctor looked around at the worried faces and decided that they needed to go and leave him to his work. He cleared the room except for Grace and Cat, who stripped Jenny of her clothes and gave her a much-needed bath when the doctor was through.

When they had Jenny settled in a clean nightgown and under warm blankets, the doctor left with instructions to send for him if there was any change. Grace gathered up the bundle of torn clothes and the filthy quilt and carried them to the kitchen, where everyone was gathered around the table. Chase went in to Jenny as soon as Grace came out.

"Caleb, take this mess out and burn it," she said as she dropped the mess into his arms.

"No!" Jamie shouted, startling them all. Jamie snatched the quilt from Caleb's hands. "This was our mother's." The look on his face was desperate as he pulled the quilt against his chest. He looked at Grace, his eyes full of despair.

Grace looked up into the deep blue of his eyes and gently took the quilt from his hands. "I'll wash it tomorrow and then I'll put it on Jenny's bed, I promise."

Jamie shoved his hair back out of his eyes and nodded wearily. His head fell forward as he fought the waves of anguish that threatened to overtake him. Grace took his arm and led him to the door. "Why don't you go get cleaned up and I'll fix you something to eat." Jamie let her lead him out the door, too tired to argue about anything. "The rest of you go on too. You're not doing anybody any good sitting around here." There was the scraping of chairs and the shuffling of feet as the group obeyed her commands.

Grace followed Jason out on the porch after everyone had left and leaned against the door frame.

"What do you think?" he asked as he looked up at the stars peeping out in the night sky.

Grace sighed and pulled her shawl close against the chill of the night air. "I think she's lucky to be alive, but she doesn't know it yet." She walked over to him. "Did you see what that animal did to her?"

"Yes." Jason scrubbed a hand over his face. "And when I'm able, I'll tell you what Chase did to that animal."

The sounds of the night filled the silence that came between them. "Do you think she'll recover?" Jason asked after a while.

"That depends."

"On what?"

"On whether or not that bastard got her pregnant." Grace's voice broke on the words, and she held her hand to her mouth, determined not to cry. Jason looked at her in shock, he had not had time to think about the long-term consequences in the rush to get Jenny home.

"How long?"

"I don't know, three weeks, a month. We'll just have to wait and see."

Jason reached out and squeezed Grace's hand as he stepped off the porch. "I'll see you in the morning."

Grace pulled her shawl up around her chin as she watched Jason disappear into the darkness. It was still late summer, but the air held the promise of a cool autumn, which meant a harsh winter would follow. Jamie came around the cabin, his hair dripping from his hasty shower. Grace was eye level with him as he walked up to where she was standing on the porch. He wrapped his arms around her waist and laid his head against her breast, something he'd never dared do out in the open before. Grace wrapped her arms around him and felt the trembling in his shoulders. "She saved my life," he said against her chest. A sob tore at him, and he fought to hold it in.

"She will be all right," Grace soothed him.

Jamie shook his head against her. "How can she be?"

"Because she's strong, and we love her." Grace gently pulled his face up so she could look into his eyes. His dark lashes were wet with tears, and he tried to blink them away, but they fell to his cheek. Grace rubbed them away with her fingertips. "You need to be strong now, she needs to know that you're here for her. Go sit with her and talk to her. Let her know that you need her to get better."

"She might not, just to make me mad."

"So make her mad enough to get better just to spite you." Jamie managed a slight grin at the thought.

Chase was half asleep in a chair when Grace and Jamie came in, Jenny's hand was lying lightly in his on top of the blanket. He was instantly alert, a lethal look on his face until he realized there was no threat at hand. Grace laid a calming hand on his shoulder.

"Chase, go get cleaned up, get some rest. You'll not do Jenny any good like this."

"I can't leave her."

"We'll take care of her, now go on." Chase did not move. "If you want, you can sleep here on the floor. Just get cleaned up first. I could smell all of you coming hours before you got here." There was a flash of humor in his eyes as he rose to obey.

"I'll be back with my blankets," he promised as he left.

"Bring mine, too," Jamie asked. Chase nodded in agreement as he left.

Chapter Thirty

Jenny was in hell, she had to be, because it was so hot. She was burning up, but she wouldn't let go of the blanket that she held tightly against her, because she did not want anyone to see her shame. Randolph Mason was there also, a sure indication that it must be hell, and he was tormenting her, trying to pull the blanket away so everyone could see his mark. She slapped his hands away just to find them on her again, pulling at her, constantly snatching at her, taking handfuls of hair, skin and blanket every time she pushed him away. *Just leave me alone,* she cried in her mind. *Please, just leave me alone.* But he only laughed, the same laugh she had heard the night her parents died, the same laugh he had used as he pounded her without mercy in her parents' bed. "Just let me die," she sobbed, but she must already be dead, because she was in hell.

Grace wrung out the cloth that covered Jenny's forehead. The cool clothes were drying almost as soon as she put them on, and Jenny's restless movements made it hard to keep them in place. "Let me die," Jenny said. Grace had to put her ear against Jenny's mouth to hear, her voice was so weak.

"No, we won't let you die," Grace said into Jenny's burning hot ear. Grace felt Chase standing beside her, the dim light of the lantern dancing on his wide bare chest and making his face disappear into the darkness.

"What is it?" he asked.

"She's dreaming."

Chase sat on the edge of the bed and picked up Jenny's hand. It fluttered against his like a baby bird, too weak to make it on its own. He brought the hand to his lips and laid his other hand against her cheek. "Jenny?" he said softly. "I'm here, you're not alone anymore." She turned her face into his hand. It was almost as if she was breathing it in, then she turned away from it, fighting once again with the demons that only she could see.

"I hear you Chase, but I can't find you." In her mind she was screaming, but the words came out a whisper. Mason wouldn't let her find him; he kept pulling her back into the furnace that was burning her alive.

"Jenny, I love you," Chase said.

"You can't, don't you see? You won't want to," Jenny cried as she slid into the heat.

"Keep talking to her so she can find her way back," Grace said as she placed a cool cloth on her forehead.

"Jenny!" Chase was calling her, she could hear him but she couldn't answer, because she didn't want to see the look in his eyes, so she stayed in hell, holding the blanket close and begging Mason to leave her alone.

"Maybe we should take the blanket off, she's so hot," Chase suggested.

Grace smoothed the blanket over Jenny's chest, noting the death grip that her hands had on it. "I don't think it would help."

Jenny kept on fighting Mason, even though she was so very tired.

The light was too bright, it was burning through her eyelids, she needed to turn away, but even thinking about moving her head made her cringe. She just didn't have the energy. *Block it out,* Jenny thought and managed to raise her hand and cover her eyes. She felt the strong, gentle touch of another hand as it smoothed back her unruly hair, and her eyelids fluttered.

"Welcome back," said a deep voice, as smooth as velvet. The light was shining in the window behind his head, but she knew it was Chase, because her heart jumped when he spoke to her. Jenny made a face at the light and she heard his laughter, and then the room was dark again. "Is that better?" he asked as he pulled her hand down.

Chase's face was etched with worry, but a slight smile touched it as he realized that the worst was over. Jenny had beaten the fever that had consumed her for the past several days. She was weak, however, that was obvious just by looking at her. The hand that had covered her face was almost transparent, and her skin had lost its golden glow. A few days in the sun and a few good meals should get her healthy again, he mused, but he was saddened when she turned away from him.

Chase had thrown her mother's quilt over the window. It framed him perfectly as he stood by the side of the bed, looking wonderful. Jenny wanted so much to feel his arms around her. She still remembered how he had held her in front of him on his horse, but it was best to put such memories behind her, best for the both of them. Her ordeal had affected him, she could tell by the lines around his eyes, and there was a sadness there also. She recognized it from when they had first met, when his mother had been killed. She had to turn away before he could see inside her. She knew that he could look into her eyes and know everything, and she couldn't stand it. He must never know what Mason had done to her, how he had branded her. It was better to let him think she did not want him because she was afraid to be with him, than to have him turn away from her in disgust.

Chase picked up the hand lying on the blanket and sat down on the edge of the bed. "Well?" he asked as he rearranged a strand of hair that was tangled around her arm.

"What happened?" Jenny croaked, and then tried to clear her throat. Chase handed her a cup of water and she gratefully took it, suddenly realizing how thirsty she was. He had to help her with it, her hands shook so when she tried to lift it. Then she realized that she needed to sit up, and she was helpless to stop him from gently pulling her up, supporting her with one arm while he helped her hold the cup with the other. His hand surrounded both of hers as she drained the cup, the water feeling wonderful on her parched throat. "I must look awful," she apologized when she was done.

"I think you're beautiful." He dropped a kiss on the top of her head, then eased her back on the pillows. "Do you remember anything?"

Jenny's mind rambled back over the past week, trying to separate dreams and hallucinations from reality. "You killed Mason," Chase nodded. "Jamie burned the house?"

"Yes. Anything else?"

Jenny shook her head; the trip home did not exist.

"Do you remember the knife in the fire?" She saw the knife flying through the air, felt the sting in her hand, but said nothing. Chase saw the panic in her eyes but ignored it. She seemed so very fragile and he did not want to push her. "You came down with a fever. The doctor said you were probably bleeding somewhere inside and we would just have to see if it healed."

That made sense to Jenny, she remembered taking some hard punches and kicks from Mason. She raised a hand to her face, where she remembered being hit. It was tender, but the swelling and cuts were gone.

"You're practically healed there, from what I can see, but you'll have to figure out your shoulder and ankle for yourself."

Her shoulder felt all right, Jenny realized when she thought about it. Her ankle felt tender when she tried to flex the foot— she'd have to stand on it to find out if it was better. As for the rest, she felt the painful itch of healing scars and willed herself not to look under the blanket, under the high-necked gown, to see the brand over her heart. She could feel it, she couldn't believe that it had not burned right through her coverings for everyone to see.

"Where's Jamie?"

"Working. We've been taking turns. Grace got tired of having both of us under foot all the time so she said we had to go in shifts. Jason's been great. He said neither one of us had to work until you were better, but we felt guilty about that so we work a little, sleep a little and stay with you as much as possible." He gave her a lopsided smile, almost like an apology, and Jenny felt her heart leap in her chest. Chase saw the spark that lit her eyes for a second and decided to push on. "I've been working on the cabin."

"The cabin?"

"Yes, the cabin. Remember Jason said we could have his old cabin to live in after we—"

"Could you get Grace for me?" Jenny hurriedly interrupted him, looking anxiously beyond for salvation.

"Sure, she's fixing dinner. I'll be right back." He couldn't hide the hurt that flashed in his eyes any more than Jenny could hide the haunted look in hers, but he knew she needed time, so he went for Grace.

"So you finally decided to join us?" Grace said to Jenny as she came into the room. "Chase is grinning like a fox. He's been so worried about you."

"He has?"

"Yes. Jamie too, but I finally had to run him off. He kept moping around and getting in my way." Grace busied herself with plumping pillows and folding the quilt that she pulled off the window. "What do you want to do first, take a bath or eat?"

"A bath sounds nice, and my hair—"

"We will take care of it," Grace went to the door. "Chase, bring the tub in here. Let's get this girl cleaned up."

"*No!*" Jenny exclaimed in panic. Grace was puzzled as she pulled the door shut behind her.

"What is it?"

"Chase—I don't want him to see me."

"He won't. He's just going to bring in the tub and fetch some water, that's all." Grace sat down on the bed and took up Jenny's hands. "I know what that bastard did to you, but it won't matter to Chase. He loves you." Jenny turned her head away, but Grace brought it back around with a finger under her chin. "It's just a scar, that's all, like Jamie's. It will heal and become a distant memory."

"How can it, when I'll know what it means."

"What does it mean? It means that you were brutalized by a man with no soul, a man who's dead and gone now, a man who will never touch you or your family again. Don't let him have that power over you. He's done enough to you in the past. Don't let him destroy your future, too." Grace smoothed back the tendrils of hair that were scattered around Jenny's face. "Now, let's get you washed and dressed and fed, and your hair brushed, and then you'll be ready to see everyone who has been so worried about you. Okay?"

Jenny nodded in agreement as she dashed away the tears that had gathered at the corners of her eyes. They heard the clumping on the porch that meant Chase had gotten the tub, and he smiled at Jenny as he placed it in a corner of the room. Grace sent him for buckets of water while she set some to heat and laid out towels. Grace had to help Jenny to the chamber pot, because her ankle would not support her; then she helped her ease into the tub. That small bit of movement exhausted her so much that she lay back and let Grace wash her hair as the hot water eased away the aches and pains that had accumulated after a week of being flat on her back.

Jenny ran a soapy cloth over her body and was shocked to find her ribs and hips sticking out prominently. She sucked in her breath when she felt a scab fall away from her breast, taken up by the washcloth, but she refused to look down, even when she caught sight of a trickle of blood out of the corner of her eye. She felt brittle and fragile, as if a slight breeze would blow her away, and wondered how she would ever find the strength to get out of the tub. She finally had to move after Grace wrung out her hair and the water began to chill and set her teeth to chattering. Grace helped her out and wrapped her hair up in a towel after she had dressed her in a long, frilly gown. Grace opened the door and summoned Chase, who was busy stirring a pot of soup that she had left bubbling on the stove.

"I need to change these linens," she explained, "and you need a dose of fresh air. Chase, take her outside to the swing and I'll bring her something to eat."

Jenny wanted nothing more than to climb back into bed and pull the blankets over her head, but Grace had already thrown the sheets onto the floor. Jenny was leaning against the bedpost, her foot barely touching the floor, but she managed to take up her quilt before it slid into a heap with the rest of the linens. Chase took it from her arms and wrapped it around her shoulders before he slid his arm down around her knees, scooping her up in his arms. Jenny had no choice but to wrap an arm around his neck as he tried to get a solid grip on her through the thickness of the quilt. Her head was against his shoulder, his hair tickling her nose, and she couldn't help inhaling his scent, the smell of outdoors, homemade soap, horse and leather, with just a hint of onion from the steam of the soup. Grace handed him a hair brush as he walked through the door with strict instructions not to yank Jenny's hair out. He laughed as he took it and commented on her bossy ways getting out of control.

Being outside again felt like hitting a wall. It was too big, too bright, too loud. Chase sat down with her in the swing, holding her tightly against him as she hid her head against his neck, trying to slow the assault on her senses. Chase didn't say a word, just pushed the swing a little with his knees until the gentle swaying calmed the rapid pounding of her heart. Her arms were around his neck, her fingers tangled in his hair, and she relaxed against him, until she could feel his heart beating against her forearm. Jenny's fingers ached to feel his skin under them, and she eased her hand down until it was pressed against his heart, feeling the pounding that had suddenly accelerated. It was all she could manage for now, it had to be enough, and he took it gratefully, turning his head to press a whisper of a kiss on her forehead.

Jenny settled against him, suddenly grateful that she was alive, that she was in a place she'd never expected to be again. When Jamie rode away from the ranch that day, she had not given thought to anything beyond the fact that he was still alive, and then she had thought of nothing but staying alive, until the desire to be dead and no longer feel the pain and despair had taken over everything else. But now, miraculously, here she was, home, and safely held in the arms of the man who loved her. She felt the strength in his thighs as he flexed them beneath her, just that hint of a movement making the swing sway gently in the crisp air of the fall afternoon. His arms held her lightly, they were a secure presence that kept her from falling to the porch floor, but did not make her feel trapped. His hair was silky against the skin of her cheek, the dark length of it warm against her pale skin.

If only life would stop now, Jenny thought. *If this moment would last forever, if I didn't have to face him, if only he didn't have to see.*

"Ready for me to do your hair?" Chase asked softly against her forehead. "I'd hate to get Grace mad at me for disobeying her orders."

Jenny did not want to move, but she also did not want to protest, so she let him slide her into the seat beside him and pull the towel away from her hair. She threw an arm over the back of the swing as he turned around and braced his outside leg against the end, giving her a barrier that would keep her from tumbling out. Chase took the brush and began with the ends, taking handfuls of hair up and brushing out the tangles until he had worked his way up her back to the base of her neck. Each little motion of the brush pulled her head back until the rhthym of the swing and the brush were in sync. When he got up to her scalp, the gentle massaging sent shivers down her back.

"Are you cold?" he asked as he stopped to pull the quilt up around her shoulders again.

"No, it just feels good."

Jenny's hair was dry now, the golden ends softly curling under, the new short growth around her hairline flying up and floating gently around her face. Her eyes were half closed in cat-like contentment and had a dreamy glow to them which Chase could not see from behind. He dropped the brush and began to massage her shoulders, moving his long fingers up and down her upper arms until she was sure she would be unable to hold a spoon if she had to.

Jenny was soon put to the test. Grace came out with a tray holding a steaming bowl of soup and several biscuits. Jenny's mouth began to water as Grace placed the tray on a small table.

"I can't even remember the last time I ate."

"Well, don't overdo it, or you'll lose it," Grace cautioned as Jenny picked up a biscuit and pulled the flaky layers apart. Just as she bit into it, Jamie came riding up to the porch, a wide grin on his face.

"Hey, you're alive!" He helped himself to a biscuit as he stepped up on the porch.

"Barely," Jenny said around her own biscuit. Chase was smiling broadly behind her as he recognized the easy banter that passed between the two.

Jamie swung a straight-backed chair over and straddled it on the other side of the small table that held Jenny's dinner. "I think you need some help with this, sis." He took the spoon and began stirring it through the soup, one russet eyebrow cocked up at Chase as if he was seeking permission.

"Bring that spoon out of that bowl and you'll wish you hadn't," Jenny said confidently from her seat in the swing. Jamie leaned back in the chair and looked at her. She had been at death's door, that much was evident from her pale looks and the great circles under her eyes, but there she sat, wrapped in their mother's quilt, the ruffle of a snow-white gown gracing her slender neck, her hair hanging long and framing her face, and her sapphire-blue eyes once again dancing with life. She did not have the strength to swat a fly, but she was sassing him, and Jamie's heart did a somersault in his chest.

Chase's hand came around her shoulder and gave her arm a gentle squeeze. *One day at a time,* Jenny told herself. *Maybe we can get through this.*

Chapter Thirty-one

Day by day Jenny grew stronger until she was able to make her way around, limping on the sprained ankle but managing on her own. She helped Grace out where she could, sitting at the table peeling potatoes or working on the never-ending pile of mending, but would then have to take a nap in the afternoon, her strength drained by the simple chores. Grace watched her carefully, marking the days but never mentioning why. Chase went back to work and spent what time he could repairing the cabin, replacing broken windows, nailing down new boards, fixing things that were broken. He wanted desperately to bring her to the cabin and make Jenny his wife, but he had decided that once again he needed to be patient, letting Jenny come around to the realization that they belonged together, and he waited, knowing that when she was ready, she would let him know.

Early one Saturday Jamie showed up at the door to Grace's cabin with Jenny's horse. "Let's go for a ride," he said to Jenny. Grace handed her a sack of food so Jenny knew there had been a conspiracy of some sort, but she went along, expecting to find Chase involved somehow. He was working on the cabin when they rode by. He stood and waved at them, sweat glistening on his bare chest from the surprisingly warm day.

"You haven't even been in there yet," Jamie commented as they rode by.

"I thought I'd wait until he was done."

"Uh-huh." They rode on in silence, letting the horses make their way. The days of rest had done Jenny a lot of good. She had started to fill out again, losing the hard angles that had been hers after the illness. She had picked up some color also, and the morning in the sun had turned her nose a soft pink. "So what are your plans?" Jamie asked as the horses plodded along.

"Plans?"

"Yeah, you know, your plans. What are you going to do now?"

Jenny looked at him in surprise and then turned quickly away. Jamie reached out and grabbed her reins, pulling her horse to a stop. He pulled his hat off and raked his hand through his hair, then turned the hat around in his hands, searching for the right angle to replace it on his head. He finally got it situated the way he wanted and put it back, arranging his hair before he placed the hat firmly on. Jenny waited, knowing he was searching for words, but she wasn't sure if she wanted to hear them.

"I never told you how much . . . I know that, damn . . ."

"Jamie, what is it?"

"You saved my life. You saved both of our lives actually, but at the time I didn't want to see that. I just want you to know that I wish it hadn't happened. I wish there was something I could have done to stop it. I'm sorry for what happened to you. . . ." His voice trailed off as Jenny reached out for his arm.

"You are my brother. I love you, that's all there is to it. I know you would have done the same for me if it came down to it."

Jamie nodded in agreement as he looked off at the mountains in the distance. "It just seems like you've made all the sacrifices and I've always let you down. Even back at the mission, I wouldn't leave when you wanted to, and—"

"Jamie, we've just had incredibly bad luck. We just happened to get in the way of some bad people. It's not your fault, it's not mine, and it certainly wasn't Dad and Momma's. Sometimes bad things happen to good people, that's all."

"But maybe things could have been different if—"

"But they aren't, so lets not dwell on it. Let's look at what we do have and be grateful for it."

"Okay," Jamie agreed after he had thought about it for a minute. "So what do you have to be grateful for?"

"I don't know. A home, friends, a big oaf of a brother."

"And?"

"And what?"

"What about Chase?" Jamie asked, looking sideways at his sister.

"What about Chase?" Jenny began to feel uncomfortable, as if walls were closing in on her. Her horse felt her tense up and took a few steps to the side. Jamie dismounted and reached up to pull Jenny down beside him. They dropped the reins to let the horse browse and made their way to a boulder that stuck up among the coarse grass.

"Chase loves you," Jamie said when they had settled on the boulder.

"I know," Jenny sighed. She pulled her knees up under her chin and wrapped her arms around her legs.

"So what are you going to do about it?"

"I don't know."

"Are you scared?" Jamie tossed a pebble into the sea of grass. "What happened was awful, but it won't be like that with Chase, I promise."

"I know, I know he wouldn't hurt me, but . . ."

"He wouldn't mind the brand, if that's what you're worried about," Jamie said without looking at her.

Jenny's head flew up in shock, and she looked at Jamie with worried eyes. "How do you know about the brand?"

"I saw it. When Jason set your arm, we all saw it."

"Who saw?"

"Me, Jason, Cat, Ty, then Grace and the doctor of course."

"Does Chase know?"

"I haven't told him. I don't think anyone else would tell him, either. That's something that's personal between you and him." Jenny laid her forehead down on her knees. "It won't matter to him."

"But it matters to me."

Jamie reached out and pulled her next to him, wrapping his long arms around her in a circle that held her tightly.

"Jenny, if you let this keep the two of you apart, then Mason has won, and I won't let what you did to save me ruin the rest of your life. I'm not worth it."

"Don't say that."

"I mean it, because if you are not going to marry Chase, then I wish you had just let them burn me that day, because I love the two of you more than anything in this world, and I want you to be happy. How could I live knowing that because of me, you aren't?"

"But it's not because of you. It's because of Mason." Jenny's voice began to tighten as she tried not to cry.

"So you're going to let him win. I can't believe that you, of all people, would let him beat you like that. What happened to my incredibly stubborn sister who wouldn't give up, no matter what?"

Jenny pushed away from his embrace. "I'm not going to win this argument, am I?"

"No." Jamie grinned at her. "Both of your answers are wrong. I'm right, and if you'll excuse me, I think I'll enjoy being right for a while." Jenny wiped some tears away, then smacked his arm. Jamie tugged on her braid, then pulled her back again for a hug. "So let's see what kind of food Grace put in that sack and then we'll go back and check out the cabin, okay?" Jenny nodded and Jamie whistled his horse over to grab the sack looped over the saddle horn. They snacked on cornbread and apples and enjoyed the warmth of the day for a while.

"So what about you and Grace?" Jenny asked when they were on their way back.

"There isn't a me and Grace anymore."

"Since when?"

"Since I broke my leg. It kinda changed things between us. It just wasn't right after that."

"Oh." Jenny looked over at his handsome face, the scar white against the bronze of his skin.

"Don't worry about me, I'll find someone." Jamie grinned at her. "Zane said he'll fix me up."

Jenny rolled her eyes. "I'm sure he knows some wonderful ladies."

"Ladies of the evening, you mean."

"I'm not sure you could actually call them ladies."

"I don't think they care what you call them, as long as you pay them." They erupted into laughter that carried them the rest of the way back.

Jamie stopped his horse in front of the cabin, grinning encouragingly at Jenny as she reined in beside him. They heard voices inside and stepped through the door to find Jason talking with Chase about the changes in the cabin. Chase was leaning against a wall, with his thumbs hooked into the top of his pants. There was a wide streak of dirt across his bare chest and down one cheek. He looked up when Jamie's frame filled the door of the one-room cabin, then a smile lit his face as Jenny stepped in behind him. Jason turned and lifted an eyebrow in surprise as Jenny shyly stood in the doorway.

"I was just telling Chase that the place hasn't looked this good in the past thirty years." Jason motioned towards the stone fireplace that filled one wall. "You'll never lack for warmth when you have this going. I remember my first winter here—I thought I would freeze to death, but I stayed very warm in here, even brought my horse in to stay with me."

"Looks like it would have been a bit crowded for that," Jamie commented.

"Jason's horse probably wasn't much bigger than you." Jenny jabbed an elbow in his side to move him out of her way. Chase's eyes began to glow like coals as she came into the center of the room, while Jamie pretended to be sorely injured from Jenny's elbow.

"Well," Jason began, "I haven't had a look at those mares lately. How 'bout we go check them out, Jamie?"

"Sounds good to me. It's a bit too crowded in here for my taste." Jamie grinned mischievously at Chase before he turned and left, followed by Jason, who gave Jenny's arm a gentle squeeze on his way out.

"Well, what do you think?" Chase asked when they were alone. Jenny looked around the empty room. It was large enough for two to live comfortably. One wall was taken up by the stone fireplace, with a corner cupboard built in beside it. On either side of the door were windows, and another window was situated opposite the fireplace wall. The back wall was solid, except for a small door that led to a privy that had been filled in years before.

"I guess it could use some furniture," Jenny said as she turned around in the center of the room.

"Yes, Jason and I were just talking about that. He seems to think he can scrounge some up from somewhere."

"Whatever he scrounges from his house will be much too elegant for this." Jenny laughed as she imagined an elegant cherry table sitting in a corner of the cabin.

"Would you rather live in a house like Jason's?" Chase looked out the window as he asked, suddenly afraid of what her answer might be.

"I was never comfortable in that house, as fine as it is. That's why I haven't moved back up there since . . . since we got back." Chase turned to look at her again, a spark igniting inside as he saw Jenny standing before him, her nose and cheeks pink from the sun, her braid a bit untidy from her ride.

"Would you be comfortable here?"

"I'd live in a tent, as long as you were there, too."

Chase felt his heart flip-flop in his chest and he took a step forward. *Easy,* he thought, *don't scare her,* but he couldn't stop himself from taking another step, then another, until he was standing right in front of her. A set of wide sapphire-blue eyes looked up at him, eyes brimming with her soul, offering up everything to him in one unguarded moment. "Jenny," he whispered, and she was in his arms.

Chase couldn't hold her tight enough. He had been holding himself back for so long, and suddenly here she was, trembling in his arms. He wrapped his hands in her hair. She raised her face, her lips slightly parted. He couldn't help himself, he lowered his mouth to hers, trying to hold back, desperate not to scare her, but desperate at the same time to have her. His kiss was tentative, searching, exploring. She did not resist, so he pressed on, his hand holding the back of her head, the other moving down her spine, pressing against her, holding her solidly against him, and she answered him, a slight gasp escaping as her lips parted further and his tongue moved inside. He couldn't breathe, he couldn't stop, he could feel himself growing hard against her thighs, and she still did not move away. Her hands moved over the bare skin of his back, kneading the muscles as she tried to find a hold on his smooth flesh, her hands tangling in his hair as she stroked the length of his spine.

He finally pulled away, dragging in air as he tilted his forehead against hers. His hands held her face as he sought to restore balance to his spinning world.

"Do you still want me?" she asked, her eyes downcast as she leaned against him.

"What do you think?" He moved his hands down her back and pushed her body against his.

"I know you want me,"—Jenny pushed him away, seeing the playful light in his eyes—"but do you want me like before?"

"I never stopped. I just wanted you to be sure."

Jenny put her hands up to his lips to stop him. "Then you need to know what you are getting."

"What do you mean?"

"You need to know about Mason."

"You don't need to tell—"

Her fingers touched his lips again, and she stepped back and began to unbutton her shirt. "I want you to know, and if you can't stand it, I'll understand. I'll leave and I won't blame you."

"Jenny—"

"Stay there, please." Jenny pulled her shirt open and pulled down the top of her camisole, turning her head away as she did so. She heard his sharp intake of breath, felt him step closer, willed herself not to tremble as he looked at the scar, still red and angry against the soft gold of her skin.

"That son of a bitch." His words were low and angry, and Jenny felt a chill go up her spine. "He died too easy." His voice broke on the words, and she turned to look at him, her hand still holding the fabric of the camisole. His eyes were smoldering, and she saw once again the image of Mason hanging on the fence, and wondered what it had been like for him to see death in Chase's flinty gaze, to know that it was coming. She hoped it was pure hell; she wished she could have watched.

Chase took her hand down and eased the fabric back into place, his fingertips barely brushing the skin as he covered the scar; the welt showed though the fine fabric. Jenny's eyes were moist as she looked at him. Her fear, her secret and her soul were laid bare before him.

"I love you." He was screaming with rage inside, but he had to hold it in, he would not frighten her with it. "I love you, Jenny. I want you with me, forever." His hand caressed her cheek, but it ached to hold his knife, to feel Mason squirm beneath it. She melted against him, tears of relief bursting forth, soaking the skin of his chest, running through the dirt that streaked that broad expanse. He held her as she cried, and his rage dissolved, becoming nothing as she grieved against him for the part of her that was gone forever. "We'll be fine, Jenny. I promise, as long as we're together, we'll be fine."

"We will?" she squeaked against his chest. Chase laughed because she sounded so funny, and he knew that he was soaking wet from her tears.

"Oh, Jenny." He pulled her against him, picking her up off her feet. "Marry me now, and we'll have dozens of babies and send them all to pester their Uncle Jamie so we can make more."

The word *babies* hit Jenny like a bucket of cold water. Her mind went back and began counting days.

"Jenny?"

"Oh, God," she said, her face going white. *Time, how much time?* Her mind whirled as Chase's dark eyes filled with concern. *Not enough*, her mind answered.

"Jenny, what is it?"

"I have to go," she sobbed. She pushed his hands away as he tried to stop her. "Please, I have to go." She ran out of the cabin to her horse, which was still standing outside.

"Jenny!" Chase was on the stoop as she mounted, the horse already in motion as she swung into the saddle with the same fluid motion that came naturally to Jamie and Chase. Chase spun around and punched the wall, hitting a board that needed replacing; the wood splintered around his hand, piercing the skin in many places.

Grace had heard Chase calling, had seen Jenny's flight from the ranch, and came running when she saw Chase holding one hand in the other, blood trickling from the wounds.

"What happened?" she asked as she wrapped her apron around his hand.

"I don't know." He ran his other hand through his hair. "I thought everything was fine . . . she was happy . . . she wasn't scared, and suddenly she just bolted."

"What did you say?"

"I told her I loved her, I wanted to marry her and make babies."

"Oh, Chase."

Chase looked at her in exasperation, and Grace pulled him down beside her on the stoop. She pulled her apron away and placed his hand firmly in her lap and began to work on a splinter.

"What did I say that was so wrong? I thought everything was out now. She showed me what Mason did, and I told her it didn't matter, that I loved her." Grace held the splinter up and flicked it into the yard. "Grace?"

Grace pulled his hand firmly in hers, holding on to it tightly. "Chase, what if Jenny is pregnant?"

His dark eyes grew wide, and he looked off in the direction Jenny had gone. "Is she?"

"I don't know, and from what just happened, I don't think she knows either. It's been almost three weeks since it happened, but I don't know what her cycle is like. It's not something we discuss." Grace kept her tight hold on his hand, knowing he could pull away at any time but hoping he wouldn't. "What if she is?"

"I love her. I've always loved her, since the first time I saw her."

"Do you love her enough?"

"Yes." He did not hesitate, did not stop to think. His heart spoke for him. "Yes, I love her."

"Go find her and tell her before she does something foolish."

Chase snatched up his shirt and started for the barn, but before he had gone ten steps, Jenny came riding into the valley. She reined up in front of the cabin and waited as Chase walked to her horse.

"Jamie was right—I always try to run away from my problems. The trouble is, no matter how far I run, I'll never be able to leave this one behind." The tears were gone, replaced by a steely resolve in the depths of her eyes. "I won't let him win," she said simply. Chase reached up, and she let him take her from the saddle, sliding down the length of him to be encircled in his arms.

"Do you know for sure?"

"No, not yet,"

"Then we'll take it as it comes." Chase placed his hands on Jenny's face, turning her eyes up to meet his own, showing her that there was nothing to fear.

Five days later, they had the answer to their question. Jenny bolted out of the cabin that morning, heading straight for the barn to saddle her horse. Chase and Jamie were out checking the herd, which had been taken to the winter pasture a few weeks earlier. Her joy was contagious when she had discovered that there were no more problems to stand in their way, that she and Chase could now plan to have the life they had wanted before, without the complications that Randolph Mason had wished on them. She covered the ground quickly, letting her horse have his head, enjoying the sweet smell of the day, the clear blue of the sky and the glorious colors that covered the mountains beyond. She finally spied a russet head towering above a sea of sweet grass, and close beside it a darker head, both bent at some task.

They had just freed a cow from a gopher hole when she rode up. The cow had stepped in the hole, and the ground around it had caved in, taking both of her forelegs down and leaving her dangling half in and half out. She wasn't hurt, just unable to get any leverage until Chase and Jamie dragged her back enough to get her feet underneath her. She ran off with a loud bawl of hurt feelings and embarrassment and joined the rest of the herd. Jamie and Chase were laughing over the cow's antics as they stomped the side of the hole to make sure it wouldn't cause any more problems. They heard Jenny's horse and looked at each other questioningly as she came flying up, then stopped so suddenly that her horse nearly sat down. She vaulted off and hit Chase squarely in the chest, so he toppled over and hit the ground with a solid "ooof," with Jenny on top of him.

"I'm not pregnant." She was smiling down at him, her hair a golden cloud around them. Chase was speechless for a moment, then wrapped his arms around her, laughing for pure joy.

"Would someone mind telling me what's going on?" Jamie demanded.

"I'm not pregnant."

"Well I should hope not. You're not even married yet. Oh . . . oh, I see." He began to stumble over the words and then his wide grin split his face. "Well, congratulations, I think." Jenny's laughter bubbled up from within, and she laid her head on Chase's chest as they were both consumed with mirth. Jamie stood watching them for a minute, scratching his head, then just walked away.

"As much as I'm enjoying this," Chase said after their laughter had subsided and they had shared a long lazy kiss, "I do need to get back to work."

Jenny did not seem inclined to move. She was enjoying the view of his regal face; he was totally relaxed for once, at peace with the world around him. His eyes were dark slits against the sun, his silky hair spread out around him on the grass, and his mouth wore a contented smile. He put his arms under his head when he saw

Jenny wasn't budging and he decided to enjoy the moment. Jenny picked a blade of grass and tickled his ears with it, then began to torture his nose, while Chase tried to keep a straight face. He finally gave up and got his revenge by tickling her stomach, throwing her off in a single movement and pinning her beneath him. Her joy was overflowing, her laughter rang out over the grass until Jamie came stomping back, complaining about having to do all the work. Chase led her to her horse and helped her mount after another long kiss, then went back to help Jamie fill in the hole. Jenny turned her horse to go and noticed that Chase had left his gun belt and knife looped over his saddle horn. She snatched the knife from its sheath as she rode by, knowing that by the time he realized it was gone, the deed would be done.

Grace's cabin was empty when she got back. The fire in the stove had been banked, and Jenny threw a few pieces of kindling in to get the flames going. When the fire had kicked up, she laid the blade in the coals, and unbuttoned her shirt. There was a wooden spoon on the counter. She tested the strength of if by striking it against the counter, and then satisfied, put it in her mouth, placing the handle firmly between her teeth. The blade of the knife was glowing red when she pulled it from the flames, and she took a deep breath as she pulled her camisole down away from the R M that was scrawled across her left breast. She laid the hot metal of the blade over the scar, obliterating the detested initials as it burned her skin. The pain made her stagger back, and she bit down hard on the spoon, crashing against a chair and falling backwards on the floor of the cabin, the blade still gripped in her hand. Tears stung her eyes as her nerve endings screamed, and blood began to seep down her breast. She spit the spoon out, the handle mangled by her teeth, and drew in a long, ragged breath. Jenny heard Grace's light footsteps on the porch and tried to sit up, but only succeeded in knocking the chair over.

Grace opened the door of the cabin and was immediately assaulted by the smell of burning flesh. "Oh my God, Jenny, what happened?" She was on the floor next to her at once, but Jenny pushed her away and scooted back until she was sitting against the wall. "What did you do?"

"Is it gone?" Jenny asked, afraid to look.

Grace looked at her with shocked eyes, her mouth agape as the reality of what Jenny had done hit her. Chase's knife was still gripped tightly in her hand, and Grace gently pried her fingers from the handle before she could do any more damage.

"Is it gone?" Jenny asked again, her head thrown back against the wall as she fought the pain. Grace filled a bowl with water and came back with a soft cloth. She laid the cold cloth on the burn, and Jenny tensed in pain.

"I think it's gone. Yes, I believe it is." Grace sat back on her heels as Jenny began to laugh. Grace began to have serious doubts as to her sanity while Jenny laughed through the tears that were flowing down her cheeks.

"We can start clean now," Jenny tried to explain. "Don't you see, it's a clean slate."

Grace smiled and gave her a hug, while trying to avoid the burned flesh of her breast. Jenny grimaced in pain again when she put her arms up. "How long do you think it will take for this to heal?"

"I believe it's already started." Grace pulled Jenny to her feet and settled her into a chair to put some salve on her burn, along with a thick padding. They had just changed her shirt and set the other to soaking when they heard rapid hoofbeats outside.

Chase kicked the door of the cabin open so hard that it bounced against the back wall before it slammed shut behind him. His face was a mixture of fear and anger as his eyes settled on Jenny, who was sitting sedately at the table with her hands folded, his knife lying in front of her. He snatched it up and returned it to its sheath before he placed his palms on the table and leaned over.

"What is going on?" he asked.

"Nothing."

Grace began to busy herself at the stove with the beginning of dinner.

"Did you take my knife?"

"Yes."

"Why?"

"I needed it."

"For what?"

"It's personal."

"You could have asked."

"You would have said no."

"Why did you need it?"

"Like I said, it's personal."

Chase slammed his fist against the table in anger, which startled Grace, who let out a little gasp. He swung his head around and gave her a look that told her she would be better off leaving, but she just smiled at him and went back to her work. "Damn it, Jenny, what are you doing with my knife?"

"It was my father's knife before it was yours, and like I said, it's personal."

"I need some answers," he bellowed.

"Be patient and you'll get them!" she screamed back. Chase straightened up and looked down his nose at her, but she didn't budge, just stared back with eyes that never wavered. Chase turned on his heel and left, muttering under his breath about Duncans, and stubborn Scots, and how the wrong person wound up with the red hair.

Chapter Thirty-two

Cat decided that planning a wedding was something she was born to do and took over all the preparations. Jenny and Chase wanted something small and simple, with just their friends, but by the time Cat was done, the whole town was invited. Chase agreed to a church wedding because it meant so much to Jenny, and Jenny let Cat have her way because she knew it was a gesture on Cat's part to make up for all the misery she had caused. Finally, on a Sunday afternoon in late October, the time arrived.

Jason was in the cabin making sure all was in readiness for the couple to start their life together after the ceremony in town and the reception at the main house afterwards. The corner cupboard was full of dishes from his own kitchen, and a small table sat in the opposite corner by the window. While the fireplace was good for warmth, it was a bit impractical for cooking, so they would continue to take their meals with the rest of the hands at Grace's cabin until they could add on a room that would hold a stove and sink. In front of the fireplace were two mismatched wingback chairs that had been delegated to the attic when Cat's mother had decorated the big house, along with an Oriental rug that had a hole burned in one corner. The other end of the cabin was filled with the big bed and wardrobe that had been Jenny's when she first arrived at the ranch. The cabin was nearly twice the size of the room the bed had been taken from, but the bed it still seemed to overwhelm it, the fine mahogany finish of the wood at odds with the rough planks of the walls. The windows were covered with white curtains, the fire was ready to be lit, a bouquet of fall foliage brightened the table, and everything seemed to be in readiness for the happy couple's wedding night. Jason shook his head at the big bed, but it had been Cat's idea, and he couldn't see a reason not to go along with it. It was covered with snowy white linens, a thick bedspread and a quilt folded at the bottom in case they got cold.

"I don't think they'll have any need for this," Jason said to himself as he ran his fingers over the quilt. Something about it tugged at his mind, and he flipped the fold over to see more of the pattern. His fingertips traced the blue of the interlocking rings, noticing the worn threads and the few stains that had not come out after Grace had washed it. Jason recognized it as the quilt they had brought Jenny out of the house in, the quilt that had belonged to her mother, but there was something else about it. He lifted a corner to turn to the backing, and was interrupted by the sound of boots on the stoop.

"Something to keep their strength up," Zane said as he placed a basket of food on the table. "Grace packed enough provisions to keep them holed up for a week." He pulled some candles out of his pocket, along with some mismatched candlesticks. "This was my idea." Jason laughed as he watched Zane arrange the candles on the mantel and one on the bedside table next to the carved angel box. "It's not the hotel, but it will do." He smiled in satisfaction.

Caleb stuck his head in the door. "Do you think it would be all right if I left my present for Chase and Jenny here?"

"I don't think they would mind," Jason said.

Caleb laid a package tied with string on the table. "It's a picture of the three of them," he explained a bit self-consciously.

"I'm sure they will love it."

"I put it in a frame, too."

Jason put a fatherly arm around Caleb as they went out of the cabin. Ty had already driven the women to church, and the men were waiting for Chase and Jamie to finish dressing. Chase was having trouble with his tie, and they had gotten tired of watching him do it over and over again. They all applauded when he made his appearance in his black suit and white shirt, and couldn't resist teasing him about second thoughts and last-minute nerves. They rode to the church in high spirits, Zane filling Chase's head with his proven techniques on making a woman happy, and Jamie threatening him every few minutes if he messed up.

"Here they come." Cat was watching from the window of the schoolhouse next to the church. Jenny tried to look over her shoulder, but Cat pushed her back. "It's bad luck for the groom to see the bride before the ceremony."

"I think we've had more than our share of bad luck. It's time for some good." Jenny swished away from the window.

"Don't you worry, darling. You've got nothing but good in front of you," Grace assured her. "Now let me fix your hair."

"I don't think I have any hair left." Jenny sighed as Grace pushed her down into a chair while Cat held her skirt up to keep her from wrinkling the fine fabric.

Cat and Grace had fussed over her hair and dress all morning until Jenny felt as if she would scream, but she patiently bore it all, knowing that it gave them pleasure to do so. They had pulled her hair up on top of her head and left a few soft tendrils down that danced along the back of her neck where a soft blue ribbon was woven among the strands. Her dress was white, as they had insisted, with a high neck and long sleeves and a series of ruffles over a multitude of petticoats. She wore pearl earrings that Jason had given her, and carried a lace handkerchief that was a present from Grace. "Something old," Grace had said when she pressed it into Jenny's hand, explaining that it had belonged to her grandmother.

A rap at the door announced Jamie's presence, and Jenny rose from her chair as Cat let him in. The two women arranged Jenny's skirts one last time and gave Jenny's cheek a kiss for luck before they left, leaving her alone for a minute with her brother.

"Wow," he said as he grinned at her. "You clean up pretty good."

"You're not so bad yourself." He was wearing a new brown suit, along with shiny new boots, and had a fresh haircut that did nothing to stop the mass from flopping down over his eyes. Jenny reached her hand up to smooth it back, and he took it in his own, bringing it to his lips. His eyes brimmed over as he softly kissed it.

"You are so beautiful."

"Thank you." Jenny looked down, her own eyes becoming moist. "I wish Dad and Momma could be here."

"They are, they're watching."

"Do you really think so?"

"Yes, I do, and I know they're happy."

"I am. I love Chase so much."

"And he loves you." Jamie placed her hand in the crook of his arm. "Let's go get married."

Jamie led her out of the schoolhouse to where Grace and Cat were waiting to help carry her skirts, and soon they were on the steps of the church, waiting for the organ music to start the procession. The doors opened, Grace went down the aisle, followed by Cat, and Jenny took a deep breath as everyone stood. In the front of the church she saw Jason standing at the podium. As they stepped through the door, Jamie ducked his head under the frame, and then Jenny saw Chase step into the aisle, looking very civilized in his suit, but still savage with his long dark hair flowing down his back. She did not remember how she got to the front of the church. She just knew she was now standing next to him, her hand in his, and words were being spoken to which she answered. When she looked down, her mother's carved silver wedding band was being slipped on her finger. She looked up at Chase in surprise and saw Jamie grinning at her over his shoulder.

"I now pronounce you man and wife," Jason said with a smile, and Chase bent to kiss her. The world stopped spinning as their lips touched.

"Will you two settle down?" Jamie whispered as Jason loudly cleared his throat. The church broke into happy applause as Jenny and Chase looked around, blinking like owls. A moment later, they managed to find their way down the aisle and out the door.

Chase handed Jenny up into the carriage which had been decorated with bows and ribbon, as had the horse. Ty was driving, and Cat was handed up next to him. Then they took off for the ranch, with their friends riding alongside, entertaining them along the way with words of advice for the coming night. A procession of carriages followed. A party was always welcome, and since the Lynches were one of the richest families around, everyone knew it would be a good one.

* * *

They had smiled a hundred smiles and shaken a hundred hands of people that they did not know. Some offered enthusiastic good wishes, and others enjoyed the lavish spread while issuing phony smiles and talked with secret disgust of the half-breed who dared to soil a white girl. Chase was not oblivious to the gossip, he just chose to ignore it. He had what he wanted, and no one was going to spoil it for him, especially narrow-minded people who did not have a clue as to who or what he was. All that mattered was that Jenny loved him, and she reminded him of it every time she reached out to take his hand during the reception. She was radiant with happiness, her face glowing each time she turned to look for him when they became separated in the crowded room.

They had been toasted and fussed over, and Chase had had enough. He caught Jenny's eye and slightly inclined his head towards the door to the kitchen. She arched an eyebrow in return and began to make her way there, politely greeting the people who stood in her way. When she was at his side, he took her hand and with a final look to make sure no one was watching they slid through the door.

Escape from the kitchen was easy, they were out the door in a flash and down the steps, where Jenny stopped to gather up her array of ruffles and crinolines for the dash down the hill. Their feet flew over grass that was silver with frost, and they laughed as they slipped and slid towards the cabin.

"I can't believe we made it," Jenny laughed as they climbed the stoop. Chase pulled her to him and kissed her, then quickly scooped her into his arms, her skirts billowing up over their heads. Jenny gave way to a fit of giggles as she pressed her skirts down and he kicked the door open and carried her through.

Someone had been there ahead of them. The fire had been lit, along with an array of candles. Chase set Jenny on the floor in front of the fireplace, and his eyes began to glow with the reflection of the coals. Jenny reached her hand up and smoothed his dark, silky hair back behind his ear, and he turned his head to kiss her hand before she took it away. His arms slid around her waist, and she eagerly pressed herself against him as he bent to kiss her again. He finally raised his head with a soft sigh and found Jenny grinning mischievously at him.

"Well?" she asked saucily. His eyebrows went up in a leer and she turned, presenting her back to him. "I think I may need some help with these." She looked over her shoulder at him, and he groaned as he saw the number of tiny buttons that went down her back.

"Who picked this dress out?"

"Cat."

"Remind me to repay the favor." He started on the buttons, his fingers amazingly nimble against her spine, and Jenny shivered in anticipation as he spread the back of the dress wide. He moved the curls aside that were dancing against her neck and planted a kiss. His hands moved the dress down as he caressed her shoulders. and soon it was bunched on the floor; her crinolines, which were tied at her waist with a ribbon, quickly followed. Jenny kicked free of the garments and turned to face Chase. She pulled his tie away as he tried to shrug off his coat, but his arms became hopelessly entangled when she pressed against him, her hands undoing the buttons of his shirt.

Jenny laughed at his frustration as he jerked at the sleeves that kept his arms behind him. He needed desperately to have his hands on Jenny, who was teasing him with her hips as she plucked at the buttons. The coat finally gave way and sailed into a chair, just as his shirt was pulled from his pants. He ripped the shirt away, not caring that one last button flew off the shirt as he flung it to the floor. He wrapped his arms around Jenny, his mouth crushing against hers as he nudged her over to the bed. Her legs gave way when they met it, and they tumbled onto the mattress.

"Jenny," he groaned against her mouth and he felt her smile beneath his lips. She unbuckled his belt and attacked the buttons. He raised himself up to help, and she eased out from under him and sat up, her legs tucked under her. He knelt on one knee before her on the bed when he had removed the last of his clothes, and reached out to untie the ribbon of the silk camisole she still wore. It fell away in a whisper, and she leaned back against the pillows. Her pantalets fell to the floor in the space of a heartbeat, and he raised himself over her as she sighed.

The movement of her breast when she sighed caught his eye, and he saw the raised skin that rippled over her heart. Chase reached for the candle that flickered on the nightstand and brought the light towards her. He looked at her face in confusion, then back at the new scar, his hand poised above it a second before he ran his fingers over the ridges of skin. Jenny raised her chin proudly, daring him to protest what she had done.

"I love you," he whispered as he set the candle down. Her arms went around his neck as he stretched out beside her.

"Love me now, Chase. Love me now . . . I don't want to wait any longer."

Her legs wrapped around his hips as he rolled on top of her and eased himself in, praying the whole while that she would not panic, that her mind would not go back to what Mason had done. Her head was thrown back, her eyes squeezed shut, and he lowered his mouth to her neck. He felt her tense as he filled her and he stopped, his will fighting his body's impulses.

Chase placed his hands on either side of her face. "Open your eyes, Jenny. Look at me." She obeyed, her sapphire blue melting into the silver of his in the darkness. "I love you."

"Chase," she whispered, and he began to move against her, holding her head steady with his hands. Her hands moved down from his shoulders to his hips, moving around to his stomach, tracing a line up to his chest. He threw his head back as her hands made the trail, then brought his mouth down to her neck, then up to her mouth again, where her lips were eagerly seeking his. He wrapped a hand in her hair, tangling the pins and ribbons that held it up as she picked up his rhythm beneath him. She began to meet him with each thrust, her hands burning across his chest. He couldn't breathe, he laid his forehead against hers, and his hair fell around them, brushing her cheeks as she gasped beneath him.

"Please, oh, Chase—" Her eyes widened as the sun exploded around her, and the impact of it carried Chase along with her, melting his spine as he went, until he could not tell where he ended and Jenny began.

When he was able, he rolled them over so that they lay side by side, facing each other. His leg hit the quilt and he flipped it up with his foot, then opened it over their bodies so that it covered their hips and legs. Jenny's face was buried in his neck. She was still trying to catch her breath, her body trembling against his.

"Are you all right?" She had yet to say a word.

"I didn't know . . . I didn't know."

"Didn't know what?"

"That it was like this." She raised her head. "Why didn't you tell me?"

"And spoil all the fun?" He grinned. "Owwww! Do that again and the fun is over." He trailed his hand down the side of her face, over her shoulder, down her arm and up under her breast. He cupped it with his hand, then bent his head to lay a gentle kiss over the scar. "I don't know if I could have done that."

"Jamie survived it, so I knew I could, too."

They were interrupted by a barrage of rocks against the roof of the cabin. "Hey, Chase, no fair sneaking off like that." Someone pounded on the window. "Hey, you need some help in there?"

Chase pulled the quilt up over their heads as they buried their laughter in pile of pillows. They heard a crash, then a loud thud. "Damn it, Jamie, we were just teasing them. You don't have to get so hostile about it." The voices drifted off; then they heard a loud "Good night" thrown in their direction, followed by peals of laughter. The sound of a door slamming drifted across the valley, and then the peaceful night sounds took over.

Chase trailed his long fingers down the side of Jenny's face in a tender caress. "I love you, Jenny." His mouth came down on hers softly, gently touching her lips. Jenny shivered at his kiss, all the way down to her toes, which began to curl against the sheets. Her head popped up and she looked down at her feet.

A vision came into her head of a young girl, dressed in her brother's hand-me-down clothes, sewing on a porch with her mother, who looked like an angel with her silvery blonde hair falling around her shoulders. "Momma, how did you know that you loved Dad?" the girl asked.

Faith looked at Ian, who was washing off the grime of a day's work, with Jamie at his side. "I just knew. The first time I met him I knew."

"How did you know?"

"My toes curled when he kissed me."

Jenny saw her father's handsome face as he came onto the porch; she remembered how his russet hair fell across his forehead as he bent over to kiss Faith; she remembered looking on in amazement as her mother's toes curled against the aged wood of the porch. She knew she would never forget the laughter that drifted up from her parents' room later that night. A soft smile lit Jenny's face as she smoothed the blue wedding ring quilt that covered their bodies.

"What?" Chase asked as she turned to look at him.

"You wouldn't believe me if I told you."

"Try me."

She told him the story, and his laughter rang out much like Ian's had so long ago. When he dove under the quilt and began to kiss her toes, she knew what had prompted her mother's giggles that night.

"What do you think our children will look like?" Jenny asked when they were settled once again against the pillows.

"Blue eyes," he said as he kissed an eyelid.

"Dark hair." Jenny ran her hand through the silky strands of his hair.

"Nice curves, if they're girls." His hands traveled over her breasts and around her waist.

"A solid behind." Jenny grabbed his firm cheeks.

"And long legs," Chase added.

"I hope we have children."

"We will, and we'll keep them safe, I promise."

"Do we have any more enemies?"

"None that I know of." Jenny yawned as she settled her head against his chest. "Go to sleep," he whispered. "We have plenty of time."

Reckless Embrace

MADELINE BAKER

Some folks say they are just two kids who should never have met—a girl from the wrong side of town and a half-breed determined to make his mark on the world. Their families fought on opposite sides at the Little Big Horn; there can be no future for them.

But when Black Owl looks at Joey, he sees the most beautiful girl in the world. And when she presses her lips to his, she is finding her way home. In each other's arms, they find a safe haven from a world where hatred and ugliness can only be conquered by the deep, abiding power of courageous love.

KNIGHT ON THE
TEXAS PLAINS
LINDA BRODAY

Duel McClain is no knight in shining armor—he is a drifter who prides himself on having no responsibilities. But a poker game thrusts him into the role of father to an abandoned baby, and then a condemned woman stumbles up to his campfire. The fugitive beauty aims to keep him at shotgun's length, but obvious maternal instincts belie her fierce demeanor. And she and the baby are clearly made for each other. Worse, the innocent infant and the alleged murderess open Duel's heart, make him long for the love of a real family. And the only way to have that will be to slay the demons of the past.

NEW HISTORICAL VOICE CONTEST FINALIST!

THE OUTLAW'S WOMAN
Tanya Hanson

Dena Clayter carries a secret. In the midst of a blizzard, the young widow harbored an outlaw. She fed and nursed the injured fugitive, frightened not of the man but of the longings he incited. She yearned for his touch, the comfort of his arms, his lips against hers, and their passion flared hot enough to burn away all her inhibitions.

Now Dena is racing across the West to try to save him from the hangman's noose. For more than just his life hangs in the balance—Dena's own future and that of their baby stands in jeopardy. And the expectant mother has to know if a bond conceived in winter darkness will be revealed as love in the light of spring.

SAVAGE LOVE
CASSIE EDWARDS

Monster bones are the stuff of Indian legend, which warns that they must not be disturbed. But Dayanara and her father are on a mission to uncover the bones. Not even her father's untimely death or a disapproving Indian chief can prevent Dayanara from proving her worth as an archaeologist.

Any relationship between a Cree chief and a white woman is prohibited by both their peoples, but the golden woman of Quick Fox's dreams is more glorious than the setting sun. Not even her interest in the sacred burial grounds of his people can prevent him from discovering the delights they will know together and proving his savage love.

WHITE DUSK
ℓUSAN EDWARDS

A winter of discontent sent Swift Foot on a vision quest, and he returned ready to be chief. Where his father brought shame upon their family by choosing love over duty, Swift Foot will act more wisely. He will lead his people through the troubles ahead—and, to do so, he will marry for *all* the right reasons.

Small Bird is the perfect choice. But for their people to survive the coming darkness, the two will have to win each other's hearts. On the sleeping mat or wrapped in furs, on riverbank or dusty plain, passion must blaze to life between the half-breed chieftain and his new wife . . . and they have to start the fire soon, for dusk has already fallen.

Dorchester Publishing Co., Inc.
P.O. Box 6640   __5094-3
Wayne, PA 19087-8640   **$5.99 US/$7.99 CAN**

Please add $2.50 for shipping and handling for the first book and $.75 for each additional book. NY and PA residents, add appropriate sales tax. No cash, stamps, or CODs. Canadian orders require $5.00 for shipping and handling and must be paid in U.S. dollars. Prices and availability subject to change. **Payment must accompany all orders.**

Name: _____

Address: _____

City: _____ State: _____ Zip: _____

E-mail: _____

I have enclosed $_____ in payment for the checked book(s).

For more information on these books, check out our website at www.dorchesterpub.com.
_____ *Please send me a free catalog.*